MUST THE MAIDEN DIE

MUST THE MAIDEN DIE

Miriam Grace Monfredo

BERKLEY PRIME CRIME, NEW YORK

MUST THE MAIDEN DIE

A Berkley Prime Crime Book
Published by the Berkley Publishing Group,
a division of Penguin Putnam Inc.,
375 Hudson Street
New York, New York 10014
The Penguin Putnam Inc. World Wide Web site address is
http://www.penguinputnam.com

First edition: September 1999

Library of Congress Cataloging-in-Publication Data

Monfredo, Miriam Grace
    Must the maiden die / Miriam Grace Monfredo.—1st ed.
        p.   cm.
    ISBN 0-425-16699-6
    I. Title.
PS3563.05234M66   1999
813'.54—dc21   99-29295
                                                          CIP

Printed in the United States of America

10 9 8 7 6 5 4 3 2 1

For Frank,
Scott and Nancy, Alyssa and Zachary,
Rachel and David,
Liz,
and Christopher, who will one day write his own

ACKNOWLEDGMENTS

—∿∿—

My grateful appreciation to

Betsy Blaustein for her relentless insistence on the Oneida Community

Lowell Garner, M.D., for his knowledge of death and dying

Katie Hamilton for her generosity and marvelous annotated transcriptions of the reference work *Youman's Dictionary of Every-Day Wants*

David Minor of Eagles Byte Historical Research for quickly and invariably pointing in the right direction

Frank Monfredo, truest critic, logic seeker, and friend

Rachel Monfredo Gee, Austin immigrant and traveling companion–guide, for continuing expertise and quick-reference memory

Scott Monfredo for his prodigious knowledge of the Bible, which saved for the maiden her good name

New York State Festival of Balloons' Jerry Rauber, Tom Derrenbacher, Florence Allen Wood (see Historical Notes— "Ballooning"), and Woody Allen

Carol Sandler, director of The Strong Museum Library, for ready assistance

And especially my publicist Nancy Berland for professionalism, unflagging support, enthusiasm, and unquenchable humor

AUTHOR'S NOTE

The major characters in *Must the Maiden Die* are fictitious, but actual historic figures appear from time to time. Interested readers will find these and other relevant facts annotated in the Historical Notes at the back of this and other novels in the Seneca Falls series.

In 1860, New York State enacted a revolutionary piece of legislation, which followed the groundbreaking 1848 Married Woman's Property Act. For more than a decade, Elizabeth Cady Stanton and Susan B. Anthony spearheaded an exhaustive effort leading to its passage. This legislation was entitled Chapter 90: An Act Concerning the Rights and Liabilities of Husband and Wife. It was adopted by the Eighty-third Session of the New York state legislature in March of 1860, and became commonly known as the Earnings Act, the first of its kind in the United States.

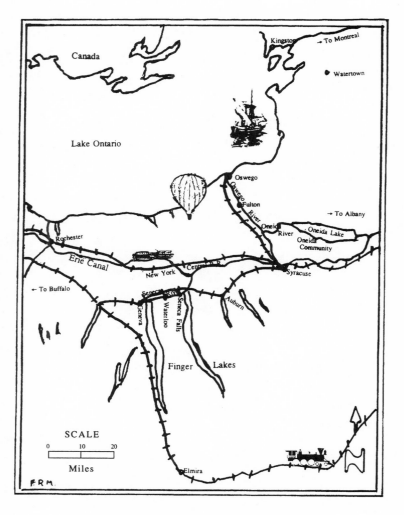

Canada

Lake Ontario

Kingston

→ To Montreal

Watertown

Oswego

Oswego River

Fulton

Oneida River

→ To Albany

Oneida Lake

Oneida Community

Rochester

Erie Canal

New York Central R.R.

Syracuse

← To Buffalo

Seneca River

Geneva

Waterloo

Seneca Falls

Auburn

Finger Lakes

SCALE

0   10   20

Miles

Elmira

F.R.M.

CENTRAL-WESTERN NEW YORK

No more alone sleeping, no more alone waking,
Thy dreams divided, thy prayers in twain;
Thy merry sisters to-night forsaking,
Never shall we see thee, maiden, again.

Never shall we see thee, thine eyes glancing,
Flashing with laughter and wild with glee,
Under the mistletoe kissing and dancing,
Wantonly free.

There shall come a matron walking sedately,
Low-voiced, gentle, wise in reply.
Tell me, O tell me, can I love her greatly?
All for her sake must the maiden die!

—Mary Elizabeth Coleridge, "Marriage"

Prologue

—⚬⚬⚬—

The adversary has spread out his hand upon all her pleasant things.

—Book of Lamentations

𝒯he girl has the quickened sense of all those who are hunted by night. Even as she sleeps she can catch the scent of danger, and now it reaches her, bringing her awake in an instant. She jerks upright on the straw mattress to listen for something she cannot yet hear. And she waits, knowing the stealth of the hunter.

The room is dark, too dark for her to see. Outside the room is a long, narrow corridor with a tall window and a table that holds a kerosene lamp. The lamp is meant to burn with a yolk-colored flame, but only for those who need its light, and she knows it will not be burning now. There is a humpback moon rising and that will be enough. She strains to hear through the darkness, listening in a brooding silence that waits to be broken by the rasp of a latch being lifted, the first furtive creak of the door. From the hall window a white sliver of moonlight will appear, and as the door begins to open, the sliver will spread like the pale flesh of a peach made to yield before its time. Then, with a louder creak, the door will swing all the way open, and the pungent odor of spirits will come to her just as she has dreamed it.

Now she hears a clicking sound. It is like the noise a rat

makes running over a tin roof, but she knows it is fingers fumbling with the latch. As the door slowly swings open, she crawls off the mattress and onto the bare floor before the man steps over the sill. When her rough cotton shift bunches above the fork of her thighs, she doesn't try to cover herself. Modesty has no meaning here.

Lying on her belly, she thrusts her forearm between the mattress and the floorboards, her hand groping until it touches the smooth bone handle of a carving knife. The one she had stolen from the kitchen the day before. She pulls the knife out and gets to her knees, inching backward until she huddles against the wall beside a crudely built cabinet. The cabinet holds one drawer, a wash basin, and a chamber pot. Aside from the mattress, it is the only piece of furniture in the room, and it cannot conceal her.

His breathing sounds labored, as if he is hurried, and when he comes into the room his spurred boot heels grate on the clean bare wood. The grating stops suddenly, and she hears his breath come faster. She knows why he has stopped. She presses her back against the wall, not needing to see to know what he is doing, and she hears the clink of his gold belt buckle as it hits the floor.

It will take him a moment to find her. Even though the room is small, each night she pushes the mattress to a different corner. Sometimes, when the smell is strong, he will stumble over the mattress, and then she can edge past him and escape through the door. He doesn't always come after her. Not if he knows there is someone in the house who is still awake and might hear.

But this time she might not get away, because his step is steady as he comes toward the cabinet. The girl grips the handle of the knife with both hands. She doesn't know if she will use it for him, or for herself, but she remembers the last time, and she will use the knife.

She hears him take another step toward her. Her palms are slick with sweat, and when she tries to tighten her grip on the bone handle, the knife slips from her grasp to drop with a clatter. With her hands outstretched she gropes in blind desperation, searching the floor, but the knife has slid beyond her reach.

Then, coming from the darkness beyond him, she hears a faint keening sound and the man's breath catches when, like a faraway echo, the sound repeats. It is a woman's voice, calling from an upstairs bedroom. The girl's room is beneath it, across the hall from the kitchen in the rear of the house. Now she hears the slither of fabric, the snick of a belt being buckled, then the thud of his boot when he kicks the door. He mutters an oath as he steps back into the corridor, and the biting smell trails after him like an engorged tail.

The door to her room closes. And with a soft click the latch drops into place. It will not be lifted again tonight; she knows this from the past. He will not return until another night.

The girl remains on her knees, listening to his boots strike each polished oak step as he mounts the stairs. She hears a door slam shut. From afar comes his raised voice, an answering voice, his again. The voices continue until another door, somewhere along the upstairs corridor, closes with a muffled rattle. His voice that has been growing louder, grows louder still. Then, as if a heavy weight has dropped, she hears a thump and the squeal of bedsprings. It could be the springs, or the faint cries, that sound to her like a small animal being tormented.

She has never once cried when he comes here. It is later that she cries.

The smell of her own sweat wraps around her like salt mist from the sea. But the only sea she knows is a picture in her mind, so sharp-etched it looks like the brown daguerreotype prints hanging in the corridor: she is running on warm sand that falls away beneath her and when she looks back over her shoulder she can see the footprints she is making.

But when she looks again, the sand is smooth and the foot-prints are gone, as if she had never been there.

Like the moth that wings too close to the flame, she leaves not a trace of her flight.

The moon has been climbing, and now a square of grime-streaked window lets watery light enter. It throws across the floor a kneeling shadow with arms bent like those of the Virgin in prayer. The girl looks down at her hands. She cannot remember finding the knife but she must have, because she is pressing the handle so hard against her chest she can barely draw breath.

And she knows what it is she must do.

MONDAY
May 27, 1861

1

—⁓⁓—

*Let us cast our eyes over the history of man, and
we shall scarcely find a page that is not tarnished
by some foul deed or bloody transaction.*

—Mary Wollstonecraft, 1794

*V*iolence does not always trumpet its coming. Its advance
may be hushed, like the creak of the stair where a predator
treads, the click of the bolt before a door opens, the whish of
the knife while it plunges. Or it may be as silent as one look
of hate sent across a room.

And the night conceals what the day will reveal.

In the predawn hours, foghorns began to sound, and the
morning gave hint of what had passed, breaking as it did
with a chill mist that rose from river and canal to wrap the
village in a tattered shroud. Bells tolled from church steeples
draped in ragged gray. And while foghorns and church bells
were frequent enough in Seneca Falls, they could mute less
commonplace sounds that otherwise might have been heard.
When the mist lifted at noon on a flawless day, skeptical
townsfolk crept out of doors, none quite believing that at last
the belated spring had come. Although nearly none could
have known what its coming would bring.

Glynis Tryon was among the disbelieving when the first
shafts of sunlight glanced off the tall, glazed windows of her
library. She decided it must be true, the return of the sun,
when dust motes flurried over her cluttered desk, and the

clear *cheerup* notes of a robin came through the door that her assistant had opened minutes before. Then she heard a faraway train whistle. With another glance at the tall pendulum clock standing against one wall, Glynis rose from her desk and went to the hooks beside the door to fetch her cloak.

She nodded to several library patrons, and called, "I'm off to the rail station again, Jonathan, for what I trust will be the last time."

The only indication that Jonathan Quant had heard came from a bob of his head. His bespectacled eyes did not raise from the pages of the book propped before him; a book whose dustcover displayed a distraught-faced, nubile young woman in the clutches of a red-caped, mustachioed man whose intentions were clearly not good. And in the event this illustration might prove too subtle for readers, the title in crimson letters blared: *A Lady in Distress.*

Glynis sighed in what she knew was futile frustration with Jonathan's long-standing passion for these popular melodramas, and went through the door to climb shallow steps to a wide dirt road. She had not thought to wear a hat that morning, depending instead on the hood of her cloak, and now she used a hand to shade her eyes against the unfamiliar sun. Like everyone else in town, she felt as if she had spent the previous months entombed.

Seneca Falls had endured the dreariest of winters, much like a prolonged illness which the afflicted comes to believe will end only with death. A blizzard in November had stripped the trees of leaves and buried the last chrysanthemums. An ice storm in April had doomed the first daffodils. And the Christmas season, the brightest note in the darkest month, had been paired with a clarion call from the Southern states, joined by a drum of hooves from the horsemen of the Apocalypse. But many had not heard or had refused to listen.

Since then, Fort Sumter had fallen to the newly formed Confederacy, the city of Baltimore had seen first blood, and the key border state of Virginia had announced that it too would leave the Union. These were events sufficient to discourage even the most sanguine of souls. At least those souls in western New York, and elsewhere in the North, who paid any heed.

Glynis, walking up Fall Street, slowed to watch robins search the warming earth, and when she passed under the tall elms that lined the road, it seemed that she could almost see their leaves unfurling to cast over the town the heart-lifting, green haze of spring. On such an afternoon as this, the reality of civil war seemed remote. But when she had seen Lincoln inaugurated in March, the city of Washington had bristled with cannon as it readied itself for siege.

She turned off Fall Street, the road that ran east and west through the center of town, then started up a side road that led to the railroad station. Just moments later, she heard behind her a rapid thud of hooves and moved quickly to the road's edge, although she could see no good reason why a horse would be urged to gallop while still within village limits. She turned as it pounded past her, catching only a glimpse of its hooded rider, who was mostly obscured by a long, dark cloak.

Despite its pace, the dapple gray horse appeared to be under control, yet the impression Glynis had from what little she could see of the rider's blanched face was that it held fear. The face also struck her as being somehow familiar. But she had lived in Seneca Falls long enough for nearly everyone in it to look familiar; everyone but the transients who worked the canal and the railroad, or those simply passing through town on the way to somewhere else. Still, as she watched the retreating horse, the rider's face nagged at her. Where had she seen it before? But then, as the hoofbeats faded down the road, a train's long whistle sounded from the east, followed by another from the west, and Glynis put everything else from her mind and walked quickly toward the rail station.

When she neared the station's cobblestone drive, she could hear a babble of male voices, and upon reaching the one-story depot she found twenty or thirty men outfitted in spanking-new militia uniforms. Sunlight glinted from a forest of steel gun barrels, many of them on the Springfield-type rifles manufactured by the Remington Arms Company in the Mohawk Valley of central New York. The canteens and haversacks slung over shoulders looked new, as did the scabbards on swords and bayonets. Some of these men were striding back and forth beside the station house, holding forth heatedly, while most were speaking quietly among themselves. A few, saying nothing at all, simply gazed down the railroad track.

They must be members of New York's 33rd Regiment, Glynis guessed, made up of companies from Seneca County who would proceed to Elmira, the central rendezvous point. From there they would head south to Washington. Lincoln had asked for 75,000 volunteer troops to guard what had become an increasingly vulnerable city. Since New York had been among the first states to respond to the President's call, this company was not the first to leave Seneca County. And, as was daily becoming more evident, it would not be the last. Some civic-minded group must have foreseen this, because the station house entrance had been draped with a red, white, and blue bunting, and there were red, white, and blue flags flying from every possible upright object. Even from the baggage carts.

Scattered here and there among the men stood a small number of women. While they were discouraged from coming to the train station—the thought being that women would bring a maudlin sentimentality to the occasion—there were always a few who persisted. These were usually young women, and, as on this day, they were far from being maudlin; most of them, dressed in pastel-colored spring frocks and straw bonnets, were lightheartedly cheerful, waving nosegays from which trailed long blue ribbons.

One of the younger women, Faith Alden, Glynis recognized because the girl worked in her niece Emma's dress shop. Faith appeared to view this leave-taking with somewhat less enthusiasm than the others; her eyes looked red-rimmed and their lids were swollen. Her hair was tied with glossy white ribbon, and she carried a bouquet of violets, perhaps given to her by the subdued-looking young man in uniform standing at her side. More than once she buried her face in the violets as if she might be hiding tears.

The few older women there forced wan smiles, as if they too might be attempting to withhold the unacceptable signs of grief.

In spite of the sunlit afternoon, Glynis experienced an oppressive gloom. She could remember well the first months of the Mexican War and the festive air of those soldiers' departure. She also remembered the men who did not come back. Like young Jamie Terhune, married for just one year before he left. His bride Jenny still kept vigil at the railroad station, sleeping at night in the baggage room and meeting each incoming train lest she miss Jamie's return. She was known as Mad Jenny, waiting for a man who fifteen years before had died in battle on the slopes of the continental divide. How could that war have been forgotten so soon?

Most of the men in town, at least most of the younger ones, believed that the "Dixie Rebellion," as they persisted in calling the secession crisis, was something that would be over shortly; just a few weeks of skirmishing before the South came to its senses, dropped to its knees, and begged a return to the Union. In the meantime, the volunteers held daily drills, marching and target shooting with others who came from their home-town militia companies. Making it still more a community affair was the fact that even the men's drillmasters and immediate officers were their friends and neighbors. And after all, they'd only signed up for ninety days. So why fret about the future?

Glynis, hurrying past the men, saw this carnival atmosphere as a celebration of failure. Not something that she wanted to watch. As she walked to the far side of the station house, several male voices burst forth with Stephen Foster's "Oh! Susanna." The singers were immediately joined by others, and yet, while the song had been so widely popular for so long that almost everyone knew the words, it was, Glynis thought, a singularly inappropriate one to be singing now. *Oh! Susanna / Don't you cry for me / For I come from Alabama / With a banjo on my knee.*

While she waited against a backdrop of men's voices rising and falling with each verse, her earlier impatience, together with a measure of anxiety, continued to grow. It was the third time today she had stood there, staring down the empty tracks. Each time a New York Central train had approached from the west, she had expected her niece Bronwen Llyr, and each time Bronwen had not appeared. But she must be on this next train. It was the last one scheduled until the following morning, and Bronwen had promised to arrive for her cousin Emma's pre-nuptial party to be held that evening. Breaking promises had not in the past been among Bronwen's shortcomings.

At last, and after a series of piercing whistles, the eastbound, twenty-ton locomotive roared around a bend, its brakes already screeching. Several minutes later brought the westbound train grinding to a halt. Now facing each other on their separate tracks, the engines followed by their long tails of passenger cars looked like two fire-belching dragons about to engage in mortal combat.

Glynis had moved away as the trains steamed into the station, spewing sparks like live volcanoes. One of these days a spark would fly too far and send the entire village up in flames. But while she had been predicting this for a decade, and although it had happened in other places, it had yet to happen in Seneca Falls. Perhaps because someone had demanded that the station house be built of brick.

When passengers began descending to the station platforms, Glynis inched forward, hoping they didn't notice how thoroughly they were being scrutinized. It would not be the first time that Bronwen, now employed as a United States Treasury agent, had traveled in disguise. In fact, she had cheerfully admitted, "It's as good as being invisible. Just consider the possibilities!"

Glynis considered many as she stood there studying each arriving passenger with a wary eye and craning her neck to see past the uniformed men now waiting to board. Although there could be no reason for her niece to disguise herself here in Seneca Falls, she might do it just for a lark.

"Miss Tryon?" said a familiar voice beside her. "Glynis?"

She looked around in surprise at the tall woman, close in age to her own early forties, in a simple dark dress; her thick brown hair, visible under a small bonnet, had been drawn back over her ears into a coiled bun at the nape of her neck. Glynis felt a warm flush creep into her face. She'd been so engrossed in the role of unmasking her niece that she'd missed the arrival of Susan Anthony.

"I'm sorry, Susan, I didn't see you," she apologized.

"No, you looked right past me. You must be expecting someone?"

"My niece. You might remember Bronwen. Bronwen Llyr?"

Susan began to smile, and the keen blue-gray eyes held an expression that said: *I would be unlikely to forget her.*

She would not, of course, actually say that. But what rose in Glynis's mind was a memory, a very clear one, of being brought to the window of her library above the canal by the noise of ducks and geese squawking furiously as they scattered in every direction. The reason for this uproar had appeared in the form of Bronwen, astride a horse that she was galloping, to no earthly purpose, along the canal towpath. As it happened, a team of mules, their towlines running to a packet boat, had been plodding along the path minding their own business. And Glynis had made what seemed to her, and surely to any other sane person, the natural assumption: that when Bronwen saw the mules she would rein in the horse. But no; she had urged it on. Glynis had sucked in her breath, wanting desperately to turn away, but unable to tear her gaze from the looming catastrophe. Then, with the aplomb of two veteran circus performers, horse and rider sailed over the mules as if they were just another programmed obstacle. The mule driver's reaction had been obvious from the clenched fists he'd shaken, and it had been a long while before Glynis could breathe normally.

And what brought this to mind at the moment was her later discovery that Susan Anthony had that day been aboard the packet boat.

But the woman was now smiling broadly. She pulled a scarlet shawl around her shoulders, saying to Glynis, "I like your Bronwen. I like all of your nieces—"

Susan was interrupted by a sudden surge of noise. The men of New York's 33rd had begun clambering aboard the passenger cars, and there was as yet no sign of Bronwen. But perhaps she was still on the train, struggling with her luggage. Although Bronwen rarely struggled; most men as a rule were more than eager to shoulder her freight. A fact of which she, at least some of the time, appeared to be blithely unaware. *Appeared to be,* Glynis thought, being the operative phrase here.

In the meantime, Susan, looking for a baggage handler and apparently finding none, went to pluck her valise from a baggage cart. After hailing an open carriage, she told Glynis, "I'm on my way to Mrs. Stanton's for a long-overdue visit, and I am delighted that it coincided with Emma's wedding date."

"Mrs. Stanton" was always called so by Susan, despite the fact that she and Elizabeth Stanton had been, for nearly ten years, fast friends and mutual supporters.

Glynis watched the woman's carriage leave, and when she turned back to the train it was with sinking hope. It now seemed certain that Bronwen would not appear. The militia men had finished boarding the passenger cars and were leaning out of the windows, while the women had lined up alongside the tracks, waving their flowers and flags. A young boy, standing apart from the others, wore an expression of utter dejection, as if he were being forced to stay behind while his friends went off to the fair.

Someone with a reed flute had begun to pipe "Yankee Doodle," which was quickly joined by boisterous singing. When the conductors went up the steps, indicating that both trains would depart shortly, Glynis began to wonder if she should consider taking up residence in the station's baggage room together with Jenny Terhune. Jenny, who at the moment was skittering toward the station house, clutching several crusts of bread.

A *clip-clop* of hooves behind Glynis made her turn to see the Seneca Falls constable, Cullen Stuart, astride his Morgan horse. An amused expression creased his face along the lines worked by time and weather, his sand-colored hair had grown shaggy around his neck and ears, and the thick brush mustache was scarcely trimmed. Not that it mattered. Cullen, like Bronwen, seemed unaware of his effect on those of the opposite gender; but in his case, Glynis had long since decided, the lack of awareness was more than likely authentic.

He leaned down to speak to her over the noise of the nearest locomotive's gathering steam. "I take it Bronwen hasn't shown up."

"No, Cullen, she hasn't. As you see."

"You sound exasperated."

She knew she did, and tried to smile. "A common enough reaction to Bronwen—"

She broke off when she found herself shouting over the deafening noise of the locomotive, the men on board yelling the last chorus of "Yankee Doodle," the young women screaming their good-byes, and over it all the reed flute shrilling like a frenzied bird.

She and Cullen waited while one train, then the other, pulled slowly out of the station. When the roar of the engines had begun to diminish, the older women allowed themselves to weep openly. And a number of the younger ones, as if they had just now realized that the party was over, had also begun to cry. Faith Alden, the wilting bouquet of violets now crushed against her face, was among them.

Cullen's earlier smile had long since faded. He had watched the departing trains with an odd expression, and Glynis suddenly wondered if he might be thinking that he, too, should be heading south. "Cullen," she began, hearing the catch in her voice, "you aren't considering—"

"So where is Bronwen?" he broke in, as if he'd anticipated her question and didn't want her to ask it.

Trying to push aside the specter of Cullen leaving for war, Glynis answered, "You know Bronwen. She changes her plans as often as she changes her opinions, wouldn't you say?"

"No, I wouldn't say. She's usually reliable enough—when she chooses to be."

Not exactly unqualified praise, thought Glynis, who had begun to worry in earnest.

"Bronwen's coming from Washington?" Cullen asked.

Glynis nodded. "But she wrote that first she wanted to spend a few days in Rochester with her family. Then she would come on here by train. Today."

"If the trains were filled with troops, though, she might have taken a packet boat." Cullen twisted in the saddle to look toward the canal. "I'll check down at the boat landing."

He guided the Morgan toward Fall Street and the Seneca River and canal, which ran below and parallel to the road, while Glynis decided she should check the telegraph office in the event Bronwen had wired. She tried not to imagine how Emma would react when told that her cousin had failed to arrive.

She was walking past the station house when a tall, fair-haired woman emerged from it. Her face was plainly distressed as she glanced around her, and she stood there at the door before taking a few steps to a nearby wooden bench. After sinking onto it, she brought up her hands to cover her face. Glynis had slowed, at first thinking she had seen the woman somewhere before, although the burgundy wool, hoop-skirted dress and cloak looked more elegant than were usually seen in Seneca Falls; the black, soft-leather shoes and kid gloves more appropriate for city streets. In comparison to her garments, the woman's fine gold hair beneath a black velvet bonnet struck a discordant note. Its disheveled appearance suggested a long train ride. Which could mean that she, despite Glynis's initial impression, was a stranger to Seneca Falls.

Glynis could not have said what made her approach the woman. It might have been the prod of memory, a sudden recollection of another well-dressed woman who, years before, had come to town a stranger, and whose life shortly thereafter had been ended by murder. A murder that could possibly have been prevented, Glynis had always felt with guilty remorse, if someone like herself had thought to inquire the woman's intent.

She crossed the cobbled paving to stand before the woman, and said cautiously, "Please excuse me if I'm intruding, but I wonder if I might be of help?"

The woman's hands dropped to her lap and startled, blue eyes met those of Glynis. "I don't know," she answered in a hesitant voice which sounded not so much weak as troubled.

"Were you to be met?" Glynis asked, although the woman did not strike her as one who would collapse over the absence of a reception.

"No," the woman answered. "But I believe there is someone I know . . . that is, I hadn't expected anyone to meet me." Her voice now sounded more steady, and she attempted a smile. "I'm just feeling somewhat overwhelmed by what I've done."

Glynis seated herself on the bench, nodding in encouragement, and trusting that the woman would go on to explain what exactly it was she had done. When she did not, Glynis gave the woman her name, then said again, "I'd like to be of help, if I can."

The woman straightened, saying, "I apologize if I've seemed ungrateful. My name is Elise Jager and I've come here from . . . from east of Syracuse, and . . ." Her voice trailed off, while she studied Glynis, but then she evidently came to a decision, because she continued, "I have reason to believe that my daughter is here in this town, but I don't know where to begin looking for her."

When she did not offer more to Glynis, her silence raised immediate questions: Why was this woman's daughter in Seneca Falls, and not in Syracuse? How on earth could a woman lose track of her own child? Glynis didn't ask. Elise Jager's wary expression held every indication of intelligence, so she must have known that her words would be heard as odd ones. And if she didn't choose to explain herself, Glynis wouldn't intrude further, not with Bronwen's whereabouts continuing to concern her. She should be off to the telegraph office.

"Perhaps you could start with the constable, Mrs. Jager," she said. Because of the gloves, she could see no ring, but assumed that if the woman had a daughter she was, or had been, married. Or, if not, that might answer the questions.

"Constable Stuart left here a few minutes ago," Glynis went on, rising from the bench and gesturing toward the canal. "He planned to stop at the boat landing, but if you don't find him there, you should try his office. Anyone in town can direct you to it. I'm on my way to Fall Street," she added, "so I'd be happy to walk with you that far."

Elise Jager had gotten to her feet, and she gave Glynis a brief nod.

"Do you have any baggage?" Glynis inquired, glancing around.

"I've had it sent to Carr's Hotel," the woman answered briefly.

As they walked toward Fall Street, Mrs. Jager said nothing more, showing little interest in the church and the school that they passed. Glynis found the woman's lack of curiosity peculiar. One would have thought, after arriving in an unfamiliar town and needing to find a daughter, she would be asking questions.

When they reached the corner of Fall Street, Glynis again gestured in the direction of the boat landing. "You may meet the constable on your way down there."

"How will I recognize him?"

"He rides a black Morgan, and he wears a badge," Glynis said, smiling. "Both horse and man are markedly handsome, so I doubt that you'll miss them." She extended her hand, saying, "I wish you well in your search, Mrs. Jager, and should you want to see me again, I can usually be found in the Seneca Falls library."

The exception to that, she thought with some irritation, being those days when she was forced to wander the railroad station like an out-of-work drifter. She stood for a moment, watching the woman walk toward the canal, then hurried on to the telegraph office.

When she'd questioned the telegraph operator, Mr. Grimes, he had been adamant: no wire had come from her niece. So where was she? thought Glynis as she emerged from the tiny cubicle of an office. She remembered much too clearly that the only time Bronwen had failed to send word, she had been in serious trouble. But what could possibly have happened to her now?

While in the telegraph office, Glynis had debated with herself as to whether she should send a wire to Rochester. But if Bronwen had simply been delayed en route—and connecting trains were often late—such a wire would cause her family needless worry.

Glynis sighed, then raised her eyes from the road, as she became aware of some commotion on the far side of Fall Street. A handful of townsfolk were standing there, pointing excitedly and shading their eyes as they gazed at the sky. Since she heard anxiety in their voices, Glynis discarded the simplest explanation: a late flock of Canada geese winging northward. As she started across the road, people began pouring from shops and offices, all pointing upward, so before she reached the others, Glynis stopped to search the cloudless sky. She blinked several times to clear her vision, then looked again. And still did not believe what she saw.

There, high over the land to the west, was something that appeared far too large to be a bird, or even a flock of birds. It bobbed slightly on the nearly windless air, and as Glynis watched, along with what had become a growing crowd, the object looked to be slowly descending.

She decided that if she were losing her mind, then she was at least not alone in madness, as the voices of those on the street were reaching fever-pitch. When her elbow was suddenly nudged, she turned to find the Morgan nuzzling her sleeve. "Cullen! What *is* that? Do you know?"

He gave her an odd smile when he dismounted, as if she were asking him the obvious. But he seemed fairly unconcerned, and while this had the effect of calming those nearby, they looked to him for an explanation. Glynis, staring upward at the now rapidly approaching object, said with some frustration, "Cullen, if you know what that—"

She broke off, because all at once she knew. It must have shown on her face, because Cullen nodded, saying, "Sure, it's a balloon."

"A gas balloon!" she said, suddenly recalling articles that she'd seen in library copies of *Harper's Weekly*. And now it did seem obvious. A pale, shimmering balloon that floated on the air like an immense, gone-to-seed dandelion. With her references now in mind, Glynis knew that it must be made of India silk contained in a net of thin, knotted silk twine.

"It's a lot bigger than the ones I've read about," Cullen said. "Must be fifty feet high, and I'll bet it weighs a ton or more. Wonder where it's going to land."

"Surely it won't land here," Glynis said, shading her eyes against the canal's reflected light. "How can it? We don't have coal gas yet, so it couldn't be reinflated to take off again."

While this seemed reasonable to her, Cullen just shook his head, and there now could be small doubt that the balloon, coal gas or not, was descending. As it came closer, Glynis could pick out, suspended from ropes that hung below the balloon, what appeared to be a large, rattan or wicker basket. And on the balloon itself, like a ship of the sky, had been painted the name *Enterprise.*

Since Cullen's announcement, the crowd had quieted, all eyes straining upward, until a voice shouted, "Look! There's somebody in there!"

Glynis felt a sudden prick of foreboding, then pushed it aside as being too outlandish to consider. She remained uneasy, though, and by the time the deflating balloon had neared the far reach of the canal, she began to think that her fear might have been justified.

She then heard Cullen's quick intake of breath, followed by, "Glynis, it looks as if there are two people in that basket. You don't think one of them could—" He broke off, shaking his head again, at the same time beginning to smile. A minute later he was laughing. "It's her, all right! I'd know that redhead anywhere."

"No, it can't be!" But even as Glynis denied it, she spotted, above the rim of the basket, a red-gold blur.

Just as the now wrinkling balloon seemed to tower above them, the crowd gasped with one voice. The rattan basket began to brush the first branches of several lofty elms, swinging erratically with a sickening, bobbing succession of jerks. Then, with a series of sharp, crunching noises, it struck the tree's lower limbs. A piercing cry—and if Bronwen's, it would be fury rather than terror—reached those standing below, and over the side of the basket appeared strands of long red hair lashing like bloodied ropes.

Glynis was barely aware of Cullen's hands gripping her shoulders. With her own hands clenched to her mouth, she watched the balloon swing slowly to one side like a ship listing in high seas, while the basket, now lurching wildly, was dragged through a tangle of whipping branches. Its occupants, if the forked limbs did not impale them first, would surely be thrown out. And no one dropping from that height could possibly survive.

2

———m———

At an altitude of a mile and a fifth I shot out of the lower westerly current, and entered the great easterly river of the sky.

—Thaddeus Sobieski Constantine Lowe, 1861

The rattan basket pitched and bucked, jerking from side to side through branches, while stripping off tender new leaves that rained down like confetti. Its occupants must have been thrown to the basket floor, because all Glynis could see of them were two pairs of hands clamped over the rim. As she craned her neck, trying to catch a glimpse of Bronwen through the maelstrom, she vowed that if her niece somehow managed to survive this horror, she would never be forgiven for participating in it. The next moment Glynis vowed never again to scold Bronwen, not even for reckless behavior. But what, if not reckless behavior, was this? How could Bronwen have allowed herself to be put in such peril?

On and on, for what seemed an eternity, the leaves and branches tossed and churned, nearly obscuring a view of the basket. Glynis had convinced herself that at any moment a young body would suddenly plunge to earth, but could not take her eyes from what she could not bear to watch.

All at once she realized that something was striking her face. It was as if she were being pummeled by tiny, stinging drops of hard rain, and everyone around her seemed to be rubbing their eyes.

"It's sand," Cullen said to her, coughing, "used as ballast. They're throwing it over the side to gain some altitude."

Sure enough, ever so slowly the balloon began to swing upward. The flurry of leaves diminished as the basket appeared to be righting itself, and suddenly, with one last breathtaking jerk, it broke free of the branches. Then the rapidly deflating balloon and the basket, with ropes now dangling from it, continued their descent, and Glynis felt the grip of Cullen's hands on her shoulders loosen.

"It's heading for the park!" he shouted to her over the noise of the crowd. Seizing her waist, he nearly threw her onto the Morgan, swinging up behind her to urge the horse forward. Dazed townsfolk parted before them like a sluggish sea, then surged after them as the Morgan left Fall Street for a side road and cantered toward the park.

Glynis, seated sideways and none too firmly on the horse, clutched the black mane and anchored herself against Cullen. She could feel him shaking, and didn't need to see his face to know he was laughing, undoubtedly thinking that the town hadn't seen this much excitement since the last fire. She couldn't help but wonder again why Bronwen continued to exercise such reckless disregard for her own well-being. Unless, of course, the balloon had been her notion of a theatrical arrival. The ultimate *deus ex machina.*

Cullen's laughter was all very well, but Glynis didn't know yet whether to laugh or to cry, not until she saw Bronwen all in one piece. And if she was whole, Glynis reminded herself, she would never be forgiven.

Just ahead of them lay the open park and, waving above it, a crinkled billow of pale, tannish silk.

"Please catch the ropes," came a booming voice from the sky. "Hold the ropes, if you please!" It took Glynis a second to realize that the voice was not supernatural in origin, but must be coming through a megaphone.

When they reached the park's grassy verge, Cullen reined in the Morgan, and his deputies Zeph Waters and Liam

Cleary could be seen running from the opposite direction. They abruptly stopped short, freezing in place as they watched the balloon basket nearing the ground. At Cullen's yell of "Grab the ropes!" the young men again sprang to life and raced across the grass.

Surprisingly, the basket bumped rather gently only a few times before coming to rest. Some yards beyond, the once huge balloon, now crumpling and wavering like a drunken ghost, began to collapse with a curious slithering sound.

Glynis slid from the Morgan's back as Cullen dismounted and tossed her the reins. Immediately he loped toward the balloon, at the same time shouting to the deputies, "Anchor the ropes to the hitching posts, then hold back the crowd! And don't let pipes or cigarettes anywhere near it!"

Glynis threw the reins over a hitching post, and whirled round in time to see her niece being hoisted to the waist-high rim of the basket by a tall, dark-haired man. Bronwen shook her head while saying something to this man, then swung herself over the rim to stand, rather unsteadily, on the grass.

Her long coat hung in rumpled folds, her red hair looked as snarled and tangled as the balloon netting, and her face was sunburned, but otherwise she appeared none the worse for her time in the sky. Twigs and leaves flew from her coat as with long strides, her balance clearly restored, she walked briskly toward her aunt. When she neared, Glynis saw the green eyes under the tumbled hair holding their familiar, expectant glitter, as if Bronwen were a magician who had just performed an impossible escape and now awaited applause.

Glynis, with a supreme effort, somehow managed to say only, "You have arrived, I see."

"It was beyond words, Aunt Glyn! Utterly glorious—well, except for the last part. As Professor Lowe says, it's like riding a great river in the sky."

"Indeed."

"You just can't imagine what it's like up there." Bronwen's arms stretched skyward. "Everything down here on the ground looks so small . . . so—are you upset?"

"*Upset?* Whatever gave you that idea?"

"You're upset! I was afraid you might be." Bronwen sobered instantly and lowered her head in what was evidently supposed to be contrition. The attempt was unsuccessful, because the sobriety quickly dissolved in a grin. And although Glynis struggled against it, she had to smile.

"Aunt Glynis, you have to meet Professor Lowe."

Glynis looked past Bronwen to see both her aerial comrade and Cullen securing the balloon. And for the second time that day, she could scarcely believe her eyes. The dark-haired man beside Cullen wore an elegant, satin-lapeled Prince Albert coat, and had just donned a tall silk hat.

"Does ballooning require formal dress?" she asked, before recalling that Bronwen frequently took such comments literally.

"The professor was at a banquet when word came that the high wind had died. He didn't have time to change, and I couldn't even wire you, we had to take off so quickly!"

"Take off from where?"

"West of here," Bronwen said, with a vague wave of her hand. Glynis began to ask the specific location of this launch, but Bronwen interrupted her with, "I'll tell you about it later. Now come and meet him."

Professor Lowe stood a shade taller than Cullen's six feet, and even had he not been in evening clothes would have cut a dashing figure, Glynis thought as she and Bronwen approached him. His sturdy frame surprised her; she would have guessed, after reading the *Harper's* articles, that an aeronaut needed to be slighter, and to weigh considerably less than this man must. A trim mustache was as thick and black as his hair, the dark blue eyes deeply set under heavy brows. When introduced, Thaddeus Lowe raised his hat and bent slightly over her extended hand. "I hope we haven't

worried you too greatly, Miss Tryon. Trees can be dangerous, I grant you, but the balloon is really quite safe."

Glynis might have argued the point; he, after all, had not
been riveted to the ground, watching in abject terror. But she
refrained, mostly because a quick grin from Cullen told her
that she would be wasting her breath.

"My niece tells me you came from west of here," she said
instead to Lowe. "I remember reading that you believe the
upper wind currents all flow from west to east, no matter
what the weather conditions on the ground. Is that right?"

"Absolutely right." He seemed delighted that she knew
something about this, and in his enthusiasm he fairly
glowed. "That's been my hypothesis, and now I feel confident that it's more than just conjecture. It's a fact! I've made
enough of these flights to satisfy myself, and to prove it to
those in science who've scoffed. That's not to say, however,
that a balloon is not influenced by ground winds—" he
turned to smile at Bronwen "—as your niece can tell you."

Bronwen shot him a peculiar look, Glynis noticed, very
much as if she were warning the man of something. Then,
possibly aware of her aunt's scrutiny, Bronwen laughed and
said, "We were nearly blown off course."

Lowe nodded. "The lower winds from Lake Erie pushed
us to the southeast."

"People would like a closer look," said Cullen, who had
been watching an excited crowd that now must be made up
of at least a third of the town, and that his deputies were
holding back with determined effort.

"They can't do the balloon much harm at this stage,"
Lowe told him. "Not if they can be kept from walking on it."

Bronwen turned to scan the crowd, then said to Professor
Lowe, "My cousin is over there and I'd like to see her for a
minute. Then we'll find you a place to stay." She turned and
walked toward Emma, whom Glynis had just seen standing
at the far edge of the crush of people.

At a gesture from Cullen, his deputies came forward with

the crowd close on their heels. The men positioned themselves to protect the silk fabric, while the increasingly loud babble of voices drove Glynis to follow Bronwen across the grass.

Emma stood there waiting, as if she had just stepped from a page of *Godey's Lady's Book,* in a flounced, hoop-skirted dress of rose-colored cambric. Long, dark brown hair was caught back with pink grosgrain ribbon, and the white velvet parasol that she held dripped with silk fringe. She accepted her cousin's quick embrace with a faint smile.

"I'm glad you're here safely, Bronwen. And thank you for coming. That was a dramatic entrance."

Glynis smiled, recognizing that Emma too had picked up the theatrical element of her cousin's descent into Seneca Falls. But Bronwen threw Glynis a quick, baffled glance before she said, "Emma, are you all right?"

Emma's dark brows raised slightly. "Yes, I'm all right. Why wouldn't I be?"

"I thought you might be annoyed that I . . . that I was late getting here."

Emma shook her head, but didn't answer and seemed preoccupied. Had seemed so for several days, and Glynis wondered uneasily if it was the wedding preparations alone that troubled her. Or if the recent argument with her fiancé, attorney Adam MacAlistair, had escalated rather than been resolved.

"The party tonight will be at Emma's shop," Glynis told Bronwen, more to divert her from questioning her cousin than anything else.

Emma seemed to pull herself back into the present with some difficulty. "Yes, we've been moving things around all day to accommodate a harp"—Emma gave Glynis an amused look—"under the baton of Vanessa Usher."

Glynis pressed her lips together to keep from smiling when Bronwen groaned. "I thought Aunt Glyn wrote me," she said to her cousin, "that The Lady Vanessa was hosting your wedding. Or is she, as usual, running the entire show?"

Emma's smile abruptly sobered. "Miss Usher is being very generous, and I'm not sure I like my wedding being characterized as a 'show.'"

"No, of course not—I'm probably still giddy from the thin air. But Emma, why shouldn't Vanessa Usher be generous? She's got more money than Midas, and she could never find clothes like the gorgeous stuff you make for her."

Glynis watched a storm gather in Emma's gray eyes, as she obviously seemed torn between defending her best customer and accepting her cousin's rather backhanded compliment. But while "gorgeous stuff" was not the most delicate phrasing, it was undistilled Bronwen and Emma should know her cousin by now. Trying to head off trouble, Glynis said quickly, "We should probably be going, Bronwen, or there won't be time to dress."

"I'm afraid I didn't bring much to wear," Bronwen said with a look of untypical chagrin. "I knew the bridesmaids' dresses were being made by you, Emma, and the balloon's basket can't hold much, so . . ."

"I've things at the shop that you can wear," Emma offered. "Actually, I've made several gowns for you—and for Cousin Kathryn, too," she added. "We're nearly enough the same size."

Size, thought Glynis, being the only thing about these young women that was the same. And Bronwen's older sister Katy—or Kathryn, as she had gently suggested that she now be called—was unlike either.

"Em, I hope you don't intend to put me in one of those steel-cage hoops," Bronwen said, "or worse yet, a corset!"

Her cousin's face gave away nothing, but her eyes went beyond Bronwen to where Professor Lowe stood talking and nodding animatedly, surrounded by townspeople who were without doubt asking about his miraculous journey. He was

so tall that he put Glynis in mind of Gulliver among the Lil-
liputians.

Emma, her gaze still on Lowe, commented dryly, "Why
don't you just ask to borrow the Professor's stylish Prince
Albert coat, my dear cousin?"

"The very thing, Em! I'll ask him."

"You know, Bronwen," said Emma in a quiet voice, "I
have always feared for your sanity." She smiled very faintly
as she turned and walked toward Fall Street, the fringe on
her parasol swaying with every step.

"*Sanity?*" Bronwen repeated to Glynis. "Emma used to
call me just plain crazy. Have I been raised in rank, do you
think?"

Glynis was trying not to think of what the next days with
these two might bring, and so nearly missed Bronwen's second question.

"What's the matter with her, Aunt Glyn? Emma's always
been on the serious side, but now she looks positively funereal. Like she's readying for a wake instead of a wedding."

"Emma has a great deal on her mind," Glynis said eva-
sively, although this, as far as it went, was true. "I assume,
Bronwen, that you're staying with me at the boardinghouse?"

"Yes, after I find Professor Lowe a room. I'll take him to
Carr's Hotel—it can't be full of wedding guests yet, can it?"
Not waiting for an answer, she turned to start back across the
grass, saying, "I'll see him to Carr's, then I'll come to the
house."

With much of the crowd slowly and reluctantly dispers-
ing, Glynis went with Bronwen toward where the balloon
was being covered with tarpaulins by Professor Lowe and
the deputies. The heap of pale silk looked as insignificant as
a melting snowdrift.

"By the way," Glynis asked her niece casually, "how was
everyone in Rochester?"

"Rochester?"

If Glynis hadn't been watching for it, she would have missed the blank look that flashed across Bronwen's face. Her niece recovered instantly with, "Oh, you mean *Rochester!*"

"Yes, Rochester. The place where you grew up. Where your family lives. Where you said you were going to visit before coming here."

"Aunt Glynis, I couldn't get home. It just didn't work out. Besides, the family will be here in just a few days for the wedding," she said quickly, as if this somehow explained her sidestepping.

While she hadn't quite out-and-out lied, she'd come very close to it. However, since they had nearly reached the others, Glynis did not press her further. Instead, she commented, "We don't have gas here to reinflate the balloon. Professor Lowe knows that, doesn't he?"

Bronwen gazed studiously down at the grass. "I expect he does by now."

"You mean you didn't tell him that before you landed?" Glynis stopped to stare at her niece.

"I may have mentioned it."

When Glynis sighed heavily, Bronwen went on, "Look, Aunt Glyn, I absolutely had to get here. Otherwise you'd never have spoken to me again."

"I suppose that's possible."

"Well, there you are. And Professor Lowe is a genius. He'll think of something!"

3

—◊—

Is it nothing to you, all ye that pass by? behold, and see if there be any sorrow like unto my sorrow.

—Book of Lamentations

The girl slowly lifted her head. When she had first wakened, it had been to the harsh caw of unseen birds and the smell of marshland, and she had found herself lying on a small mound of earth tufted with grass. Now she could see that a short distance beyond her the grass sloped downward to meet a vast expanse of water, desolate and murky except for a few silver glints from a sun dipping low in the sky. The air bore a dankness that felt on her skin like laundry just pulled from tubs of lukewarm water.

The girl did not know how long she had been there. She held a hazy recollection of a loft in the carriage house, a horse rearing, and the sensation of falling. Only that; nothing more.

When she tried to pull herself upright, her head throbbed and her left arm hurt her, and when she looked down at it she saw a wound, as if somehow the top layers of skin had been torn apart. She fell back on the grass and lay there until the pain eased. A black snake undulated past, gliding silently into the water, and she heard overhead the cries of wild geese and the trill of smaller birds. From closer by came the murmur of water lapping at stalks of reeds and cattails.

The girl, moving carefully to favor the arm, tried again to pull herself upright, but now the weight of her wet cloak held her down. A few pieces of straw clung to the black wool as she raised herself to a kneeling position. When she saw the stark gray stumps of dead trees jutting from the water, she wondered if, before she had been thrown from the horse, she had somehow reached the edge of the vast Montezuma Marsh. But why would she be there? She couldn't seem to remember.

She looked down at her hands that were shaking as if they were birch leaves, and saw splotches on them that looked like smears of dried blood. And then it came; an image of wavering water and a prone body and the long handle of a knife, and above the body she saw the reflection of her own face.

The girl closed her eyes, grinding her fist against her forehead until it hurt so much she had to stop. The image lost its sharpness and gradually faded.

She tried to get to her feet, and fell back on the grass when her legs would not hold her. Her arm ached, and when she inched backward on her knees away from the water, her head throbbed with the rhythm of heartbeats. But then, over the throbbing, she heard a rustling noise. It came from behind her. It was moving closer, and with it came the sound of something splashing through water.

She had to get away. When she again tried to stand, she toppled over but did not cry out. The splashing sound came closer. She lay still and shut her eyes tightly, as if by not looking she could make the terror disappear. Then she heard what sounded like an animal panting, and something cold nudged her bloodied hands.

The smell of wet fur made her open her eyes. She looked into the face of a large dog that crouched before her as if ready to spring. Its keen gaze was trained on her with the intensity of a guard warning its prisoner not to move, so the girl lay still. But when she looked into the alert, brown eyes, her fear began to lessen. She recognized the dog as a shepherd, like the one she had known as a child; its undercoat of russet and white was overlaid by long dark outer hairs, as if the dog's back and head had been stroked with a sooty hand. Its erect ears twitched slightly, and when it rose from its crouch and moved sideways, she saw behind the dog a pair of worn, mudcaked boots below ragged trousers of jean cloth.

From somewhere she heard a moaning sound, and it came to her that the sound might be of her own making. But she could not talk, so that must not be. She was afraid to raise her eyes until the boots took several steps toward her, and when she forced herself to look up, the man was standing in front of her; a gaunt man with a heavy beard and wild dark hair that hid most of his face. But when he stepped toward her again, the hair fell away so she could see, staring down at her, fierce black eyes.

She tried to crawl away from him, but the dog sprang to its feet to block her path. The man bent down and reached for her shoulders, saying something she could not make out, and she tried to cry with her eyes what she could not cry with her voice—no . . . no . . . no . . . the words in her head going on and on like the lament of a small, snared beast.

The dog began to circle her while making a deep warning growl, the thick ruff of hair around its neck rising. When the man bent down again, the girl felt his hands slide under her arms, and then she was dragged forward on her belly. Still circling, the dog barked sharply as she tried to twist away from the man, clawing at his boots with her hands while the pain in her head and her arm sliced through her fear like a butcher's knife. Her arms had no strength. It seemed as if they were no more than bare branches tossed by the wind.

She thought the man said, "Stop struggling," and he looked down at her with a face of anger, and then she knew that he would force her. He would cover her mouth with his hand and pull up her skirt, pressing her under him into the silent marsh. The water would cover her face and then she would die.

When she felt herself being lifted, the fear stopped her breath. She strained for air, and the last thing she saw were the fierce dark eyes boring into her own.

4

—ᴍ—

Seneca Falls—upon [the] Seneca River, was in-
corporated April 22, 1831. It is a station on the
N.Y.C.R.R. [New York Central Rail Road] and the
Seneca Canal. The fall is 51 feet and furnishes an
abundance of water power which is greatly im-
proved. It contains 7 churches, the Seneca Falls
Academy, a union school, 2 newspaper offices, ex-
tensive manufactories of fire-engines, pumps, ma-
chinery, iron and woolen goods and a great
variety of other articles. Population about 4,000.

—from an 1860 *French Gazetteer*

Glynis stood at the window of the dress shop, looking out
onto Fall Street and watching gold-edged pink clouds in the
western sky fade into twilit mauve, while behind her the
plucked strings of a harp caroled softly under the murmur of
women's voices. The murmur was oftentimes punctuated by
soft laughter.

During daylight hours the view from the front window of
EMMA'S, a shop that sat tucked among others, was usually a
fairly lively one of horse-drawn farm wagons and carriages,
mule teams and their drivers, chickens and geese, the odd
sheep or cow that had somehow gotten loose, and even an
occasional black-and-white Berkshire sow and her young;
the last always bringing to the town a measure of excitement
while everyone ran around trying to capture the slippery lit-

tle porkers. There was also a bewildering number of cats and dogs, the sounds of whose ancient, mutual loathing could make the livestock and everything else within hearing distance miserable.

In the hours of early morning, and again at noon, Fall Street bustled with farmers, shopowners and customers, mill and factory workers, bankers, a few lawyers, doctors and one dentist, the constable and his two deputies. Now the road was nearly deserted. A few minutes before, Glynis had seen Cullen and the Morgan pass by at a fast clip. Cullen had looked deadly serious, so there likely had been a fight at one of the taverns down along the canal.

Something nudged her memory, and it was only then that Glynis remembered her encounter at the rail station with the troubled Mrs. Jager. But given what had followed that meeting, it was hardly a wonder that it had slipped her mind to ask Cullen if the woman had managed to find him.

Glynis turned back to what Emma called her "showroom" and the gathering of a dozen or more women friends, and a few of her favorite customers, as well as her employees Lacey Smith, a runaway slave come north years ago on the Underground Railroad, and young Faith Alden, whom Glynis had seen earlier at the rail station; the girl's eyelids still looked swollen. Most sat on small sofas and chairs provided by Emma's best customer, Vanessa Usher, while several of the younger women were on decorative pillows placed on the thick, green Brussels carpet. The smell of coffee and tea, and rhubarb pies and cinnamon cakes, floated over colorful drifts of paper and trailing ribbons, because many of the gifts had already been unwrapped.

Vanessa Usher sat in one corner, her fingers running up and down the harp strings in a rippling glissando. When finished, and after some well-earned applause, she rose from behind the instrument and glanced over the gifts, saying, "My dear Emma, what a treasure trove you have here."

It was one of those rare moments when Glynis found herself in complete agreement with Vanessa. Draped over a chair back was a large signature quilt, each of its cream-colored squares signed by a member of the Seneca Falls Ladies' Sewing Society. White lace-edged sheets with scalloped and embroidered pillowcases, ivory linen tablecloths and napkins, linen bath towels, and woven table runners and sideboard scarves were carefully folded to be tucked into a rosewood dowry chest bestowed by Vanessa.

Against a sofa stood a framed, parchment copy of the *Declaration of Sentiments,* which Elizabeth Stanton had written for the first women's rights convention, held in Seneca Falls some thirteen years before. Tonight Elizabeth had managed to escape her seven children and husband for a rare evening out, having left them all in the care of Susan Anthony; she'd earlier presented the *Declaration* to Emma with a smile, saying, "Hang it over your stove!"

"Aunt Glyn?" Emma's call brought Glynis back to the present. "Look at this. What do you suppose is in here? Can anyone guess?" she asked.

She'd just unwrapped a tall, elegantly carved mahogany box sent to her by Helga Brant, Emma's wealthiest customer and wife of merchant-importer Roland Brant. Since Mrs. Brant was not present, there was now considerable speculation about what the splendid box might hold.

"A sterling silver rolling pin?" suggested Elizabeth Stanton, with a wry smile.

When Emma raised its hinged lid, nothing could be seen but two silver-and-bone handles fitted into slots. Only when withdrawn did the gleaming steel blades of carving knives become visible. Glynis wondered briefly if the knives might have been made by members of the Oneida Community near Syracuse, who were known for their fine steel. She didn't wonder aloud, certainly not on this particular occasion, since these people were also known for their communal sexual practices, which for more than a decade had outraged the congregations of established churches. At Oneida, conventional legal marriage simply did not exist.

The twilight was beginning to fade, and as the room inside the shop grew dim, Lacey and Faith started to light the kerosene parlor lamps, while Emma turned up the two wicks of a molded glass pedestal "wedding lamp" that she had earlier unwrapped. Rainbowed light flared inside the pair of opalescent fonts, accompanied by the onlookers' appreciative murmurs. Emma's eyes seemed to sparkle, and for a moment she looked to Glynis like many another young woman approaching her wedding day. But when she glanced up and caught her aunt's eyes, a small pucker formed between her brows. The frown said that Emma had not forgotten the conflict that had begun the day before.

She had come to the library yesterday afternoon, her face drawn with what Glynis had initially seen as fatigue. But when Emma then asked if they could go to Glynis's office, more than simple fatigue had surfaced.

"I don't know what to do," she'd said as Glynis closed the door on the library proper. "Can you talk?"

"Yes, I shouldn't be needed for a few minutes."

Shouldn't be needed, that was, if her assistant Jonathan Quant could raise the eyes buried in the pages of a new dime novel long enough to take care of business.

"What is it, Emma?" she'd asked with concern. Although this was not the first sign of trouble, it appeared to be something more than a simple spat.

"It's about Adam," Emma answered. "We've had an argument. A serious one."

Glynis had at first doubted that young attorney Adam MacAlistair, having finally convinced Emma to marry him, would in any way jeopardize his hard-won victory, and she wondered if her niece might have exaggerated the situation. Emma had disabused her of that.

"Have you noticed," she had begun, "that all the militia

men who are going South have new uniforms? And that the uniforms are homemade?"

Glynis nodded, but although she had noticed, she hadn't thought much about it, and couldn't imagine where Emma's question might be leading.

"Aunt Glynis, if we have a real war—and from the talk these days it seems likely—there will be a demand for many more uniforms, hundreds of them. Most women don't have the time to sew them by hand, so I suggested to Adam that perhaps I could make them at the shop. Naturally, I'd have to purchase additional Singer machines and hire more women, and that would need ready cash. So I asked Adam how I might go about obtaining some start-up money. I thought perhaps I could make a contract with the government."

Glynis knew she was gaping at her niece; she was flabbergasted that Emma had come up with such a scheme. Although she supposed she shouldn't be surprised—Emma had always had a good head for business.

"And what did Adam think of that idea?" Glynis asked, trying to contain her own distaste for viewing a catastrophe as a money-making venture. Nonetheless, there were no doubt many others who would see profit in a war.

"Adam thought it was, he said, 'a mercenary scheme.' And I suppose you do, too. But someone is going to profit from the demand for uniforms, so why shouldn't it be me? And he seemed still more upset that I'd have to expand the business. Aunt Glyn, you know we've argued about my keeping the dress shop after we're married."

When Emma had first come to Seneca Falls two years ago, her consignment work for the shop's previous owner, Fleur Coddington, had quickly gathered customers. Less than a year later, she'd had opportunity to purchase the shop from the Coddington estate. Adam MacAlistair had offered—eagerly offered—to advance to Emma the money required. After all, so Adam's reasoning had gone, since he intended to marry Emma, her debt to him would simply be canceled upon their betrothal. But at the time Emma had declined both his money and his proposal. In the end, it was Vanessa Usher whose co-signature had guaranteed the bank loan.

But now it seemed this issue was to be revisited. "I thought the matter of your shop had been resolved," Glynis said cautiously. "That Adam had agreed, even if reluctantly, that you should keep it."

"I thought so, too," Emma agreed, "but just this morning he brought it up again. He doesn't want his wife to work, even though I made myself hoarse trying to explain, again, that the dress shop is not what I consider work."

Glynis felt reasonably certain that defining the word *work* was not the problem.

"But now," Emma continued, "I'm worried about something else. I'm afraid, Aunt Glyn, that after we're married, Adam might insist on selling the shop. And then what, if anything, could I do about it?" As she spoke she twisted the large, glittering ring on her left hand, a circlet of diamonds surrounding tiny blue sapphires which formed the initials A.M.

Glynis told herself to say nothing. This was between Emma and Adam. She should not even open her mouth. For all that, after a moment or two of studying the look of misery on her niece's face, she said, "Emma, have you ever thought of putting something about this down on paper?"

"Like a contract, you mean?"

"It's not unknown—I think it would be something like a trust agreement. Adam certainly would be aware that such a thing exists, although I'm not really sure that you need it, Emma. Last year's passage of the Earnings Act should—at least I *think* it should—protect your shop even without a special agreement."

Prior to that, however, a married woman could not sell or give away property she had acquired prior to or during her marriage without her husband's written consent. As the eighteenth-century British jurist Sir William Blackstone had portentously stated: "A husband and wife are one, and that one is the husband." The American Revolution, for whatever other tyrannies it might have overthrown, had not freed married women from the chains of English common law.

"But even so," Glynis went on, "you should investigate the new law, because while conveying property is one thing, the conduct of the business itself might well be another. You could ask Jeremiah Merrycoyf. . . ." She paused, then said, "No, on second thought, Jeremiah won't do." Merrycoyf was Adam's law partner and would probably refuse to become involved. And rightly so.

"I don't want to rely on some law, anyway," Emma said. "But if I had something specific to hold onto, a legal document signed by Adam, that would satisfy me."

Glynis did not want to probe too deeply into the contradictions of her remark. "You would trust Adam's intentions, then?"

"Oh, absolutely, once he'd signed something."

Emma had given this qualification without a moment's hesitation, and apparently without even a hint of irony. And had then added, "But if Adam doesn't agree to it, I don't know. . . ."

Her voice had trailed off at Jonathan's knock on the office door, and she'd left the library shortly thereafter.

As Glynis now looked at her niece's expression over the twin flares of the wedding lamp, she was fairly sure that the issue still had not been settled.

An hour later, as the guests were leaving and as Glynis stood rolling up yard upon yard of ribbon, she realized she had not seen Bronwen for some time. She asked Emma if her cousin was, in fact, still there.

"I think she's asleep upstairs in my bedroom," Emma answered, but as if she were so preoccupied that her cousin's absence had barely registered.

"Asleep? Surely not!" snapped Vanessa Usher, her violet eyes flashing like polished gems as she pulled a hood of black velvet over her harp.

"I wouldn't be surprised," Glynis said. "Bronwen has had an exhausting day."

"Yes, I heard all about it—as who in this town did not," Vanessa retorted. "Far be it from me to criticize your relatives, Glynis, but that particular young woman seems to have small regard for decorum."

Emma, despite her distracted manner, had begun to smile, quickly turning her head to hide it, but Glynis experienced a perverse kind of relief. During the course of the evening, the fair Vanessa had appeared so subdued, so nearly resembling the image of a beatific Renaissance angel, that Glynis had wondered if the woman might be ill. Clearly it had been a temporary condition. And undoubtedly, since Vanessa must know how infuriating she could be on occasion, this restraint had been for Emma's sake. Glynis did not doubt for a moment that the woman adored Emma, at least insofar as there was room in Vanessa's affections for anyone other than herself. And Glynis had speculated before now that the loss of Vanessa's sister to consumption, several years before, had left a void that perhaps Emma had come to fill.

"Don't concern yourself with all those extra chairs," Vanessa told Emma. "I'll have a servant pick them up tomorrow. You should get some rest, dear—that is, if your cousin hasn't usurped your bed."

"It's a large bed," said Emma softly. She leaned over to bury her smile in an immense bouquet of lilacs and iris, trailing ivy, and long white satin ribbons that had arrived in the hands of a delivery boy just before the party had begun. The attached card read: "To my beloved Emma." The large, self-confident scrawl of Adam MacAlistair required no signature.

After Vanessa had left—sharply warning her two belea-guered servants to handle the harp as if it were bone china—Glynis and Emma went upstairs to the several rooms above the shop. Emma, raising a glass chamber lamp by its handle, stopped at the door of one of her workrooms. "Want to take a quick look at the gowns for the wedding?"

"Yes, of course. Are they finished?"

"All but mine and Bronwen's. Before everyone got here tonight, though, I persuaded her to stand still long enough for a final fitting."

She opened the door and Glynis, holding her own lamp, followed her niece into the cluttered room. Although it was strewn as usual with bolted fabric and spools of ribbon and yards of lace trim, and although in the eye of the hurricane sat two Singer sewing machines, what Glynis first saw, draped over a dress form, was Emma's wedding gown. It shone softly as if creating its own light, a white waterfall of gleaming satin with froths of delicate, point d'Alençon nee-dle lace and droplets of seed pearls.

"Emma, it's absolutely beautiful! I've never seen any-thing to compare."

Emma smiled, put down her lamp on a sewing table, and pointed to two other dress forms holding pale green brides-maid gowns, trimmed only with white satin sashes and, at the flounced hems, tiny white satin roses.

"Green is not a traditional color, of course, and at first I had planned to have pink," Emma explained. "But then I re-alized that Bronwen would look terrible in it, while Aunt Gwen and Cousin Kathryn can wear any color in the rain-bow."

Glynis nodded at the thought of Kathryn, transformed al-most overnight—or so it seemed—from a rather plain girl, who had lacked the early good looks of her sister and her cousin Emma, into a real beauty.

"And pink is not by any means your color either, Aunt

Glyn," Emma said, and Glynis heard not the slightest intent of meanness, but rather the voice of an artist.

"Here's yours," Emma said, lifting from a standing rack a hanger that held a gown more silvery green than those of the bridesmaids. The color reminded Glynis of sea foam. She was to stand in for Emma's mother, who had died two years before. Her sister Gwen, Bronwen and Kathryn's mother, would be matron-of-honor, and Gwen's gown, which Emma was now holding up, was a darker shade of the same green. All of them would look, Glynis thought, like spring willows surrounding a white rose.

They went back out into the short hall, and when Emma opened the door of her bedroom, they found Bronwen, who was indeed asleep, sprawled face down across the bed's coverlet.

"Should I wake her?" Glynis asked.

"No, let her be. I can sleep around her, although I'm not very tired," Emma said softly, her eyes suddenly grave. "I can't imagine why, but I guess it's from worry about the wedding. I haven't even talked to Adam today, Aunt Glyn. I just couldn't find the time."

Glynis, noting Emma's swift change of mood from the lightheartedness of the sewing room, might have thought that all else would have been secondary to clearing the air with Adam, but did not say so. And when she went down the stairs, she almost called, *Don't underestimate Adam's generosity,* but on second thought decided that would sound patronizing. Emma had good sense.

Outside the shop, and while Glynis walked down a few marble steps under a green-and-white-striped canopy, she heard hoofbeats coming toward her. She peered into the soft darkness that was barely relieved by the kerosene lanterns on posts along Fall Street, and saw the black Morgan just rounding the corner of State Street. Cullen reined in the horse beside her.

"Glynis, I'd hoped to find you here." His voice held an uncharacteristic tension.

"I saw you go by earlier tonight, Cullen. Did something happen down at one of the taverns?"

"Something happened all right," he said harshly, "but not at a tavern. It was at the Brant house. Roland Brant was found dead."

"Cullen, no! How can that be? He always looked like such a healthy man. What did he die of, or don't you know yet?"

"He didn't die of bad health, I know that. Brant had been stabbed. The knife was left in his chest, so there's no question he was murdered."

5

—⚏—

Go where it chooseth thee,
There is none that accuseth thee;
Neither foe nor lover
Will the wrong uncover;
The world's breath raiseth thee,
And thy own past praiseth thee.

—Dora Read Goodale (nineteenth-century
poet), "The Judgment"

Glynis drew in her breath and took an unsteady step toward Cullen. "Roland Brant's been murdered? Who did it?" was all she could think to say, and even then the words emerged as a whisper.

"Don't know yet. His family seems to be bearing up fairly well, but no one admits to knowing anything about his death. I left Zeph there at the house to make sure they all stay put."

Cullen glanced around, apparently for passersby, and though there were none, swung down from the Morgan, saying quietly, "No need to send the whole town into an uproar tonight."

Glynis nodded, and kept her voice lowered when she told him, "Roland Brant's wife was invited to Emma's party, but late this morning she sent her regrets. Her note simply said that she was indisposed, which I took to mean that she was unwell."

"She didn't mention any illness to me," Cullen said.

"Mrs. Brant's health has been less than robust for some time. It would certainly be understandable if she didn't elaborate, Cullen, especially given the circumstances."

"Guess that makes sense, but she seemed mighty calm for someone who'd just learned of her husband's murder."

"Why? When did it happen?" Glynis asked, knowing full well that the question was really none of her affair, except for the fact that Cullen had chanced upon her. But curiosity, never her most commendable or repressible trait, overcame discretion. She also simply could not find it credible that a man of Roland Brant's substantial vitality was dead. Much less that he had been a victim of murder.

"Don't know when he died," Cullen answered. "The last time anyone recalls seeing him—seeing him alive—was around nine o'clock last night. Family and servants all agree on that time. Mrs. Brant claims that earlier this evening, when her husband didn't appear at supper, she sent one of the servants to look for him. The servant, a fellow named Clements, says he found Brant's body on the floor of his library."

"What time was that?" Glynis asked.

"Around six. But it looked to me as if Brant had been dead for some time, and I think it's damn peculiar that no one discovered his body sooner. On the other hand, it's a big house. And Clements says it was a hard-and-fast rule that Brant was not to be disturbed when he was in his library. Brant was also known to take frequent, overnight business trips."

"But Cullen, what made you think he'd been dead for some time?"

"He was stiff. Rigor mortis doesn't set in until a few hours after death. Maybe even longer if the weather's cool. I'm hoping the doctor will answer that one, so we can try to guess at the time Brant died. I'm on my way now to get her, or—" Cullen motioned toward the shop "—is Neva still in there?"

"No, she couldn't stay long. Several children at the Women's Refuge have been sick, and she'd been with them round the clock, so she was worn out. By now she's probably home with Abraham."

"And will not be happy about being rousted out again," Cullen commented dryly. "Well, it can't be helped. I want her to see Brant's body before it's moved."

If the circumstances hadn't been so grim, Glynis would have found Cullen's insistence on Neva Cardoza-Levy amusing. When Neva had first come to town four years ago, Cullen had been as disturbed as many others at the idea of a female doctor. But in a matter of months, she had proven herself more than capable, and Cullen, to his credit, had openly voiced his change of heart. Only six months ago, he'd succeeded in having Neva appointed deputy coroner of the village, a heretofore unheard-of position for a woman. Not that she and Cullen didn't continue to snipe at each other, and sometimes argue heatedly, the arguments nearly always centering on the taverns and alcohol that Neva believed responsible for at least half the ills she encountered in the practice of medicine. The primary reason, in fact, that she had opened the Seneca Falls Refuge for Women and Children.

"Glynis, while I'm fetching the doc, I'd like you to go to the Brant house," Cullen now said—in an overly nonchalant manner which made her suspect that this was not a spur-of-the-moment request, but something he'd planned to propose all along. "Someone might slip," he added, "and say something useful to you."

"You can't think that one of Roland Brant's own family murdered him," Glynis protested. "That's not only dreadful, but seems far-fetched."

"Not any more far-fetched than the notion of a stranger

just walking in and stabbing Brant in his own library! Besides, Glynis, you know his family—"

"I don't know them at all well," she broke in.

"Doesn't matter how well. They might say more to you than they have to me."

He took a lantern from a post and handed it to her, saying, "There's a near-full moon rising and you probably won't need this, but take it anyway."

Not giving her time to further object, he remounted the Morgan. "If you start walking now, I'll catch up with you before you get to the house."

"The Brants will resent my intrusion," she argued, but remembered to keep her voice down. "And if a family member was cold-blooded enough to murder Roland Brant, and then remain there at the house . . . well, why should that person suddenly become rattled enough to say something incriminating? Forgive me, Cullen, but I don't think this is a very good idea."

"I do."

"But I'm not adept at this sort of thing."

"You're as adept as anyone else around here, if not more so," he said, turning the Morgan and urging it forward before Glynis could think of a more persuasive argument.

She stood watching him ride down Fall Street, wondering as usual why she possessed so little backbone. She should have simply refused Cullen; although it had occurred to her that the Brant household must be in a terrible state. While she'd seen Roland Brant infrequently, he had always been generous when donating money to the library, and there was the possibility she might be of some help if one of his family needed it. She owed the man that. Moreover, regardless of what Cullen might expect, she hadn't actually consented to do anything more.

She swung the lantern back and forth a few times and, still debating with herself, reluctantly began to walk up State Street. Why on earth would someone murder Roland Brant?

It was true that he had considerable wealth, and that he was subject to the predictable envy levied against one who had much when others had little, but it was hard to imagine that envy alone could kill. Still, what other possible reason would there have been for his murder?

When Glynis turned west onto another dirt road that ran more or less parallel to Fall Street, she was still finding it inconceivable that Roland Brant could be dead. She remembered the Brant family's arrival in Seneca Falls some ten or eleven years before, and since then the man had been a dominant figure in the village. A philanthropic member of Trinity Church, he had also contributed to other charitable institutions; his importing business had apparently been highly successful, thriving even during financial recessions when others had failed. Just within the past year, R. Brant & Sons had purchased on foreclosure a large, stone building along the canal, converting a bankrupt harpsichord factory into a company warehouse.

And Brant had, to all appearances, been devoted to his family—his wife, two sons, and a daughter-in-law—all of whom lived in one very large house. A house which, now that Glynis thought about it, stood so far back from the road that isolation might have been at least one consideration. Moreover, while the place was being built, carriage traffic on Fall Street had been snarled for days by dray wagons weighted down with deliveries of live evergreen trees. Almost everyone in town had been inconvenienced by this project, and almost everyone had speculated about its cost. And to what purpose? Rather than move half-grown trees, why not simply plant seedlings that would mushroom in a few years' time like every other tree in western New York?

And now, as she came upon a gravel drive nearly hidden from view by a thick stand of hemlock, Glynis realized that she hadn't been aware of just how dense the trees fronting the road had become; she'd had little reason to pass this way often and especially not at night. It looked as if a forest had sprung up there, and if she hadn't known that a house sat somewhere behind it, she probably would have missed the drive altogether. Although Cullen had been right about the moon, and the lantern wasn't really necessary, she had no intention of extinguishing it until he came. And where was he?

Then a slight breeze ruffled her hair, bringing with it the sound of hoofbeats from some short distance down the road. It must be Cullen's Morgan, and she might as well start for the house, because while the night held the balmy warmth of the day, it would soon start to cool.

Gravel crunched under her high, laced shoes as she followed the initial curvature of the drive and almost immediately began to wish she had waited. The hoofbeats seemed to have faded, although it might be that the trees were so dense they absorbed the sound. It hadn't occurred to her that the entire length of the drive itself would be overgrown, but to either side of the graveled path the trees and shrubs had been pruned back only enough to permit the passage of a coach. Other than that, they'd been allowed to reach the height and density of impenetrable walls. Clearly, the Brants liked privacy. Which meant they did not like intruders. What had Cullen been thinking when he sent her here? Likely as not, he hadn't been thinking about anything other than a murder taking place in his town.

Holding the lantern before her, Glynis raised her skirt with her free hand to walk more quickly and searched her mind for a distraction. Just how good was a librarian who couldn't recall a few random phrases to divert herself? Something soothing, such as poetry. Someone trustworthy, such as Longfellow. What did he write about murmuring pines and hemlock? *This is the forest primeval. . . .*

She should think of something else. While she watched her feet, and refusing to look anywhere but down, the lines came to her in a rush: *Be lion-mettled, proud, and take no care / Who chafes, who frets, or where conspirers are. /*

Macbeth shall never vanquished be until / Great Birnam Wood . . .

This was not working. Her fixation with *woods* she could understand, even tolerate, but Macbeth? Possibly the most notorious murderer in all of literature?

Again quickening her pace, and searching for the words to curse Cullen's devious idea and her own spineless compliance with it, she tripped over a tree branch lying in the gravel. The lantern swayed and clanked while she regained her footing, but when forced to look up, she saw some yards ahead a boundary to the nightmarish woods. Beyond lay an open grassy expanse broken only by four or five lofty fir trees, their lower branches pruned away so they resembled immense umbrellas spread beside a rectangular, three-story, Italianate-style house. Like many such houses, its architectural design included a square, central tower as though endeavoring to pass itself off as a castle. Although Glynis thought she saw shadows flit before wavering candlelight in the tower's top dormer window, she could locate only a few scattered lights in what must be the first-floor rooms. Otherwise the house appeared dark. The flat-roofed structure had about it a forbidding presence, squatting there amidst the firs like a great brooding beast.

But since she could not hear the sound of hooves, or of anything else behind her, and since she refused to remain one second longer in the forest primeval, she cautiously went forward, beginning to wonder how Cullen expected to explain her appearance to the Brant family. As she neared the house, she again tripped, stumbling over something at the edge of the drive. Her balance restored, she once more took a cautious step forward, and now the toe of her shoe struck something substantial. She pulled aside some hemlock branches and lowered the lantern, bending down to look more closely at what she guessed must be another branch. But what she saw shining there in the gravel simply could not be. She straightened, thinking that a rush of blood to the head might have caused her to hallucinate. Setting the lantern down on the gravel, she slowly bent over again. And stared, disbelieving, at what appeared to be the largest diamond ever taken from a mine. Only slightly smaller than the palm of her hand, its many facets sparkled in the lamplight like that of a brilliant crystalline jewel.

Slowly Glynis reached down to pick it up. Its sheer heft then told her that what she held was a crystal paperweight. They had first become popular in Europe several decades before, and while American glass factories were now hard put to keep up with demand, this one resembled those made by the famed Baccarat factory of France. Had she not been standing on the drive of an extremely wealthy man, this would have seemed an absurd idea; but it was not, she decided, any more absurd than finding the crystal to begin with, lying in the gravel like a carelessly discarded rock.

What was she now to do with it? The small velvet reticule looped over her arm was not sturdy enough to bear the weight. But she could hardly just leave it there; it was valuable and also somewhat dangerous should a horseshoe or carriage wheel strike it. She transferred the paperweight to her left hand, and picking up the lantern with her right, again walked toward the house.

As she crossed what had become a formal, brick drive, she saw for an instant a small reddish glow—from a cigar or cigarette?—beside one of the Corinthian columns of the front porch, but it abruptly disappeared. Glynis gradually began to realize that she did not smell the lilacs and iris and lilies of the valley which the late spring had caused to bloom concurrently, thus drenching the entire village of Seneca Falls with perfume. No such scent was present here, nor were there any blossoming shrubs or flower beds around the house. Instead, thick evergreen yews crowded against the foundation walls.

And then, coming from the darkness, a hand shot out to seize her left arm in a vise-like grip.

Glynis braced her feet in an attempt, a futile one, to wrench loose from her captor, and in doing so nearly lost the paperweight. But when she managed to shakily lift the lantern, its light caught the glint of a gold belt buckle, which for no good reason she found reassuring. "Who's there? And please release my arm."

The man let her go, but stood his ground. "What are you doing here?"

Glynis could smell tobacco on his breath, he was that close to her, but her fear began to lessen, and she asked, "Mr. Brant?" This seemed a reasonable guess, as the man's pale, clean-shaven face looked fairly young, and he certainly was not Zeph Waters.

"Yes, I'm Erich Brant. I repeat, what are you doing here?"

"I apologize for intruding, Mr. Brant. I'm Glynis Try—"

"I know who you are," he interrupted, "but that doesn't answer the question."

If he'd recognized her, why had he seized her so roughly? And since she could see a half-smoked cigarette between the fingers of his left hand, he must have been on the porch and so had seen her approaching. But he deserved an answer.

"Constable Stuart asked me to come," she said. "He thought perhaps I might be of help. And I am sincerely sorry about your father." She had almost forgotten the crystal still clutched in her hand, and now, while her first impulse was to hold it out to the man, some instinct made her conceal it in the folds of her skirt.

Erich Brant gave her a curt nod. "I should probably apologize if I frightened you. I thought you were just someone intent on gawking. I imagine we'll have plenty of that in the next days."

Glynis silently agreed that he might be right. "I'm sure the constable will do what he can to prevent that," she began, then stopped as a door slammed, and a figure hurtled from the porch. She didn't see Zeph touch ground more than once before he stood beside them.

"Mr. Brant, I asked you to stay in the house," Zeph said brusquely. There was irritation on his face, dark as ebony wood beside the fair one of Erich Brant.

And Erich's face also held irritation when he said, "I came outside for a smoke, deputy. I assume I'm not being kept a prisoner in my own home?"

With the sound of horses now coming up the drive, Zeph was spared the obvious answer: that because Erich Brant's father had been murdered, the son was indeed a prisoner, at least until Cullen Stuart had finished questioning him.

Moments later, the black Morgan, and a roan mare that Glynis recognized as belonging to Abraham Levy, were reined in beside the porch. Dr. Neva Cardoza-Levy's bobbed brown hair, damp with perspiration, clung to her forehead and cheeks, and though she looked tired, Glynis thought, she dismounted in her usual brisk manner. This was remarkable in itself, since Neva, who had lived most of her life in New York City, had never been astride a horse until several years ago. But she had no patience, she'd said, with the time and effort involved in readying a carriage, so had learned to ride despite her intense distrust of horses, describing them as "skittish equine idiots."

Cullen, in an aside to Glynis as he tied his and Neva's reins to the hitching post, muttered, "Shouldn't have taken me this long to get here. But the doc wasn't too eager about coming, to put it mildly."

"No, I wouldn't imagine so," Glynis said under her breath. "And she's not the only one."

Cullen obviously chose to ignore this. And Neva, with a quick glance sideways at Glynis that said she'd overheard the exchange, nodded shortly to the others and headed for the porch, carrying her black leather valise.

"Just a minute!" Erich Brant said to her sharply. "What are you going to do with that?" He gestured at the valise.

Cullen started to say something, but Neva cut him off with, "I don't know that I'm going to do anything with it,

Mr. Brant. But where I go, it goes!" Before Erich could further protest, Neva turned on her heel and marched up the porch steps.

"Doctor," Cullen called, "before you go in, there are some questions I want to put to Mr. Brant here."

Neva paused on the porch, and waited.

Glynis now held out the crystal paperweight to Cullen, telling him, "I found this back there at the edge of the drive."

Glynis saw in his eyes the same incredulity she had at first experienced.

Erich, frowning, said, "That paperweight is my father's—he brought it back from a business trip to Europe."

"Was it made by the French Baccarat company?" Glynis asked him, reasoning that she should know as much as possible about her serendipitous discovery.

When Erich shrugged, Cullen asked her, "You found that along the drive?"

After Glynis nodded, Cullen gave her a quizzical look, then motioned for her and Erich to follow Neva.

Erich immediately objected, "I think my family's had about all the intrusion and questioning it can take for one night, Stuart. Why can't this wait until morning?"

"Because your father has been murdered, Mr. Brant," Cullen replied in a conversational tone, although Glynis knew that the faint emphasis he'd put on *Mister* meant he was becoming provoked, "and murder unfortunately makes privacy next to impossible—especially for your family."

There had been no overt note of irony in Cullen's voice, but Glynis, growing steadily more uncomfortable, had heard it there nonetheless and could only assume that Erich Brant had heard it too. For a moment it seemed as if he would refuse to cooperate, but then with a slight twitch of his shoulders, he went up the steps to the porch and leaned against a pillar, his arms crossed over his chest.

Cullen turned to Zeph, said something that Glynis couldn't hear, and a minute later the deputy mounted the Morgan and turned it toward the drive. As Zeph rode off, Cullen started up the steps. Glynis stayed where she was, hoping to think of some excuse to avoid going inside. The dark blue shingled exterior of the house had been given cream-colored trim that should have made it more hospitable looking; however, the heavy, elaborate dormers that had been constructed like brows over windows that arched toward the roof line had created the stare of a many-eyed gargoyle. She tried to push aside as fanciful her sense of foreboding, but her mind kept harking back to Macbeth's castle of death.

Then she saw a curtain suddenly fall across an open upstairs window, and the light behind it—a light not there some minutes before—was quickly extinguished. The secretive gesture chilled her, suggesting as it did that someone who preferred not to be seen was furtively watching and listening.

"Are you coming?" Cullen said to her over his shoulder.

"I guess I don't have much choice," she answered. And, still carrying the heavy crystal paperweight, with reluctance she climbed the porch steps.

6

—∽∽—

The time at length arrives, when grief is rather an indulgence than a necessity and the smile that plays upon the lips, although it may be deemed a sacrilege, is not banished.

—Mary Shelley, *Frankenstein*, 1818

When Glynis reached the top porch step, Cullen suggested that she should continue on into the house. Since refusing to do this would mean having to engage him in public debate, she left him with Neva and Erich Brant, then passed beneath a fanlight window as she stepped over the threshold. This brought her into a large foyer leading to a massive, oak staircase, and a first-floor corridor that resembled a long, dark tunnel. What illumination there was in the entryway came from an etched, glass-globed lamp on a low table, its light too dusky for her to pick out details in the framed daguerreotypes hanging on the wall. After she had set down the crystal paperweight beside the lamp, its facets reflected a warm golden glow. This provided but meager comfort, because while moonlight as white as frost crept through a window at the far end of the hallway, the dark around her felt ominous.

The instruments of darkness tell us truths, quoth the hapless Banquo to Macbeth, and Glynis decided that if her memory sent her one more warning by way of these macabre passages, she would leave here forthwith, and Cullen be hanged.

The bare marble floor seemed to amplify the click of her heels, distinctly announcing her coming to any who might care to know. And perhaps someone did care, because ahead of her Glynis saw the back of a hoop-skirted figure disappearing quickly down the corridor.

To her right was a castle-proportioned dining room, the only thing in it clearly visible being a silver tea service that shone resplendent on an extended mahogany table; around it lurked the shadows of high-backed chairs, but Banquo's ghost was mercifully absent. To her left was what must be the front parlor. Glynis paused to brace herself before entering it, and then, with strong misgivings, went through an ornately framed archway. She stopped short just inside the lamplit room.

For a long moment she feared that she had somehow stumbled back into the woods, as in every corner of the parlor stood tall, thickly leafed rubber-plants and long-fronded ferns in brass tubs, these set amidst statuary of nude nymphs and satyrs strategically draped with English ivy. Underfoot lay a thick, floral-patterned carpet.

The wallpaper, what little of it wasn't concealed by massive gilt-framed mirrors and paintings, consisted of thin, dark green stripes alternated with stripes of pink roses. Overstuffed couches to either side of the marble fireplace were upholstered in rose-colored velvet, a number of plump chairs were covered with yellow and pink floral-patterned damask, and over the windows hung draperies of green velvet fringed and tasseled with pink silk, looped back and held by brass sunflower medallions. Numerous footstools bloomed with needlepoint chrysanthemums, throw pillows with needlepoint poppies. A nest of small tables held runners of crocheted daisies. Overhead, a candlelit brass chandelier dripped with leaf-shaped crystal baubles, and under it stood a round table draped with a damask cloth featuring pink and white peonies.

The dizzying, overall effect, Glynis thought, was much as

if a deranged gardener had tried to compensate inside the house for the absence of flowers outside it. Admittedly, the furnishings only accentuated what had been for some time a popular decorating trend, but she couldn't help longing for her own relatively spartan bedroom. And as a clock buried somewhere in the foliage chimed the hour of eleven, she again reproached herself for allowing Cullen to send her to this house in the first place.

Because of the cluttered furnishings, Glynis took another long moment trying to sort out individual items; the candle lighting even made it difficult to tell if there was anyone else in the room. Then something that sounded like a smothered cough brought her gaze to a rosewood chair. And to the widow of Roland Brant. The woman sat stiffly upright, motionless, with a colorful, crocheted afghan over her knees, and but for the black bodice of her gown, she might have been a chameleon, so well did she blend into her garden surroundings. Something stirred on the afghan, the sound apparently bringing to life a white, long-haired cat curled at the woman's right side, and which Glynis had mistaken for a mohair pillow. The cat raised its head briefly to blink copper eyes at its mistress and received for its exertion a pat from a slightly palsied hand. It ignored Glynis altogether.

Helga Brant, given her repeated illness, should have appeared frail, Glynis thought, but the woman in some way, perhaps by her erect bearing, did not give the impression of frailty. Although she did look wafer-thin. Her complexion was the yellowish white of old lace and her graying, ash-brown hair, parted in the middle, was swept back over her ears into a chignon caught in a black-threaded net caul. Although the woman lacked the rounded, hunched shoulders and slackened skin of the chronically ill, it was commonly believed that Mrs. Brant was a semi-invalid who seldom left the house; when she did venture out, as for instance to visit Emma's dress shop, she was accompanied in a four-passenger brougham coach by one or two of her servants. Glynis recalled Emma once saying that Mrs. Brant seemed to have no difficulty standing for the time it took a gown to be fitted or a hem to be pinned.

The widow now was dressed in a high-necked, somber black bombazine gown. As befitted mourning, it was black unrelieved by even so much as a trace of white lace at the sleeves or throat, or by even the silver chain with its small sterling and seed pearl cross that Glynis had always seen her wear.

"Mrs. Brant, please accept my condolences," she said, crossing the room to extend her hand. "Constable Stuart asked me to come in case there was something I might do for you."

Her hand was taken in a surprisingly strong grasp. The grasp instantly loosened as if Helga Brant had momentarily forgotten, and then remembered, her ailing condition.

The faded hazel eyes that looked up at Glynis were dry, and when Mrs. Brant said, "That is kind of you, Miss Tryon," her words carried more than the usual hint of a German accent. "The servants are naturally rather unsettled," she went on, "but I believe they might make tea if you would care for some."

Glynis didn't know what to think; should she be reassured by the widow's display of remarkable self-control, or be concerned that Helga Brant might be in shock, and beyond comprehending the violent death of her husband? She was about to decline the offer of tea when Mrs. Brant reached for the braided cord that would summon a servant, and gave it a tug.

"Maybe the lady would prefer something stronger, Mother," said a male voice at the far corner of the parlor. The voice was accompanied by the chink of glass.

Startled, Glynis spun round to see Helga Brant's younger son, Konrad, standing at a richly carved mahogany pier table. Soft ash-brown hair curled over his linen collar, and while his coloring was similar to that of his mother, in voice and posture he resembled almost exactly his blond brother, Erich. Glynis, in fact, had initially been sure it was Erich who had spoken.

At the moment, Konrad was pouring into a tumbler what the bottle's label showed to be the blended dark whiskey called Kentucky bourbon.

"Care to join me, Miss Tryon?" Not waiting for a reply, Konrad briefly raised his glass to Glynis before throwing back his head and downing the bourbon in several swallows. "Damn it," he unexpectedly muttered, "if Kentucky votes to secede, I'll have to stop drinking its bourbon. Certainly a most deplorable hardship."

Glynis couldn't sense which to him would be more of a hardship: Kentucky's secession or the want of its bourbon. Or possibly it was both, because bringing the tumbler down hard on the table, Konrad stretched out his right hand again for the bottle. "So one more for the Union and President Abe!" he roundly declared.

"Konrad, I'd prefer that you didn't indulge," Helga Brant objected, in a firmer tone than Glynis would have thought her capable.

"That's right, Konrad, my sweet," came another voice, this belonging to a shapely, dark-haired woman, probably in her early thirties, Glynis guessed, who had just entered the parlor. She had slipped sideways through the doorway, to accommodate her wide, black hoop skirt; in so doing, she did not seem to note, or care to note, that her revealing neckline, not quite in keeping with the occasion, had edged down to reveal still more.

She waved the wine glass in her hand at the bourbon bottle, purring to Konrad, "Mama thinks you've had enough of that. Remember, dear boy, you must mind your mama!"

Konrad ignored them both by pouring himself another generous measure of bourbon.

The woman, whom Glynis had belatedly recognized as Erich's wife, moved with lithesome grace to the table, where she brushed her hand slowly over the young man's cheek. And while the voluminous skirt made it impossible for her to brush any more than a hand over him, the gesture was clearly intended to be intimate. When it evoked no visible response from Konrad, his sister-in-law smiled up at him in a faintly taunting manner, and reached around him for a decanter.

The decanter might have contained wine, although Glynis was too distracted by the unnatural atmosphere of the room to pay much heed. She had the sudden notion that perhaps these people were not the immediate relatives of a recently deceased man, but were a company of actors; impersonators hired by a family too distraught to face outsiders.

Erich's wife now looked over at Glynis with lustrous eyes, dark as jet beads in the ivory oval of her face. "I don't believe we've ever been formally introduced, Miss Tryon. I—"

"No, Tirzah, probably not," Konrad broke in. "I doubt you'd have much occasion to visit a library." He turned to Glynis, saying, "Tirzah doesn't read, you see. But no one mourns this lack, particularly not my brother, for whom *beauty is its own excuse for being.* A mawkish defense if ever I heard one—and who was it who said that?"

Glynis, confused by this abrupt turn, and by the sardonic half-smile that he directed at her with brows raised in question, responded reflexively, "It was Emerson." Then felt a flush rise as, to her embarrassment, this earned a prolonged look of appraisal from Konrad.

"Ah, yes, Emerson," he said, fingering a small, metallic American flag pinned to the lapel of his box coat. "And happily, unlike our beauteous Tirzah, you evidently read, Miss Tryon—which must be a decided advantage for a librarian."

Again came the smile that was not a smile, and this time Konrad lifted his glass to his sister-in-law before tossing back the drink as he had the previous one. Glynis wondered how long he had been at this.

Tirzah, having cheerfully disregarded him, now said to Glynis, "As you see, Miss Tryon, my brother-in-law has very bad manners. Would you care for a glass of port? Surely my venerable mother-in-law won't object to that! Then again she might, so we shall all have to humbly beg her forgiveness."

After Glynis murmured a refusal, she stole a glance at Helga Brant, and found the woman watching her daughter-in-law with a disconcerting intensity. Then her gaze moved to Glynis. For a brief instant their eyes met, before Mrs. Brant looked away.

To Glynis's profound relief, she heard Cullen's voice coming from the hall. When he didn't materialize, she nodded to the others, and started for the doorway. And nearly collided with the dining room's silver tea service. The servant carrying the tray—at least Glynis assumed the man was a servant, since he had a deferential manner that no one else in the house seemed to possess—stopped and bowed briefly. Then he stepped aside to allow her past him.

Glynis came face-to-face with a pinch-faced woman in a black maid's uniform, who had been following the man and was holding a plate mounded with something that was covered with a large white damask napkin and smelled like freshly baked pastry. Glynis tried to move aside, but the woman swayed directly into her, sending fruit tarts flying in all directions.

The maid gasped dramatically, sank to her knees, and began sobbing. Since everyone else in the room seemed to be frozen in place, Glynis bent over the woman and put a hand on her shoulder in an attempt to apologize—for what she wasn't certain, but the poor woman must have felt humiliated, and something had to be done. The woman shoved Glynis's hand away, while continuing to sob with a rising intensity that sounded dangerously close to hysteria.

"Phoebe, do calm down," said a male voice beside Glynis. Konrad Brant lifted the distraught woman to her feet and, while nearly dragging her from the room, said to Glynis over his shoulder, "Not to worry. She does this every so often. Clements," he added, "please see to Miss Tryon."

Glynis felt a hand grasp her elbow, and she was whisked from the room by the servant Clements, who deposited her in the hall and, with another short bow, immediately returned to the parlor. Someone, probably at Cullen's direction, had placed several lanterns in the hallway, thus diminishing the gloom.

Sobs interspersed with prolonged wails from the end of the corridor implied where the unfortunate Phoebe had been taken. Then a door closed, the sobs ceased, and Konrad reappeared. He passed Cullen and Neva, who were standing in the hall, and gave Glynis a wry smile before he disappeared again into the parlor.

Cullen and Neva waited near a door beyond the dining room. They were both looking toward Glynis with incredulous expressions, but she decided that lest her sanity be questioned, she would not even try to explain the scene in the parlor. And if that slightly ajar door by which Cullen and Neva stood led to Roland Brant's library, she would go no farther. Neither would she return to the Brants, none of whom she could characterize as grieving, at least not in any sense that she understood. They were unmistakably tense, yes. In shock, perhaps. But not grieving.

She had paused at the foot of the oaken staircase, but Cullen now motioned for her to come forward. If she shook her head, he might not see it. If she spoke to him, it could bring Konrad and Tirzah out into the hall with wine and bourbon glasses in hand. The quantity of spirits being consumed in the parlor was guaranteed to rankle Dr. Cardoza-Levy, and it might be best to avoid this; western New York was in the forefront of the temperance movement, and Neva had been known to deliver a lecture on abstinence for less cause than what she would find in this house. Glynis doubted that a lecture would prove fruitful here. And it would prolong their stay. Then the sound of steps at the top of the staircase gave her no choice. She quickly went down the long hall, passing by another door, as Erich descended the stairs.

He paused at the foot, sending the three of them a glowering look before going into the front parlor, which behavior Glynis found more appropriate than what she'd witnessed of the other family members till now. Erich, at least, seemed to have grasped the fact of his father's murder. Or it might be, she thought uneasily, that for good reason he'd had more time to adjust to it. She suddenly wondered if Roland Brant had made a will. And who in this house stood to gain most by his death?

"Glynis, I'd like you to take a look in there," Cullen said when she reached him, gesturing into what must be the dead man's library.

"Whatever for?"

Neva ran a hand over her eyes in obvious fatigue. "For one reason, because I would like to leave this madhouse and go home!" she stated. "But the good constable here insists that we continue a discussion that would be better left until tomorrow. I am not doing any autopsy tonight—I'm too tired to even think straight! So let's get your thoughts, Glynis."

"Thoughts about what?"

"The library," answered Cullen. "I want your impression of it. And by the way, Clements thinks that when he found Brant's body, the outside door of the library had been closed and bolted—although he grudgingly admitted he might be mistaken about that. But he swore that he'd bolted that door himself last night. Said he always checked it."

As Glynis had dreaded, there seemed little hope of avoiding this task, as from experience she knew that Neva and Cullen could continue to argue for some time. And she, too, wanted to go home.

"Very well," she said, "but I don't know what good it will

do." She drew in a breath, let it out, and walked into Roland Brant's library. The room held a pungent, unpleasant odor that she tried in vain to ignore.

A pendant kerosene library lamp suspended from center ceiling gave adequate light, and polished the tooled, dark leather spines of volumes that almost filled two floor-to-ceiling bookcases. Some other volumes, though, lay strewn over the floor, their spines cracked and their pages torn, causing Glynis to wince. A desk with papers scattered in disarray over its surface, and behind it an overturned leather-covered chair, stood in front of a curious-looking door. It consisted of small panes of glass, much like one of the tall, mullioned windows in her own library. She'd never seen anything like it before, and wondered if the door had been acquired during Roland Brant's frequent travels. The glass door stood with its drapery drawn aside, and when she went to it and turned the brass handle, the door readily swung open onto a small, bricked terrace. The servant Clements had said the door had been closed and bolted; Glynis saw now that the brass bolt could only have been shot home from inside the room. And none of the small panes of glass appeared to be broken, or to be newly glazed.

Against another wall of the library sat heavy mahogany cabinets, one of which, from the intricately shaped keyhole on its door, was obviously a safe. Its hinged door stood open. When Glynis bent over to glance inside, she could see several steel boxes with their lids raised and a jumble of leather folders. Presumably Cullen had asked if anything had been removed. She also presumed, since the open safe and the room's disorder so clearly suggested robbery as the motive for Brant's murder, that he might want her to look for something less obvious.

A grouping of small chalk-and-ink etchings of Rubensian nudes hung on the only wall lacking cabinets and shelves. Several of the etchings were askew, as if disturbed during a struggle; otherwise the room, in stark contrast to the parlor, was free of ornamentation. Glynis took a hesitant step around the desk and looked down. There, on a rich burgundy and blue Persian rug at the desk's far side, and thus concealed from the view of anyone passing in the hall, was the rigid corpse of Roland Brant, the bone handle of a knife protruding from his chest.

Although she had been expecting it, imagining it, the reality struck a hard blow, against which she could not have prepared herself. She backed up against the desk for support, and stood there in an attempt to merely observe. Cullen wanted her impressions and she would fail him, she knew, unless she could move past this numbing impact.

The scene looked so incongruous, notwithstanding that sudden death always looked that way, but this death looked particularly wrong, Glynis thought, brushing fitfully at her eyes. Roland Brant had been a man whom she thought of as vigorous, capable, forceful in presence. The position of the body seemed telling: rolled partially on its side, the forearms stiffly raised, the fingers curved like claws.

Although a rather short man, he had been sturdily built and should have been able to defend himself. Unless his killer had caught him unawares. Which could point to a stranger, in spite of Cullen's dismissal of the notion as farfetched. Brant might have surprised a thief already there inside the room when he entered. Or, if Clements had erred about the door being bolted, and if Brant had been seated at his desk, the thief could have come in behind him and Brant's reaction had not been quick enough.

Then, too, she unwillingly conceded, the killer could have been someone familiar to him; someone who he had learned, but learned too late, meant him harm. Else why the curved fingers that might before death have been clenched into fists?

She forced herself finally to move from the desk to stand at the feet of the corpse. Whenever she had seen Roland Brant, he had been without exception well-dressed. Yet here there was no frock coat, and the collar had been detached from the cotton—not linen—shirt, its four buttons at the top undone. He had not been dressed to go out. Not on business, at least. The shirt was tucked into his trousers held by a belt with a monogrammed gold buckle, and there was no sign of slashed fabric around the embedded knife. Whatever blood there had been was difficult to make out against the arabesque pattern and dark color of the rug.

As she began to bend down to look at the rug more closely, an odd blotch of red caught her eye. At first she thought it was blood. But when she moved her head to one side, it flashed light. She went down on her knees and reached under some strewed papers beneath the desk.

When she rose to her feet again, she held the clear glass dome of a paperweight, so smooth and slippery that she had nearly dropped it. Enclosed in the glass was a single, waxy red rose that looked as if it had been dipped in paraffin. A picture jumped to her mind, one that had accompanied an article on glassmaking which she had read some time ago in a library copy of the respected journal *Scientific American;* the picture of a paperweight called the Millville Rose. While its gaudiness had not appealed to Glynis either then or now, it was becoming a popular, relatively inexpensive collectors' item.

The Millville Rose had been featured in the same article where she had learned of the Baccarat factory. The manufacturer of costly, crystal paperweights.

She stood looking down at the desk surface on which she had already noted an overturned brass library lamp, and a pen-and-ink stand. When she moved aside the scattered papers, she could find no other paperweight there. Surely at such a time as this, the peculiar appearance of the two she had all but accidentally found must have some significance. Though what could be their link to Roland Brant's murder?

She shook her head in bewilderment, then stepped back from the desk and knelt to study the carpet again. Roland

Brant's face was turned slightly away from her, and it was only now that she noticed a slight mark on the left temple, nearly covered by graying blond hair. Glynis glanced at the rose paperweight, wondering if it was heavy enough to have made the bruise. She picked it up and hefted it, deciding that it weighed more than enough, but if the paperweight had been used as a weapon, surely it would not have been left there in the room. Not when it could easily have been carted away. Before she placed it on the desk, she turned it slowly in her hands, looking the smooth glass over carefully. There were no scratches, nothing she could find to indicate that it had been used violently.

The corner of the desk, which she thought Brant might have fallen against in a struggle, likewise seemed to bear no evidence of violent contact that she could see, even with careful inspection.

Before she left the room, she took one last look at Roland Brant's face. The bluish pallor and the absence of expression distressed Glynis more than anything else. It was a face she remembered as being ruddy with health and strong of feature. There was little hint of either now.

When she stepped back out into the hall where Cullen and Neva waited, Cullen looked at her closely, and asked quietly, "Are you all right?"

Glynis nodded, relieved that he didn't ask for her impressions. But he wouldn't yet, not with the family right down the hall. She felt, though, that she should say something about Roland Brant.

"It's an elegant room, and it looks like him," she offered, unable to conceal the wistful note she heard in her voice. "If I'd ever thought about it, the room is just what I would have expected."

Neva gave her a long-suffering look. "That room, Glynis," she said, fatigue registering in every syllable, "is not really what we're concerned with here—"

She stopped as Erich abruptly emerged from the parlor to

come toward them. "Seen enough?" he said shortly. "Now can we have some privacy?"

"You can as soon as my deputy comes back," answered Cullen evenly. "You know, don't you, Mr. Brant, that there will have to be an autopsy?"

"Autopsy! Why, for God's sake? My father was stabbed to death. That certainly seems clear enough. The library's been ransacked, and the property deeds and bank notes kept in the safe are missing. As I told you. So instead of wasting time on an autopsy, why don't you spend it on finding his thieving killer?"

In spite of Cullen's bland expression, Glynis watched the muscles along his jaw tighten. But he would not lose control; that knowledge in the past had often been reassuring to her, and few times more so than now.

"Mr. Brant," he said, "I'm sorry for what your family is going through. And I'd like to spare you any more aggravation, but in a case of suspected murder, a postmortem exam is—"

"I refuse to allow it," Erich said, cutting off Cullen in an uncompromising tone. "An autopsy can't be performed without my permission."

"Then I'll get a court order. It will be done, Brant, whether you agree to it or not."

At this, Neva gave a soft groan. A request for a court-ordered autopsy meant the doctor would need to prepare an affidavit of merit. She backed up against the wall as if she needed support, and sent Cullen a black look.

Now a distant rumble, coming from beyond the house, turned everyone toward the entrance door. Glynis hoped it was Zeph returning, as by this time she'd guessed where he had been sent earlier. She followed the others out onto the porch to watch a team of gray horses drawing a black, silver-trimmed hearse emerge from the woods. Even Erich remained silent while Zeph brought the hearse to the front entrance, reined in the team, and jumped down from the driver's seat.

Erich again found his voice. "I will contest an autopsy," he said now to Cullen, and Glynis wondered if the man could be trying to maintain the upper hand rather than expressing some deeply felt conviction. He did not impress her as unintelligent, therefore she wondered just how far he would carry his opposition. But Cullen would not back down, she knew that. Not if it took until dawn, or a midnight ride to the home of a judge for the court order.

"Listen, Brant," said Cullen, his voice still steady, "we can do this the easy way, or you can make it unpleasant. Have you asked how the rest of your family want to proceed? Your mother may have a different opinion."

"My mother need have nothing to do with this," Erich answered. "I will not permit some brazen female calling herself a doctor to violate my father's body."

To Glynis's surprise, Neva said nothing in reply to this, but simply gazed upward at the hazy stars of a warm, moonlit night. No one spoke for an uncomfortable length of time, during which Zeph climbed the porch steps and went to stand beside Cullen, obviously waiting for instructions.

Cullen said, finally, "O.K., Brant, if that's the way you want it. I'm impounding your father's body until I have a court order for the autopsy."

"You can't do that!"

"I'm doing just that. Zeph, get some of the servants to help bring Mr. Brant's remains to the hearse."

Erich moved swiftly to block the young deputy's path. When Glynis saw Zeph's hand go to his holster, and although she trusted his judgment, she grasped Neva's arm to remove them both from a possible confrontation.

Neva, however, stood firm. "I understand that you're upset, Mr. Brant," she said. "In your place I would be, too. And I wouldn't necessarily want a male doctor—if the circumstances were the same—handling, say, my mother's autopsy. So if that's your objection, then as you certainly know, there's another doctor in town. And Quentin Ives is a good man. But there's no sense in—"

"I don't need to be patronized by you," Erich snapped. "And I'll fight your or anyone else's desecration of my father's body."

The entrance door suddenly swung open, and Erich's brother stepped out onto the porch. "What the devil's going on?" Konrad asked. His words were more distinct than Glynis would have expected, since he still held the glass tumbler, and it again looked to be empty.

"Nothing that concerns you," Erich told him.

"It concerns me that you're behaving like an ass, Erich." Konrad pointed toward a parlor window. "Mother has heard this whole sorry thing from in there, and you might give some thought to her sensibilities. In any case, you can't stop Stuart from taking Father's body."

"Keep out of this, Konrad! You gave up any right to talk about sensibilities long ago. Remember, you were here in this house at Father's indulgence—and you are now here at mine. But I warn you, my patience is not unlimited."

Glynis saw a shadow move in the doorway.

"Erich, please stop this!" Helga Brant stood just inside, leaning on a cane, with her eyes fixed on her older son. "Enough has been said here," she added, "and Constable Stuart is clearly determined to do as he feels necessary. Neither you nor I will likely dissuade him."

Konrad started to speak, but his mother stopped him by saying, "No, let us have no more airing of our differences." She turned again to Erich. "I have instructed the servants to assist the deputy." Her eyes held those of her son, a long look that did not waver, and then, after motioning for Zeph to enter, she went back inside.

Erich brushed past the others and strode down the porch steps. At the edge of the brick drive, he stopped and turned back to those on the porch. "There will be no autopsy. Count on it!"

He then walked rapidly toward what looked to be a carriage house and stable.

Glynis, as she turned to Cullen, caught from the corner of her eye a glimpse of Erich's wife standing just inside the doorway. Tirzah's face seemed to hold the same bitter anger as that of her husband. But anger, Glynis had learned, sometimes looked much the same as grief.

When Konrad followed Zeph inside, and Neva went down the steps and walked toward the hearse, Cullen said in an undertone to Glynis, "Wait for me out here, and I'll see you home."

"Cullen, I don't want to ride in that hearse."

"You don't need to. Zeph and Neva can get Brant's body back to town and I'll take you with me." He motioned toward the back of the hearse, where Glynis now saw that the Morgan was tied. "You're not walking home alone, Glynis."

"I'm not arguing with that."

"Can't think why I let you come here by yourself to begin with," he said, shaking his head as if he had just realized this.

"Your mind was on other things then, Cullen." And he couldn't have known, she thought as he went back inside, that she'd be foolish enough not to wait for him.

She went down the steps, intending to talk to Neva, and had just reached the drive when she heard someone call to her.

"Miss Tryon? A moment please?"

She turned to see the servant Clements, with whom she earlier had nearly collided, coming toward her. He was a heavy man, balding, and he bore what appeared to be a perpetually sour expression. Clements had sworn up and down, so Cullen said, that the last time he'd seen Roland Brant alive was a few minutes before nine o'clock the previous evening, when he took to the library a bottle of whiskey and a clean tumbler. He did this every night, the man had also sworn.

"Yes, Clements, what is it?" Glynis asked him.

"Mrs. Brant—that is, Mrs. *Roland* Brant—has retired to her room. She cannot be further disturbed tonight. But she requested that I inform you of something. Constable Stuart inquired earlier if all the servants were here and accounted for. We thought they were. But we've found that one has gone missing."

"*Missing?* And you've only now discovered it?"

"She's just a kitchen maid, madam. Indentured to the Brant household." He gave Glynis a less disdainful look when he added, presumably in earnest, "It is said that she's been cursed."

"What on earth do you mean, she's *cursed?*" asked Glynis, then instantly regretted the skeptical edge in her voice, which would achieve nothing with someone who believed in evil spells. And Clements was hardly alone in this belief.

Since the man was now eyeing her with distaste, she tried again with more caution. "Please tell me how this girl is cursed."

"They say she has been struck dumb."

"By that, do you mean she's witless? Or do you mean the girl is mute?"

"She never says a word. Not for a year now."

Did that mean this girl *could* not talk—or *would* not talk? "I see," Glynis replied, hoping the man would be encouraged if she acted as if she understood him. "Clements, why didn't any of the servants know until now that she was gone?"

"What with Mr. Brant being . . ." He paused, swallowed, and continued, "That is, it seems no one noticed her absence today. But now that we've had time to reflect, it appears that she hasn't been seen since early last evening."

TUESDAY
May 28, 1861

7

He hath led me, and brought me into darkness, but not into light. He hath set me in dark places as they that be dead of old. He hath hedged me about, that I cannot get out.

—Book of Lamentations

The girl had been awake for some time, lying as still on a marsh-grass pallet as the dead lie in the dark of their graves. The pallet was thin and spread on a dirt floor. When she had woken once before this, she had found herself wrapped tightly in a coarse wool blanket, and when she had twisted the injured arm, the pain made her gasp. It must have been heard, her gasp, because the sudden light of a torch was thrust in her face, blinding her, and she'd heard the anxious whine of a dog. A liquid that smelled like the thick, biting odor of spirits was poured into her mouth, and she choked and gagged, but had been made to swallow it. And as she lay there now, a picture came into her mind of a man with hair hanging over fierce dark eyes. His lips moved as if he were saying something to her, but she was too afraid to listen. He made her swallow something else, thin and watery with a taste more bitter than that of chicory.

She could now see a pale light coming from somewhere, and she wondered if it could be the dawn. She rolled her head to one side. The light filtered across her in thin gray stripes, and she saw that it came from a small, square opening overhead and from between chinks of the logs that were stacked one on top of another to make a wall. She rolled her head from the wall to see a dark heap a short distance away. It looked like a mound of earth. When she tried to lift her head to see more, the wool wrapped around her made only a whisper of sound, but the dark mound heard and rose up and came toward her. She lay still, her eyes shut fast, fear running through her as a chill stream runs, and then she felt something rough and warm and wet on her cheek. And she knew it was the tongue of the dog.

She opened her eyes to look into the gleam of the dog's brown gaze before it settled down against her side with the warmth of a sun-baked rock. The heat of its body eased the cold, and the sound of its steady breathing made her think of waves lapping against a shore. Or the wings of a moth slowly fanning in flight.

She must have slept again, because suddenly she felt the air around her stir, and when she heard a faint hissing like that of steam from a fire, it made her afraid. The dog was gone, and strong morning light came through a door opening in the opposite log wall, where a flap of canvas had been pulled aside. Then she heard footsteps and a man, a man she thought she had never seen, walked through the opening, carrying something in his hands.

When she sat up and tried to inch back against the log wall, she saw that she was no longer bound tightly in the wool, but her left arm felt strangely heavy. She didn't know why, and she couldn't look at it and watch the man at the same time. He had stopped just inside the door opening. And then she saw his eyes. They told her this was the man who had come upon her in the swamp, with his fierce dark eyes and the shepherd dog at his heels. His hair was as black as his eyes, and now it did not hang over his face but was brushed back and fell to his shoulders, shining like the mane of a horse. And the beard on his face was gone, leaving only a shadow in the hollow of his cheeks, so he must have just shaved the beard off. What he carried looked like an iron fry pan, and whatever was in it hissed and spattered as if the pan had just been taken from hot coals. And she could smell fish.

When the man started toward her, she shrank back against the wall. He stopped again, and stood staring at her, while the dog came forward and stood in front of her with its tail sweeping the dirt floor like a long-handled feather duster. Then it sank to its haunches and looked up at her with its keen gaze.

A few feet away from her was something that looked like a big tree stump made into a table, and the man took a few steps, bent forward, and put the pan on it. Then he turned and started back toward the cabin opening. The dog rose quickly, and its nose was nearly into the fry pan before the man, without looking around, said, "No, Keeper. No."

Even though the man had said this in a low voice, the dog dropped to the dirt floor like a stone. Then the man snapped his fingers, and the dog rose and went to him, tail swirling, and they left the girl alone with the fresh-smelling fish that made the juice in her mouth run.

With her eyes on the door opening, she started for the table and the pan. It was then she understood why her left arm was heavy; it was wound with a thick, clean cotton cloth like a bandage. Her arm didn't hurt much anymore. But she saw, too, with a quick thrust of fear, that the wet cloak and the muslin dress and the shift she had worn were gone. Now she wore a large, yoked shirt, coarsely woven, and jean-cloth trousers that bunched around her waist, held with a piece of rope like a drawstring instead of a belt. Even though the trouser legs had been rolled up, they dragged in the dirt. They looked, the shirt and the trousers, like what the man wore, but the shirt was not too big for him and the trouser legs only went to the ankle of his boots. She didn't want to think of the man taking off her clothes, so she looked at the pieces of fish in the pan, lying crisp and brown beside what looked like fresh dandelion greens. She started to pick up the fish with her fingers, then heard a sound outside and quickly backed away as the man came though the opening.

He laid a small, carved wooden scoop in the pan and put down a tin cup of steaming liquid that smelled like sassafras tea. As he turned to go outside again, he said over his shoulder, "You should eat."

It was only a minute or two before the dog came back alone. It crouched in front of her and watched her eat, its eyes going back and forth between her mouth and the pan, with its ears pricking forward at every bite. When she had almost finished, she looked quickly at the opening of the cabin, and gave the dog the last piece of fish. The dog gulped it down and licked her fingers, its tail brushing back and forth, while she ran her hand over its fine-boned head. Then hot tears came and she pushed the dog away.

When the dog jumped to its feet, she saw that the man had come back inside, and was leaning against the wall of the cabin, watching her. She wondered how long he had been there, and how angry he would be if he had seen her give the fish to the dog after he had said, "No, Keeper." But his eyes did not look so fierce, so perhaps he didn't think it was bad, what she and the dog had done.

The man took a step toward her. She started to back away from him, but he dropped to a squat where he was.

"Does your arm hurt?" he asked in a low voice, the same voice he had used with the dog.

She looked at the dirt floor, wiping her hands on the bunched, jean-cloth trousers.

"It was a bad cut," he went on, as if she had answered him, and then asked her own question. "I had to hurt you to get the dirt out, though, so I poured some whiskey over it, and some into you. It should be better now. If it's not, I can give you some more willow bark."

That must have been the bitter liquid he had made her drink. She shuddered, remembering, and maybe he knew why she shuddered, because suddenly he smiled. Then she saw that he was not as old as she had thought; not young, but not very old, either.

"All right," he said. He was still smiling, and now his voice, rich and clear, made her think of the call of a wood thrush. "No more willow bark. Unless it hurts again. But you have to tell me that."

He was watching her, and she was afraid he would be angry when she didn't answer. She ducked her head, so he wouldn't see how afraid she was.

But he must have seen, because he said, "I know you're scared—you look scared—but you don't have to be. What's your name?"

She moved back a little, waiting for the anger.

"I won't hurt you," he said, and a line came between his brows as if he were troubled. And then he said, "From the looks of it, you've been hurt enough."

He got to his feet, saying, "I know you're not mute because you cried out." She saw the question in his face. She looked away from him.

"Do you understand what I'm telling you?" he said. "You must be able to nod, or shake your head, because you're not deaf, are you?"

She couldn't look at him. Tears were smarting behind her eyes, and that frightened her almost as much as he did, because she couldn't think why she should be crying. Maybe because he kept talking in that clear thrush voice, and asking her questions she couldn't answer.

"Why were you in the swamp?" His face looked as intent as the dog's had looked while she was eating the fish. "The closest town is Seneca Falls. Are you from there?"

She wanted to tell him no. No, she was not from Seneca Falls. But even if she could tell him that, he might know it wasn't true.

He went to the doorway, and stood there for a time with his arms crossed over his chest, just looking at her. "If you won't, or can't talk," he said, finally, "I'll have to go into town—find out who you are. You can't stay here. If I wanted company, I wouldn't be living in a swamp."

When he said that, that he would find out who she was, she felt her breath go out of her. She struggled to her feet, and she could feel hot tears running down her face, the fear so thick in her throat that she thought she would not be able to bring in air again. She was shaking her head with her hair slapping against her face. And she knew he was watching her.

He took several steps toward her, stopping when she cringed back against the wall. The dog let out a short whimper and came to her side to lick at her hand.

"I won't touch you," he said, "if that's what you're frightened of." It was not a question, but his face looked as if it had been. "Or is it because of what I said? About finding out who you are?"

This time it was a question, and all she could do was look at him.

"How can I know what you want unless you tell me?" he said. "I'm not a mind reader."

She put her hand to her throat, and she could hear herself gasping for air to come in.

He came toward her again, and this time he didn't stop when she shrank against the wall, but stood right in front of her. He didn't touch her, he just stood there with his thumbs hooked under the waist of his trousers.

"All right," he said, "I'm going into town. I don't go any more than necessary—I have no love for that place, believe me—but I need to find out who you are, and where you belong. If I go by way of Black Brook, I should be back by dark. I'll leave Keeper here with you."

She tried to see him through the blur, and she tried to stop the tears, too, and she couldn't. He raised his hand slowly and reached toward her face, but when she shied away, his hand dropped to his side.

"My name is Gerard," he said to her. Then he turned, and went outside. She heard him say to the dog, "Stay, Keeper. Stay!"

She waited until the sound of his footsteps faded before she went to the cabin doorway. He was striding down to where the water met the land, and to where a bark canoe lay nearly hidden in clumps of marsh marigolds the color of churned butter.

She stood there with the dog beside her and watched him push the canoe out into the marsh. Once, before he climbed into it, the dog whined and took a few steps forward as if to follow him.

The man Gerard said, "No. Stay, Keeper!" and the dog sank to the ground, muzzle on its front paws, its eyes fixed on the man in the canoe.

When the man dipped the flat-bladed paddle, it sliced through the air with flashes of silvery light as he struck out over the desolate stretch of water. She watched him until, shrouded by mist and the tall marsh weeds at the mouth of Black Brook, he was lost from sight.

8

We are fond of talking of the mysterious things in nature—of earthquakes, volcanoes, whirlwinds, pestilences, and other marvels of the material world; yet these do not begin to compare in strangeness and importance with the developments of the human heart. . . . The great questions of our future history do not turn upon marvelous phenomena in the heavens or under earth, but upon the play of human passions.

—the June 1861 issue of
Harper's New Monthly Magazine

It was the clatter of wagons outside one of her bedroom windows, closely followed by the neighing of horses, the barking of dogs, and the boisterous shouting of men, that finally roused Glynis. Otherwise, she thought, glancing at the clock on her bedside table, she would likely have slept until noon. But what could be going on out there? It sounded as if half of Seneca Falls had suddenly converged in her landlady's front yard.

She threw on her green silk undress and rushed to the window, where it became clear that the commotion was not in Harriet Peartree's yard, but in the one next door, belonging to Vanessa Usher. Cayuga Street had been transformed into a crazed jumble of heavy dray and rack wagons. More were arriving every minute, while a dozen burly men hailed one another with gibes and laughter as they milled around the jammed road. Glynis smiled at their exuberance, thinking it possible, given the past months of foul weather, that some of these men had not met since the previous autumn.

She opened the window on the warmth of a sunlit morning and leaned her arms on the sill. Although most of the men below were still fraternizing, some of them had begun to haul from the wagons scores of flowering trees. Heavy burlap wrapped the clumps of soil around roots of shadblow and crab apple and wild cherry and plum, all of which were nearing full bloom. It made for a magical scene, and only that particular year, with its miserable, cold, wet spring, could have brought these trees into flower at the same time, bursting into color practically overnight. Glynis decided that this horticultural wizardry, usually left to the whims of the weather gods, must have been summoned by a wave of Vanessa's wand and was now, even as Glynis watched, materializing directly at her door. And the reason for this feverish activity, it had slowly dawned on her, was Emma's approaching wedding. On the first day of June, a mere four days hence.

Plans for the ceremony and reception to take place on the spacious Usher grounds had been in the making for months. Ever since the very second, Glynis suspected, that the woman had learned of Emma's engagement. And Vanessa, given the artistry she had shown on prior occasions, would undoubtedly produce the most beautiful wedding ever beheld in western New York. Even if she had to move heaven and earth to do it.

Earlier in the year, a pragmatic Emma had cautiously asked her, "If the wedding is held outside, what will we do if it rains?" To which Vanessa had replied, "It wouldn't dare rain!" Thus disposing of the heavens. And apparently, from the look of things on Cayuga Street, this was the day the earth moved.

But how, and from where, did Vanessa conjure all those trees?

Burnham Woods come to Dunsinane. Glynis sank to the edge of her bed, the previous night looming in her mind and her delight in the morning draining away. She glanced at her clock again, and now noticed a coffee cup and saucer on the bedside table. When she picked them up, the coffee pale with cream the way she liked it, she found a note underneath.

Aunt Glyn—

So where were you *last night? Out carousing somewhere, and with the handsome constable too, I wager! Have some errands to run, but I'll see you later, here or at the library.*

Love, B

Just where would Bronwen think one could carouse in Seneca Falls? Other, that was, than the taverns along the canal, in which a woman who valued her reputation would never set foot. Or care to. Neva Cardoza-Levy had done it once, in an effort to close down Serenity Hathaway's place, but Neva was by nature more dauntless than most.

However, since carousing was a far cry from what Glynis had actually been doing until after one in the morning, she sighed, and took a swallow of very cold coffee.

Then went to her wardrobe cabinet and, her spirits raising slightly, eyed the dove gray French muslin gown Emma had made for her during the past winter. At last a day had arrived that would be warm enough to wear it. And Emma had said that, although she didn't approve, a full crinoline would be sufficient—Glynis shared with Bronwen a stubborn refusal to wear hoops. Before gathering up her hair with a set of tortoiseshell combs, she brushed out its nighttime braid, noticing that while it was many shades darker than Bronwen's hair, the vinegar rinse Emma had insisted she begin using had brightened the reddish-brown considerably. She glanced into her mirror and pulled down a few strands of hair to soften her cheekbones, deciding she was becoming more than a tad vain in her advancing years. Then told herself it was Emma's influence: *Aunt Glyn, you must heed the fact that, whether you want to be or not, you're a walking advertisement for my shop.*

Glynis made a face at herself, wondering if next she would be required to wear, chained round her neck, a sign blazoned EMMA'S. Then she pulled several more strands of hair around her face. And applied a touch of light rouge. It was, after all, finally spring.

When she reached the downstairs kitchen, Harriet Peartree was there, watering pots of herbs on the sunny windowsill, and turned to give her an appraising glance. "You look lovely, particularly after what I would call a late night."

"Yes, a very late night," Glynis agreed while she poured herself another cup of coffee. "And now it's a late morning, so I can't go into much detail, but—"

"Don't need to," Harriet broke in, her chin-length hair swinging about her face like glossy, silver fringe. "The whole town's in an uproar. And I don't mean about what's going on out there," she added, tossing her head in the direction of the noisy street. "Everybody knows by now that Roland Brant's been murdered."

"How did the news get out so quickly?"

"Glynis, you know how word travels in this town. Like lightning, especially something like this! It's in the *Courier,* too—extra edition. The newspaper hadn't even come yet, though, when your redhead shot out of here at the crack of dawn."

"Bronwen? Why, what time did she leave?"

"Which time? She's been back twice since then. First time I heard her banging around down here, it was before six."

"Where could she have gone that early? And she must not have stayed with Emma, so when did she come back here last night?"

Her landlady's brows lifted as she said, "I don't know exactly when, but it was certainly long before you did."

"Harriet, you're looking at me as if you think I was . . . was out carousing!"

Finally, with that, came Harriet's good-natured laugh. Followed by a more sober, "As a matter of fact, after I'd heard what happened at the Brants', I guessed you were probably with Cullen Stuart."

Glynis nodded, while she spread apple butter on a muffin. "For reasons known only to Cullen, he insisted I go out there to the Brant house."

"I should think so."

"Why do you say that?"

"Cullen Stuart's a good man, and a smart one, but he's not . . . what's the name of that detective in those Poe stories you made me read?"

Glynis smiled around the muffin. "I didn't make you read them, Harriet, I just suggested them. And the name's Auguste Dupin, but if Cullen's not Dupin, surely I'm not either. So what did the newspaper say?"

"That Roland Brant had been stabbed. In his own house. Is that true?"

"You can always believe what you read in the paper." When Harriet chuckled, Glynis added, "As it happens, this time the *Courier* got it right. That part, at least. What else?"

"Not much. On the one hand, Constable says there are no suspects yet. On the other hand, he wants anyone with information about the Brants' kitchen maid to come forward. Seems as if the girl's gone missing, so she sounds like a good suspect to me. But you probably already know that."

"Did the paper give a description of her?"

"Only a general one. Could fit any number of girls in this

town. Age sixteen or seventeen, the paper said—blond hair, blue eyes, and pretty. That right?"

"That's what we were told last night. Did the *Courier* mention anything else about her?" Glynis wondered if it had reported that the girl was mute.

"Just her name. Said it was Tamar. Tamar Jager."

When Glynis reached the corner of Fall Street, the first thing she noticed were the people standing in small, restless knots along the road, some of them gesturing toward the stark stone factories and warehouses that stood on the south side of the canal. She guessed, from their anxious, inquisitive expressions, that they were discussing Roland Brant's murder. And were thinking that if it could happen to him, with his castle house and his solid stone buildings and his substantial wealth, it could happen to anyone.

Then, while waiting for several wagons and buggies to pass before she could cross the road, she saw Bronwen just emerging from the telegraph office.

Her niece stopped on the plank sidewalk, obviously reading a wire, then stood looking up at the sky with a studiously rapt gaze. But when Glynis waved at her, Bronwen quickly stuffed the rectangle of yellow paper into her pocket; the pocket of a leaf green dress, buttoned from neckline to hem, and notably lacking hoop, or ruffles or flounces. It was what Emma called the new, princess style, and clearly she had taken some pains to accommodate her cousin's dislike of frills. But while the young woman in the dress resembled nothing so much as an elegant wood sprite, Glynis found herself less interested in Bronwen's looks than in her continued, strangely furtive behavior.

A loud rattle of wheels made Bronwen scurry to stand at the edge of the road beside Glynis, and together they watched as a dray wagon turned down Cayuga Street, this one massed with what looked to Glynis like shrubs of pink-blossomed mountain laurel. She couldn't be sure, but they didn't look like a Seneca Falls crop.

"Just look at those!" said Bronwen. "I'll wager they came from the greenhouses at Mount Hope Nurseries in Rochester." And since Bronwen had grown up next door to these nurseries, her father being a horticulturist for them, Glynis took her word for it.

"They must have come here by rail," Bronwen went on, "so it has to be costing The Lady Vanessa a fortune!"

"I expect so. But when Vanessa decides to do something, she usually spares no expense." Glynis thought that Bronwen was just a little too enthusiastic about the shrubs, and wondered if the purpose here was to distract. "Well, Bronwen, what have you been doing this morning?"

"Oh, nothing much." Her niece at first did not meet her eyes, but then went on more openly, "I did have breakfast with Professor Lowe at Carr's Hotel, though. And I was just coming to Peartree's to find you, because your assistant Jonathan Quant said you hadn't been to the library yet. Cullen Stuart wants you. At his office. As soon as you can get there."

"I hope he put it more graciously than that," Glynis said.

"A little more," Bronwen agreed, grinning. "But he did say to tell you that he'd tried to see the woman you mentioned to him last night. The one staying at Carr's Hotel, too. A popular place!"

"Mrs. Jager?"

Bronwen nodded, saying, "She's supposed to be at Cullen's office in—" Bronwen paused, presumably looking for the time, and glanced in a window of Erastus Partridge's Bank of Seneca Falls "—in about half an hour."

"In that case, I'd better tell Jonathan."

"I already told him. There weren't too many patrons there and he was just dandy, Aunt Glyn, sitting cross-legged on the floor unpacking crates of books."

"What books were those?" Glynis asked anxiously, with red-caped villains and nubile innocents leaping to mind.

"He said they'd just come from London."

"Ah, those finally arrived. Well, then, Jonathan might keep his mind on what he's doing, because there are no dime novels or melodramas in that shipment. At least I hope the British have not succumbed to them." She also fervently hoped that *Silas Marner,* George Eliot's new novel, was among those in the shipment. Although the stacks of books to be read on her library desk and her bedside table were reaching perilous heights.

"I'll walk to Cullen's office with you," Bronwen said, "because there's something I need to tell you."

At last some answers, Glynis thought as they started up Fall Street. "I'll be glad to listen," she said. "What is it?"

"Just that Vanessa Usher, and everybody else, is probably going to a lot of trouble for nothing. Because I don't think there will be a wedding."

"What?" Turning to stare at her niece, Glynis nearly stumbled into the crates of rhubarb and asparagus stacked in front of Monroe Groceries.

"I thought I'd better tell you," said Bronwen. "Not that I care much about Vanessa, but people are coming from out of town for this. I asked Emma weeks ago to send an invitation to Tristan Marshall in Pennsylvania. I don't know if he's coming, and neither does she. I doubt he's too concerned with things like RSVPs. You remember Marsh, don't you?"

"Yes, I remember him," Glynis answered. Clearly Bronwen did too, else why the invitation to a young man her cousin had never even met. "But what *is* this about there being no wedding?"

"And besides my family in Rochester, aren't Uncle Robin and Emma's brothers traveling from Illinois?" Bronwen was referring to Glynis's brother and nephews.

"Yes, of course they are, but for heaven's sake, Bronwen, just what are you basing this prediction on? No, wait, don't answer that yet. Let's go down there." She pointed to a bench in a small grassy patch remaining between the shops built on the shallow slope to the canal. "There's no need to air this for the whole town."

"I don't think the whole town would be interested," Bronwen remarked as they walked down the slope. "The only thing anybody's talking about is that murder. I can't remember—when I used to spend summers here, did I ever meet Mr. Brant?"

"You might have. His son Erich usually competed in the horse race at the fair, and he probably was there the summer a few years ago when you won it. I'm sure you recall that incident."

"How could I forget? Being disqualified just because I was a girl!" Bronwen threw herself down on the wood-slatted bench, the memory plainly still galling.

Glynis sat down beside her and glanced around them before she said, "We seem to be alone. Now, why do you think Emma's wedding may be called off?"

"I overheard something in her shop. I didn't mean to eavesdrop, but I could hardly help myself, they were talking so loudly."

"Emma and Adam?"

"You already know about it?"

"Bronwen—"

"Oh, I guess that would be pretty obvious."

"Will you please not draw this out, and just tell me?"

"O.K. After I left the shop last night, I realized that I'd forgotten to take the hair thingamabob that Emma's insisting we wear. For the wedding. The one that looks like it's not going to happen—"

"My patience, Bronwen, can wear thin very fast."

"Sorry. When I went to the shop to get it this morning, I used that back delivery door. I heard Emma talking in the front room, and I thought she was with a customer, so I just went upstairs for the hair thing. But then I heard Adam

MacAlistair's voice, too. And they were both beginning to sound . . . upset. Well, at that stage I was more or less trapped upstairs, and I couldn't think what to do. Not without embarrassing all of us. And besides, I didn't know then it was going to get worse."

"They were having a disagreement?"

"No, I'd say it was more like a fight."

"About Emma's shop?"

"You *do* know!"

"Bronwen, just tell me what happened."

"Do you want a long blow-by-blow version, or should I just summarize it?"

"Dear Lord, give me strength!"

"I'll summarize. Emma told Adam that she wanted an agreement drawn up before the wedding. It sounded like something that says after they're married, the shop is still hers. Emma's. So she can do with it what she wants."

"Yes, and . . . ?"

"And Adam said he was disturbed that Emma would insist he sign something, because he'd already given his word to her about that. Besides, he said, the new law about married women's property makes her shop . . . ah, I think he used the word 'secure.' "

"To which Emma said?" Glynis prodded.

"That she didn't trust the law. That the law in the past hadn't done women much good, so why should she rely on it now? And, she said, she didn't want to involve the law anyway. She just wanted Adam to sign a piece of paper. Which, when you think about it, Aunt Glyn, doesn't make a whole lot of sense—Emma doesn't want the law, but does want his signature? I mean, after all, a signed document does tend to make you sit up and think: 'legal!' "

"Just go on, Bronwen. Really, when you report to Treasury, does it have to be dragged out of you?"

"You're not Treasury. And I'm trying to give you the flavor of it. Where was I? Oh, and then Emma said that when

she took out a loan to buy the shop, the bank made her sign
a contract. And that if bankers have signed contracts, she
thought *she* was entitled to have one, too."

"And then?"

"And then things really went to pot!"

"Bronwen, please!"

"You said you wanted it short. But Emma sounded like
she'd started to cry and Adam didn't sound too happy either.
Said Emma must not trust him—and how could they have a
marriage built on distrust? You know, Aunt Glyn, he has a
point there."

"Could you please not editorialize, at least not yet."

"But that's about all of it. No, wait, there were a couple
more things. Adam really hit the roof when Emma asked
him what would happen if, later on, he changed his mind?
And made her give up the shop? Or said she could keep it,
but couldn't work in it? And if he did *that* . . ." Bronwen
broke off, frowning. "I just want to make sure of Emma's
exact words here. She said to Adam, 'If you won't let me
work in my shop, then do I have the right to make you give
up your law practice?' "

Bronwen hesitated, as though giving her cousin's question fresh consideration. Then she continued, "Adam said,
of course not! There was no comparison. And that he would
be the laughingstock of western New York, if it leaked out
that his betrothed had asked him to put his signature on
something so . . . so . . . I think he said 'demeaning to my
professional integrity.' And that his word was his bond, and
so on and so on and so on."

"Which it is," Glynis murmured.

"So you're on Adam's side, too?" Bronwen asked her in a
surprised tone.

"I'm trying very hard not to take sides, Bronwen. Was
there any more?"

"Yes, because then poor Emma really started crying. It
sounded as if she was gasping like a netted trout on every

other word. She said what if something were to happen to Adam? Something like him dying? *Big* gasp there! Sorry, Aunt Glyn. Anyway, how would she survive after that? she asked him. Because if he let her keep the dress shop, but in name only, and decided that someone other than herself should run it, then she would lose control of the business and might inherit a worthless property."

"Which, unfortunately, is a very real prospect."

Bronwen's eyes widened. "Ah, yes . . . I guess it could be, what with the war and all. And, now I think about it, Adam didn't answer that. But it might have been because . . ."

Since Bronwen's voice had stopped, Glynis asked, "Because what?" before she realized that her niece was grinning.

"Well, all of a sudden Emma's sobbing sounded muffled, and then things got very quiet—if you know what I mean."

"Probably, but could you be a little more explicit?"

Still grinning, Bronwen nodded. "Since I thought this might be my chance to get out of there, I sneaked down the stairs, and peeked around the doorway into the front room. And, just as I'd suspected, Adam had his arms around Emma and . . . it was a pretty scorching scene!"

"I see," Glynis said, trusting Bronwen knew that her smile was for the choice of words and not for Emma's predicament.

"Anyway, as I was creeping out the back door, I heard Adam mumbling something about he and Mr. Merrycoyf being the best lawyers around, and that they would know what was best for her. Which was not too humble of him, I guess, but he's probably right, don't you think?"

"I don't know what to think."

"Now can I editorialize? Because we're supposed to go to Cullen's office, remember?"

Glynis stared at the sparkling water of the canal, and wondered how much she might have contributed to this issue between Adam and Emma.

"For a while there, Adam sounded truly put out," Bronwen said. "And I'm not sure I blame him. After all, this is a fine time for Emma to bring this up—four days before the wedding!"

"She might not have thought seriously about it before."

"How could she not think about it? Why did she agree to marry Adam if she doesn't trust him to keep his word?"

"I don't think she mistrusts him . . . precisely. Bronwen, try to look at it from Emma's viewpoint."

"But Adam *said*, and I heard him say it, that she could keep her shop! And it sounded to me as if this wasn't the first time he'd said it."

"Emma is wary with some reason. She's seen women who have lost what they brought into a marriage," said Glynis carefully, trying to think how to explain it. "For instance, some time ago, a young woman—whose parents had very little money—married one of the most charming men you could imagine. He told everyone, when he arrived here in town, that he came from a wealthy New England family, that he'd graduated from Harvard, et cetera, et cetera. Before the wedding, and because the father of this young woman had nothing else to give her in the way of dowry, he turned over to his daughter the deed to his small property and house. I know all of this because Emma made a beautiful wedding gown and told the couple that she would wait for payment until they were settled."

At least, Glynis thought, she did have Bronwen's complete attention.

"To make a long story short," she went on, "four or five months after the marriage, this very charming man found another young woman to charm, and then threw his wife and her aging parents out on the street. And the law said that he could do it, because what had been given to his wife therefore belonged to him."

For a moment, Bronwen just stared at her. "That's the

most awful . . . what an absolute bast— . . . scoundrel. The man *and* the law! Did Emma get paid for the gown?"

Glynis sighed. "That's hardly the point I'm trying to make. But no, she did not."

"Adam, though, is not a scoundrel," said Bronwen soberly. "I know his parents died when he was young, and he had to work all the while he was in law school, but he's been a lawyer here now for some time. We all know him. And know he's a decent man."

"Yes, that's true. But Emma loves her work."

"More than she loves Adam? Again, why did she say she'd marry him? She has to know that she's really stuck forever if she goes through with it. That she can't just turn round the day after the wedding and say: Whoops, I guess I shouldn't have done that!"

"Emma is rarely impulsive, so I doubt that would be the case."

"Well, what is the case? Frankly, Aunt Glyn—and maybe I shouldn't say this—but I think Emma's got some brass questioning *my* sanity! She couldn't find anyone nicer than Adam MacAlistair. He's honest and smart, clean, works hard and makes money—*and* he's good-looking. He's just a peach! Pick of the litter!"

Glynis had to smile. And she found the order of Bronwen's priorities not only telling but reassuring. "I agree with the sentiment, Bronwen. But this is something that Emma has to sort out for herself."

"And in the meantime, while she's 'sorting' it out, what are the rest of us supposed to do?" With that, she sprang to her feet, her neck craning in the direction of the bank's tower clock.

"Why, what are you thinking of doing?" As Glynis asked this, she too glanced at the clock, and rose from the bench. "There's something else you haven't told me," she said to her niece. "From where did you and Professor Lowe leave— I mean, of course, leave in the balloon?"

Bronwen stood straightening the rumpled skirt of the green dress with the sun glancing off her hair in bursts of copper light. Her green cat-eyes gazed first at the towpath, then studied the sky, and she said, suddenly, "Speaking of impulsive, remember the time I jumped the mules with Cullen's Morgan?"

"I'm not likely to forget it. You didn't answer me, though."

"Aunt Glyn, I . . . we left from Cincinnati. In Ohio."

"Cincinnati? But why there?"

"That's where Professor Lowe was meeting . . . someone. His wife was there, too. His French expatriate wife, Leontine. Who's beautiful and sweet-tempered and a former actress and he adores her—in the event you're wondering about that! And as far as your other question . . ."

She stopped, while Glynis waited, feeling with unhappy certainty that Bronwen was about to lie to her. And that she herself might be to blame. Was she forcing Bronwen to lie, by asking too many questions that really weren't her business? Her niece wasn't a child anymore, although that was often hard to believe. Perhaps even harder to accept.

Bronwen brightened, though, saying, "I have work to do. And you have work to do, and while we're waiting on Emma to sort herself out, everybody has *something* to do— except maybe Vanessa Usher. You know, Aunt Glyn, if The Lady Vanessa were smart, *she'd* marry Adam!"

Again Glynis was forced to smile. What else could she do?

When they reached the turn from Fall Street that would bring them to the fire station, and to Cullen's office in the rear of the building, Glynis stopped at the corner and said, "Bronwen, we shouldn't mention Emma's situation to anyone else, all right?"

"Of course, and I wouldn't have mentioned it to anyone but you. Listen, Aunt Glyn, I need to see Professor Lowe soon, but would you mind if I meet Mrs. Jager?"

Surprised, Glynis said, "No, I don't mind, not if Cullen and Mrs. Jager don't. But I'm curious—as to why you want to meet her, that is?"

Bronwen shrugged, and then shot her aunt a sideways glance, eyes glittering. "Because I'm curious," she said. "It seems to run in the family."

9

—On Jan. 6, 1832, local [Seneca County] newspapers carried the following ad: John Shay of Fayette offers 6 cents reward for runaway indentured girl named Catherine Sherman.

—On Nov. 23, 1832: the same paper announced that: Jeremiah Stuck offers $5 for strayed steer.

—from Seneca County History, edited by Betty Auten, historian

When Glynis and Bronwen reached the door of the constable's office it stood partly open, and Glynis heard not only Cullen's voice but, to her surprise, also that of Adam MacAlistair. Evidently Bronwen recognized Adam's voice, too, as she gave Glynis a look laden with guilt. With a shake of her head, Glynis stepped into the familiar room, her niece following her.

Adam had been standing near the door, and after a perfunctory greeting, he said to them, with something less than his customary zest, "I should be on my way now." He turned back to Cullen, saying, "You understand my situation, then?"

"Yes, sure. But are you certain you can persuade Jeremiah Merrycoyf to come out of his so-called retirement?"

"I think so. He can be obstinate, but the need to rescue a damsel in distress is something his conscience probably won't let him avoid. Or, so I trust. But it's impossible for me, for obvious reasons, to take on this case right now. Especially since I imagine it could be a complicated one."

"And a nasty one," Cullen added.

"That, too."

Adam started to step outside, but then, as if reluctant to leave, he turned and remained standing in the doorway. The late morning sun brightened his sleek, brown cap of hair, but did not erase the smudges under his ordinarily alert, hazel eyes. Glynis had already noticed that his face looked paler than usual. Clearly Emma was not the only one to be losing sleep.

"Miss Tryon," he said now to Glynis. "Miss Tryon, I think you believe—at least I hope you believe—that I will do everything, *everything,* within my power to assure Emma's future happiness. But I would appreciate hearing you say so."

Glynis felt a poke between her shoulder blades and heard the swish of Bronwen's skirt. She also saw, from the corner of her eye, Cullen's thoroughly bewildered expression. Whereas she was caught off guard by Adam's request, she supposed she shouldn't have been; while another man would never have broached the topic so openly, certainly not in the presence of others, Adam was not just another man. His reason for it, of course, must be the quarrel with Emma. And, knowing Adam as she did, he would want to know where she stood—and the devil take conventional decorum. No wonder Bronwen liked him. But then, so did she.

"Adam," she said, carefully, "you and I have been acquainted for some time now—for even a longer time than you have known Emma—and so I have never for one minute doubted your intentions toward her."

His responding smile came with its usual reflection of self-confidence and good humor. "Thank you—Aunt Glynis," he said with a chuckle, and even before Bronwen's startled laugh came, he had turned and was gone.

"The lad's bold, *Aunt Glynis,*" said Cullen, grinning. "But what was that all about? Kind of late in the day to be assuring you of his good intentions, isn't it?"

"Assurances of good intentions are always welcome," Glynis answered, smiling herself.

"But Aunt Glyn," Bronwen began, "you didn't exactly say—"

"Tell me, Cullen," said Glynis, deliberately cutting off her niece, whose moments of insight did not always need to be aired, "what were you and Adam saying about Jeremiah's retirement? Not that anyone really believes he has retired."

"No, but he likes to think we believe it." Cullen rounded his desk, waving Glynis and Bronwen into straight Shaker chairs, and closed the door before he answered. "I thought I'd better discuss the Brants' missing servant girl with a lawyer, mainly because you were told that she was a mute. If she's accused of a crime, she'll need to be represented. We don't know yet that she's a murderess, and I don't want her taken advantage of when she's found. *If* she's found, that is."

"Has anyone come forward yet with some idea of where she might have gone?" Glynis asked.

Cullen shook his head. "But I've just wired the Seneca County Sheriff's Office with a description of her. The one we got from Clements at the Brant house last night. And somehow it got into this morning's newspaper."

"The *Courier* didn't mention that she was mute, though, Cullen. Why was that, do you suppose?"

"Maybe whoever wrote the story wasn't told. I don't know where the newspaper's information came from—do I ever know?"

"I guess it might be important."

"Why?" This came from both Cullen and Bronwen.

"Because I wonder if this girl has always been mute. Something Clements said last night about her being cursed. . . ." Glynis saw their dubious stares and felt slightly foolish. "It's probably not crucial at this point."

"I'm waiting to organize a search party," said Cullen,

"until after I've talked to this Elise Jager you told me about. I left a message for her at Carr's Hotel earlier this morning—desk clerk there said she didn't respond to a knock on her door, so she must not have been up yet. But she should have received it by now. I assume she wants this Tamar found as much as we do. If, as she told you, she's looking for a girl she claims is her daughter."

"The way you phrased that, Cullen, sounded as if you're doubtful."

"Do you have a question about Mrs. Jager?" asked Bronwen. "About her being the girl's mother, I mean?"

"Seems strange to me," Cullen answered, "that she told you, Glynis, she didn't know where to look for the girl. And she didn't make much of an effort to find me yesterday. I was available, at least until the—The Descent!"

Bronwen, whose eyes had been fixed on Cullen's desk clock, tore her gaze away long enough to grin.

"I agree," Glynis said, "I think it's strange, too. Though the woman was very reserved. I regret now that I didn't try harder to gain her confidence. But at the time," Glynis added with a glance at her niece, "I was too concerned with Bronwen's whereabouts."

Bronwen murmured, "Sorry," but didn't look overly so.

"Although it occurs to me," Glynis said, "that we've jumped to a conclusion here. Because the surname Jager is the same, we're assuming that the missing servant girl from the Brant household is the one Mrs. Jager is searching for, but the name could be coincidental."

"Just how many people in this town," Cullen asked with skepticism, "do you know named *Jager?*"

"None," Glynis said, "but it's a German name and we have a sizable German population here. Just because I don't know any—"

She left off at a firm knock on the office door. As Bronwen, at a nod from Cullen, rose to answer it, the door opened from without, and the flaxen-haired Elise Jager stepped into the office. Glynis, with less on her mind now as compared to the day before, thought how striking the woman looked; perhaps this was in part due to her height, because her nose and jaw were too prominent, her blue eyes too small, to call her beautiful, or even pretty. But she unquestionably was not commonplace.

"Are you Constable Stuart?" she said to Cullen, her face betraying little anxiety, Glynis noted. Could the woman not have heard the uproar in town? Perhaps not, if she knew no one and had not seen a newspaper.

When Cullen nodded and stood up, she said, "I'm Elise Jager. I understand you wish to see me."

Glynis rose to reintroduce herself. Bronwen also stood, and for a moment abandoned her watch on the clock to give Mrs. Jager what Glynis thought was an exceptionally thorough going-over. And she wondered again why her niece was so curious about this woman.

"Yes, Mrs. Jager," said Cullen, after sending Glynis a look that said he'd also noted the woman's coolness. "If you'll have a chair, I need to ask you some questions. I understand from Miss Tryon that you are here in Seneca Falls to look for your daughter?"

"Yes, I am." Elise Jager went to the straight chair and lowered herself into it, her movements uncommonly graceful, something else about her that Glynis had not noticed the day before.

"And you're from the Syracuse area?" Cullen asked.

"Yes."

Glynis had reseated herself, and Bronwen, who remained standing behind her, muttered under her breath, "She isn't going to make this easy, is she?"

Glynis, hoping that Elise Jager hadn't heard, shifted on the chair to direct a dark look at her niece. But Bronwen's attention was again on the clock. This excessive concern with the time not only mystified Glynis, but had begun to worry her, making her uneasy as to what Bronwen was brewing up now. Surely it was something. At one point Glynis had even speculated that it might have to do with the Treasury job—which would explain the furtiveness—but she'd discarded that notion as stretching imagination just too far. Bronwen was here in town for her cousin's wedding. And Treasury could hardly be interested in that.

Cullen, if surprised by Mrs. Jager's apparent ignorance of the town's current events, and the shortness of her responses, did not give any indication of it, but looked at the woman with a level gaze. "What is your daughter's name?"

"Her name? Why, it's Jager, of course. Tamar Jager."

And that took care of that, thought Glynis with disappointment. She had hoped against hope that the missing servant girl and the daughter of Elise Jager were not one and the same. But she found it more than curious that this elegantly dressed woman had a daughter who worked as a servant. She studied the guarded Mrs. Jager. How would she react when informed of her daughter's possible involvement with murder?

Glynis didn't have to wait long to learn, however, as Cullen waded right in, leaning forward in his desk chair to tell the mother that her daughter had disappeared, probably at or about the time her employer, one wealthy and well-respected Roland Brant, had been stabbed. Then, while the woman simply stared at him blank-faced, he sat back in his desk chair. And waited.

As did they all. For a long moment Glynis wondered if Elise Jager had even heard Cullen, because her reaction seemed so empty of emotion. But her hands in black kid gloves gave her away; they were tightly clasped in her lap, the soft leather stretching like a second skin over her fingers.

Then Bronwen, with a last quick glance at the clock, moved toward the door, saying, "I have to leave now. I hope that you find your daughter, Mrs. Jager."

She opened the door, but then she slowly turned back and said to the woman, in an offhand manner that Glynis knew was staged, "Oh, by the way, is Tamar's father here in Seneca Falls? He would, I assume, be Mr. Jager?"

Elise Jager was without doubt not prepared for this, as her mask of indifference dropped, her face bearing a confused array of expressions before it settled into one of dislike. Glynis could hardly blame her.

Bronwen, however, did not wait for an answer to her question. Before the silence that followed it could be broken, she was out the door.

"Excuse me," Glynis said, and quickly got up to follow her niece.

"Just what was *that* about?" she demanded, catching Bronwen as she started for Fall Street.

Bronwen fidgeted, rocking on her feet as if preparing to run. "I'm going to be late—"

"Late for what?"

"I can't stay any longer! But make that woman answer my question, Aunt Glyn, because something's wrong back there," she said, tossing her head in the direction of Cullen's office. Then she sidled away from Glynis, saying, "I'm sorry, but I have to go. And don't *worry* about me!"

Then, picking up the skirt of the green dress, she turned and darted off like a dragonfly.

Glynis stood watching her with once again the usual response: a mixture of utter exasperation and concern. Bronwen was up to no good, she told herself as she walked back around the firehouse. And what exactly could she do about it? Again, as usual, nothing. She did ponder, briefly, the possibility that her sister Gwen, instead of giving birth to Bronwen, had simply found her one day under a toadstool.

When she went back inside the office, murmuring an apology for her abrupt departure, Cullen eyed her with curiosity. Mrs. Jager simply eyed her. As if Glynis, like her niece, should be viewed with extreme caution.

"Mrs. Jager has just told me," Cullen said to Glynis, "that her daughter was not employed by the Brant family."

Glynis must have looked as confused as she felt, because he explained, "It seems that Tamar was indentured to them."

"Indentured?" Glynis echoed. For a fleeting second she wished Bronwen was there to blurt: *Why?*

"Can you tell me when she was first indentured?" Cullen asked the woman, which to Glynis's mind began a tortuous, roundabout route to get where he wanted to go, although he must have earlier determined that this would be the best way, perhaps the only way, of reaching this woman.

"Several years ago," answered Elise Jager.

When nothing more was forthcoming, Cullen said, "Would you please be more specific? We need as much information about your daughter as possible."

"I don't understand what difference it could make," she said, drawing herself up on the chair. "Frankly, Constable Stuart, I find these questions from you and your acquaintances extremely intrusive. My only purpose in being here is to find my daughter."

Glynis saw the instant that Cullen's mind, and hence his tactic, changed; his eyes narrowed and he sat forward at the edge of his chair to say in a clipped manner, "And frankly, Mrs. Jager, I find your answers to these questions unsatisfactory. Let me make things plain for you. Miss Tryon has been of invaluable assistance to me in the past. Plus, I thought you might be more comfortable with another woman here. And while her niece Miss Llyr may not always proceed in the most tactful fashion, she is at present a United States Treasury agent. Which means she is employed to be, as you put it, 'intrusive.' "

Elise Jager's face was beginning to blanch. In the meantime, Glynis, for the life of her, couldn't see what bearing Bronwen's occupation had on any of this.

"Now, whether or not you find my questions intrusive, Mrs. Jager, is of no concern to me," Cullen continued, "because your daughter has become, for the time being at least, a principal suspect in a murder investigation."

Elise Jager's hands unclasped and she gripped the seat of her chair. "That's absurd!" she gasped.

"All right," said Cullen, sitting back, "then suppose you tell me why it's absurd."

"Tamar wouldn't harm anyone! Ever!"

The woman's voice carried passion and conviction, and perhaps, Glynis thought, her wall of reserve had been breached.

"Go on," Cullen said.

"Why would you even think she's committed some terrible crime? She's just a child!"

"A child?" Cullen asked. "How old is she?"

"She'll be seventeen next month."

Cullen's brows lifted slightly at this, but Glynis understood: to many a mother almost any age would still make her daughter "just a child." And now that Elise Jager's facade of indifference had been removed, Glynis again had the sense—the same one she'd had when first seeing the distressed woman the day before—that she seemed somehow familiar. But Glynis wouldn't interrupt to ask anything now. Not when Cullen had finally gotten through.

"You told me that your daughter had been indentured several years ago," Cullen said. "What exactly is 'several'?"

"Two. Two years."

"So she was fourteen, fifteen at the time?"

Elise Jager nodded. Glynis, seated in a chair beside her, looked at the woman's strong profile, and saw eyes suddenly made softer by the moistness of unshed tears.

"How did that come about—that your daughter was indentured?" Cullen asked her, his tone now considerably milder, as if he, too, had seen the tears.

She hesitated, as though making a decision, just as she had done with Glynis the day before, then explained, "That was not by my hand, Constable Stuart. I had no choice. My husband, Tamar's father, made the decision. And all the arrangements. He and I are . . . we've been separated for some time now."

Glynis quickly got to her feet and went to the office window, the anger she felt so strong that she feared she could not contain it unless she forced herself to move. There was silence in the room behind her as she stared out at the canal, seeing wave upon wave of petitions asking, pleading, begging that the law be changed; the law that gave a father sole custody of a married couple's children—*absolute custody*—allowing him to sell those children into servitude despite the frantic, heartbroken objections of their mother. The law that gave a father the right to take a child from its mother in all cases of divorce, no matter how reprehensible the behavior of the man, or how venial the purpose. A father could be a drunkard, an adulterer, a profligate spender, a wanton degenerate, and still retain custody of his children.

For two years Susan Anthony had canvassed the state in pursuit of legal reform. To gather signatures on the petitions, she'd delivered lectures all over the state, covering hundreds of miles between cities and towns by stagecoach and train, by sleigh and canal boat, through summer heat and winter blizzards. And it was mostly through her efforts that the New York legislature had finally the previous year granted to women some rights to their purses and to their children. A married woman now shared with her husband equal custody. And this reform had been brought about by the tireless campaigning of the unmarried Anthony. And by the articles and written speeches of Elizabeth Cady Stanton, who, although tied down with seven children in Seneca Falls, still managed to wield a powerful pen.

Glynis heard Cullen shuffling papers on his desk. She took a deep breath before turning back to the room to say, "Are you aware, Mrs. Jager, that New York State has recently passed a new law, Chapter 90, called the Earnings Act? It also addresses the custody of children."

"Yes, I just learned of it," the woman answered eagerly.

"That's why I've come here. The indenture period was supposed to be for five years, but I want Tamar released from it now. Can you tell me, Constable Stuart, how I would go about asking for custody of her?"

"Go to the Seneca County Court House in Waterloo, and talk to the clerk there. He should be able to tell you how to file an application petitioning the court for your daughter's custody. The circuit judge isn't there right now, but I'm told he'll be back in a day or two. He could probably hear your request then."

"I'll go there this afternoon," Elise Jager said. "And thank you, Constable."

Glynis glanced at Cullen with curiosity. He had been writing something on a piece of paper, and when he looked up his face was grim.

"I think you may be in for a rough time," he said to Elise Jager, "and your daughter is going to need legal representation." He stood, leaning over his desk to hand the paper to her. "Jeremiah Merrycoyf is one of the best attorneys in western New York. I've written down the address of the Merrycoyf and MacAlistair law offices on Fall Street. Tell him of your daughter's situation. If he's reluctant to become involved—which he might be since he insists that he's retired—I'll try to intercede for you. And so, I'm sure, will Miss Tryon."

When Elise Jager took the paper from him, her eyes threatened to overflow. "Thank you, again, Constable. And you, Miss Tryon. I hope you'll forgive . . ."

"That's O.K.," Cullen said. "I'm going to get a search party under way, and for that I'll need a complete description of your daughter."

"But I haven't seen Tamar for two years."

Glynis turned back to the window as Cullen handed the woman more sheets of paper, saying, "Just do the best you can then, when you fill these out. I know you want to find your daughter, but I need to find her, too. And regardless of whether I like it or not, she is still the best suspect I have in Roland Brant's murder."

Elise Jager's face flushed as she said, "But Tamar would never—" She broke off at what might have looked like an inflexible stance on Cullen's part, but Glynis knew better. He was a fair man, and would search for the woman's missing daughter whatever the reason.

Elise Jager took a handkerchief from her purse, and after wiping her eyes she said, "How long do you think it will be? Until you find her?"

"I can't say. At the moment we don't have any leads as to where your daughter might have gone, and this is a big county. Parts of it even I haven't seen. There are thousands of acres of marshland, and if someone really wants to stay lost . . ."

He stopped as Glynis whirled round to send him a look of appeal.

"We'll do our best, Mrs. Jager," Cullen said with firmness. "With luck, we'll find your daughter. That's all I can tell you right now." He turned to Glynis saying, "I'm going back out to the Brant place late this afternoon. Need to talk to the family and servants again, now that we have a little more to go on. Since Zeph and Liam will be heading the search party, I'd like you to come with me." His face bore the ghost of a smile when he added, "You know the women there, remember?"

"Constable, I want to see the Brants, too," Elise Jager said, looking up from the forms Cullen had given to her. "They had Tamar there for two years!"

"No," responded Cullen somewhat sharply, "I don't think that would be a good idea. At least not yet. Your daughter is a murder suspect—the Brants are not likely to greet you with open arms. Wait until I have more information. I assume that you aren't planning to leave town anytime soon, right?"

Elise Jager looked bewildered. "No. No, of course not."

"Good. Don't. You can be reached at Carr's Hotel?"

"Yes."

"Cullen, I'll be at the library," Glynis told him, "and I need to stop at the Women's Refuge before I leave with you for the Brant place."

"O.K., I'll come by there after I get the search started. I need to talk to the doc, anyway."

"Mrs. Jager," Glynis said to her, "if you want me, I'm usually at the library—above the canal at the corner of Fall and Cayuga Streets. But if I'm not there, you can leave a message with my assistant, Jonathan Quant."

As Elise Jager was thanking her, Glynis suddenly remembered what she'd wanted to ask the woman. "Can you tell me how long your daughter Tamar has been . . . has not talked?"

"What?" The blue eyes widened in what had to be genuine surprise. "Not talked? Whatever do you mean?"

Since Glynis had her answer, she shook her head, saying only, "I understand she is a rather quiet girl?"

The woman's shoulders relaxed, then slumped. "Yes, she's always been shy."

Although she feared Mrs. Jager might resent it, Glynis could not keep herself from briefly touching the woman's shoulder before she left, saying, "We'll find Tamar."

At least, she thought, I pray that we do.

It was only when Glynis reached Fall Street that she recalled the question Bronwen had put to Mrs. Jager. And that it had not been answered.

10

Already, we begin to cry out for more ammunition, and already the blockade is beginning to shut it all out.

—Mary Boykin Chesnut, 1861 entry from
A Diary from Dixie.

The two men stood several feet apart, facing each other, the set of their shoulders uncompromising. During their argument, the intensity of which waxed and waned, both continually glanced about to make certain they could not be overheard. They had carefully isolated themselves, so they thought, under an oak of great age that grew on a slope overlooking the port city of Oswego, New York. The only objects within hailing distance of the men were a few empty hay wagons.

The city of Oswego lies on the southeastern shore of Lake Ontario, the smallest of the Great Lakes but eventual heir to all of their waters that flow to the sea; waters funneled east to the Atlantic by the powerful, rapids-frothing St. Lawrence River. Below the two men, the port hustled with activity under a bright noonday sun.

The Oswego River and canal also empty into Lake Ontario. The city itself straddles the river, and when the men—one English, the other American—looked to the high banks east of it, they could see a symbol of their century-old hostility in the brick Fort Ontario, reconstructed after the British burning of 1812. Due north of the men, and too far across the shining water to see, lay the Canadian shoreline and another port city, that of Kingston, Ontario.

But these two men were more absorbed by what sailed on the water than by what stood on the land.

Lake schooners and three-masted frigates plied the lake and mouth of the river, as did one-masted sloops, trading ships, canal packets, and fishermen's boats, and even an occasional bark canoe. Both men turned their eyes often to scan these voyagers. Only the American, however, studied anew the half-mile distance between the Oswego-Syracuse Railroad and the wharves. These wharves at midday were swarming with dockworkers, and the smell of the fisheries reached even the men standing under the oak. Overhead in a cloudless sky, gulls screamed and wheeled in endless, searching arcs.

The slender, hawk-faced Englishman took from a pocket of his gray-wool morning coat an immaculate white handkerchief and dabbed the perspiration on his clean-shaven upper lip. "And those are the terms, my good man," he said with a restrained smile. "You are quite welcome to reject them, although I would not advise it."

"We had a deal," snapped the robust American, who had taken off his short box coat and slung it over his shoulder to hang from an index finger. "And this is the third shipment. You can't suddenly change the terms now!"

"Oh, but indeed I can. And it is not I but you who have proposed changing the original agreement. Thus the situation is somewhat different than when we implemented the initial shipments. And in the meantime, your Mr. Lincoln's blockade of the southern Atlantic ports has limited my options."

"We had a deal!" the American repeated. "It's not my fault the damn shipment is three days early! And your options are not the issue here."

"Ah, but they are, you see—"

"No, I don't see. *You're* not running those rifles to the South."

"And there is the rub." The candor in the Englishman's voice belied the shrewdness in his eyes. "You misled me, as well as my associates in Britain, into believing that we would simply be shipping the rifles to Canada, and that would be the end of it. And now I have learned, to my consternation, that you expect an additional, and more hazardous, course of action. Since that course is out of the question, I may be forced to look elsewhere for markets. Of which there are many. I've just come from the South and demand there is high. But to supply that demand will almost certainly involve the blockade—"

"Just a minute. I'm taking the lion's share of the risk here. My partner and I are the ones smuggling those rifles—and bayonets—into the South. Let's not forget that."

"To my contacts in the South. Let us not forget *that.*"

"What the hell is there to argue about?" the American demanded. "So the Enfields are arriving early. All I'm asking is that you *unload* the damn things! Once that's done, I'll get them the rest of the way. But Seneca Falls," he added, "is forty miles from here."

"Ah, yes, Seneca Falls. Nonetheless, our original agreement, if you remember, called only for the Enfields to be shipped from London across the Atlantic to the Gulf of St. Lawrence. And then up the river to—"

"We've been over that!" interrupted the American, anger flushing his face. "I admit we made a mistake. We figured the canal bypassing the rapids at Montreal could handle a deep-draft ship. That the guns could come straight up the river to Kingston. So, we were wrong!"

"Yes, and because of your error, the guns must be brought almost two hundred miles overland from Montreal. As if that were not complicated enough—no, do not interrupt me again!—you insisted that we put them aboard a Canadian ship and sail them to this port. And my partners agreed to that, although under some duress, if memory serves me. But that was *all* the agreement covered."

"I told you," said the American, "we've had a problem with ready cash. It's nothing that can't be fixed in a few days. But you say you won't unload! And you won't wait without more money!"

"I cannot wait. The rifles are in Montreal, due to reach Kingston today or tomorrow. And will immediately be loaded onto a Canadian ship. Every minute that ship rides at anchor in port is costly."

The American wiped his hand across his forehead. "You know this takes careful planning. One small hitch and—"

"My dear man, I hardly need to be lectured about planning." The Englishman's eyes took on a brighter glint. "Just what is it that you are not telling me?"

"Nothing. There's nothing to tell. Except the damn shipment is early and . . . and I don't have the men to unload it. But again, why the hell can't *your* crew unload the guns?"

"Quite simply because I refuse to violate the law of the United States."

"Oh, c'mon!" the American jeered. "Since when did you get so law-abiding? I'm not a fool—you're just playing my partner and me for more money. And don't act self-righteous! You'll do anything to see the Confederacy succeed so your cotton supply is protected. You and your associates are involved in this up to your greedy necks."

"Not so. I merely bring our rifles through international waters. What happens to them after that is none of my concern. And, my good man," the Englishman added, "even our greed, unlike yours, does not embrace treason."

The American's look of exasperation heightened, and his glance went again from the limestone railroad station to the wharves. "All right! If you won't unload, then just hold the ship up in Kingston."

"I believe that is what I suggested earlier."

"No, what you *suggested* is that this delay will cost plenty."

"Regrettably, that is correct. And now having come full circle we are back precisely where we started," said the Englishman. "Those are the terms. If you accept them, I will hold the ship in Kingston."

"I need to talk to my partner. It's a lot of money, de Warde!"

The Englishman's eyes widened into the intent black stare of a raptor, and his voice carried a dangerous edge. "Don't *ever* again call me by name. *Not ever.*" Then his face relaxed, and he went on as if nothing untoward had occurred. "I'm afraid, however, that I cannot afford to wait for consultations. Do you accept the terms or not?"

The American, who had been looking northward across the water, now returned his gaze to the other. At last, he shrugged. "You've taken advantage of this, you bastard— but it looks like I have no choice."

"Excellent. And I am certain, now that we fully understand each other, that this can continue to be a mutually beneficial arrangement. Good day, my dear sir."

Colonel Dorian de Warde gave the other man a pleasant smile before turning to walk down to the harbor. The American stood for only a moment, directing a resentful glare at the back of the Englishman's gray morning coat, before he started at a run for the rail station.

Neither man had paid much attention to the empty hay wagons parked a short distance away. Nor did they see the lone figure who now crawled out of one from beneath a false floor.

And who also took off at a run toward the city.

11

—m—

Dr. Elizabeth Blackwell, returning to this country from England about the time of the breaking out of war, fresh from an acquaintance with Miss Nightingale, and filled with enthusiasm, at once called an informal meeting at the New York Infirmary for Women and Children. . . . A public meeting was then held on April 26, 1861 at the Cooper Union, its object being to concentrate scattered efforts by a large formal organization [called] the "Woman's Central Relief Association of New York."

—History of Woman Suffrage, edited by
Elizabeth Cady Stanton, Susan B.
Anthony, and Matilda Joslyn Gage

$\mathcal{A}$fter leaving Cullen's office, Glynis was walking down Fall Street toward the library when she saw Bronwen dash from the telegraph office. She then darted across the road to the entrance of Carr's Hotel. Glynis stood puzzling over her niece's behavior, until she remembered that Professor Thaddeus Lowe was staying at the hotel. Bronwen had mentioned that she needed to see him, and she might have found a place with gas available to inflate the balloon—a place most likely to be Rochester or Syracuse. That could explain the telegrams. But it alone could not explain Bronwen's newly acquired obsession with time.

Glynis again reminded herself that Bronwen's business

was not also her business, and that her sister Gwen would be there soon enough to ride herd on her daughter. Despite an aroused curiosity, she had other pressing things to do at the moment. And no doubt she'd have opportunity to talk with her niece that evening.

In late afternoon, Glynis found herself again on Fall Street, now trudging in the opposite direction toward the side street on which Dr. Neva Cardoza-Levy's refuge was located. Her arms and the large canvas bag slung over her shoulder were laden with books, mostly children's literature. Jonathan had said he would bring along the remaining ones she'd designated for the Women's Refuge after he'd closed the library, but Glynis had promised the children's books and she knew that some of the youngsters there were waiting for them.

There had been no further sighting of Bronwen. Nor had Emma been at her shop; perhaps she was with Adam. Which Glynis hoped was a good sign.

After she had turned off Fall, and was nearing the refuge, she thought about the time, several years before, that she'd first seen the place. She had just returned from a year in Springfield, Illinois, at the home of her brother Robin, where his wife Julia had languished for months before dying of consumption. Glynis, on the day she'd returned with Emma to Seneca Falls, had gone to the refuge, which Neva had written about with such enthusiasm. She remembered her first impression: that the abandoned warehouse with its stark brick walls and few windows, most of them broken, had evoked an image of nearby Auburn Prison.

Since then, however, things had improved, often as a result of generosity on the part of anonymous donors. Neva had told of arriving at the refuge on more than one morning to find awaiting her, from unknown sources, such things as feather mattresses, or wooden chairs, or crates of eating utensils, bowls, rag dolls, clothing, and on one occasion, a Franklin stove.

There were also the efforts of a small but disparate group of men: Neva's husband, hardware store owner Abraham Levy; Lacey Smith's husband, the blacksmith Isaiah; the young deputy, Zeph Waters; and even Adam MacAlistair. New windows had been cut in the warehouse walls to let in more light. Broken glass had been replaced. Partition walls had been erected. And now grass surrounded the building where there had once been only hard-packed dirt; or, still worse, a sea of mud. Several of Cullen's sturdy, curly-horned merino sheep tolerated the children and kept the grass cropped short. The yellow bloom of forsythia bushes now spread against the brick walls, and stout, young oak trees held rope swings. Here and there patches of scarlet tulips and white candy tuft bloomed in the sheltered places where children's feet did not tread.

And then, of course, there was the new addition. From a not-so-anonymous donor.

Glynis would never forget the morning, nearly a year ago, when Neva had arrived at the library, looking very much as if she had suffered a severe shock. She had collapsed into a chair in Glynis's small back office, and dropped on the desk a letter and a banknote. As it turned out, the amount of the banknote had been amply sufficient to cause shock.

"Glynis, just look—look at those numbers," Neva had said. "Those are four zeros! I simply cannot believe it."

"No, I can't either. Who is it from?"

Neva had gestured toward the letter. After Glynis had finished reading it, she suspected that she had looked as stunned as Neva.

"Vanessa Usher is donating all this money to the refuge?" Neva said, disbelief making her voice crack. "Do you think it's the woman's idea of a practical joke?"

"If so, it's an expensive joke," Glynis answered. "This note is drawn on the Partridge Seneca Falls Bank, which is about the most solvent bank in the state. And after our counterfeiting episode here, I pretty much know a genuine note when I see one, Neva."

They had just sat and stared at each other. Until at last Neva had ventured, "O.K., what do you suppose she wants in return?"

Glynis had replied, after only a moment's hesitation, "I think I can guess!"

And now, as she stepped onto the narrow stone walk in front of the converted warehouse, Glynis had to smile at her bull's-eye prediction. There was no possible way to avoid seeing it, since foot-high letters carved across the fieldstone entrance of the new addition read: THE VANESSA USHER CHIL-DREN'S WING.

Neva had not put up so much as a token resistance. She had not even batted an eye when writing a letter to the *Courier,* the purpose of which had been to publicly thank Miss Usher for her most beneficent and selfless generosity.

Glynis left the books in the hands of eager youngsters and went looking for Neva. She found her in the rear yard, seated on a bench under a blossoming, white-plumed horse chestnut tree and reading what looked to be a long letter; Neva in repose was such an uncommon event that Glynis disliked having to disturb her. But Neva called to her, patting the vacant portion of the bench beside her.

"I take it Cullen isn't here yet?" Glynis asked after seating herself and inhaling deeply; a row of lilac bushes just beginning to bloom sent over the yard their peerless fragrance. From the front of the refuge came the high, clear voices of children playing in a warm, hazy, sunlit afternoon.

"No, but he stopped by early this morning," Neva answered, tucking strands of tightly curled hair behind an ear, then waving at Glynis several sheets of paper. "I was looking over this affidavit I just wrote—for Cullen to submit with his request for a court-ordered autopsy on Roland Brant. I had time to do it because the children who were sick yesterday have all made a fast recovery, and none of the others have been stricken."

"What good news that is, Neva!"

"Yes, and I think the sickness was caused by milk—milk that sat around too long on a warm day. It makes me more certain than ever that Pasteur's research with airborne bacteria is on the right track. And I've been insisting that everyone's hands are washed before handling food—it seems to help keep these illnesses—whatever they are—from spreading like wildfire from one person to another."

"Do you think a cure will ever be found for consumption—tuberculosis?" Glynis asked her, thinking of Julia Tryon and Vanessa's sister Aurora.

"We need to find out what causes it—and there's just so much we don't know," Neva answered, her wide brow creasing like a folded fan as it did when she concentrated. "But remember, until a half century ago we didn't know much about smallpox either. Now we're on our way to seeing it someday wiped out, maybe even within this century. When you think of the people who've died where a simple inoculation would have saved them . . ." Neva's voice broke slightly, as if she couldn't listen to her own words.

"You seem more agreeable to an autopsy today than you were last night," Glynis said.

"Last night I was exhausted! Besides, I had another look at Brant's body after Zeph and I got it to the icehouse. I think there's something odd there, Glynis."

"Odd?"

"Yes, to do with the stab wound. But I'd better not speculate. Although this court order may take a day or two—Erich Brant's attitude has not changed, according to Cullen, and apparently the judge is off somewhere on circuit and won't be back until tomorrow. At the earliest."

"In that event, I guess we should hope that Roland Brant's funeral won't be held the same day as Emma's wedding."

"What a thought, Glynis! How do you come up with these

things? Too much imagination, that's how—makes for a worrier. But don't listen to me. I'm a fine one to talk! So, is Bronwen's sister Kathryn coming from New York City for the wedding?"

Kathryn, for the past five months, had been nursing at the New York Infirmary for Women and Children, founded four years before by Drs. Elizabeth and Emily Blackwell and Marie Zakrzewska.

"Yes, she's coming," answered Glynis with a smile. Of her three nieces, she thought, Kathryn was the one most like herself.

Neva nodded. "Good. Unfortunately, I think we're going to need battalions of nurses very soon. But the only one who appears to recognize that is Elizabeth Blackwell. It's foresighted of her to begin organizing a relief association," she added, "because if this hideous affair in the South escalates . . . Men and their wars! If to keep themselves amused they have to be firing guns at something, then why not line up all their politicians and have a turkey shoot! Really, Glynis, if women ever manage to get their hands on the vote, I trust the first order of business will be to banish guns!"

"There would certainly be enough of us to do it," Glynis agreed. "Which may be one of the reasons men don't want us to have the vote."

"Then let them keep their breech-loading muskets," was Neva's response. "With those things they're just as likely to kill themselves as to hurt someone else. One truly has to wonder what was in the minds of those forefathers of yours when they wrote up the Constitution."

"Since Colt revolvers hadn't been invented yet, we can be fairly certain they didn't foresee one of those in every hand. But why *my* forefathers?"

"So far as I know, Glynis, there were no Jews invited to that party." Neva scowled darkly. "Those men and their Constitution have other things to answer for, aside from the matter of guns. Their provision for slave-holding is the reason for this dreaded mess we're in now. And then there's the small matter of their exclusion of women. I think it's high time we took another look at that one-sided, flawed document."

Neva seemed to consider this a moment before she continued, "Do you know what Elizabeth Blackwell is actually doing? She's involving New York's society women in her relief group—a brilliant stroke! My cousin Ernestine Rose wrote to me about it. Now maybe some of that money will be put to good use."

Glynis nodded. "We can only hope they don't all demand to have their names carved in stone."

Neva, glancing at the new wing, laughed.

Before Glynis next spoke she took a quick look around for possible eavesdroppers, and then said, "If it isn't betraying a confidence, Neva, can you tell me if Roland Brant's wife—or rather his widow—is a patient of yours?"

"Yes, I can tell you, and no, she isn't my patient. And she wouldn't be."

"Why not?"

"Because I've learned, Glynis, that women with the most intimidating husbands are the ones least likely to see a female doctor."

"I would guess that's probably true."

"You would?"

"I didn't say it was good. But the point is, does Helga Brant look ill to you?"

"I haven't noticed."

"You haven't?"

"Glynis, I don't view everyone I meet as a potential patient, you know," Neva stated. "I've got enough of those as it is. But why are you asking about Helga Brant?"

"I'm not sure. Just a guess, perhaps, that she could be stronger than she looks."

"That may be, but strength is relative. I met Roland Brant on occasion, and I doubt very much that his wife, or few oth-

ers for that matter, could have matched him for strength—
physical or mental. If that's what you're referring to."

"Not precisely, but again, true enough, I suppose."

"That's one of the qualities I like about you, Glynis. You
nearly always sound agreeable, even when you're not agreeing."

"Well, I'm agreeing now. At least I think so. And I'm not
even certain why I'm asking you this. It's just that—that
several things don't seem to fit," Glynis said slowly.

"Then, knowing you, I'd say there's a pretty good chance
that things *don't* fit," Neva replied. "I can't tell how, or even
if, this might relate to Helga Brant, but there's another thing
I've learned. That some women, when they're terrified of
having more children, manage to become chronic invalids.
Which means they are frail. Untouchable. It's their only way
out of the so-called marital obligation. And it may not even
be, on their part, a consciously planned escape. I'm certain
you know what I mean."

"Of course I do. And tragic though it is, it makes some
sense. I'd just never thought of it that way before."

"Well, why would you? You're not married!" Neva gave
her a sideways glance. "This despite the fact, I might add,
that two of the very few good men around are—"

"Neva, please. Let's not get into that."

But she readied herself, because Neva shifted round on
the bench to launch a frontal maneuver, saying, "We haven't
had any chance to talk, Glynis, since you came back from
Washington. Did Jacques Sundown come with you?"

"No, he didn't. Jacques put me on the train and —"

"But Sundown is here. I saw him just this morning."

"That's not likely," Glynis said, straightening on the
bench. "At least I don't think it is. Are you sure it was
Jacques you saw?"

"Glynis Tryon! How could any woman who wasn't half-
blind, and half-dead, mistake that man for someone else? Besides, he was on that black-and-white paint horse of his,

heading up Cayuga Street. But you really didn't know he was here? No, from the look on your face I guess you didn't—"

"Neva," Glynis interrupted, as she'd just heard, below the high voices of children, another, deeper voice, "I think Cullen's just arrived."

Glynis grasped the side of the small, covered buggy as Cullen turned the horse onto the side road that led to the Brant house.

"Got the buggy at Boone's Livery," he'd said at the refuge, handing her up onto the black leather seat, "because it looks like rain."

Light wind had begun to stack the southern sky with rolls of fleecy gray cloud, but the air remained warm.

"Has the search party for Tamar Jager been organized?" Glynis asked him now.

He nodded, saying, "But it's a bad time of year to ask men to leave their fields. The Seneca County Sheriff's Office sent a couple of deputies, so that's a help. What men there are have fanned out from the Brant place with descriptions of the girl."

"Apart from the girl being mute, it's rather a vague physical description, isn't it?" Glynis asked.

"The blond hair narrows it down some, but yes."

"Cullen, when we were at Brants' yesterday, did you find the family's attitude—well, unusual?"

"Hard to say. Unusual in the sense that they sure didn't seem to be grieving Roland Brant's death, yes, but maybe they're a tougher bunch than you're used to seeing. If we could just find that girl! Biggest headache is that we don't have any notion where she might go, or even in what direction she'd head—north, south, east, west."

The shadow of something flitted across Glynis's mind, gone before she could really see it.

"I worry about the girl being mute," she said. "The men in the search party are aware of that, aren't they?"

"Yes, but I know what you mean. Zeph and Liam will

handle it all right, and I think I impressed on the others that they shouldn't scare her, but not all of them are my men. Plus the dogs alone might frighten her."

"You're using dogs to track her?"

"Glynis, of course I am. She could be anywhere! Got a piece of her clothing from Brants' last night, hoping the dogs can pick up her scent. Don't forget that this Tamar is possibly Roland Brant's killer—I can't think her disappearance is only a coincidence. But I admit that I also can't think of a motive for a servant girl to kill Brant. Unless he caught her stealing from his safe."

"I suppose so," Glynis said, "but Roland Brant was a strapping man, certainly more than able to defend himself against what we've been told is a slender girl."

Cullen nodded, and said, "Don't worry about the dogs. They're all hounds—most of them bloodhounds—so they won't harm her."

"But how could she know that?"

"Couldn't. Not unless she knows dogs."

They rode in silence for a time, Glynis watching the freshly plowed fields and the recently awakened woodlands, their shades of green brilliant against a sky grown increasingly gray, and she heard scattered drops of rain pinging against the roof of the buggy.

Brants' hemlock appeared, and then Cullen guided the horse onto the curving, gravel drive. Today the distance to the house seemed to Glynis to be half that of the night before, the forest more untamed than ominously primeval. The only sound was the rattle of the wheels and the spring rain spattering against the roof of the buggy. And the occasional, distinctive call of a bird seeking a mate.

When the house came into view, Glynis decided that daylight had not improved its character. It still had about it an unpleasant, brooding look.

12

Calamities came to them too, and their earlier errors carried hard consequences; perhaps the love of some sweet maiden; the image of purity, order, and calm had opened their eyes to the vision of a life in which the days would not seem too long . . . but the maiden was lost.

—George Eliot, *Silas Marner,* 1861

Cullen brought the buggy up the Brant drive to the hitching post by the porch steps, reining in the horse beside a dun-colored mare and another carriage. By now his face had lost its relaxed look. Glynis had seen him do this before; distance himself from everything else to concentrate solely on the problem at hand. It required discipline of a kind that to her did not come readily. Moreover, she had observed that the mind of many a woman seemed to run on more than one track, invariably changing course to accommodate the needs of those in her path.

The misty gray drizzle continued, and Cullen, rooting around under the buggy seat, at last unearthed an umbrella. He handed it to Glynis, saying, "At least with this rain everyone we need to see will probably be indoors and accessible. Before we left last night I told them all to be here this afternoon. Let's see which ones choose to make themselves scarce—other than our missing servant girl, who's looking more guilty every minute."

She couldn't necessarily agree with him, at least not yet. The young Tamar, who had been indentured without any choice in the matter, and without her mother's consent, might have had other reasons for running away; although the fact that she was mute would make it even more difficult to get at the truth. And while there could be any number of possible explanations for a girl's mysterious disappearance, nearly all of those that Glynis imagined were unpleasant ones.

"I expect you want me to talk to the women?" she asked Cullen.

"I think that's best, but last night the manservant Clements sought out you, not me, so maybe you should deal with him."

She waited while Cullen climbed from the buggy and tethered the livery horse to the hitching post beside the dun mare. As he rounded the buggy to help her down, she said to him, "I think Clements came to me because it was what Helga Brant wanted."

"Even so," Cullen said, "if he's going to jabber on about curses and evil eyes you'll have more patience with him than I will. The main thing is to try to pick up inconsistencies in these people's stories . . . but you know all that, Glynis. If we had some idea of when Brant died it would be easier—but without an autopsy we're going into this blind." His hands caught her waist and he lifted her from the buggy.

A voice from the porch said, "Back again? Just couldn't keep away from our cozy little household?" It was Konrad Brant's greeting. "You must lead a singularly uneventful life, Constable Stuart."

"You know what to ask," Cullen said to Glynis under his breath before he turned to Konrad.

"Yes, I'm back and it probably won't be the last time," Cullen answered him. "Is everybody in the household here?"

Konrad nodded and motioned toward the other carriage.

"Not only that," he said, "we've even got an extra body for you."

He sounded remarkably cheerful, Glynis thought, and she looked for a glass in his hand. It was there, and it was filled. Did this young man exert himself in any way other than self-indulgence? Glynis recalled the words of Konrad's brother Erich the day before; something to the effect of Konrad's having been allowed to live there only through his father's forbearance, and being now subject to his, Erich's. Which made her again wonder if Roland Brant had made a will, and if both sons had known its terms. Konrad, however, had not protested when Erich had seemed to say that the house was now his. But there were too many ifs to hazard speculation.

As she and Cullen went up the steps to the porch, someone from inside said, "Oh, hell, it's the constable again." The speaker had not attempted to keep his voice down, and almost immediately Erich appeared on the other side of the open door.

Glynis couldn't have explained what made her glance aside at that moment. It might have been a quick movement where she expected none, or the flash of a gold belt buckle; but glance she did, in time to see Konrad pitch the contents of his glass into an empty clay planter. Cullen was looking toward the doorway and couldn't have seen it, because Konrad's curious deed was done so adroitly that he had only to shift a foot to make it appear that he'd turned to gaze out at the rain.

Erich stood aside for Glynis and Cullen to enter, saying, "Do you always bring your lady friend on official calls?"

When Cullen said nothing, Erich went on, "I'd appreciate it, Stuart, as would the rest of my family, if you'd make this fast. We've already suffered the inconvenience today of half a dozen of your men and their hounds tromping around the property. For no good reason, because that girl's been gone too long for dogs to pick up her scent."

"I was told last night that no one knew when she'd disappeared," Cullen said. "So how do you know how long the girl's been gone, Brant?"

Erich scowled without answering. Cullen waited for the implication of his question to sink in, before saying evenly, "I expect Miss Tryon and I will be here as long as it takes to get the job done. The more cooperative you are, the faster it'll go."

"My mother's not at all well, so I trust you can leave her in peace," came Konrad's voice from directly behind Glynis. "And if I were you, Erich, I'd watch my step with this handsome librarian. Word has it that she's a regular Madame Dupin. Which is undoubtedly why she's here."

Glynis did not turn and acknowledge the gibe—it could hardly have been a compliment—and so caught the frown of confusion on Erich's face and the twitch at the corner of Cullen's mouth. But Konrad's comment made her wonder if he knew that she'd seen his covert disposal of the bourbon.

She followed a light, metallic tinkling and found Erich's wife, Tirzah, in a small music room off the parlor, a room Glynis had not even noticed the night before. The woman was seated at a harpsichord, dressed in flounce-skirted black silk with white lace at the throat and wrists, her fingers moving expertly over the keyboard. She looked up as Glynis entered the room, and brought the baroque piece to a premature end.

"Handel?" Glynis asked as she walked to the mahogany harpsichord, admiring the rich warm glow of its finish. She looked for sheets of music, but there were none in view.

"Yes, Handel," Tirzah said, looking somewhat surprised. "Are you a musician yourself, Miss Tryon, or an educated listener?"

"A little of both," Glynis answered. "I play the flute on occasion."

Tirzah rose from the bench on which she'd been seated, saying in a lethargic voice, "I play often, because there's little else in this house to do. But I'm sure yours is not a social call, is it?" Without waiting for an answer, the woman went to a window that faced the carriage house and stable, and stood staring at something outside.

Glynis took a few steps forward, and looked past Tirzah to see through the blurred, rain-spattered glass a stableboy walking a grassy track, slowly leading a gray horse with a white wrapping round one of its forelegs. Again she had the peculiar sensation of something nudging at her mind, as had happened in the buggy with Cullen, but could not bring whatever it was forth into light.

"A dreary day for a dreary business," Tirzah commented, absently brushing her skirt, then looked down, saying, "I do believe the worst thing about someone in a family dying is the obligation to wear black—which I detest. I suppose it would create a scandal of monstrous proportions if I were to show up in red satin at my father-in-law's funeral, don't you agree?" she asked, turning to Glynis with a bland expression.

"I expect it would create some talk," she answered cautiously. She couldn't read Tirzah well enough to be certain of her motives in voicing what most would consider disrespect, or at least in poor taste. But she might simply be trying to shock, which seemed more in keeping with what Glynis had observed about the woman the day before. Tirzah's provocative behavior with Konrad could have been merely a game to offset boredom, a flirtatiousness rather than the less innocent implication it had suggested at the time. Whichever it had been, though, it had clearly offended her mother-in-law, Helga Brant. But that had likely been Tirzah's intention.

"Some 'talk' would be a godsend!" Tirzah now replied. "It is utterly tedious living way out here, isolated from almost everything. And now having to wear black . . ."

She left the rest unsaid as if it were too tiresome to be spoken.

Glynis thought she should find out with whom she was sparring. "The custom in China," she told Tirzah, "so I've heard, is to wear white for mourning. And you would wear the red satin at your wedding."

"What an extraordinary piece of information," Tirzah said, and Glynis thought she saw a glint of amusement in the jet eyes when Tirzah continued, "Do you suppose I might take up residence there—in China, that is—until this thing is over?"

"But you'd have to come back here at some point, wouldn't you?" Glynis asked, encouraging comment.

"Oh, by then it wouldn't matter, because this depressing place would have been sold—" Tirzah stopped abruptly, and gave Glynis a sideways look as if suspecting that she might have been led to say more than was wise. Then she turned back to the window. "I'm sure you didn't seek me out, Miss Tryon, to talk of foreign customs. What is it you want to know?"

Having already learned more than she had expected, Glynis said merely, "Constable Stuart is trying to account for everyone's whereabouts before your father-in-law's body was found."

"Do we know when he died?" Tirzah responded, her mouth curving in the satisfied smile of someone playing a trump card.

"No, we don't know."

"Well then, all I can tell you is that I retired early Sunday night," Tirzah said, walking back to the music bench and seating herself. "In fact, I recall that it was barely dark when I went upstairs. And my husband joined me shortly afterwards." Her fingers moved to the keys, and with her back to Glynis she said in obvious dismissal, "Is that all, Miss Tryon?"

"Yes, thank you. I'll tell the constable what you've said." Glynis added, "It may be that he'll want to speak with you further himself."

Several jarring chords followed her into the parlor and on through to the corridor.

As she turned toward the kitchen, which she guessed was at the rear of the house, Glynis saw that Clements had just opened the door of a dumbwaiter between the dining room and Roland Brant's library, and was placing on it a tray. The smell of tea and of chicken broth made her think the tray was meant for Helga Brant, since Konrad had said she was unwell. Glynis waited until Clements raised the tray by pulley, closed the door, and went back down the hall, all the while studiously ignoring her.

When she approached Roland Brant's library, she heard muffled voices coming from it. Assuming one of them must be Cullen's, she paused in front of the closed door.

"So where the hell are they?" The questioner's voice was unfamiliar. "I've got to have those names!"

The reply came from Erich, his voice harsh when he said, "Why didn't you get them from Father when you were here on Sunday—you argued with him long enough! And how should I know where they are? They could even be at the warehouse for all that. But it wasn't my practice to snoop in my father's desk drawers, and I suggest it shouldn't be yours either, Jager!"

Jager? Glynis was so stunned, she didn't move quickly enough when she heard the click of the door handle. But it was already too late to rush away, lest she look even more like the guilty eavesdropper that she was. Thus, as the door swung open, she managed to stand her ground.

When Erich saw her there, his expression underwent several changes, finally settling into the one which seemed to reflect his most consistent emotion: anger. Before that, though, Glynis thought she'd glimpsed a fleeting look of apprehension. When speaking so loudly, had he forgotten there were strangers in the house? It seemed unlikely. Although anger could often overrule caution. She reminded herself, however, not to underestimate Erich's intelligence. He might just be covering his tracks should anyone have over-heard his visitor's remarks.

"You appear to spend a great deal of time standing in this hallway, Miss Tryon," he said to her. "Is it time well spent?"

"It will be," Glynis replied, hoping she didn't look as un-easy as she felt, "that is, if you can direct me to the kitchen."

Erich, remaining in the doorway and thus blocking her view of the library, gestured to his right. She heard a rustle of papers coming from behind him, and apparently Erich also heard it, as he started to turn, but stopped himself, say-ing, "Did you want something else?"

Glynis first wondered where Cullen was and if he knew this man Jager was here; then tried to think how she could confirm that the man behind Erich was Elise Jager's hus-band and the girl Tamar's father. Erich obviously had no in-tention of introducing him. Now if Bronwen were there, she would simply ask the question, not in the least concerned with how forward it might sound.

Glynis swallowed to relieve a throat suddenly gone dry, and hoped that her voice would carry when she said, "Mr. Brant, is that gentleman behind you the missing girl's fa-ther? Tamar Jager's father, I mean?"

The rustle of papers in the library ceased while Erich stood glowering at Glynis.

"Missing?" This came from the fair-haired man who had just appeared behind Erich. "The girl's missing?"

So he didn't know, Glynis thought, at the same time ques-tioning what kind of father would not even bother to see his daughter when he arrived, and would call her "the girl" in-stead of by name. The answer, of course, was the kind of fa-ther who would sell his daughter into servitude.

Erich stepped back inside the room with the evident in-tention of closing the door in her face, but the other man put his hand out to hold it open. "Who's this?" he demanded of Erich, pointing at Glynis. "And what's she talking about?"

"My name is Glynis Tryon, Mr. Jager," she answered him.

By now she was too angry to worry about her voice not carrying. "I take it you didn't know that your daughter wasn't here?"

"This is a private matter and none of your affair, Miss Tryon," Erich said, but his tone was less belligerent than it had been, and Glynis thought she might even detect a hint of nervousness. Then she heard the thump of boots descending the stairs.

"Sorry, Brant," said Cullen, coming up behind Glynis, "but nothing that goes on in this house is private anymore. Think I told you that last night. Now, why don't we all go inside there," he motioned to the library, "and talk this over."

It was not a question, because he took Glynis's elbow and propelled her into the room, forcing the other two men to move back. The light in the library was dim, although the brass desk lamp was lit. The surface of the desk still held scattered papers, but obviously they had been gone through, because there now were some on the carpet and the seat of the straightened chair. The safe stood open.

Cullen closed the hall door behind him.

"All right," he said to the fair-haired man. "Let's get an answer to the first question. Are you Tamar Jager's father?"

Jager, sturdily built and probably in his late thirties, retorted, "And just who the hell are you?"

"Constable Cullen Stuart. Now suppose you answer my question."

"I'm Derek Jager."

"Tamar Jager's father?"

"Yes."

"And what brings you here, Mr. Jager? I heard you indicate that you didn't know your daughter was missing, so you couldn't have come to see about her."

Glynis watched Derek Jager, thinking not for the first time how quietly intimidating Cullen could be when he chose. His voice hadn't even been raised, but Derek Jager had begun to look less arrogant.

"I'm Roland Brant's business associate," Jager said. "Or I was."

"That isn't an answer. Why are you here?" Cullen repeated. "And while we're at it, where are you from?"

"From east of here—"

" 'East of here,' " Cullen interrupted, "doesn't quite do it, Jager. Again, where are you from?"

"The Syracuse area. So I didn't hear about Roland's death until I saw it in the newspaper."

"The Syracuse paper?"

"Yes."

"And you came here to . . . ?"

"To express my condolences to the family, naturally," Jager said, annoyance flushing his face.

Cullen turned to Erich, who was looking at Jager intently. "That sound right to you, Brant?"

It seemed to Glynis that Erich hesitated slightly before he answered, "As he just said, Stuart, he was a business associate of my father's."

"Does that explain why Jager was here in your father's library—as your man Clements just told me he was?" Cullen said, his expression skeptical.

"Yes," Erich said, and with a sharp glance at Glynis he added, "we were looking for some paperwork that Derek needs."

"What kind of paperwork?" Cullen asked.

Derek Jager frowned. "I can't see as that's any of your concern, Stuart."

"Maybe; maybe not," Cullen said, "but we'll leave it for now." He then turned to Glynis.

"Mr. Jager," she asked, "do you have any idea where your daughter might have gone?"

"How would I know that? And what's it got to do with all these questions?"

"Aside from the danger your daughter might be in, Jager, which doesn't seem to worry you much," said Cullen, not bothering to hide the disgust in his tone, "she's suspected of killing Roland Brant."

"That's ridiculous. Why would she do that?"

"Good question," agreed Cullen. "Why *would* she do that?"

"I have no idea."

Cullen again turned to Glynis. "Anything else you want to ask?"

She knew he wanted her to leave, probably because he thought things would become more unpleasant as he made the two men go over the same ground again. Leaving them was fine with her. Although she couldn't imagine how much more unpleasant it could get than to stand there and listen to Derek Jager talk about his daughter as if she were some stranger about whom he had less than a passing interest.

"I do want to ask Mr. Jager," she said, watching both the man and Erich closely, "how long his daughter has been mute?"

"What are you talking about?" Jager said, then looked at Erich. "The girl's not mute."

Erich's expression seemed cautious when he answered, "It's true, Derek. She doesn't talk. Not for some time now."

"That's crazy!" Jager retorted.

"When was the last time you saw her?" Glynis asked.

"It . . . it must have been . . . maybe a few months ago."

Glynis knew by the look crossing Erich's face that Jager was either lying, or hadn't seen his daughter for so long a time that he couldn't even recall when last it had been.

She gave Cullen a brief nod that meant he should follow her out into the hall, then turned and left the room, her dislike of Derek Jager so bitter she could taste it.

"Cullen," she whispered after he'd pulled the door closed, "I only overheard a few sentences, but Derek Jager was in there looking through the desk. More important, he apparently had been here on Sunday."

Cullen's eyebrows lifted. "That so? I'll ask him about it.

But since Roland Brant and Jager were business associates, it might have no connection to Brant's murder."

"I was on my way to the kitchen when I heard them in the library," Glynis told him. "Since Tamar was a kitchen maid here, the cook very possibly knows more about her than anyone else."

Cullen nodded and turned to open the library door. He paused, however, to say quietly, "You shouldn't have been here alone with those men, Glynis. Don't let yourself get cornered—somebody in this house could be a killer, remember."

"I could scarcely forget."

As Cullen returned to the library, Glynis heard a muffled sound, as if someone were choking, that seemed to come from the front parlor. She backtracked down the hallway to find a servant there in the room; the Phoebe with whom she had collided the previous night. The woman held a feather duster in one hand, while the other hand searched in a pocket of her apron. She glanced up and saw Glynis, just as she was withdrawing a handkerchief from the pocket.

"Oh, it's you," Phoebe said, sullenly. She applied the handkerchief with zeal to her red-rimmed eyes, then blew her nose vigorously.

Her age was difficult to determine, but Glynis guessed it might be about the same as her own. The woman's dull brown hair was skinned back into a tight bun, which only accentuated her sharp features, and the blotches on her pallid skin indicated that she had been crying for some time. Glynis, despite the sulky greeting she'd received, felt some sympathy for the woman. She appeared to be the only one in the household expressing grief at Roland Brant's passing.

"Phoebe, I'm sorry about the awkward incident last evening," Glynis began. "It certainly was not your fault, but my own clumsiness."

"Yes," said Phoebe, more emphatically than was called

for, Glynis thought. "It *was* your fault. But nobody takes no mind of us servants."

How on earth did one respond to that? wondered Glynis unhappily, since in this house it might be true. "I do apologize, Phoebe," she said.

The woman shrugged, blew her nose again, and after stuffing the handkerchief back in her pocket, began applying the duster to bric-a-brac on a small round table covered with a damask cloth, which was patterned with blue morning glories. Her cleaning efforts left something to be desired, since dust particles flew into the air only to settle again in approximately the same place. Phoebe did not seem to notice.

Glynis cleared her throat—probably coated with dust motes, she guessed—and said, "I wonder if I might ask you some questions?"

The feather duster paused in mid-flight, and Phoebe eyed Glynis with distrust. "What right you got to do that?"

"Ah, well . . . Constable Stuart has asked me to assist him."

"Why you? Why can't he ask me hisself?"

Because by now, Glynis thought, he would have shaken you until your teeth rattled. "He has a number of other people to see," she explained.

"People more important than me," Phoebe pronounced. "Well, for your information, I know more things than I'll tell you."

Glynis attempted to sort this out, decided she couldn't, and in some confusion plunged ahead. "What things won't you tell?"

Now Phoebe looked confused. After a slight pause, she said, "I know more than you'd think I know."

"I'm sure that's true," Glynis agreed wholeheartedly. Perhaps her tactics needed revision. The direct approach might work best. "Phoebe, where were you on Sunday evening—the night before last, that is."

"I was in bed."

A clear, concise answer to a question laden with ambiguity. "What time did you go to bed that night?"

"Same time I go every night."

"And that is?" If the woman said *bedtime,* Glynis vowed, she would leave her to Cullen's tender mercies.

"Nine o'clock."

Emboldened, Glynis said, "Did you hear anything unusual during the night?"

The feather duster, which had been winging over the frosted globe of a lamp, stopped again, while Phoebe stared at her in unmistakable disgust. "How could I hear anything if I was asleep?"

"Ah, an excellent point," Glynis conceded, now determined to see this through, although she would exact from Cullen a fitting reward.

"Phoebe, I can't help but notice that you seem to have a great many responsibilities in this house," Glynis commented, and watched Phoebe's feather duster hover momentarily while she preened. "Tell me," Glynis went on, praying that she was finally on the right track, "do you also clean the upstairs bedrooms?"

"Course I do. Who else?"

"Oh, no one else I'm sure would be as capable as you. And those rooms would include, I suppose, the demanding task of taking care of Mr. and Mrs. Roland Brant's room?"

"Ha! Wish it was only one room! They got separate bedrooms—connected by a door. Some folks do, you know," said Phoebe, unaccountably edging closer to Glynis.

Glynis nodded, sagely she hoped, and smiled as if she were well-acquainted with this arrangement. "Yes, indeed," however, was all she dared say, lest she interrupt the fruitful intimacy with Phoebe that she suddenly seemed to have established.

Phoebe took the bait, whispering, "It's 'cause the missus, well, she don't want to be fussed with, if you catch my meaning?"

"I catch your meaning precisely," answered Glynis. "And since you're so familiar with the family's habits, did Mr. Brant's bed require making up yesterday?"

"Come again?"

"Did his bed look as if it had been slept in Sunday night?"

Glynis saw instantly that she'd erred, as Phoebe whipped the handkerchief from her pocket, shaking her head furiously.

"The poor man," Phoebe began to wail, but not before she'd choked out, "didn't even get a decent rest before he died."

This stopped Glynis cold. But then, wondering if she could snatch another minuscule victory from the jaws of near-defeat, she recalled something that Clements had said to her. Could this woman conceivably have been its source?

"Phoebe, did you have much contact with the girl, Tamar?"

The feather duster fluttered, then hung suspended in the air, and Glynis realized that not only had the wailing abruptly ceased, but she had the woman's riveted attention.

"*Her?*" Phoebe blurted. "Oh, no! No, you wouldn't catch me near that one!" She sent Glynis a sly look, adding, "She's been cursed, you know."

"No, I didn't," Glynis said, cautiously. "Why is that?"

"So's she can't spread her evil talk. Struck dumb, she was, and that's what happens to them who's in bed with the devil."

"I see. When did this take place—the girl being struck dumb?"

"I dunno *when*. I just know why!"

"How long have you worked here?" Glynis asked.

"Maybe close on a year."

"And the girl never spoke during that time?"

"Course not. I told you, she's cursed! I figured that out for myself."

"I'm sure you did," Glynis agreed, beginning a retreat to the parlor doorway.

"Now she's gone—and you know where?"

Glynis pulled up short. "No, where *has* she gone?"

"To sleep with Satan, that's where! You mark my words, when she's found, she'll be lying with the Lord of Darkness!"

Glynis started to step through the doorway, but paused again when Phoebe said, "And you know what else? Poor Mr. Brant—she killed him! He wouldn't have died, not otherwise. But she killed him!"

Her voice choked, and she was applying the handkerchief as Glynis turned slowly and asked, "What makes you think that?"

"Cause that's what evil women do. She put a spell on him to make him die!"

Glynis quickly stepped out into the hallway. And it was believed by most, she thought, that this had ended more than a century and a half before with the horror at Salem. But to those like Phoebe, that women were witches and willing consorts of the devil was still the explanation for the unexplainable.

She leaned back against the door frame as the sound of renewed sobbing reached her.

13

—⁕⁕⁕—

Her fingers fumbled at her work
Her needle would not go;
What ailed so smart a little Maid
It puzzled me to know.

— Emily Dickinson, circa 1860

Glynis waited in the hallway outside the parlor until she could regain some balance before approaching the Brants' cook. She had just started down the corridor to the kitchen, when she thought she heard her name called.

And, again, "Miss Tryon?" The voice came from the upstairs.

Glynis turned and went back to the foot of the steps. Above her on the landing, Helga Brant stood leaning on her cane, and was apparently not as unwell as Konrad had earlier portrayed.

"If you have a moment, Miss Tryon, I should like to speak with you. Will you come up, please?"

"Yes, of course," Glynis said, thinking herself fortunate to have dodged Konrad, an unlikely, bourbon-breathing, knight-errant guarding his mother's drawbridge. Or, perhaps he was more chivalrous than drunk; since she had seen him pour out his bourbon, she'd guessed he might be making an effort not to further distress his mother. Although it might be that he feared his brother Erich. Word in town had it, so Cullen said, that Konrad had been ousted from medical school because of his dissolute behavior. A rumor borne out as true apparently, if Erich's comment the previous night was any indication.

Glynis lifted the hem of her dress before climbing the steep flight of stairs to the landing, where Helga Brant was lowering herself onto the long bench built under a stained glass window. A moment later, the white cat sprang from the banister to land on the woman's lap with the lightness of a snowflake.

After a swift, covert glance had shown Glynis that all the doors along the upstairs corridor were closed, she seated herself next to Mrs. Brant.

"What a magnificent window," she said, looking up at the stained glass, composed of pearl-white lilies and red poppies delicately traced against a field of brilliant emerald green. The flower motif obviously extended beyond the parlor. Had perhaps crept into every corner of the house like overgrown ivy. Every corner, save Roland Brant's library.

Helga Brant, stroking the cat with a tremulous right hand, while her left grasped the edge of the bench, also gazed upward at the window, saying, "It is magnificent, isn't it. My father had it shipped to me from Munich as a wedding gift. Munich, in Bavaria," she added. "He knew, naturally, how much I love flowers."

And yet she had no garden, Glynis thought with sadness. But she made herself smile in response, hoping that the woman's usual restraint would lift to reveal something more about herself. "Did you grow up in Bavaria, Mrs. Brant?" she asked.

Although there was more than a touch of sorrow in the woman's voice, she smiled faintly and nodded, saying, "But it was so long ago, my growing up. My mother, too, loved flowers, Miss Tryon. For some time, my father employed five full-time gardeners, and Mother kept them busy every minute. The rose bushes alone took two men to care only for them. There were so many roses that their scent carried throughout the region where we lived. Oh, we had splendid large gardens then, known for miles around. It was rather like living in a park."

Her father must have been a man of considerable wealth, Glynis assumed. But she shouldn't try to make assessments now; there would be time later to comb through this information.

"As you may have noticed," Mrs. Brant was saying, "there are no gardens here. My husband did not like flowers."

She said it in such a way, her voice tight with emotion, that Glynis despaired of finding the right words to respond. Even if Roland Brant had not liked flowers, would it have been such a hardship for him to allow his wife something she cared for so much? It was a side to the man Glynis wouldn't have expected.

She was spared a response, as Mrs. Brant said then, "But enough of the past. I asked to speak with you, Miss Tryon, because I want to know if there has been any word of the kitchen maid. Has she been found?"

"I'm afraid not. At least not yet. Constable Stuart has men searching for her, though. Mrs. Brant, do you have any idea where the girl might have gone?"

"None at all. I have asked myself that repeatedly, but I cannot think of anyplace. I am rather fearful for her safety. As Clements told you, I believe, she does not speak."

"Yes, he told me. But it seems that she wasn't always mute, was she?" Glynis didn't want to reveal to the woman what had been Elise and Derek Jager's reaction to this matter, but wasn't sure why she didn't. She had learned, however, that with this sort of thing she should trust her instincts.

Helga Brant was staring up at the window when she said, "No, the girl wasn't always mute."

"When did she stop talking, do you know?"

"Well over a year ago, as I recall."

"Did there seem to be any reason? By that I mean did something specific happen that might have caused it?"

Helga Brant gave her an odd look. "Such as what, Miss Tryon?"

"Well, for instance, had she been ill? Did she have the measles or the pox?"

"Not that I'm aware of. Although, there was the incident of . . ." Helga Brant's voice trailed off, and she appeared reluctant to say more.

"Mrs. Brant," Glynis urged, "anything that you can tell us about the girl might be of some help."

"Well, she did love animals," the woman said with some hesitation. "I recall one time, when the maid Phoebe was ill and the girl had to clean the bedrooms—which she had never done before—she became distraught when she found Konrad's butterfly collection. And then, the day my husband had to shoot a horse that had been lamed, the girl was inconsolable."

"Was that close to the time she stopped talking?"

But Helga Brant's face had suddenly blanched, and beads of perspiration began to form on her upper lip. She put a hand to her throat, saying, "I really can't remember, Miss Tryon."

"Are you feeling ill?" Glynis asked, alarmed by the abrupt change in the woman.

"No. No, I'm quite well, but I am rather tired. If you will excuse me, I believe I must say good day to you."

Glynis rose and started to ask if she could help Mrs. Brant to her room, but the woman was already rising with the aid of her cane. And Glynis sensed she would be embarrassed, or even offended by an offer of assistance. Meanwhile, the white cat, having jumped to the floor, streaked off as if pursued by the hounds of hell.

Mrs. Brant took a few unsteady steps to the stair railing and pulled on the bell cord there. A moment later a door along the upstairs corridor opened and Konrad Brant appeared, just as Clements came running up the steps, taking them two at a time, belying his apparent age.

"Mother," Konrad said anxiously, "are you having another spell?"

"I am simply fatigued," she said, her voice more firm than frail. Then she turned to Glynis and said, "I trust you will let me know, Miss Tryon, when the girl is found?"

She looked at Glynis as if she expected an answer, but before Glynis could do more than nod, Konrad intervened. He took one of his mother's arms and motioned for Clements to take the other, and with Helga Brant between them, they led her to a nearby door. When Konrad opened it, Glynis had a brief glimpse of a rose-colored bedroom, which looked as cluttered as the parlor. Then Konrad closed the door behind them.

She was standing at the top of the stairs, reflecting on what might have caused Mrs. Brant's sudden malaise, when Konrad emerged from the room. He seemed surprised to find her still there. "Mother is resting comfortably now, Miss Tryon. And I'm sure you're wanted downstairs."

Meaning she was not wanted upstairs.

"I hope your mother is all right, Mr. Brant."

Konrad smiled and nodded, obviously waiting for Glynis to leave.

As she descended the stairs, it occurred to her that going up and down them might be difficult for Mrs. Brant. She would probably require assistance, which, if no one were there to help, could make her a virtual prisoner in the upstairs bedroom. But then, Konrad and Clements appeared to be highly solicitous of Helga Brant. And Clements also seemed to be always present.

The smell of freshly baked bread and roasting chicken met Glynis before she entered the large kitchen, two of whose windows looked out onto the same grassy track as did that of the music room.

"I'm Glynis Tryon," she said to a wiry Negro woman of middle age, who was standing at a table and rolling dough with practiced motions. "Are you Addie?"

"Yes'm," came the reply. The woman barely glanced at Glynis from large hooded eyes in a square face the color of cherry wood. Her sinewy arms were dusted with flour, and she wiped her hands several times on her long, cotton apron. It was rare to see a cook so thin, Glynis thought, although she recognized the woman.

"I know your cousin Isaiah Smith," Glynis said to her. "His wife Lacey is my niece's assistant at *EMMA'S* dress shop. And I think I've seen you in town at the Fourth of July picnics."

Addie gave Glynis a longer look, and nodded, then picked up two thinly rolled circles of dough and draped them over the pie plates. As she lightly pressed the dough into place, Glynis said, "Constable Stuart is asking everyone in the household about Roland Brant's death, and I offered to talk to you. Would you mind answering some questions?"

"Don't s'pect I have a choice." Addie turned to the far end of the table to throw several handfuls of flour into an immense bowl filled with pieces of cut rhubarb steeping in sugar, then tossed the mixture with a long-handled wooden spoon. "I got to get these pies done, though."

Glynis went to the table in the center of the room. "May I sit here?" she asked, motioning to a high wooden stool.

The woman brought the bowl closer to the pie plates, and with raised eyebrows she said, "Nobody ever asked leave to sit in this kitchen before. Go ahead."

"Addie, were you here in the house Sunday night?" Glynis asked, perching herself on the stool.

"I was home. Never sleep over here 'less there's a big doin' early the next day," Addie answered, spooning the rhubarb mixture into the pastry-lined pie plates. Glynis could feel her mouth pucker even as Addie poured in more sugar, then sprinkled a half cup of raisins over the top of each filling.

"Where is home?" she asked.

Addie's glance said she thought this was no one's business but her own. She answered, however, "Same road as Isaiah and Lacey, but down a piece from them." She gave Glynis another hooded look, before she added, "You can ask them, Lacey and Isaiah, about that, 'cause I stopped there on my way home Sunday. Don't like working on the Sabbath, but I got to keep my job."

"Do you remember what time it was when you left here?"

"Not exactly, I don't. It was before dark, though."

"Were all the family members here in the house at that point?"

"Missy, I don't know where the 'family members' were. I stay in here, they stay out there. I like it that way." She spoke the last sentence slowly, as if Glynis should take particular note of her preference, while she began to roll out dough for the top crusts.

"I apologize for intruding," Glynis said with a sigh, "but I'm afraid this has to be done. Surely you want to see the one who killed Mr. Brant brought to justice."

The rolling pin paused a moment as the woman looked directly at Glynis, her expression one that was impossible to interpret. Glynis waited to see if Addie would comment, but she only looked down again and continued to roll out the dough.

"How long have you worked here?" Glynis asked, wishing she could leave the unfriendly kitchen, the brooding house, and the peculiar Brant cadre altogether.

" 'Bout a year and a half," Addie replied, after taking a knife from a drawer and beginning to cut off strips of dough to form latticed crusts.

"So the girl Tamar had already been working here for some time when you came?"

Addie shrugged. "Guess so."

"Addie, was she here, or not?" Glynis asked, trying to keep impatience out of her voice and aware that she was not succeeding.

"She was here."

"What did you think of her? Did you like her?"

"Didn't think of her at all. She was just a kitchen maid—not worth thinking about. No more'n these nosy questions of yours."

Glynis got off the stool and went to stand across the table from the woman. "I've apologized for intruding, but whether you consider them worthy or not, Addie, these questions have to be answered. You have a choice, you know. You can talk to me now, or Constable Stuart can demand that you go to his office at the lockup to answer them. Frankly, I think you have too much dignity to want that. But it's up to you."

In return for what she immediately recognized as an ill-advised outburst, Glynis was forced to stand and wait while the woman began laying the strips of dough in a crisscross pattern across the rhubarb filling. When Addie had finished one pie and had started on the other, she finally relented. "So what else you want to know?"

"I want to know what the girl Tamar was like. For instance, did she talk to you?"

"Didn't talk to no one."

"Did you ever hear her say anything? Anything at all?"

The floury hands stopped moving, and it seemed to Glynis that the woman was about to answer, but then she pressed her lips together and said nothing.

"Do I understand," Glynis persisted, "that you never heard the girl make a single sound?"

Addie shook her head, the flour dust flying. "Didn't say that. You asked about her talking, not about her making sounds. I heard her cry a couple times."

"When?"

"Mornings, sometimes, she'd be crying when I came in. But she always stopped, soon as I told her to do something."

"So she wasn't a girl who wept often?"

"I wouldn't say she was weepy, no." Addie picked up a pie and with the knife began trimming away the excess dough of the crust, twirling the plate on her upturned fingers like a circus juggler.

"What reason did you think Tamar had for crying?" Glynis asked, watching the pieces of trimmed dough falling away with Addie's deft strokes.

"Told you, I didn't think."

The second pie was undergoing the knife when Glynis ventured, "I suppose anyone in the house would have access to those knives in the drawer. Or are you, as you indicated earlier, the only one—the only one other than Tamar—who is allowed here in the kitchen?"

Addie quickly set down the pie and looked at Glynis with a startled expression. "No. No, anybody could come in here and get a knife," the woman hastily replied.

"Anybody, including the girl Tamar?"

Again, Addie seemed about to say something, and stopped herself. Instead she simply nodded.

"I'd like to hear what you were about to say, Addie. If there's something Constable Stuart should know, then—"

"She took a knife," Addie broke in. "The girl, she pinched a carving knife a couple days ago. She thought I wasn't watching, I guess, but I saw her take it to her room."

"Did you tell her that you'd seen her take the knife?"

"Why should I tell her? She must have needed it for . . . for something."

"For what?"

"I don't know."

"Addie—"

"I told you I don't know for what! Maybe for protecting herself or something!" Addie had begun to look alarmed. Which would get them nowhere.

Glynis thought it best to change course. "Why don't you show me Tamar's room?" she said, her hope of the girl's innocence fading.

Addie nodded at this request with surprising cooperation—perhaps relieved that she was not to take the sole brunt of suspicion—and led Glynis to a small room across from the kitchen.

The room seemed to contain little that would tell much about the girl: a rough commode cabinet, a blanketed mattress on an immaculately clean, bare wood floor, and several hooks on the door, from which hung a nightdress and wool sweater, a towel and washcloth. High up in the wall, a small amount of gray light struggled through a square of grimy window glass.

Glynis went to the cabinet and opened its door to find an unused chamber pot. Its one drawer held a pair of cotton stockings, several undergarments, and two carefully folded cotton dresses, all clean and neatly mended. On top of the cabinet sat a half-melted candle in a crude, sheet metal holder, a small Bible, a hairbrush, and a wood carving of a butterfly with its wings spread in flight. A flight like that of the girl, Glynis thought. But to where had she flown?

She recalled then what Helga Brant had said about her son's butterfly collection and Tamar's reaction to it, but she could see no link between that incident and this carving, other than Tamar's apparent fondness for butterflies. When Glynis started to push the drawer closed, she felt it catch as if something were jamming it. She reached in and ran her fingers along the back of the drawer until they encountered an object, and she pulled out a slim volume of poetry. With a librarian's eye she saw that the book was well thumbed even though the title page indicated a fairly recent printing date. A handwritten inscription on the flyleaf read: *"For yon fair and silent maid."*

The signature was a scrawl, impossible to decipher except for the unique lettering of a *B* similar to that monogrammed

on the gold belt buckle of every male Brant Glynis had encountered. She balanced the spine of the book on her palm,
letting the pages fall open to those most likely to have been
often read. It wasn't an infallible system, but it was the best
available.

The poem was Byron's *Childe Harold's Pilgrimage,* the
pages opening to the first canto, and Glynis saw faint pencil
markings under several lines: *Maidens, like moths, are ever
caught by glare. / And Mammon wins his way where Seraphs might despair.*

How odd to find this passage singled out here, Glynis
puzzled; to her the meaning of the lines conveyed a scorn for
those young women who were blinded by the wealth of certain men, thus casting aside others more deserving. But this
particular young maiden did not seem to have in any way
benefited, if she had indeed been attracted to wealth like a
moth to light. It didn't fit.

Unless, perhaps, the passage had meant something quite
different to the reader who had wielded the pencil. And who
might not have been the girl Tamar at all, but the giver of the
book. The girl's mother? No, wrong initial. One of the
Brants? Konrad seemed the most obvious, although his
brother or father, or even his mother, might have suggested
to Tamar that here was a lesson to be learned. But would any
of them take such pains with someone all seemed to think of
as just a kitchen maid?

And now, glancing back at the cabinet, Glynis considered
the likelihood that what she had taken to be a butterfly
might, instead, be a moth.

She put the book back in the drawer where she had found it.

Noticing that Addie had left her, having probably gone
back to reclaim her kitchen, Glynis went to look again at
the muslin nightdress. On closer examination, it appeared to
be a new garment, edged in lace and possibly never even
worn, as out of place in this austere room as the gaudy rose
paperweight had been in Roland Brant's library. The paper-

weight—strange that it should come to mind, Glynis thought, trying to recall if she'd seen it today amidst all the clutter on his library desk. She didn't think she had, but would look again before she and Cullen left.

She stood in the doorway to take one last survey of the room, and her gaze fell on the Bible. She went to pick it up, again letting the book fall open. To Lamentations. Which certainly seemed more appropriate to an indentured servant girl than Byron's footloose pilgrim.

So what more did she know of the girl now? mused Glynis, as she closed the door of the room behind her and started again for the kitchen. Naturally, the first thing that she, or almost any librarian, would note was that Tamar presumably could read. While the Bible was in plain view and possibly placed there by someone who felt she should have it—whether or not she could read it— the volume of poetry appeared to have been purposefully concealed. The girl was neat and obviously clean, as the wood floor looked to have been well scrubbed. The window, though, was dirty, which might only mean that the girl was not tall enough to reach it. Tamar had very few clothes, unless they were kept somewhere else, which seemed improbable. She had nothing in the way of unessential personal belongings except the carving and the book of poetry; while Glynis might consider poetry to be an essential, undoubtedly no one else would.

When she stepped into the kitchen, Addie was taking a glazed, roasted chicken from the stove, and she greeted Glynis's return with what appeared to be a look of stoic resignation. The smell of the chicken and roasted potatoes made Glynis yearn for Harriet Peartree's homey kitchen.

"Addie, when did you last see Tamar?"

"Don't remember exactly."

"Try."

There was a pause as Addie closed the stove door. "After Sunday supper. When I left, the girl was in here washing dishes."

"Can you think of any reason—any reason at all—that Tamar would want to harm Mr. Brant?"

Addie looked at her for a moment, then turned away abruptly and began to scrape flour and dough from the table top. Glynis again had the feeling that the woman had been about to say something but bridled herself.

"This is very important, Addie," she coaxed. "I give you my word that whatever you say to me will not be repeated to your employers. If you're worried about that."

Addie whirled round to say, " 'Course I'm worried about that! I need this job, Missy. Got three young 'uns and no man to help me. You think I'm goin' to shoot off my mouth about what goes on around here? And I sure got no reason to trust your word, either."

Glynis shook her head. "No, I guess not," she sighed, "and I can understand that. It's just that everything seems to point to this girl as being Roland Brant's murderer. But if she wanted to rob his safe she had plenty of opportunity to do it when he wasn't around. And there appears to be no other motive for her to kill him."

Addie stood there staring up at the ceiling for some length of time, and Glynis began to wonder what might be overhead. Surely the upstairs bedrooms.

Unexpectedly, Addie offered, "Things, they aren't always what they look like, Missy. Big houses like this one can cover a lot."

Glynis leaned over the table toward her. "What kind of things, Addie?"

"That's all I'm goin' to say! That's all!"

From the determined look on the woman's face, Glynis believed her. But obviously Addie knew something that she was reluctant, or afraid, to voice.

From the corner of her eye, Glynis caught a sudden shift of light and she turned toward the windows. The rain had stopped, the sky had begun to clear, and from a lowering sun the kitchen was gradually becoming suffused with an amber glow.

A squeal of metal hinges made her turn back to see that Addie had opened the stove and was inserting her fist inside it. She held it there; then, after a short time yanked her hand out. "Hot enough," she pronounced, placing her pies on a rack. Then she closed the door with a clang, looked directly at Glynis and, emphasizing each word, said, "The men in this house have big appetites."

Immediately, Addie turned on her heel and walked quickly out of the kitchen.

Glynis, stunned into silence, stared after the woman, while a flurry of thoughts crowded her mind, along with the unpleasant sensation of something crawling up and down her spine.

Addie couldn't have intended what she'd said to come across as it did, she told herself. Glynis would have discarded it entirely, but for that remark of Phoebe, unstable though she was, about Tamar being in bed with the devil. Glynis's first reaction had been that the maid was simply jealous of Tamar's prettiness and the extra attention it might have brought the girl. But perhaps in that disturbed mind there was some twisted strand of truth.

No; she thought, this wild flight of nonsense was just her own imagination fueling what had to be a particularly dreadful speculation. And Neva had already accused her this very day of possessing too much imagination.

But what if Roland Brant had caught one of his sons with the girl in her room? And had in appalled rage, attacked that son, only to be felled himself. His library was next to Tamar's room, and it would have been an easy matter for either Erich or Konrad to drag the body into it. The floor of the girl's room had been immaculate. Was that because someone had been forced to scrub blood from it, explaining why there had appeared to be so little in Roland Brant's library?

And Tamar, if she had witnessed the murder, could have run away because she was terrified she would be next.

No, Glynis told herself again. Her speculation rested on a house of cards; Addie had been referring to her pies. And about them feeding hungry, craving, desiring . . . the synonyms for *appetite* rushed through her head. The plague of a librarian who read too much! Could she be as obsessed with young females led astray as was her assistant Jonathan? When the lurid dustcover of *A Lady in Distress* rose before her, Glynis shook off the image with disgust.

If she were to suggest this to Cullen . . . She couldn't suggest this to Cullen. She turned again to look through the window, mainly to free her mind of thoughts that insisted on clinging with the tenacity of leeches.

The sun was throwing light over the grassy track and she saw again, more distinctly now, the stable boy and the horse with a white wrapping around its . . . *A dapple gray horse!*

She rushed out of the kitchen to find Cullen. The shadows clouding her memory had all at once cleared like the sky, and she knew in which direction the Brants' servant girl had been going. A girl whom Glynis had probably seen in town on occasion, which is why the frightened, pale face had looked vaguely familiar—and why her mother a short time later had also looked somewhat familiar. A cloaked girl on a galloping, dapple gray horse, who had passed Glynis on her last trek to the rail station the previous afternoon.

Yet the horse was here now, its foreleg injured in some way. Had it alone found its way back? If so, what had become of its rider?

The girl Tamar had been heading north. North, toward the vast swampland of Montezuma Marsh.

14

—⌇—

$\mathcal{T}$he girl sat at the end of a fallen birch log some yards from the cabin. On the ground beside her lay the shepherd dog, his white-frosted chin resting on the toe of her boot. The dog was not asleep. Every so often his prick ears twitched and his muzzle came up, his black nose searching the moisture-laden air. Then the girl would put down the fish she was cleaning and look toward the water.

She stroked the dog's head now as she glanced west toward the dipping sun. The earlier rain had stopped, and the clouds slowly drifted away, leaving wide patches of blue, the color so clear and clean the sky looked as if it had been scoured. Overhead, a large crow came into view, circling once before it swooped down to perch on the woodpile near the cabin. As the crow landed, the dog's nose quivered; otherwise he didn't move. But the girl still found the friendliness of the big, chunky bird to be a wondrous thing. She reached into her pocket, as she had done a number of times that day, and held out a handful of corn kernels.

The first time the crow had come, she had been sweeping the cabin floor with rushes bundled together with twine. There was nothing else for her to do, not while it was so wet outside. The crow had suddenly appeared, hopping into the doorway on its spindly legs, just beyond where she had been standing. It had cocked its head to fix her with a darkly glinting eye, its look saying: *I am here. Now do something.* When she did nothing but stand and stare back at it, wondering why the dog was not chasing the bird, was not even barking at it, the crow sidled up to the barrel placed under a porch-like overhang just outside the doorway. It looked at her again as if it were waiting for something.

Then, with a noisy flapping of wings, the crow hopped up onto the barrel. It perched there, and began pecking at the barrel's closed lid with its stout black bill, all the while making harsh *cah*ing sounds. When she took a few steps forward, the crow flapped to the ground and again stood as if waiting. The girl, upon lifting the lid, found that the barrel was more than half-filled with dried corn. She scooped up some of the kernels to scatter on the ground, but since the bird seemed so fearless, she slowly bent down with the corn and opened her hand.

The crow, without hesitation, hopped forward to pick each kernel from her palm. When her hand was empty, the bird lifted on its shining wings and was gone. But it came back again and again. The man Gerard must have fed the crow, she had thought, else how could it have known where the corn was stored, and have been so trusting as to eat from her hand? And the dog had paid the bird no mind, because he must have come to expect it.

Now, after the crow had spread its wedge-shaped tail and iridescent purple-black wings to again take to the sky, the girl picked up the tin cup of spicy, boiled sassafras tea she had made from dried bark. She had found the bark stored in a jar on a shelf in the cabin, along with clusters of arrowleaf tubers that grew at the edge of marshlands. After she had fried the tubers over the man Gerard's fire pit, she had covered them with the lid of a tin pot to smother the smell—the potato-like smell that made her think of the kitchen in which she had worked. The kitchen and the room across from it, in which she had slept. And thinking this brought back again the half-formed, nightmare memory of a knife's bone handle in shadowy darkness. Was it from the knife that the blood on her hands had come?

She shook her head, trying to dislodge the memory. The dog stared up at her, then scrambled to his feet to put his muzzle in her lap as if he knew she was afraid. When she bent down to press her forehead against his, she wished that she could tell the dog how grateful she was for his nearness and for the guard that he kept. He could not guard against memories, but there were other dangers.

Sometime earlier, when the rain had first begun to slack some, she had left the cabin and dug mudworms to bait the hook of a fishing pole she'd found propped against a cabin wall. Then she'd carried the pole and a tin pail to the edge of the marsh, and in a short time she had hooked a dozen small bluegills. On the way back to the cabin, the dog, who had been trotting beside her, suddenly stopped dead in his tracks.

The ruff on his neck rose. She heard a faint buzzing sound, but before she could see what was making it, the dog jumped in front of her and, barking sharply, began lunging at something in the marsh weeds. A moment later a rattlesnake, big around as her ankle, slithered off into the tall grasses. The dog chased it a short distance, but must have judged the snake to be no further threat, because he soon came trotting back to the girl with his feathered tail switching back and forth.

She had knelt down to bury her face in his ruff, wanting to tell him what a fine dog he was, but the words would not come out. They could not get past the clogged part of her throat that felt as if it were packed with moist wool. The feeling had been there for a long time. She knew it was there so that she would not speak.

Never talk of this. Never speak of it, or great harm will come.

She wrapped her arms tightly around herself, trying to shut out the voice.

Never talk . . . never speak . . .

All at once the dog gave a high-pitched bark and went dashing to the water's edge, his tail sweeping behind him like wind that made the tall grass flatten. A canoe had just appeared, making its way across silver-streaked water toward the girl and the dog.

The man Gerard pulled the canoe up on land and stowed the paddle, and all the while the dog jumped around him, barking joyously. The girl, standing apart from them, watched as the man stopped to stroke the dog's head, saying, "All right, Keeper, I'm back now. It's all right, boy."

She thought she should try not to be afraid of this man. He had not hurt her when he could have. He had helped her when he didn't have to. Not all men were dangerous, she knew that. One man had already taught her that some men did not have to be feared. And this man Gerard, who treated his dog with respect, and who had taught a wild bird to trust him, might be safe for her to trust. She would try.

But when he came toward her, a newspaper tucked under his arm, she took a step back. He stopped, and said, "Were you all right here?"

His eyes did not look fierce now, but he wore an expression that she did not understand. He stood very still, looking at her, and she saw something sorrowful come into his face. It made her less afraid. And he said again, "Were you all right?"

She would try to trust him. She looked at the dog, and then she nodded.

He nodded back at her, then sniffed the air, and he turned toward the fire pit. "Something smells good. The arrowleaf tubers—did you cook them?"

She pointed at the covered pan beside the pail of cleaned bluegills ready to be fried.

"You waited for me to come back?" he asked. "Haven't you eaten anything at all?"

She went to the corn barrel, lifted the lid, and pointed to the sky. And then he smiled at her. His smile made her feel like the crow must feel when it lifted on its shining wings, and she wanted to trust the man Gerard.

"So Crow was here," he said, still smiling. "The little beggar. But I hope you had more to eat than dried corn."

She went to the fire pit, and with a stick of green wood she stirred the coals until they glowed. The fish would fry quickly.

They ate sitting on the birch log, now and then feeding pieces of fish to Keeper, and tossing kernels of corn to keep Crow at bay. But when they had finished, Gerard said to her, "I found out some things in Seneca Falls today. Your name is Tamar, isn't it? Tamar Jager."

She inched farther away from him on the log.

"Why does that upset you—my knowing your name?"

She couldn't tell him. And she wasn't sure she knew why.

"The newspaper says that you were indentured to the Brant family—the Roland Brant family. Is that true?"

She started to get up from the log, but he reached out and took gentle hold of her arm. "You don't have to be frightened of me," he said. "I think you know that now, don't you?" He let go of her arm then.

She thought about the dog and the crow, and she sat down again.

"The paper says that the Seneca Falls constable is searching for you. Did you know that?"

She looked at him and shook her head, reaching for the paper. He held it away from her, saying, "You can read, then?"

When she nodded, he said, "You'll have the paper in a minute. But first, I want to ask you something. And no matter what you answer, it will be all right—just as long as it's

true. I need the truth, so I can help you. Do you understand?"

What truth did he need? Why should he have to help her?
She nodded at him, though, so he would know that she understood about telling the truth. It seemed important to him,
so she looked straight at him and nodded again.

He was watching her very closely as he said, "The night
before last, someone killed Roland Brant. I need to know if
it was you who did it."

The ground under her feet suddenly seemed to be churn-
ing, throwing up small black specks that swam before her
eyes, and the moist wool in her throat was growing so big
that she couldn't breathe. Her fingers clawed at the log she
sat on, and she started to fall forward.

Gerard caught her shoulders and pulled her back onto the
log, and then he got into a crouch in front of her. "I don't
care if you killed Brant or not, Tamar. I just want the truth.
But you didn't even know he was dead, did you?"

Shaking her head back and forth, her hair whipping across
his face, she grabbed her throat with both hands, pulling at
her skin so there would be room for air.

Gerard took her hands from her throat and held them in
his, saying, "All right. Don't be afraid. It's all right." He
reached out and stroked her hair just as he had stroked the
head of the dog. He kept saying it was all right, but how
could it be? The man Brant was dead.

"It's damp out here," Gerard said at last, "and you're
shivering. We'll go inside and I'll make a fire in the woodstove. Then I'll tell you about Roland Brant."

He pulled her to her feet and led her toward the cabin. The
dog bounded ahead of them, still happy, still trusting the
man.

It seemed strange to her that once inside the cabin she had
felt safer. And she was warm again. Gerard had wrapped a
blanket around her and had fired the woodstove, and they sat

on a wooden bench in front of it. He had handed her the newspaper, then lit an oil lamp so that she could see to read.

Now, as she gave the paper back to him, she was afraid again. She must have shown the fear, because he took the paper away and said, "I don't think you killed Brant, Tamar. If only because you looked so stricken when I told you. But something happened to make you run away. That's what you were doing, wasn't it—when I found you last night? Running away?"

She didn't know, and when she tried to remember, all that came to her was the darkness and the knife. The newspaper said that Roland Brant had been stabbed. Did she only dream his death—or had she actually stabbed him? She put her hand to her throat, wishing she could describe these questions to Gerard. She tried to tell him with her eyes, but she knew that he couldn't understand.

"There were hoofprints on the earth when I found you, near where you were lying," he was saying now. "Had you been on a horse?"

She nodded. Yes, she had been on a horse, but she couldn't remember why. She gazed down at her hands, afraid that the blood might appear again, then looked up at Gerard.

He got to his feet and went to take down the guitar she had earlier seen hanging on the wall. She had heard a guitar played before, and it had seemed like magic—the music that suddenly came from strings that had been silent until someone's fingers made them sing.

Gerard played the guitar with the dog Keeper lying at his feet. The music was soft and it made her feel quiet inside, as if she were asleep but could still hear it. And she tried not to think about remembering.

She didn't want him to stop playing, but he stood the guitar against the bench, and he asked her, "Do you feel safer now?"

She nodded.

"Good," he said, going to stand in front of the stove, "because I want to tell you a story."

Her eyes went to the books on the shelves, but he said, "No, this is a real story. About real people. About a man who worked hard all his life. The man had a wife and a son, and he took care of them—by making the things that make music."

Gerard smiled then, slowly, but she thought his eyes looked sad.

"The man built string instruments," he went on. "That guitar I just played was his. And he built banjos and dulcimers and even harpsichords. Do you know what they are?"

Yes, she knew. There had been a harpsichord in the music room of—but she didn't want to think about the house. She nodded so Gerard would tell her more.

"This man had a factory where he made the instruments. It stood down along the canal in Seneca Falls. One day, about six months ago, this man discovered that the mortgage loan he had gotten from the bank—a loan to build the factory—had been sold by the bank to another man. And this man, the second man, wanted the factory for himself. He told the first man to pay him the money that was due on the loan, or he would take possession of the building. The man who made instruments didn't have the money to do that. He'd fallen a month behind in the payments because his wife was sick, and he needed the money to pay for her treatment and medicine. He told the other man about this, but the man said, 'That's just too damn bad!' "

The girl was watching Gerard, and she saw his eyes begin to glisten. She had never seen a man close to tears, and it made her own eyes fill. And she thought she knew who the first man was, because Gerard had his guitar. He must have seen that she knew, because he came and sat down beside her on the bench.

"So my father lost his factory," he said, "and then he couldn't work. And my mother, without money for medi-

cine, died shortly after that. I wasn't here then. I had a schol-
arship to a university in Ohio and I was there. I didn't know
anything until a telegram came, telling me that my parents
were dead. On the night my mother died, my father shot
himself."

Tamar felt tears washing down her face. She wished she
could say something to Gerard, but all she could do was put
her hand on the bench next to his. He picked up her hand
and held it, and even though her heart was hurting for him,
she felt like the bird lifting into the sky.

Gerard dropped her hand, then got to his feet and went to
stand by the stove. "I didn't go back to the university," he
said, and now his voice sounded more angry than sad. "And
I live out here, alone, because I've been afraid that otherwise I might kill someone before I was ready to do it—the
man who took my father's factory and his life. Do you know
who that man was, Tamar?"

She felt herself go cold with fear.

"He deserved to die," Gerard said, his voice tight and his
eyes fierce again. "It was Roland Brant."

15

———〰〰———

*He impaired his vision by holding the object too
close [said Dupin]. He might see, perhaps, one or
two points with unusual clearness, but in so doing
he, necessarily, lost sight of the matter as a whole.
Thus there is such a thing as being too profound.*

—Edgar Allan Poe, "The Murders in the
Rue Morgue," 1841

Glynis perched on the edge of her four-poster bed, once
more reading the note which had been left on her night table.
What was she to tell her sister Gwen? That question disturbed her almost as much as the contents of the note.

And she had already been sufficiently disturbed that day
by the various disclosures at the Brant house.

It had been early evening when she'd finally returned to
her boardinghouse, uncomfortably warm in the humidity
left by the earlier showers and drained of energy. She had no
sooner walked through the front door when Harriet Peartree,
perspiring in her jean-cloth gardening outfit, had come hus-
tling down the hall to say, "Your redhead has left. Gone.
Flown the coop, so to speak."

"Bronwen? Whatever do you mean?"

"She came rushing in here saying she needed notepaper.
That she didn't have time to explain, but would leave you a
message—I imagine it's up in your room. Then about five
minutes later she left with that little valise of hers."

Glynis had by this time started for the stairs, but paused with her hand on the banister's newel post to ask, "Do you remember what time that was?"

"Afternoon—probably an hour or two after midday." Harriet turned toward the kitchen, saying, "Just came inside to warn you. I'm working in the back garden if you want me."

Glynis hurried up the stairs, thinking that this mysterious flurry of activity must have come shortly after she'd seen her niece burst from the telegraph office and dash across the street to Carr's Hotel. But what reckless course could Bronwen be pursuing now?

As soon as she stepped into her room, she saw the note propped against her clock. Since she thought that, Bronwen being Bronwen, it would be prudent to sit down before reading it, she went to her wing chair beside the window and unfolded the notepaper.

Dear Aunt Glyn,

I hope you won't be too *upset about this, but I have to leave town. Temporarily. Professor Lowe and I found out that Rochester would be the best place to inflate and launch the balloon, so we're catching the next train out with it—no small amount of baggage even when it's deflated!*

I'm sorry I've had to be secretive, but there are things I just can't talk about. And you're so good at solving puzzles that I hardly dared say anything for fear you'd figure out what was going on before—well, before it actually went on*!*

I'll explain it all when I see you at the wedding. If there is *one. And please, DON'T WORRY ABOUT ME!*

Love,
B

Glynis sighed; saying *don't worry,* when it came to Bronwen, was like saying *don't breathe.* Why on earth did her niece think she had to accompany Professor Lowe and the balloon to Rochester? Lowe had seemed quite a reasonable man, but Glynis now realized she had badly misjudged him. Which was inexcusable on her part, because, after all, how reasonable could a man be who insisted on flying? Without wings. How could she have been so blind?

Nonetheless, it seemed that together Bronwen and Thaddeus Lowe, an incautious duo if ever there was one, were embarked on what Bronwen had chosen to describe as "things I just can't talk about." How reassuring!

Further disturbing was Glynis's present conviction, based on the phrasing of the note, that Bronwen's Treasury job must be the explanation for her shady behavior. Glynis should have credited this before now, but she'd kept discarding as outlandish the idea that the wedding of Bronwen's cousin in Seneca Falls and the business of the U.S. Treasury Department could somehow coincide. What possible interest could Treasury have in western New York? And how did Professor Lowe fit into the picture?

But there was nothing Glynis could do about any of it. Except serve as the object of her sister's wrath when Gwen arrived in Seneca Falls to hear that her youngest daughter had once again evaded restraint.

Glynis pulled off her dress and crinoline, then unpinned and brushed out her hair, before slipping into her flowing, forest green silk undress; another of Emma's lovely creations. She padded barefoot down the stairs and into the kitchen, just as Harriet was coming in from the garden, ruddy skin laved with moisture, and silvery hair plastered to her face and neck.

"It's as hot as August out there," she panted. "The flowers are exploding with the heat—I've never seen tulips and dogwood and iris and lilacs blooming at the same time. The peonies are ready to pop, and so is the mock orange. And here, just a few weeks ago, I thought we were entering another ice age."

"It has been the most peculiar weather," Glynis agreed.

Harriet nodded. "Well, I'm stiff as a board from working out there, so it's a cool shower for me, then I'm off to bed. And thank heavens for Dictras Fyfe!"

The non sequitur startled Glynis until she realized that Harriet referred to her former boarder, Mr. Fyfe—now living with his daughter's family in Syracuse and close to eighty years of age by Glynis's calculation—who had built a wooden shower stall behind the kitchen. Its tank being attached to the cistern on the roof, the recent rain would have filled it.

"You look fairly wilted yourself," Harriet said, over her shoulder. "I'll save some water for you."

"Thank you, Harriet. I thought I'd use the shower after I eat something. I'm nearly faint with hunger."

"Cold chicken and potato salad's in the icebox."

Glynis, showered and once again in her undress, sat in the kitchen waiting while water came to a boil for tea. Harriet had long since gone to bed and the house was quiet, with only a creak now and then from beams contracting as the heat of the day lessened, although the air was still unseasonably warm and humid for the end of May. Almost as if the frigid spring had overnight melted directly into midsummer. Meaning that for another four days, Vanessa Usher, by sheer willpower alone, would have to hold in abeyance the opening blossoms on her new flowering trees. Which Glynis had no doubt that Vanessa could do.

The question remained, however: in another four days would there even be a wedding? Glynis had stopped at the dress shop on her way home, and she'd only had to glimpse Emma's forlorn face to know things had not yet been set to rights.

"Adam keeps going on about some law!" Emma had told her. "Chapter 90, he claims, is the answer to all my worries.

Just what I need to reassure me most—some legal mumbo jumbo that I won't even be able to understand without a lawyer to translate it. Which, under the circumstances, seems a little like sending a fox to guard the henhouse!"

"But you believe Adam will be truthful when he's answering your questions, don't you?"

"Yes!" had come Emma's response, quick and unequivocal. "That is, if I know what questions to ask."

It did seem somewhat ironic that a law written by male legislators, to be interpreted by male lawyers, was being touted as the answer to a maiden's prayers, Glynis thought now. Still waiting for the water to boil, she sat looking out at Harriet's garden. The pink dogwood, the purple lilacs, and the opening flowers made bright splashes of color against the twilit sky. It made her think of the grounds of the Brant house and the absence there of any such blooms.

That afternoon, after she had told Cullen about the dapple gray horse and rider that she'd seen heading north, they had immediately gone to talk to the stableboy.

At Cullen's questions, the stocky, freckle-faced boy had fidgeted and said, "The horse, he come back late last night. No, sir, I didn't see he was gone until I was muckin' out the stable yesterday. Then, when I tells Mr. Brant—yeah, Mr. Erich Brant—he got powerful angry about the horse bein' gone. But it was gettin' dark, so's there was nothin' to be done for it 'til morning. But, like I said, the horse found his way home by hisself."

"And he was injured when he came back?" Glynis had asked, pointing at the wrapping around the gray's foreleg.

"Yes, ma'am. First I thought he'd tore somethin', but he's better now, so I guess it ain't too bad."

"Was he saddled when he got back here?" asked Cullen.

"No. But the girl could ride bareback 'cause I seen her do it."

"Why do you say that?" Glynis asked him. "About the

girl, I mean. Do you know for a fact that she's the one who took the horse?"

The boy pushed a lank piece of hair out of his eyes. "Who else would 'a done it? She's gone—nobody else is," he added somewhat defensively.

"Yes, of course," Glynis said quickly. "I just wanted to make certain. But tell me, did the girl ride often?"

"Not no more," the boy said. "Not after Mr. Brant, he . . ." His voice trailed off and he shifted his feet as if his boots were too tight.

"Which Mr. Brant? And after he did what?" Glynis prodded.

The boy looked toward the house. "I don't reckon I should say—"

"Yes, you should say," Cullen interrupted. "Now answer Miss Tryon."

"It was Mr. Roland Brant—him that's dead now," the boy said, looking uneasy.

"Can you tell us how long you've worked for the Brants?" asked Glynis.

"A couple years."

"So you were here when the girl first came?"

"Yes, ma'am."

"I see. Now, what were you saying about the girl not riding anymore?"

Before he answered, the boy again glanced toward the house. "Well, one day," he said, "after the girl been ridin' one of the old mares, when she come back, Mr. Brant he ran out of the house with his shotgun. He said he saw the horse was limpin'—"

The boy stopped, and Glynis saw that he was hesitant to speak, perhaps even fearful. He shook his head at Cullen, and began to back away. "Mr. Constable, sir," he said, "I gotta go to the stable."

"You're not going anywhere, son, until you finish this," Cullen said.

Glynis turned to him and murmured under her breath, "Perhaps it would be better if you left me alone with him for a few minutes." She added, "I think he's scared."

Cullen, his expression thoughtful, eyed the boy briefly. Then he shrugged and strode off toward the house.

"Why don't we walk to the stable," Glynis said to the boy, "while you tell me what happened that day? And your employers," she added, "don't need to know that you've talked to me."

She started in the direction of the stable, and after a moment of what appeared to be indecision, the boy fell into step beside her.

"You were telling us," she said, "that Mr. Brant came out of the house with his shotgun. He said the horse was limping?"

The boy glanced over his shoulder uneasily, then nodded. "But I didn't see that mare limp," he said. "And the girl said she didn't neither—"

"Excuse me," interrupted Glynis, "but the girl actually *said* the horse wasn't limping?"

"Yeah, she did."

"So at that time she could talk?"

The boy stopped walking and stared off for a moment. Then he turned to Glynis and said, in a surprised tone as if he'd just realized it himself, "Yeah, she could talk then."

"All right, I'm sorry to have interrupted you. Please go on."

"You won't tell no one?"

"I won't tell anyone in the Brant family that you've mentioned this," she answered.

The boy gave her a searching look, and must have been satisfied, because he started walking again, saying, "O.K. Like I said, that mare was sound, far as I could tell. But Mr. Brant, he said he got to shoot the horse 'cause it was lame. The girl, she says no, and she starts cryin', and she throws herself against the mare, and Mr. Brant tells her to stop talkin' and to get outta the way. I can see he means it, so I pull the girl off. And then he shot that old mare."

Glynis drew in her breath, but could say nothing, and she kept walking. By the time they had reached the stable, she was able to ask the boy, "What did the girl do, after . . . after the mare was shot?"

The boy answered slowly, "It was like she went crazy or somethin'. Screamin' and cryin'. Mr. Brant, he said she was . . . was . . . I dunno what he said, but he slapped her real hard. And he says to her . . ."

The boy's voice broke off.

"Yes? Can you remember what he said?" Glynis had prodded again, noticing that the boy's face had gone pale.

"He said to her somethin' like, 'See what happens when you talk?' And I think he said, 'Don't ever talk again.' Or somethin' like that."

"And can you remember," Glynis had said to him, "if that's when the girl Tamar stopped speaking?"

The boy had looked distressed when he'd said, "Yeah. It just now come to me. She didn't talk no more after that. Never talked again."

Glynis, her memory of the afternoon's conversation still fresh enough to be distressing, now heard the kettle whistling, and she rose and went to the stove. While waiting for the chamomile tea to steep, she recalled what she had said to Cullen about Roland Brant on the drive back to town.

"It's like peeling away the layers of an onion. And discovering that the onion is not as wholesome as it had first appeared. There were obviously qualities of Roland Brant's character that most people never saw. Other than his family and household staff."

"Better not put too much faith in what the staff says," Cullen had told her. "Brant could be tough when it came to business—probably carried over to his staff."

"What do you mean by 'tough'?" Glynis had asked him.

"I was reminded of it just today. Remember when, about half a year ago, Brant foreclosed on that harpsichord and dulcimer factory down by the canal?"

"Yes, of course I remember. And then Andre Gagnon shot himself. Roland Brant claimed that he was sorry about the foreclosure. That he hadn't known Mr. Gagnon's wife was ill, only that Gagnon had fallen months behind in his payments. And that he thought Gagnon killed himself because he'd been distraught over his wife's death."

"That's what Brant said," Cullen had agreed. "I thought of it because I saw Gagnon's son in town today. What was his name? If you recall, the son at the time said his father's suicide was Brant's fault, and that he would—Would get Brant! My God, Glynis, maybe that's it!"

"You think Andre Gagnon's son might have killed Roland Brant?"

"He sure as hell threatened to!" Cullen had responded. "If he really believed Brant was responsible for his father's death, I'd say he had a pretty damn good motive, wouldn't you? And motive is what we've been looking for."

"But why now? Andre Gagnon died months ago. Why would the son—what *was* his name? Gerard!—why would Gerard wait until now to kill Brant?"

"The need for revenge can drive a man for a long time, Glynis. Maybe Gagnon's son had no opportunity before now. Maybe he needed time to work out a plan. Who knows? But I think it needs investigating."

"Where does Gerard Gagnon live?"

"Don't know. Although somebody said he was out in the Montezuma—"

"The *swamp?* Cullen, that's the direction the girl was heading! But it must be just coincidence."

"And maybe it's not!" Cullen had slapped the reins over the horse's back. "I'd better call in that search party, and regroup it fast," he'd said. "But they can't go into the swamp at night, so the earliest we can concentrate the search there will be tomorrow morning. There's an outside chance that if we find Gagnon, we'll find the girl."

The girl again, Glynis now thought, as she carried the cup

of tea up the stairs to her bedroom. After putting the cup down on her night table, and realizing that the room was still unpleasantly warm, she took off the silk undress and pulled a white cotton lawn nightgown from a bureau drawer. She couldn't remember ever before wearing something as thin as the lawn this early in the year. There seemed to be no air at all coming through the window that overlooked Harriet's garden, so she went to open the one on Cayuga Street, hoping to catch a cross breeze. But the night was still, as quiet and calm as death. Which was not a comfortable simile tonight, Glynis thought as she climbed into bed and reached for her cup of tea. Her mind roiled with questions, and without the chamomile she'd never get to sleep; she took several swallows, then set the cup back on the table.

The moon was nearly full and climbing, its light streaming like cool white sunshine through the garden window. She turned down the wick of her lamp and sat back against the pillows, twisting her hair into its nighttime braid.

There were so many odd details that accompanied Roland Brant's death. How many of them were important to the murder, and how many were extraneous?

For instance, Roland Brant's library. Before she and Cullen had left the house that day, Glynis with reluctance had gone back inside to see if the Millville Rose paperweight was still there on Brant's desk. It was obvious that the earlier clutter of papers had been hastily straightened, but the rose paperweight was gone. In its place sat the beautiful Baccarat crystal, its facets making it gleam under the desk lamp like an immense cut diamond. But where was the garish wax rose? And why had it been there to begin with?

And then there was the window door. Today she'd looked at it again, and could not find a way—other than breaking one of the glass panes—for the bolted door to be opened from the outside.

She had sought out Clements to inquire about it, although she was rather intimidated by the heavy man. He had been found in the parlor, admonishing Phoebe about ashes that had been left in the marble fireplace.

Glynis had stood waiting while Phoebe protested.

"It's not my job!" she'd complained. "It's that witch's job to clean the fireplace."

"She's not here, so it's your responsibility," Clements had said briefly in a voice that carried a cool authority. "Don't squabble about it. Just do it!"

Phoebe's face had looked flushed and angry, but she got down on her knees and began to sweep out the ashes.

"Clements, you told Constable Stuart," Glynis had begun, "that when you found Mr. Brant's body, the library's glass door was closed and bolted, is that right?"

"I have been giving that some thought, Miss Tryon, and I really cannot say with certainty that the door was bolted."

"You don't remember?"

"No; no, I don't. It ordinarily is kept bolted, but I may have done it myself, after I found Mr. Brant . . . Mr. Brant's body. It was rather a shock, naturally, and since I always check that the door is closed and bolted before I leave the room—as I did Sunday night—it might have been that yesterday I did so again without thinking."

Although Glynis could imagine doing something like that herself under duress, she'd had the distinct sense that Clements was lying to her.

But she had decided to abandon that tack for the time being, as the man had clearly become irritated.

"Apparently Mr. Brant had been dead for some time when you found him, Clements. And it was early evening before anyone went looking for him?"

Clements gave her a curt nod.

"Isn't it odd that no one went into that room during the day?"

"Not at all odd," he answered briskly. "The hallway door to the library was closed, and I can assure you that no one

would interrupt Mr. Brant at his work. And it was not unusual for him to spend the entire day in there."

"I see. Would that mean he was also accustomed to skip-
ping breakfast and the noon meal?"

Clements looked annoyed. "Mr. Brant was accustomed to
doing as he pleased. And, as you may have noticed, Miss
Tryon, this is a large house."

In which to lose oneself was the implication, Glynis
thought, and countered with, "But there are any number of
people in this house, staff as well as the family."

"The staff does not roam the entire house at will."

He was clearly going to resist saying more about this, no
matter how many ways she asked the same thing. "Very
well, Clements. But again, it's not possible for you to say
with certainty whether or not that glass door was bolted
when you found Mr. Brant's body?"

"That is correct." Clements gave Phoebe a quick glance,
then turned his back to her and said in a slightly lowered
voice, "In fact, I can recall several times when the door was
left unbolted. Servants can be careless, Miss Tryon."

Glynis jumped at the sudden clatter of metal against marble, and looked past Clements to see Phoebe retrieving a
short-handled shovel that she'd apparently dropped, spilling
ashes over the hearth. She turned to glare at Clements's
back, and then shook her head at Glynis.

"Perhaps while the maid is working, you might step into
the hall," Clements said, leading the way before Glynis
could resist. Once out in the corridor, the man said, "I have
things I must attend to, Miss Tryon. Will that be all?"

"Not quite," Glynis answered. She'd seen that the dark
rings under his eyes were more pronounced than they had
been the night before, and she wondered if Clements was losing sleep because he had felt genuine affection for Roland
Brant, or because the disaster had occurred on his watch, so
to speak. Or perhaps there was a less benign explanation.

"I do have another question," she said to him. "It's about

the paperweight, the Baccarat crystal one I just saw in Mr. Brant's library. Of course it wasn't there last night." She wondered if Clements had been the one to find it on the hall table where she'd left it.

"I beg your pardon, Miss Tryon, but it was there. That paperweight has been on Mr. Brant's desk for years, and I can assure you that it has never left that room."

Glynis looked at him in astonishment. "It was not there when I went into his library last night, Clements. I am absolutely certain of that." She did not say more.

Clements's eyebrows raised very slightly, and it looked to Glynis as if he was peering down his nose at her. In addition, his voice took on the tone of someone talking to a young and not very bright child when he said, "With all due respect, Miss Tryon, I have been employed in this house for many years, and that crystal paperweight has always been on Mr. Brant's desk."

Glynis doubted that this was the time to accuse Clements of lying either to protect himself or to protect someone else. Or even of being so distraught over the discovery of Roland Brant's body that he truly hadn't noticed the crystal had been gone. In which case, who placed it back on the desk? Phoebe?

"Will that be all, ma'am?" Clements replied, not bothering to hide a note of disdain.

Glynis sighed, feeling a sudden, unexpected sympathy for Phoebe. "Yes, Clements, that will be all."

He gave her a meager, very meager, bow and went off down the hall.

"Pssst!"

Glynis turned at the sound.

"Pssst!" hissed Phoebe again, standing in the parlor doorway. "C'mere!"

"Yes, what is it?" asked Glynis, thinking that she wasn't often summoned this way.

"That old buzzard," Phoebe stated, looking down the hall. "He's full of himself, he is. But that door you asked about? The one in Mr. Brant's library?" Here Phoebe had begun to reach for her handkerchief and Glynis feared a repeat performance of the sobs.

"Yes, Phoebe," she had said quickly, "what about the door?"

"It was *always* bolted. *Always.* Even during the daytime. Mr. Brant, he gave strict orders—said if he ever catched anyone leaving it unbolted he'd fire 'em on the spot!"

"Phoebe, did you by chance find that crystal paperweight on the hall table last night? And put it back in Mr. Brant's library?"

The woman had given her a cunning look. "I ain't telling."

Glynis, having taken a last, long swallow of tea, now placed the cup on her night table and lay back against the pillows. Phoebe was without question an unreliable source, and was probably vindictive enough to contradict Clements no matter what he'd said. Even so, he might have deliberately lied about the door being occasionally unbolted, thinking he would be protecting the Brant family by making it look as if an intruder, gaining entrance through an open glass door, had been the killer. Rather than someone in the household. As he'd perhaps lied about the paperweight.

And if the outside door *had* been bolted, then whoever killed Roland Brant must have been someone with whom he was familiar and had willingly admitted to his library. A stranger outside the house could easily have been seen through the glass. As could an enemy. As could anyone whom Brant believed he had no reason to fear.

Glynis now agreed with Cullen; it was hard to imagine a thief risking discovery in that long hallway in order to rob the safe—providing the thief even knew where the safe was located. Erich had said, however, that property deeds and banknotes were missing. But had they been stolen? Or was their disappearance a ploy by the killer to make it appear that murder was incidental to theft; that Roland Brant had caught the thief in the act of robbery and had been overpowered? And had this ploy been designed to cover a crime that in truth had sprung from a more sinister but as yet unknown origin?

Glynis, by now tossing fitfully in her bed, recalled the curiously small amount of blood that had been present when the body was removed and the Persian rug lifted. But last night, Neva had said she couldn't give an opinion as to that until she'd done the autopsy. There could be a logical explanation: a single thrust of the knife would have caused a large amount of blood only if the knife had been withdrawn. Which it hadn't.

Glynis lay staring up at the intricate shadows of tree branches playing over the moonlit ceiling. She wondered if she was focusing too much on the details entangled in Roland Brant's murder. Thus missing the forest for the trees.

But there were other things; minor, seemingly peripheral things, she supposed, still they nagged at her.

Erich's wife, Tirzah, had indicated that she wanted the house sold. This would seem to suggest that Tirzah knew Roland Brant had made a will, and that her husband would inherit the bulk of what must be a considerable estate; it might or might not have been common knowledge among the family members. It was a question that neither Glynis nor Cullen had asked. But they should have. That estate, or the knowledge of who would inherit it, could be a motive for murder. And how, if the house *was* sold, would Helga Brant then fare? The law of dower provided that a widow was entitled—with or without a will—to one-third of her husband's real estate, but it didn't specify which one-third. So Mrs. Brant might possibly stand to lose her home.

And why had Derek Jager been there today? And on the previous Sunday? Cullen had said that when he questioned Erich and Derek Jager further, both agreed that Jager had stayed for only an hour. But the man could have returned later that night, been admitted through the outside door, and killed Brant.

Glynis suddenly thought of the question that Bronwen

had put to Elise Jager: *Is Mr. Jager in town?* While in retrospect it had been an interesting question, what had Bronwen in mind when she'd asked it?

Although Derek Jager had been a business associate of Brant's, he was probably not the only one, so why did Erich allow the man free access to his father's private papers? Or did Jager just steal secretly into the library and begin a search for the mysterious names? If indeed it was names for which he'd really been searching. After all, Jager had lied when saying that he'd learned of Roland Brant's death in the Syracuse newspaper. As Cullen had pointed out later, the Syracuse paper had not even received the story in time to carry it in this morning's edition.

Then there was the girl Tamar. The unknowns surrounding her became darker and murkier with every step: her inability or refusal to speak; her relations with a father who had sold her into servitude, and with a mother who had taken so long—or so it seemed to Glynis—to find and free her; and, of course, her untimely disappearance. If the girl hadn't murdered Roland Brant, why had she run away? Unless she had witnessed his murder, seen his murderer, and thus feared for her own life.

And what about Gerard Gagnon's threat? . . . No, Glynis moaned, and rolled onto her side; she could not sleep if she continued this futile speculation. She closed her eyes, determined to also close her mind.

And heard an eerie sound outside the garden window.

It began as a soft, wailing cry; scaling upward, not in volume but in pitch, to a long preternatural howl. The hair at the nape of Glynis's neck rose, until she identified it.

The call of a wolf. Jacques Sundown's clan spirit.

16

For, lo, the winter is passed; the rain is over and gone. The flowers appear on the earth; the time of the singing of birds is come, and the voice of the turtle is heard in our land.

—Song of Solomon

Glynis had to struggle upright through a tangle of sheets before leaving the bed and going to the window. The grass directly below her, and the garden beyond it, merged into a wide, pale river of moonlight flowing over and around the shapes of trees and shrubs. For a brief moment, she saw in motion a low-slung creature of silver and black, flecked with white, and with eyes that glinted like ovals of gold. It streaked into the shadows, and then, standing there beneath the window, was Jacques Sundown.

She turned back to the room, searching in the relative darkness for her undress; finding it, she slipped it on, then made her way out of the bedroom, flinching at the slight creak the door made as it swung open. Before she descended the stairs, she paused outside Harriet's bedroom and listened for the soft, steady breath of sleep. When she heard it, she went down the stairs and followed the moonlight flooding through the kitchen windows. She turned the key in the lock of the door, went down a few steps, and walked toward the tall man who stood waiting there.

He never changed. Never. The glossy black hair falling to

his shoulders, the smooth coppery skin, the high cheekbones and strong features; the half-Iroquois, half-French blood that had made him a taciturn loner, moving to his own inner rhythm with the lithe grace of a mountain cat, the swiftness of a wolf. Those who threatened him learned that, like the cougar and the wolf, he could be deadly.

Cullen had often said that Jacques was silent and distant. Not always.

Glynis didn't speak until she was within a yard of him. "I heard you were in town, Jacques."

"You weren't."

"No, I've been out at the Brant house. Roland Brant has been murdered."

"I know. Word gets around."

She waited, not asking why he'd come, or for how long he would be there. Over the years, she had at last begun to understand his ways.

He, too, seemed to be waiting; the flat, brown eyes looking down at her as if they'd just happened to meet on Fall Street. That would change.

When the tension between them had stretched to the breaking point, he said, "I can't be here long."

"I thought as much. Word gets around."

She caught the trace of a rare smile before he extended his hand and took hold of her wrist, his eyes in the moonlight beginning to warm. "We can't stay here."

"Harriet's asleep."

He started to lead her across the grass, saying, "You know the rules."

She pulled back, stopping them both. "Since when have the rules applied to you?"

"There's always been the one, says you can't be seen with me. Not at night. Not if you want to stay in this town. I expect you want to do that." He added, "When you don't, let me know."

As they began to walk again, Glynis felt herself slipping on the damp grass. "My feet are bare," she said.

Jacques cast a swift glance around, then continued to scan the yard while he reached for her, sliding one arm around her waist, the other under her knees, lifting her as if she weighed no more than a sack of feathers to carry her over the grass. His long strides took them past the garden and Glynis could now see, hidden among the pines at the rear of the yard, his black-and-white paint horse. The scent of lilacs and lavender drifted sweetly across the quiet air, and moths fluttered over night-blooming moonflowers.

"So much for rules," Glynis said when he lifted her to the horse's back. In a single fluid movement, Jacques vaulted onto the paint, his eyes undergoing the strange alchemy that could turn them from cool brown into the gold of the wolf.

"Nobody to see us," he said, turning the paint in the direction of Black Brook. Glynis knew where he was headed. It was a short distance, less than half a mile. A place from which could be seen the reservation where he had once lived.

The paint moved through the warm night, the sky an arc of black where even the glitter of stars was dulled by the brilliant moon. Jacques reined in the horse at the crest of a low, rounded hill; below the small clearing, lofty fir trees spread their long, fringed branches like wings. He swung her down and took a blanket roll from behind the saddle.

They shook out the blanket over thick, fragrant clover, and Glynis, after seating herself, tucked her feet under the silk skirt of the undress. He stood for a time looking down at her, then pulled a tobacco pouch from inside his leather jacket, and began to roll a cigarette, his fingers working with deft precision.

"How is he?" Jacques said, now staring north toward Black Brook reservation.

"Cullen's fine, Jacques. But if he hears you are in town . . ."

Glynis let her voice trail off. Jacques would know what she meant.

"He'll get over it," Jacques said. "Always does." He was still standing, the smoke from his cigarette rising into the windless air as a ragged white feather.

"Where have you been since Washington?" she asked, breaking again the velvet quiet that surrounded them despite the distant chorus of spring peepers, the occasional soft *whoo* of an owl.

"With McClellan."

"The railroad man?" Jacques had acted as scout for the Ohio & Mississippi Railroad, of which George McClellan was president.

"The military man. He commands the Ohio volunteers. War's going to heat up soon down there along the Ohio River."

Ohio—why the sudden tug at her memory? "There's no hope left, then," she asked, "for another effort at compromise?"

"You've been south," Jacques said. "You want to compromise with slaveholders?"

"No."

"Then I'd say there's no hope."

"But most Southerners aren't slaveholders, Jacques. And I don't think many of them want war. "

"Then they better speak up fast."

"You didn't say where you've been with McClellan."

Jacques crumbled the remains of the cigarette, than sat down beside her. "Cincinnati."

Glynis thought that she couldn't have heard him correctly. "Did you say *Cincinnati?*" When he didn't answer she repeated, "Cincinnati, in Ohio?"

"Think there's only one."

"In that case," Glynis said, "it must be a lively place with so many people coming and going!"

Jacques leaned forward to look into her face. In the moonlight, his own face was the deep, rich color of live coals, ready to flame at a single stroke. "Who's coming and going?" he asked.

The sudden flash of amusement in his eyes, so unusual that it caught her unawares, nonetheless told her that she was on the right path.

"Bronwen traveled from there with a Professor Thaddeus Lowe," Glynis answered. "In a balloon! Cincinnati apparently being such a crossroads, though, I would guess you knew about that?"

"I knew about it. Lowe's balloon was stored there. McClellan lives there."

"But Bronwen doesn't have any connection to Cincinnati, so what was *she* doing there?"

"Following orders."

"Whose orders?" she asked. "Rhys Bevan is her superior at Treasury." He was the head of its Special Detective Service, and Glynis had met him several years before when he investigated a counterfeit ring operating out of Seneca Falls. So she added, "Don't tell me that Rhys Bevan lives in Cincinnati."

"I won't. He doesn't. He was there two days."

"Cincinnati, the Mecca of the East. And I suppose Bronwen's orders included a command not to discuss whatever it is she's doing?"

"Bevan made her swear to it. It was a test. He figured if she could keep something from you, she could stand any kind of questioning."

"She passed the test."

"I know. Sounds like you figured it out anyway."

"Just that Bronwen wasn't in Seneca Falls solely for her cousin's wedding. Have you seen her?"

"Today. Not for long."

"And did Rhys Bevan make you take a secrecy oath?"

"I don't take oaths. You should know that."

"Will you tell me, then, what Bronwen's involved in?"

"What do you want to know?" He had taken her braid in his hands and begun to untwist it, his fingers separating the strands of hair as deftly as they had rolled the cigarette.

"For a start," Glynis said, "what on earth is Lowe's connection with the U.S. Treasury Department?"

"Salmon Chase. He's Treasury secretary," Jacques said. "He's not from Cincinnati."

Glynis smiled, even though her uneasiness about Bronwen was growing. "Then how is Chase involved?"

"He heard about Lowe's flights from McClellan. Had Lowe meet Lincoln. Lowe says balloons can be used for aerial reconnaissance of Confederate troop positions. McClellan thinks it's a good idea. So does Lincoln. He wants a trial run."

"Here?"

"Why not here?"

"Because the last time I looked, Jacques, there were no Confederate troops in western New York."

"That's why it's here. Lowe doesn't much want to get killed. Wants to know how close he can get to a target without catching bullets."

Glynis let out a long breath. Even if she accepted the premise that humans were meant to be airborne—and it seemed she had no alternative—she still thought this sounded unreasonably hazardous. She was almost too afraid to ask, "And Bronwen's role in all of this?"

"She's a Treasury agent. She's lightweight. She doesn't scare easily. That's about it."

"No, I don't think so," Glynis said, wincing as she turned her head, forgetting that Jacques held her hair.

"What don't you think?"

"I think there's more to it," Glynis persisted.

"You always do."

Again Glynis caught the trace of a smile, while Jacques began to weave his fingers through her hair.

"Well, why are you here?" she asked.

"I know the terrain."

"But you won't be in the balloon, will you?" Glynis countered, trying to concentrate on Bronwen's safety. "Jacques, what is it that you're not telling me?"

"You have to keep quiet about it."

"I will."

"I know that. Bevan said you shouldn't be told—said you'd worry. I know you better than he does. You'll worry more if you're left guessing."

"So please tell me."

"You heard about Lincoln's blockade of Southern ports?" When Glynis nodded, Jacques went on, "Couple of times in the last month, British rifles—Enfields outfitted with sword bayonets—got smuggled into Virginia. Overland. Looks like they first came in by ship from Canada. Nobody knows where they went after that. Treasury's got an idea, but that's all it's got. There's no proof."

"Jacques, please don't tell me that some unbalanced mind thought of using a balloon to track British rifles."

"That's what Bevan thought. Lowe did too."

Evidently, she decided, she'd misjudged the sanity of both these men, although Rhys Bevan had in the past exhibited a flair for the theatrical. And at the outset, from the moment he'd taken her niece into Treasury's detective service, Glynis had feared the worst if Rhys and Bronwen were paired. To be proved prophetic now offered little consolation.

"Looks like your British friend de Warde might have a hand in this," Jacques said.

"Oh, not Colonel de Warde! He's involved?"

"Been spotted in Kingston, Ontario. And Oswego at about the right times."

"He's a treacherous man, Jacques! You know he's an espionage agent—and Rhys Bevan knows it, too."

"De Warde can guess he's being watched. I don't think he's stupid enough to handle the guns himself."

"No," Glynis agreed. "He always makes someone else do his dirty work."

"Treasury wants to find out who's doing his dirty work this time. And how the guns are leaving the North."

"But why are you involved?"

"This was put together fast," he said. "Maybe too fast. Bevan needs a ground man to lead his agents. They got to Oswego yesterday, but don't know their way around. I have to ride there tonight."

"I wonder if any of those agents can ride," Glynis said, her concern deepening. "The ones I met in Washington were city men. Driving carriages was the extent of their experience with horses."

"That'll be interesting." Jacques's shoulders twitched in what, on a more demonstrative man, would have been a shrug, before he said, "Word came from an agent in Montreal that a shipment of Enfields got there yesterday. Looks like they're headed for Kingston. We figure they'll come across the lake in the next couple of days."

"Well, that explains Bronwen's fixation with the telegraph office. She's been haunting that place ever since she got here—every hour on the hour, apparently. She was checking with Treasury, wasn't she, about when the guns were due to arrive in Montreal?"

"That's it."

"But then I don't understand. She left a note, saying she and Lowe were going to Rochester, *west* of here, to inflate the—ah, yes; the balloon rides on wind currents flowing east. And Oswego is north of here, so they have to launch from the west. I don't think I much like the sound of this."

"Too late now."

"But why are you here, Jacques, and not already in Oswego?"

"You sure you need to ask that?"

Glynis felt him gather and lift her hair, and then his fingers moved across the back of her neck.

"I have another question," she said.

"Is Oswego going to be risky? Maybe."

"Unfortunately, I'm certain of that, and I don't want to think about it. No, this concerns Montezuma Marsh. You know that area better than anyone. Where might a man live there for any length of time? And could a young woman survive in the swamp?"

"Not alone. There's a cabin or two on high ground along the western edge. Maybe quarter mile due north of where Black Brook flows into it." His hand began to move down her spine, making the silk of the undress whisper softly.

"I think it's getting late, Jacques."

"Think you're right."

When they rode back into the stand of pines behind the garden, Glynis said to him, "I'm afraid for you and Bronwen. This Oswego scheme sounds so dangerous."

Jacques slid off the horse and lifted her down. "Some people don't mind danger. It's the ones left behind who mind the most."

Glynis nodded, then forced herself to smile, reaching up to lay her hand against his cheek. "Please watch over Bronwen, if you can. And be careful, Jacques."

"O.K." He caught her hand, and held it fast.

WEDNESDAY
May 29, 1861

17

———✺———

Have they not sped? have they not divided the prey? to every man a damsel or two.

—Book of Judges

An early morning fog was lifting from the village, and bells in the church steeples were striking the hour of seven as Glynis hurried up Fall Street. Like an ominous ball of fire, a red sun sat above the eastern horizon; rain before nightfall, she thought, raising the skirt of her cream-colored muslin dress above her ankles to walk quickly over the dirt road without stirring up cloudlets of dust. She had overslept, and now feared she wouldn't reach Cullen before the search party left. And when she turned the corner and headed down the slope to the firehouse, the road in front of it looked all but deserted.

After she'd rounded the brick building, she saw a handful of unfamiliar-looking men and several spavined horses standing on the towpath a short distance away. The men were unshaven and unkempt, and several were passing a bottle back and forth; Glynis felt it safe to assume that they were not in the employ of the law. More than likely they were drifters. They would wait to pick up a few hours' of work, then spend what little money they'd earned at Serenity's, or at one of the numerous other taverns along the canal. At least two of them could be bounty hunters, because they carried shotguns and bore the greedy, predatory look of men who hunted humans for money. Not a savory crew. And clearly Cullen was not around or he would have moved them on.

She went to his office door and, finding it open, stepped inside to see lanky young Liam Cleary seated in Cullen's desk chair. He set down his mug of coffee and stood up, wiping a freckled hand across his mouth.

"Constable Stuart's left already, Miss Tryon."

"How long ago?" she asked, trying not to let guilt over her belated arrival defeat her purpose.

"Left at dawn, couple hours back."

"He was headed for the swamp, I suppose?" Glynis asked. When Liam nodded, she said, "How many men did he take?"

"Besides Zeph and his bloodhounds? Maybe a half-dozen others."

Eight men to search the twelve-mile-long swamp with no idea where to start looking. In some places Montezuma Marsh was as much as eight miles wide; with thousands of acres to cover, they would never find the girl. But the east side of the marsh fronted Cayuga Lake for some distance to the north, so they might rule out that area.

"Liam, did the constable say where he was going to start the search?"

"Said they'd begin at the south end of the swamp. Near Dermont Creek."

"Where it flows into Cayuga Lake?" When Liam nodded again, Glynis said, "Then he plans to go up the west side of the marsh?"

"Guess so."

At least the searchers would be traveling in the right direction, Glynis thought, then asked Liam, "And other than Zeph, who were the men with Cullen?"

"There were a couple from the Seneca County Sheriff's Office and . . . lemme think now."

Glynis waited with impatience while Liam consulted his memory. Since that might take some time, she tried to nudge him along by asking, "Was Abraham Levy one of them?"

"Oh, yeah." He then went on to name three others, one of which, to Glynis's surprise, was Adam MacAlistair.

"Mr. MacAlistair went? Really?"

Liam grinned. "Yeah, he said he might as well do something useful to take his mind off his troubles. Isn't he supposed to be getting hitched pretty soon?"

When Glynis sighed, Liam added, "Guess that's the trouble he meant!"

Glynis did not feel compelled, under the circumstances, to comment on this. "Liam, I need to reach Constable Stuart with some information as quickly as possible. But I imagine he wants someone here in the office, which is why you aren't with him?"

"Told me I was in charge here, yeah. So I don't dare leave for any length of time, Miss Tryon. Constable, he'd skin me alive if I did."

While Glynis knew this was youthful exaggeration, she also knew Liam wouldn't disobey Cullen, no matter whose life, including his own, might be threatened. So who else might be available to carry a message to Cullen? There was Danny Ross, smart and reliable enough, but why hadn't he gone with Cullen in the first place?

When she asked Liam this question, he answered, "Danny said he had to help his mother install some new kinda water pump in the laundry. He said Mr. Gould let them have the pump for half price."

Danny was the oldest son of Daisy Ross, who, more than a decade before, had been left a young widow with five small children. Daisy had opened Seneca Falls's first "Professional Laundry" with a bank loan guaranteed by attorney Jeremiah Merrycoyf; a widower, Merrycoyf had said he liked the idea of clean, ironed shirts. Long hours of backbreaking work by the Ross family had made the laundry into one of the town's most successful small businesses.

But Glynis thought that Daisy would spare her son for an emergency. She said so to Liam.

"O.K., Miss Tryon, I can fetch Danny if you'll watch things here for a minute—reckon that would be all right with the constable. But what is it you want Danny to do?"

"I've been told," she said, "that there's some high ground a quarter of a mile north of where Black Brook flows into the western part of the swamp. A man that the constable is looking for could be there. And Tamar Jager could be with him. If Danny Ross could just take word to the constable . . ." She hesitated, shaking her head, having realized that Danny would have trouble even locating Cullen. But then she remembered hearing that the boy was a good hunter. "Liam, please bring Danny here and I'll tell—"

She broke off, as a sudden noise in the doorway made her turn to see one of the men she'd noticed loafing on the towpath; one of those who she'd guessed might be bounty hunters. A stocky man, he swaggered into the office, carrying a shotgun, a sly smile creasing his bristled face. A long white scar ran from one eye down the length of his cheek, and several of his front teeth were missing; which, along with his scruffy clothes, Glynis thought uneasily, lent him the look of a ruffian in one of Jonathan's favorite novels.

"I know them parts of that swamp," the man said, gruffly. "Any reward posted for them two?"

Glynis said, "No!" at the same time that Liam said, "Yes." "Which is it?" asked the man.

Glynis tried to catch Liam's eye, but in vain, because he answered obliviously, "There's a reward for the girl."

"I'm sure it's not much," Glynis said quickly, as she couldn't imagine anything more terrifying for Tamar Jager than to be confronted with this man. "Not much at all," she added, sending Liam another frantic look of appeal.

The man grinned. "Don't need much. Got nothin' else to do, so I think I'll just give it a go. Take my pal here with me."

He turned slightly, and Glynis saw behind him a short, thin man with a long scrawny neck who had about him the sharp-eyed look of a turkey vulture. And like a vulture, he was obviously taking the idea of a scavenger hunt more seriously than his grinning companion.

The heavy man now asked with profound good humor, "You want this girl dead or alive?"

"Alive! She is not to be harmed in any way," Glynis said icily. "The girl is not a criminal, and furthermore, Mr. . . . I don't believe I caught your name."

"Name's Sledge, pretty lady. Glad to make your acquaintance."

"To be truthful, Mr. Sledge," Glynis stated, in the most forceful tone she could manage, "I don't believe your assistance will be necessary. The constable and his search party are more than capable of finding the girl. I think, in fact, he will be back here with her shortly. So you see, there's no point in putting yourself out for no reason."

Having despaired of Liam's support, she was surprised to hear him pipe up, "Yeah, I think Constable Stuart can find her all right with the men he's got. Hope so, anyway."

"Wal, now, if it's all the same to you," the stocky man said cheerfully, "I think me and my pal here will just take a looksee. We're damn good—begging your pardon, ma'am—at tracking fugitives. I bet we find her faster'n your constable!"

With this he backed out of the office and motioned to the smaller man, and they strutted toward the horses.

Glynis whirled to Liam, saying, "Why did you mention a reward? They would just as soon kill her, or Lord knows what else, as—" She stopped, because Liam looked so abjectly shamefaced. "Never mind, Liam, it's done now. But bring Danny Ross here as fast as you can. Those two men mustn't find that girl!"

18

*I have been hunted like a bird by those who were
my enemies without cause.*

—Book of Lamentations

The girl sat on the birch log in the silvery, warm afternoon, feeding kernels of corn to the crow and watching Gerard stack logs. The shepherd dog lay on the ground beside her. Every now and then she glanced at the sky, where a red sun had begun to descend into the haze that hung over the swamp; it looked angry, she thought, as if its red ball might suddenly burst and hurl down chunks of fire.

Gerard's movements were quick and sure as he re-arranged the logs in the woodpile to make, he said, "A cave to hide you if anyone comes."

She must have looked frightened, because he added, "I don't think anyone will come. Who would think of searching for you so far north of town? Besides, from the look of that sky, we're due for a storm soon and that will keep everyone away."

The girl nodded, and she tried to smile. She hadn't smiled in a long time, though, and her mouth felt strange, like it belonged to someone else. But Gerard stopped shifting the wood and stood smiling back at her, so she guessed that she had done it right. Maybe smiling was something that, after you had done it once, you didn't have to learn it again.

The dog Keeper raised his head and gave a contented yawn, then settled back to doze. Moments later he sneezed in his sleep, as cottonwoods growing near the edge of the marsh were sending out small white tufts that floated on the strangely still air like iridescent motes of silk.

The crow, demanding more corn, gave a harsh caw and rose on its feet to flap glossy dark wings. It made the girl remember that, the night before, she had dreamed about a dark shadow pressing her into the ground so she couldn't breathe. She must have been gasping, or crying, because she woke to Gerard kneeling beside the straw pallet, stroking her hair and saying, "It's all right, Tamar. Don't be frightened." And Keeper's muzzle was resting on her arm while he whined softly and gazed at her with his alert, bright eyes.

Then Gerard had said to her, "I think someone has hurt you. Hurt you badly. Is that true?"

She had tried not to cry, but she felt the tears come, washing down the sides of her face and into her hair. When she struggled to sit up, Gerard had gently eased her back against the straw pallet, and had blotted the tears with his fingers.

"You don't have to be afraid," he had said. "No one will hurt you again. Do you believe me?"

She had believed him. And, believing, she had gone back to sleep.

Now she smiled again, and reached down to fondle Keeper's head. So she felt the dog's first tremor. A second later his nose twitched, and he sprang to his feet.

Gerard stopped what he was doing and looked at the dog. "Keeper? What's the matter, boy? You smell something?"

The dog's ears went forward and he gave a low growl. When the girl got up from the log, her heart leaped, because from the distance came the faint sound of dogs baying. The crow took several hops before it lifted into the air with a great flap of wings and soared off into a sky that was now darkening like tarnished silver.

The girl looked at Gerard. Were the dogs baying for her?

He motioned for her to stay where she was, then he turned and ran inside the cabin. He came back out with a long length of rope. "Keeper, come!" he called.

The dog came, but he was still growling, his nose pointing south in the direction of Black Brook. Gerard looped the rope around the dog's neck. "Quiet. Quiet, boy!"

The dog stopped growling, but his body trembled. The baying still sounded far away.

"Tamar, we need to leave here," Gerard said.

Shaking her head, she pointed to the cave he had made in the woodpile.

"No, that won't work, not now," he said quickly. "The hounds would find you there in a minute. We have to leave fast!"

He took her hand and pulled her toward the canoe.

Keeper, trailing the rope, ran ahead and jumped into the long, narrow boat, then stood growling as Gerard led the girl to it.

"Get in," he told her. "Sit on the bottom and don't move around."

Gerard's eyes worried her because they had grown so fierce, but she knew that was because of the hounds and not because of something she had done. She climbed into the canoe, and he lifted a pointed end, thrusting it into the water, then scrambled in behind her and snatched the paddle she handed to him. They glided north from the shoreline and out into the swamp as a long roll of thunder came from the west.

Gerard, dipping and swinging the paddle, looked at the sky. "I hope the storm holds off," he said to her. "We should stay on the water so the hounds can't track us. The men won't know about the canoe, not right away. They'll think we've run, until the hounds track our scent to the shore. And that should give us some time."

Keeper had stopped growling and sat on his haunches with his muzzle resting on the bow of the canoe. The girl looked beyond the dog to the murky water ahead of them. Thunder rolled again, but it was still distant.

"We'll be all right on the water," Gerard said, "unless it gets too shallow. Or the storm hits. But about a mile north of here, if we can make it that far, there's a place where White Brook flows into the swamp. If the brook's deep enough we'll take it. In summer we wouldn't have a chance, but the rains this spring may give us the depth we need."

His voice was tight, and she listened carefully, even though she thought he was talking to himself and not to her. But he was in trouble because of her. The hounds and the men weren't chasing him. It was because of her that he'd had to leave his cabin and hide in the swamp like a hunted animal. She twisted around and reached out to touch his shoulder, then shook her head and pointed to the shore.

As if he read her mind, he stopped paddling and took her hand. "No, I'm not putting you ashore," he said. "This is not your doing, and I won't leave you."

But it was her fault.

He held her hand tightly when he said, "No. I didn't have to run. It was my decision." She started to turn away, but he said, "Look at me, Tamar. Look at me!"

He reached out and took her chin in his hand to make her look into his fierce eyes. "We'll be all right. Tell me that you believe me."

She tried to tell him, but no sound came. He raised his hand and curled his fingers around her throat. "I think you'll talk again someday," he said, "and I want to hear your voice."

Then he began to paddle once more through dark water that reflected the gathering clouds overhead. The canoe followed the shoreline just beyond where green willows drooped and brown marsh reeds grew thick, skirting the ghostly dead tree trunks that rose out of the water like gnarled fingers pointing toward the sky. A red-tailed hawk perched high up on one, watching, and the girl could hear wild geese calling and the occasional cry of a loon. Above them, black clouds began to swirl. But there was no wind blowing, and no rain fell.

Then the canoe trembled and stopped, and she could hear scraping underneath her.

"We're snared on something," Gerard said, leaning over the side of the canoe.

The girl looked toward shore, where a clump of willows stood a short distance away on what looked like solid ground. She plucked at Gerard's sleeve as he poked the paddle down through the water, and she pointed at the trees.

He looked up and followed her finger to the willows, then shook his head, saying, "Unless we're trapped here, I'd rather stay on the water. That thunder doesn't sound much nearer. Maybe the storm will miss us."

When he raised the paddle, it came up dripping with long thin weeds. "It's too shallow here, and we're caught on something," he said, using the paddle like a pole to push them backwards.

Keeper suddenly jumped up and began to growl, his nose quivering in the direction of the shore.

Without warning a shotgun blasted. And pellets hit the water some distance ahead.

"Get down!" Gerard shoved the girl flat and tried to grab the snarling dog, who looked ready to leap from the canoe. "That can't be from a search party. The hounds are still too far away, and they're behind us. Maybe it's just a hunter and he's not shooting at—"

Another charge of shot sprayed the water, and it was closer than the first.

Gerard leaped from the canoe, the water and weeds rising halfway up his calves. "C'mon," he whispered to the girl, reaching for her. "We're a sitting target. Running may be what he wants us to do, but we won't have a chance staying here. We'll head for those willows. Keep your head down!"

The girl tried to grab the dog's rope as Gerard lifted her

out of the canoe, but Keeper jumped from the bow into the water just as another shotgun blast sounded. A spray of shot to the south of them bent the tall reeds and cattails.

They splashed through the water, Gerard pulling the girl, with the dog plunging just ahead of them. She managed to snatch Keeper's trailing rope, terrified that to protect them the dog would dash toward the gun when they reached higher ground. The water was still knee height as they neared the willows. A few big drops of rain fell, and thunder rolled with a closer grumble of sound, but the shotgun was silent.

The girl, sliding on the shifting mud underfoot, felt as if she were trying to swim upstream; the wet trousers belted with string around her waist weighed her down, and her boots were filling with water, dragging her backwards while Gerard pulled her forward. He was slipping, too, and she thought they would both sink beneath the water, sucked down and strangled by the twisting weeds.

But all at once the water became shallow, and then she felt her feet touch more solid ground. And now the growling dog, having gained firm footing, nearly yanked the rope from her hand.

"Keeper, quiet!" Gerard's voice was low, and the dog stopped growling, but he lunged at the end of his lead.

Gerard took the rope from her and seized her hand, and then they were running toward the shelter of the trees to where they could hide behind the dense, sweeping branches. When they reached the willows, they crouched down, panting as hard as the dog. Light rain began to fall.

They waited there, crouching, for a long time, but the air over the swamp didn't stir. The storm was coming, though, because the birds had stilled, and the air smelled like metal. The girl's skin prickled, but maybe it was just because she was so scared. A pattering of rain on the willow leaves was the only sound she could hear. Then the dog began to whine softly, but Gerard gave the rope a quick jerk. Keeper sank to the ground, quivering but quiet.

To the west, a streak of lightning was followed by a deep rumble of thunder. They waited. Finally Gerard whispered, "That storm will hit soon. Maybe the gunman's left, or he's gone in the other direction. I'm going to take a look."

The girl drew in her breath while Gerard took a step forward to see around the trees. Silence. He took another step, and the silence was broken by the explosive bark of the shotgun.

The gun was much closer.

Keeper lunged at the end of the rope, and Gerard grabbed the girl's hand. They ran over the spongy ground, dodging cottonwood trees and dragging the dog, who kept trying to run toward the gun. From somewhere behind them, another blast sent shot that brought down a shower of leaves, and now they could hear a pounding sound that must be the hoofbeat of horses.

They reached a thick clump of cottonwoods and squatted down to listen. The pounding hoofbeats had stopped. But the girl heard the baying of hounds coming closer, and through the spattering rain, a rising wind carried the faint shouts of men.

Lightning snaked over the swamp, and thunder boomed like a drum. The rain was still light. The girl, her clothes soaked with swamp water, clenched her teeth to keep them from chattering and put a hand to her neck. Her hand was shaking and the inside of her throat felt raw, as if something was tearing at it with sharp claws.

A sudden explosion of shot ripped the bark of the trees just in front of where they were squatting. Gerard pointed at another clump of cottonwoods to the left of them, and near the trees was a waist-high mound of sparsely grassed earth.

"Head for that," he whispered, again quieting the dog. "And run! No matter what happens, keep going! I'll be right behind you. Now, go!"

She didn't want to leave him, and she shook her head. Then he lifted his shirt and pulled a hunting knife from the sheath hanging on his belt.

"Go on!" he breathed, and the fierce look in his eyes and the knife gleaming in his hand made her turn and run, just as she heard a charge of shot spitting into the ground behind her. Lightning zigzagged, and overhead a thunder clap sounded like another shotgun, making the ground underfoot vibrate. She could see ahead of her a knotted mass of tree roots, and tried to jump over them, but the heel of her boot caught. She fell headlong, sprawling on the damp ground.

"Get up! Keep going!" came Gerard's shout from somewhere behind her. Scrambling to her feet, she caught a glimpse of him from the corner of her eye, and she knew that he was waiting, making himself a target so she could get clear. She hesitated, heard him snap, "Go!" and she ran.

When she reached the mound of earth, she whirled to see the man and dog racing toward her, and then Gerard reached out and pulled her to him. They crouched behind the earthen mound, Gerard's knife gripped in his hand, and listened for either a man or a spray of shot. They waited, while the rain fell, and the wind whipped through the cottonwoods.

Between rolls of thunder, the girl could hear the hounds baying just to the south of them. The wind was beginning to decrease, and the next peal of thunder sounded farther away. Gerard had his arm around her shoulders, and she could feel his warm breath against her cheek when he whispered, "Those hounds are getting nearer, but they're still farther away than the shotgun. And I don't think the constable would be shooting at us. So who the hell is?"

The girl shivered, and he pulled her closer so that her head pressed into the hollow of his shoulder. "Stay, Keeper!" he said to the dog, who had started to creep forward. A softer rumble of thunder signaled that the storm was moving on, but the barking hounds sounded as if they were closing in fast.

Then, suddenly, the shotgun roared, sending particles of dirt flying into their faces. When Gerard brought his hand up to wipe his eyes, the rope was yanked from his grasp as Keeper lunged forward, scrabbling over the mound and down the other side. Again the shotgun cracked.

The girl wrenched herself away from Gerard and ran around the earthen mound after the dog. She heard the shotgun again, and yards ahead of her Keeper jerked, then flattened. Still snarling, he began to crawl forward on his belly. Through a veil of rain, the girl saw blood running from the dog's shoulder. At the same time a glint of metal flashed in the trees ahead, and a thin, sharp-faced man holding a shotgun stepped from behind the trunk of a cottonwood.

The girl ran forward, hearing Gerard yell behind her. Keeper had stopped moving, and lay still. Even so, the man had raised the gun to his shoulder, and was now aiming straight at the dog.

"No! Don't . . . don't shoot!" the girl screamed, her throat ripping open, her voice bursting in her ears. "Keeper! Keeper. . . ."

She threw herself at the dog as the shotgun exploded.

19

---∽∿∽---

*A poor young girl of the lower orders, cajoled, or
ruined, more or less, is of course no great matter.
The little baggage is turned out of doors . . . and
there is an end of her.*

—W. M. Thackeray, *The Adventures
of Philip,* 1861

Glynis sat in Cullen's desk chair, holding the most recent
copy of *Harper's New Monthly Magazine* and attempting to
read, by the light of a kerosene lamp, the current installment
of William Thackeray's latest, serialized novel. Her eyes,
however, skimmed over the lines unseeing. Just as they had
done most of that afternoon and early evening.

After renting a livery horse for Danny Ross to take her
message to Cullen, she had walked to the library, where she
tried to work. Unable to concentrate, she finally gave it up in
late afternoon. When she had stopped at the dress shop, it
was to see a still-miserable Emma, who nonetheless persisted in plans for her uncertain wedding.

At last, unable to distract herself from worrying about
Bronwen and Jacques, Glynis had gone back to the firehouse to worry about Cullen and the girl.

But where *was* Cullen? The time on his desk clock now
read nine, and she could see through the open, office door
the late May twilight beginning to fade. A few minutes before, she had insisted that Liam Cleary should go home for

supper. Although he had been light-headed with hunger, he had left with great reluctance.

The night was quiet, and the air coming in through the doorway and open window felt fresh and cool, cleansed by the storm. Glynis had turned back to the magazine, but then leaned forward over the desk, positive that she had just heard the sound of hoofbeats. After a minute or two, she decided that horses were indeed drawing closer, and she rose from behind the desk, went to the door, and stepped outside. By the time she had rounded the firehouse and looked up the short slope, a number of dogs and horses and men had collected at the far side of Fall Street. Two of the horses and their riders shortly broke away and headed west; she guessed those were the Seneca County sheriff's men returning to the village of Waterloo. But had the girl been found?

She waited impatiently while the remainder of the group rode toward her: Cullen on the Morgan, and Zeph with his two bloodhounds loping to either side of his horse; Adam MacAlistair; the bounty hunter Sledge; a man with dark hair whom she couldn't at once identify; and Danny Ross, who was leading a horse which had slung over its back something that resembled a sack of grain. Glynis watched anxiously until they came close enough for her to see that the body on the horse was probably that of Sledge's otherwise absent partner, and not the girl, or a member of the search party.

The other men from the village had most likely gone straight on home. But there was no girl with those who remained.

Cullen pulled up the Morgan beside Glynis and dismounted. His dirt-smudged face looked tired, his expression was grim, and his first words to her consisted of, "Where's Liam Cleary?"

"Don't be angry with him, Cullen. I insisted that he go home for supper," Glynis answered. "But what happened? Did you find the girl, Tamar?"

"We found her all right. But not before two bounty hunters did." He turned to his deputy and said, "Zeph, get Sledge into the lockup. Danny, take the body to the ice house—Abraham Levy said he'd meet you there. And thanks, lad, for your help."

Glynis took a few steps toward the horse that Danny Ross was about to lead away, moving in only close enough to confirm that the body was that of the second bounty hunter.

"C'mon, Gagnon. We're going inside," Cullen said to the dark-haired man, whom Glynis could now see was Andre Gagnon's son, Gerard. The young man looked extremely agitated, and his hands were bound.

"Cullen, please," Glynis said to him, "tell me what happened?"

"Let's go into the office," he replied in a low voice. "I want to keep this out of the newspaper for as long as I can. But it's probably a lost effort, since the search party heard the confession."

"What confession?"

Cullen shook his head and strode toward his office. Glynis gathered in her skirt to pass the black-and-tan bloodhounds, whose ropy tails were switching back and forth as they gulped a pail of water, and she followed the men into what had become a crowded room. Zeph was just disappearing with the no longer grinning Sledge, taking him to one of the holding cells in the rear of the building. Sledge did not look entirely unwilling to go, perhaps spurred by the prospect of a square meal.

It seemed to Glynis that Gerard Gagnon was unwilling to go anywhere. What had he confessed to? Surely not Roland Brant's murder, as even with his hands bound, Gagnon's stance was combative as he said angrily, "You can't throw a man in jail for no reason, Stuart! What charge are you holding me on?"

"You just killed a man."

Glynis found herself confusedly trying to follow them;

was this the confession to which Cullen had referred? And where was the girl?

Adam MacAlistair, who until now had been unusually quiet, said to Cullen, "It was apparently a clear case of self-defense on Gagnon's part. Even Sledge admitted that. Zeph said he saw the whole thing, and he agreed Gagnon acted in self-defense. Agreed with no qualification."

"I'm holding you, Gagnon," said Cullen briskly, as if he hadn't heard Adam, "for interfering with the law, for harboring a possible fugitive, and for assaulting a deputy. And in about two seconds, I'm going to add resisting arrest. Besides," he said, "I'm doing this partly for your own good. Until you calm down, you're a danger to yourself as well as to the entire Brant family."

Glynis stared in bewilderment at Cullen. And when she looked at Gerard Gagnon, his expression was one of desperation. But so, she assumed, was her own, as by now she was frantic to learn what had become of Tamar. And who had confessed, and to what? Apparently, from what was being said, it could not have been to the death of the bounty hunter.

"I need to be with the girl," Gerard said, his voice as desperate as his expression.

Cullen replied, "There's nothing you can do for her now, Gagnon."

"Cullen," Glynis said, unable to remain silent, "what has *happened* to her?"

"She was shot!" Gagnon said accusingly, "because your constable here thinks she's a killer. As if anyone could believe that a frail girl was capable of murdering that pig Roland Brant!"

"O.K., that's it!" Cullen said.

"Gagnon, don't say any more," Adam intervened. "I'll represent you, but for now keep your mouth shut. We can ask Miss Tryon here to keep you informed of the girl's condition—"

"Then she's alive?" Glynis broke in.

"She's been taken to the refuge," Cullen answered, his eyes on Gerard Gagnon, as if expecting the young man to attack momentarily, bound hands or not. "And Adam, if you want to represent Gagnon, that's fine with me. But he stays here tonight, regardless."

Zeph reappeared to say, "Let's go, Gagnon," indicating the short hall to the cells.

"Give me a minute," Gerard insisted, and swung to Glynis. "Miss Tryon, please go to the girl, make sure she's well cared for. And for God's sake, don't let her be taken back to the Brants'!"

Glynis found herself nodding, despite Cullen's scowl.

"And please," Gerard added, "let me know how she is?"

"Yes, of course I will. She's in good hands with Dr. Cardoza-Levy, though, I promise you."

Despite her attempt to reassure him, Gerard Gagnon, as he was led off, did not look any less distraught. And Glynis continued to wonder in what condition the girl had been when brought to Neva. But apparently, she would have to see for herself, since no one seemed inclined to tell her.

When the door had closed behind the other men, Cullen said to Adam, "That was a surprise—you saying that you'd represent Gagnon. Isn't that a conflict of interest, since you and Merrycoyf are law partners, and he's representing the girl?"

"Let's say I think Gagnon needs a lawyer, Cullen. Are you planning to press those charges? If so, we'll worry about a conflict of interest later."

"I doubt that I'll press them, especially if he's cleared of murder. But Gagnon needs a night or two in jail to cool down. He's holding every last member of the Brant family responsible for his father's death. And you heard Zeph tell how he went after that bounty hunter. I'm not saying Gagnon didn't have good reason. He probably *was* defending himself and the girl. But he's damn good with a knife, and you just listened to his opinion of Roland Brant—who was stabbed, if you recall. How do I know Gagnon didn't murder Brant? How do you or anyone else know that?"

"Presumably the murderer knows," suggested Glynis. "But will one of you *please* tell me who has confessed?"

The two men exchanged a look before Cullen answered, "On the way back here, Tamar Jager all but admitted she killed Roland Brant."

"Cullen, no. Was she in any condition to know what she was saying? And what *is* her condition?"

"I don't know the answer to that," Cullen said. "All I can tell you is that she repeated, 'My knife, my knife,' over and over again. Gagnon tried to keep her from saying more—a little ironic, since she was previously mute—but when I asked her point-blank about the knife she said, 'My knife killed him.' "

Glynis grasped at the straw of hope, saying, "Then she didn't actually admit that *she* killed him."

"No, not precisely," said Adam. "But taken in its context, it did sound like a confession."

Glynis looked at Cullen. He nodded at her, then said, "That's why I want it kept quiet for now. The newspapers will jump all over what she said. And frankly, I think Gagnon's a good suspect. Could be that's why he tried to shut the girl up—before she incriminated him. For all I know, they were in it together. The girl could have let Gagnon into the house Sunday night or the following morning, and she could have given him the knife that killed Brant. I can't discount what she said, Glynis."

Before she could respond, Zeph returned. "Kept those two as far apart back there as I could," he said flatly.

"Zeph, see Miss Tryon to the refuge," Cullen said. "And she wants to know what went on at the swamp, so go ahead and tell her." He said to Glynis, "He's the one who saw it all."

He looked exhausted, Glynis thought. She started for the

door, then turned back to Cullen. "Shouldn't Elise Jager, the girl's mother, be told?" she asked.

"Yes, now that you mention it," Cullen answered. "When Liam Cleary gets here, I'll send him to Carr's Hotel for Mrs. Jager."

Glynis hesitated before she said with reluctance, "And the father?"

Cullen shook his head. "I thought he might join the search party, but Erich Brant told me Jager was planning to leave town."

She shouldn't be surprised, Glynis thought, given Derek Jager's previous behavior toward his daughter, but this latest example of indifference was disturbing, nonetheless.

She and Zeph left the office with the hounds trailing them, and as soon as they reached the road, Glynis said, "All right, Zeph, what happened? But first tell me, how is the girl?"

"Don't know. We took her straight to the doc. She was in shock, the doc said. And she took some shot from that bounty hunter. Doc was trying to work on her when we left. That's all I know."

His dark, square-jawed young face was somber in the fading light, his eyes not as alert as usual; he too looked exhausted. "Where do you want me to start?" he asked Glynis.

"At the beginning."

"Right. Search party split up when we got to the swamp. Constable and me, and MacAlistair—he isn't exactly a woodsman—we went on due north. Mr. Levy and the others from town struck out to the northwest, and the sheriff's deputies were going as far east as they could before hitting the lake. When Danny Ross caught up with us—said he had followed hoofprints—we were about two miles north of Dermont Creek. Danny's a good tracker, you know that?"

"Yes, I'd heard it somewhere. Apparently Danny stayed with you three?"

"Yeah," Zeph answered, and gave her a tired smile. "He said it beat installing a pump in the laundry."

"I'm sure."

"Anyhow, we knew from your message where to look. Went on north, and when the dogs started baying we knew something was ahead. Were almost to Black Brook when we heard a shotgun. Went off a couple of times. It sounded close. Not too hard to tell the distance on account of the air being so still—you know, right before the storm?"

Glynis nodded. Right before the storm.

"The dogs lit out, and we followed them. Couldn't go straight-away—had to ride around some fingers of swamp a few times, or we would have gotten to the girl and Gagnon sooner. Too bad about that."

They turned off Fall Street as Zeph was saying, "Just by chance, the dogs and I were the first ones there."

No, thought Glynis; it wouldn't have been chance. Given the opportunity, Zeph would always take the lead. He was the one to have on your side in a tight spot.

"I tethered my horse and tied the dogs—they don't much like a fight unless they're forced into it, and they can't always tell the good guys from the bad. Anyway, I came in at an angle behind the bounty hunters," Zeph went on. "If you can believe it, they were firing at a mound of dirt! The one named Sledge saw me, and he put down his gun. His partner, though, a runty guy, was some yards ahead and looked like he was really enjoying himself. Then I saw a dog come over the dirt mound, and that lunatic with the gun, he shot at it. Right after that, the girl came running after the dog, and she was screaming something—"

"She was screaming?" interrupted Glynis.

Zeph nodded. "And Gagnon was behind her yelling—and then that damn bounty hunter shot her. Good thing she was still moving when he did, or he would've killed her for sure."

"Unfortunately I'm not surprised," Glynis said.

"I started after the guy," Zeph went on, "same time as Gagnon was running toward him, but Gagnon got to him first. Man moved fast—nobody faster, except Jacques Sundown when he's after somebody—and he, Gagnon, already had this runt on the ground by the time I reached them. He'd stabbed him a couple of times in the chest. Must have hit the heart because that bounty hunter died quick. And the constable and the others got there right about then."

"Dear Lord, Zeph. What a nightmare!"

"Yeah, it was that. Gagnon got up, shoved me away, and ran back to the girl and the dog. And that's about it. We managed to get Gagnon and the girl—he wouldn't let go of her, and she wouldn't let go of the dog—onto the dead guy's horse. Made Sledge bring the body on his horse until we got to the refuge."

Glynis took a minute to collect her thoughts before asking, "So there's no question, Zeph, that Gerard Gagnon acted in what looked to you either like self-defense, or in defense of the girl."

"No question. After that bounty hunter shot the girl and the dog, he was loading to fire again. He didn't get the chance, only because Gagnon got to him first. That runty guy was a real born killer. I was sideways to him, and I could see him grinning away while he was loading to shoot again. I thought I'd have to kill him myself to stop him. So, no, there's no question in my mind."

The refuge was directly ahead, but Glynis had a few more things to ask. "Zeph, you're very observant—how did the girl behave toward Gerard Gagnon? Or didn't you have an opportunity to notice?"

Zeph paused before he said, "When she was on the horse, holding the dog, she sort of crumpled up against Gagnon. Like she felt safe that way. Is that what you mean?"

"That's exactly what I mean. Now, one last thing. Did you hear what the girl said about the knife? The knife that presumably killed Roland Brant?"

"Yeah, I heard. Doesn't look too good for her, does it? She's a little thing, though. Hard to believe she could have killed Brant, but that's just my opinion." Zeph gave Glynis a sardonic glance before he said, "And once or twice I've been known to be wrong."

When they reached the refuge entrance door, Glynis thanked him, then watched him stride toward Fall Street with the bloodhounds loping along beside him. Despite his obvious fatigue, his shoulders were straight and his gait easy, and it made her heart lift, as it always did, to see over the past seven years the profound change in Zeph—the son of runaway slaves. She just prayed he would not become involved in the war.

The war. For the hundredth time that day she thought of Bronwen, and of Jacques, already caught up in it, even here in the North. But since she couldn't endure for long the thought of either of them endangered, she drew in a deep breath of the sweet-smelling night air, then turned and opened the refuge door.

Aside from the Vanessa Usher Children's Wing, the large warehouse space had been divided by partition walls into sections to accommodate sleeping rooms for women and a cooking and eating area. A front quarter of the warehouse held what Neva called her dispensary, and it was to there that Glynis went.

She assumed that Cullen would not want her to tell Neva of the girl's confession, so she would need to be careful about what she said, she told herself, before knocking softly on the dispensary door.

"Yes?" came Neva's voice.

"It's Glynis. Shall I come in?"

"Yes! And thank God, you're here!"

20

She weepeth sore in the night, and her tears are on her cheeks .

—Book of Lamentations

When Glynis opened the dispensary door, the light from two softly glowing kerosene lamps showed Neva bending over a bed. A still figure lay covered with a white cotton sheet. And Glynis at once feared the worst.

Then Neva straightened, and said, "I hoped you'd come, Glynis, when you heard the girl was here. I need your help."

Glynis went to the bed where the girl lay; although it wasn't really accurate, she thought, to call her "a girl," when Tamar was in fact almost seventeen. But she looked so . . . frail. That was the word Gerard Gagnon had used to describe her, and it seemed appropriate. And Glynis now saw why the girl on horseback had looked vaguely familiar to her Monday afternoon when passing her on the road. Tamar had been with Helga Brant at least once in Emma's shop when Glynis had also been there; although it must have been more than a year since then, and Glynis could not recall whether the girl had spoken on that occasion.

But where had Tamar been on Monday *before* Glynis saw her? From what she and Cullen had been able to learn, no one in the household could recall seeing the girl at all that day. The question was, when Tamar left the house, had Roland Brant been dead?

The girl's long blond hair was tangled, and one arm that rested on top of the sheet was wrapped in bandages. Beside the bed, a shepherd dog lay stretched out, a long strip of white cotton bandage wound around its shoulder. As Glynis approached, the dog gave a low growl and tried to rise, but Neva put her foot on its rump and said, "Lie down and be quiet!"

The dog, to Glynis's surprise, at once obeyed.

"This fellow did not make things easy," Neva said. "He apparently thought I was attacking the girl. Tried tying him up outside, but he howled like a banshee."

"The dog was injured, too?"

"He had some shot in his shoulder. After I muzzled him, I took it out fairly easily. He was good about it, and he obeys commands. It was only earlier, when I worked on the girl, that he became aggressive. But really, Glynis, treating dogs—for this I became a doctor?"

"You say that at least once a week," Glynis answered, bending over to look at the girl. "How serious are her injuries?"

"I think I removed all the shot from her arm, but there's always the danger of infection."

"She doesn't seem feverish," Glynis commented after laying the back of her hand on the girl's forehead. "And she seems to be sleeping peacefully enough."

"It's laudanum-induced sleep, though," said Neva. "I had to give her some so she wouldn't keep the others awake when she cried out. Fortunately, the women who are here at the moment are in the new wing."

"Do you mean that she cried while you were taking out the shot?" Glynis asked, wondering if the girl, possibly in a delirium, had again referred to the knife.

"No, that's not what I mean. There's another problem, Glynis."

"Another problem?" repeated Glynis cautiously.

"When they brought her here, Zeph told me what went on in the swamp. The girl threw herself on the dog, and she suffered not only pellets in her left arm—which had a cut as well—but she also has at least one lodged in her upper left thigh. I say at least one, because she wouldn't let me get a good look."

"I'm not sure I follow you," Glynis said. "She wouldn't let you look at her thigh wound?"

"That's right. She let me take out the pellets in her arm with barely a sound. But then, when I tried to see the one in the thigh, she became so frantic that I gave it up. And the dog was ready to take a chunk out of me. I didn't want to tie the girl down—while she seemed terrified, I wouldn't have called her delirious—so I gave her some laudanum to calm her, just a while ago, and decided I'd wait for you."

Glynis bent over the girl again and brushed from her forehead a strand of hair as pale as corn silk. *Corn.* The image brought to mind a kitchen; the Brant kitchen and Addie's disturbingly ambiguous words: *The men around here have big appetites.*

Glynis turned to Neva and asked, "Did Tamar understand what you were planning to do? Did she ask anything, say anything at all?"

"I have no idea if she understood," Neva answered. "I tried to tell her, but she was crying and fighting me, so she might not have heard. And yes, she did say something, which surprised me, since I thought she was supposed to be mute. She kept saying 'No!' and 'Don't hurt me,' over and over. At that point it struck me as peculiar, since it was after I'd worked on her arm, which couldn't have been painless."

So she had been surprised by the girl speaking. Which meant that Neva didn't know about Tamar's apparent confession, and there had been no more talk of a knife, or she would surely have mentioned it. "When you took out those pellets, Neva," Glynis asked, "was she covered with the sheet at the time?"

Neva frowned in thought. "I think so, yes. I had to get her clothes off because they would have interfered while I was working on her. Besides, they were soaked with rain and swamp water."

"And did she object? When you took off her clothes?"

Neva frowned again. "Not much, as I recall. Although she was in shock then—she may still be. Why, do you think her reaction was due to modesty?"

"I don't know."

"That's possible, but whatever the case, I have to remove that pellet."

"Can you do it now," Glynis asked, "while she's asleep?"

"I hope so. I didn't give her much laudanum, though. It can be dangerous to someone in shock, and it's pretty much a matter of guesswork as to what's the right amount. If she comes out of it while I'm working on her and carries on like she did before . . . well, that scalpel is sharp."

Neva moved to a large table at the far side of the bed, which held a tin tray of instruments, among them a scalpel and forceps. "I have to go to the pump to wash these," she said, picking them up along with a tin basin filled with bloody water.

"Neva, her mother should be here soon, I expect."

"She has a mother? I thought she was indentured to the Brants because she was orphaned."

"Yes, I can see why you might have thought that. It's rather a long story."

"Tell me when I get back," Neva said over her shoulder as she left.

Glynis pulled one of the two straight chairs in the room closer to the bed and sat down. Softly, she said, "Tamar?" to see if the girl's sleep was sound.

She stirred slightly, but didn't open her eyes. Glynis took a lower corner of the sheet and began to slowly lift it.

Almost immediately, the girl grabbed the sheet with her right hand, and her eyes opened; large eyes the bright blue of October skies. "No, don't hurt me," she said, her speech slurred, Glynis assumed, by the laudanum. But at least she was speaking.

When the dog began to growl, Tamar's eyes closed; she must feel protected, Glynis decided, and guessed that the shepherd probably belonged to Gerard Gagnon.

She thought it best to take the dog outside while the girl was quiet. Glynis had to coax some before he limped after her, and then not willingly. Once outside, it occurred to her that he might try to find his master—and Gerard did not need him as much as the girl did—so she tied him to a hitching post. Then she stood gazing down the road to see if Elise Jager was coming. The moon was rising to outline the factories and warehouses along the canal, and she looked for the one that had been owned by Andre Gagnon before Roland Brant had foreclosed. She thought it might be the stone building directly across from the library. If so, there had been little activity there in the past days, she recalled.

Finally, seeing no one approaching, she went back inside to wait for Neva, and heard the dog whimper as she closed the door. She experienced a pang of longing for her terrier Duncan—gone many years now but still so sorely missed that she could not bring herself to have another—and she almost relented and brought the shepherd back inside. But he would be unmanageable if he sensed the girl was in distress.

"Good—you took the dog out," Neva said when she came back. "Her mother isn't here yet?"

"No, although she must have been notified by this time."

"Well, let's get this over with."

"Tamar's half awake, I'm afraid," Glynis said, and told Neva of her experiment.

"Then we'll have to tie her down."

When Glynis started to object, Neva added, "I can't wait for infection to start."

"No, I suppose not. It just seems so—"

"So heartless," Neva said, moving to the table where two additional lamps sat. "But letting her die would be more heartless, wouldn't you say?" She turned up the two lamp wicks.

Glynis sighed, and nodded. Moreover, the girl didn't protest when they loosely tied her hands with cotton cord to the bed's spindled headboard. Glynis hoped that Tamar's earlier reaction might have been a reflex, perhaps to the sheet rubbing against her wound.

But as soon as Neva lifted the sheet, the girl began to pull at the cords.

"Tamar," Glynis said to her, "Tamar, it's all right. Dr. Cardoza-Levy is just trying to help you, and it will be over soon."

Neva was meanwhile swabbing wood alcohol over the swollen area of the girl's thigh, muttering, "Who knows if and how this works, but Dr. Ives swears by it. And much as I dislike alcohol in any form, if it helps to ward off infection, I'll use it."

Tamar was by now straining at the cords, saying, "No, please don't hurt me." She still sounded dazed from the laudanum, and Glynis thought this protest was due to something other than the pain of her wound, especially since Neva had barely touched her yet.

But then Neva started to probe with the scalpel. "No, please no!" the girl cried softly, tossing her head back and forth, her eyes open and wild with fear.

"Glynis, hold her legs down," Neva said crisply, "she's thrashing around too much."

"I don't think I can bear to do this," Glynis said with mounting distress. "She's so terrified."

"You have to do it," Neva retorted, "or else we'll need to tie her legs down, too."

Glynis tried to comfort the girl by talking to her quietly while Neva worked, but her efforts were in vain, as Tamar continued crying, "No, no," over and over again in a drugged voice. And outside the shepherd dog barked and howled as if he were mad with despair.

Glynis returned from the refuge kitchen with two cups of tea, and after handing one to Neva, she sank into a chair. She had felt such pity for the dog that as soon as possible she'd brought him back inside, but not before he had managed to waken all of Seneca Falls, Glynis was sure. Now he was again stretched out beside the bed of the sleeping girl.

She reached down to stroke the dog's head, and said with feeling, "Neva, I could never be a doctor!"

"Days like this one," Neva answered, after taking a swallow of tea, "I don't think I can be either. But at least the scurrilous bounty hunter responsible for those injuries"—she motioned to the girl—"is now rotting in hell. And don't look at me like that, Glynis. Just because I'm a doctor doesn't mean I can't also subscribe to the ancient justice of an eye for an eye, et cetera. He probably murdered more than one person with that shotgun, and the girl could easily have been killed. You saw the size of that pellet!"

Yes, she had seen it; thankfully there had only been the one.

There then came a sudden knocking at the outside entrance door. When Glynis went to answer it, Liam Cleary stood there, shivering slightly in the cool night air. He told her that he'd come because Cullen had said Gerard Gagnon would drive them to drink by his constant demands for information about the girl.

"Come inside, Liam. We need to keep it as warm as possible in here."

After she'd closed the door, Glynis said to him, "You can tell Gerard Gagnon that the girl is holding her own. Dr. Cardoza-Levy removed all the shotgun pellets, and Tamar is sleeping quietly. So is his dog."

He nodded and turned as if to leave.

"Wait, Liam," Glynis said. "Mrs. Jager hasn't arrived here yet. Did you see her at Carr's Hotel?"

To her astonishment, his face began to color, the blush extending to his carrot-colored hair. "Yes, Miss Tryon, but . . . that is, I saw her, but I didn't exactly talk to her. Not much."

"Well, what did you do?" Neva asked, coming out of the dispensary.

"I didn't do anything. She was . . . that is, she had . . ."

"Liam," Neva snapped, with what Glynis knew to be the impatience of fatigue, "what is the matter with you? Just spit it out!"

Liam swallowed, and mumbled, "She, Mrs. Jager, she was in her, ah, undress."

"That's hardly scandalous," Neva said, eyeing Liam narrowly. "You've surely seen a woman in a dressing gown before."

"But that's not exactly all," Liam said, now staring earnestly at the floor.

"All of what?" Neva demanded.

"Well, I guess she was . . . was . . . was entertaining. Yes, that's what she was doing!" he said, obviously thankful for his inspiration. "She was entertaining."

"Entertaining whom?" Neva asked. "Her husband?"

"Ah, no. No, Constable Stuart said that he, Mr. Jager, left town today." Liam gazed with pitiful eyes at Glynis, evidently seeking support, but she was too bewildered to help him. And she also wanted this sorted out.

Neva must have decided to change tactics, as her approach became milder. "All right, Liam—steady as you go, boy, and let's try this again. Who was with the woman?"

"I think he must have been a gentleman caller," Liam said with unexpected brightness. "Yes, I think that's what he was."

Glynis and Neva exchanged a look.

"Did you recognize him?" Glynis asked.

"I didn't see much of him," Liam said, blushing again.

Neva asked with characteristic bluntness, "And just how, exactly, was Mrs. Jager entertaining him?"

"Ah . . . well, that's . . . that's hard to say," Liam stammered. "He didn't seem to have many clothes on."

This brought them all to silence.

"And you're sure you don't know who this gentleman was?" Glynis finally asked gently, as she thought that Liam had made himself about as clear as he was capable of doing.

"No."

"Then how can you possibly know he was a gentleman?" Neva persisted. "With few clothes on!"

"Well, I don't know," Liam said. Then he added, "But I'd like to think so."

Which, Glynis decided as she sent Neva a shake of her head, was altogether a most reasonable and charitable answer.

"Were you able to give Mrs. Jager the message about her daughter?" Glynis asked him, when he began to back toward the door with a determined expression.

"I tried to, Miss Tryon. But she closed the hotel room door so fast, I don't know if she heard me."

These were Liam's last words before he yanked open the refuge door and sped off into the night.

After Neva and Glynis had spent a long moment staring at each other, they went back into the dispensary. Neva checked her sleeping patient, then sat down and took a long swallow of tea before saying, "Liam Cleary is not a fool, so why does he insist on acting like one? Didn't you want more from him, Glynis, about Mrs. Jager?" she added. "You, whose curiosity is notorious?"

"I thought we had gotten as much as we could without embarrassing poor Liam further," Glynis murmured.

Neva looked sideways at her. "You are unquestionably a better person than I."

"No. You save lives, Neva."

"In an indirect way, so do you. You have an uncanny ability, Glynis, to associate the most dissimilar subjects. You take one thing from here, one thing from there, then add them together and come up with an answer of three! Cullen Stuart should just sit back and relax, because sooner or later you'll figure out who killed Roland Brant. Now, not that I want to change the sordid subject of murder, or even the sordid, if fascinating, subject of Elise Jager's callers—"

"We don't know that it's necessarily sordid," Glynis protested, although not very strongly. "There might be a perfectly respectable explanation."

Neva's brows raised. "If you say so. But I'm due in Waterloo tomorrow to urge granting of the Brant autopsy request, which means some sleep would be welcome. And we need to discuss something before Abraham arrives and drags me home. You're sure you don't mind staying here tonight?"

"Not at all."

Neva nodded, and glanced again at the girl. "You did see that bruising, didn't you? On her inner thighs?"

Glynis sighed. "Yes, I saw."

"Those are not fresh bruises," Neva stated. "They look to have been made at least a week or ten days ago. Maybe more, because Tamar is malnourished—no one that thin is healthy—and she probably doesn't heal well."

"Yes."

"Yes? You sound, Glynis, as if this is old news to you. How long has she been with that Gagnon man?"

"Not long enough," Glynis answered. "Not to have done that. Unless she's known him longer than I think she has. But I've met Gerard Gagnon, and I really don't think he's to blame."

"Then who is? It's not only those bruises, there's been other tissue damage in her genital area. In my opinion, that girl has been violated. And certainly not willingly, if her behavior tonight was any indication."

"I'm afraid I think you're right."

Neva moved forward to the edge of her chair, and stared

at Glynis. "Why are you so composed about this? You don't even seem shocked! Does that mean you knew about it?"

"No, not for certain, not until now. But I had begun to suspect it."

"Which is why you asked those questions earlier?"

Glynis nodded.

"Well, who has done this?"

"I'm not sure. Not yet."

"Since she lived at the Brant house, was it one of those men?" Neva asked, her voice strident with anger.

Glynis didn't immediately reply. When she did, it was to say, "I wonder—and I'm only guessing here—if perhaps Gerard Gagnon knows the answer. Tonight Cullen said something to the effect that Gerard seems to hold all the Brants responsible for his father's suicide. But Andre Gagnon's death might not be the sole reason for his son's implacable hatred of that family. Earlier tonight, Gerard was adamant, desperately so, that Tamar should not go back to the Brant house."

"I would think that goes without saying."

"Not necessarily," Glynis replied. "Remember, her father sold her into servitude there. I very much doubt that he would give a second thought to sending her back—although surely he doesn't know about the harm done her there! He may be callous, indifferent, but I can't believe he would condone that kind of brutality. And now we have to worry about her mother's judgment—I've been uneasy about her before tonight, although my reasons may not be good ones. But Neva, that poor girl! She has no one. Nowhere to turn, except possibly to a young man who is now sitting in Cullen's jail." Not that she thought he belonged there.

"So what should—"

Neva broke off at a knock on the refuge door. "That will no doubt be my weary husband," she said, as she got to her feet. "We'll talk more about this tomorrow, Glynis."

Abraham had opened the door, but then stood leaning against the jamb, looking just barely able to keep awake.

"You must be exhausted, Abraham, after that search," she said.

"It has not been one of the shorter days of my life," he agreed. "Are you coming home," he said to Neva, "or do you need to sleep here tonight?"

"No, Glynis has offered to stay with the girl." She turned to say, "You know what to watch for, Glynis. Redness, swelling, fever, the things I listed. And if anything changes—"

"Yes, I'll come and get you."

But as Neva and Abraham left, Glynis did not feel as confident as she had sounded. There remained the very real possibility that Tamar's apparent confession had been genuine. And that she had indeed murdered Roland Brant.

After checking the sleeping girl once again and finding her forehead cool, and her bandages free of blood, Glynis turned down the wicks of the two lamps still burning. She lay down on the other dispensary bed, fully intending to simply rest.

Sometime later she was wakened by a clattering crash. Followed immediately by a series of barks. She pulled herself upright to see Tamar crouched at the edge of the other bed, and staring with frightened eyes at the tin tray of instruments that was still vibrating on the wood floor. The dog had stopped barking and was now investigating, skirting the tray warily.

Glynis slid off the bed, and stood in place, being careful to keep her distance from the girl while saying to her, "Don't be frightened. It's only the doctor's instruments making that racket."

The girl looked at Glynis, the confusion expressed in her face clearly adding to the fear revealed in her eyes. The dog, however, had returned to stand in front of her, his tail switching back and forth, and when Tamar looked down at him, her expression changed to one of less fear.

"Yes," Glynis said, "the dog is fine, Tamar, as you see. My name is Glynis Tryon, and I'm a friend of . . ." A friend of whom? she asked herself, her mind still somewhat clouded with sleep. Certainly it wouldn't ease the girl's distress to say a friend of the Brant family. Or of the father who had sold this girl into a servitude of immense harm.

"I'm a friend," she repeated, leaving it there. "I met you once in my niece Emma's dress shop, but I don't know if you'd remember that. And I'm the town librarian," she added, for no particular reason other than that she herself would have found this a reassuring fact to know about a stranger.

The fright in the girl's eyes had lessened. It was probably due more to the presence of the dog than to anything else.

"Did you need something?" Glynis asked. "For instance a chamber pot?"

The girl gave a nearly imperceptible nod. Glynis went to the table and pulled the chamber pot from beneath it. Still keeping her distance, she said, "You may be unsteady on your feet, so I'll help you, if you like."

The girl shrank back against the bed, and Glynis quickly added, "Or you can hold onto the spindle of the headboard until you know whether you can stand without dizziness. Then I'll leave you by yourself."

The girl gave her a long look, then put her hand on the wooden spindle and immediately stood up. A moment later, she sank back down, a sheen of perspiration appearing on her forehead.

Glynis, whose impulse was to go to the girl, remained where she was with effort, saying, "It's a terrible feeling, isn't it? I was once sick in bed for a number of days, and afterwards, when I first tried to walk around, I decided I'd rather be sick again." She smiled tentatively at Tamar. "It passes, though, once you've been on your feet for a while."

The girl seemed to be studying her, the outright fear replaced by a guarded expression. She again tried to stand, but this time she did it more slowly, and with one hand placed on the dog's back. When she finally straightened, she seemed to be fairly steady.

"I'll be right outside the door if you need me," Glynis told her as she crossed the room. "Please don't be afraid to call. We're the only ones here, except for a few women who are sleeping in the wing of the refuge."

As Glynis left the room, she could feel Tamar watching her. She pulled the door closed with some misgiving, but the girl did not look feverish and the laudanum appeared to have worn off. Better that she be given some privacy, than to intrude on her unnecessarily. And surely the dog would bark if the girl fell. Glynis's concern was more about the fact that Tamar hadn't spoken. Had she again withdrawn into silence?

Moonlight coming through the large warehouse windows was so bright that Glynis could read the clock on Neva's desk. A few minutes past three. The girl had been asleep for some hours; as had she, Glynis thought with a start of guilt. But apparently no harm had been done, unless Tamar had been lying there awake and in fear.

A few minutes later the dispensary door opened, and Tamar stood gripping it while the dog danced around her feet. She pointed at the chamber pot, then at the dog. Although Glynis thought she knew what the girl meant, she waited to respond, hoping Tamar would speak.

The silence stretched, and just as Glynis was about to give up, the girl said, "Outside. He needs to go outside."

"Yes," Glynis said with relief, "I'll put him out for a few minutes. And while he's gone, I'll make us some tea, all right?"

The girl didn't respond, but continued standing there.

"It would help," Glynis said, "if you could tell me the dog's name."

"Keeper," said Tamar.

"Keeper," Glynis repeated, smiling. "A good name for a shepherd—keeper of the flock. Is he Gerard Gagnon's dog?"

Tamar's face changed, apprehension in her expression. "Is he . . . ?" She had drawn in her breath, and didn't seem able to finish the question.

"Gerard is fine," Glynis answered, which was not completely candid if being jailed was any measure, but she noted the immediate easing of anxiety in Tamar's face. It reassured her that Gerard Gagnon had not been the one to brutalize this girl.

"I'll put Keeper out," Glynis said, "but would you please go back to the bed? I doubt if you're very strong yet, and I'm afraid that you might fall."

The girl said nothing, but backed away from the door and edged toward the bed. When she lowered herself to the edge of it, Glynis nodded, then called the dog to the door.

Tamar said nothing when Glynis brought her the tea. But she drank it readily enough, seated on the edge of the bed, and even took a few bites of the corn-bread biscuits that Glynis offered. But since the girl still looked pale, Glynis asked if she didn't want to lie down again. Tamar gave her another long look, then lay back. In the meantime, Glynis had been debating with herself as to how much she should tell the girl if she asked the actual whereabouts of Gerard.

She didn't ask, but curled on her side with her back to Glynis. After turning down the lamps again, and stepping over the dozing Keeper, Glynis started for the other bed. She was stopped by the sound of a soft sob. The dog immediately jumped to his feet; at least he, Glynis thought, was recovering quickly. But she wondered if Tamar would be able to recover from what she had suffered.

Leaving the lamps low and relying on the moonlight, Glynis pulled a chair up next to the bed and sat down.

"I'd like to help you if I can," she said, cautiously reaching forward to smooth the girl's hair. Tamar didn't pull away. Glynis thought this remarkable considering what the girl had been through, and it gave her hope that Tamar might still be able to trust.

"To help you, though," Glynis told her, "I need to know a few things. You don't have to answer, but I hope you will trust me."

There was no response from the girl, but she remained still.

"I expect you probably want to know about Gerard Gagnon," Glynis said to her, and was rewarded with a quick nod of Tamar's head. "He's here in town," Glynis went on, "and he was healthy when I last saw him. Unlike you, he wasn't shot."

At this, the girl rolled onto her back to look at Glynis. "He's all right?" she asked.

"Yes, although he's worried about you, Tamar. He sent . . ." Glynis stopped, again doubtful as to how much she should say about Gerard's circumstances.

"Where is he?" Tamar asked.

The girl plainly had some strength of will, or she couldn't have survived this long, and while Glynis didn't want to upset her more, she also didn't want to lie to her. "He sent a deputy here to see how you were," Glynis answered, hoping this might be enough.

"A deputy? Why?" Tamar asked, looking straight at Glynis, but with her fingers kneading the sheet.

"Constable Stuart thought it best that Gerard stay at the lockup overnight, because he was very angry about what had happened to you. The constable was afraid that he, Gerard, might try to punish those responsible."

Glynis waited.

Tamar continued to gaze at Glynis, then at last asked, "Did the man with the shotgun run away then?"

"No, that man is dead," Glynis answered. "Gerard killed him before he could shoot at you again."

"But if the constable knows that . . . Does he know?"

"Constable Stuart and a search party were looking for you. Do you remember, before the man with the shotgun came after you, that hounds were baying?"

"I remember."

"Those bloodhounds belong to one of the deputies who was searching for you. The dogs led the constable and his men to where you and Gerard were being attacked by two bounty hunters with shotguns. And to answer your question, yes, the constable knows that to protect you Gerard killed one of the men."

"Then why is he in the lockup?" Tamar asked and struggled upright, her eyes again beginning to widen with fear.

Glynis helped the girl to sit up, and plumped a pillow behind her, at the same time wondering if she'd done the right thing in saying so much. And now, it was too late to back away. "Constable Stuart is questioning everyone who knew the Brant family," Glynis said, watching the girl closely, "in an attempt to discover who killed Roland Brant."

The girl's eyes fluttered, and she clutched at the sheet. "Gerard didn't kill him," she said in a whisper. "Does the constable think he did?"

"Constable Stuart thinks he might have had reason to kill Roland Brant," Glynis told her.

"No, Gerard didn't kill him!" Tamar said, her eyes in the moonlight now brimming with tears. "I killed him."

THURSDAY
May 30, 1861

21

—∿—

"**SERVANT GIRL CONFESSES TO MURDER OF LEADING CITIZEN**" blared the boldface headline. Neva, having just arrived at the refuge, had hurled the morning newspaper onto the table in the heretofore quiet kitchen where Glynis sat drinking coffee.

While Glynis gaped at the paper, Neva threw herself into the nearest chair. "This is absolutely monstrous!" she stormed. "Glynis, do you have any idea where that wretched paper could have picked up such a thing? Aren't there laws against slander? Why doesn't someone take a horsewhip to the editor of that contemptible rag? Why aren't you *saying* something?"

"I'm numb," Glynis replied. She had also just awakened a short time before.

She pulled the paper toward her to read the first lines of the article.

The investigation into the murder of distinguished Seneca Falls merchant and philanthropist Roland Brant has concluded with the capture of his killer. Tamar Jager, an indentured servant in the Brant household, confessed to the heinous crime when she was seized yesterday in the area of Montezuma Marsh. Miss Phoebe Jones, another servant at the Brant estate, said she was not surprised to learn that Jager was a murderess, and went on to state that she had always known "the girl was queer in the head."

Glynis could read no more. "This is worse than I would have imagined," she said, pushing the paper away in disgust.

Neva had jumped from her chair to pour herself a mug of coffee, and now began pacing around the table. "How can they print something like that?" she exclaimed, her face flushed with anger. "I was with that girl for hours and she said nothing about Roland Brant. Nothing! And you were with her all last night—" She suddenly stopped pacing and gave Glynis a direct look, the question in her eyes explicit.

"Did you see Tamar this morning?" Glynis asked quickly. "She seems much better. At least to my mind, she does."

"She was asleep when I just looked in on her," said Neva slowly. "Glynis, did she tell you something?"

"She woke just once to use the chamber pot," Glynis answered, truthfully. "She slept much of the night, as did I. But Neva, I really need to go home now and . . ."

Her voice trailed off as she saw that Neva was studying her with narrowed eyes of skepticism. Glynis knew how rapidly her friend could spot evasion, and she was badly botching her evasiveness; she simply hadn't expected the newspaper to print the story so soon.

She sat there in discomfort while Neva asked, "Why do I think that you're trying to change the subject? And that you're concealing something?"

Before Glynis could form an answer, Neva, each word pronounced with deliberation, went on, "I've just realized that you don't seem irate, or even surprised at the newspaper report that Tamar has confessed to murder."

"Oh, I'm surprised—"

"Let me finish, Glynis! If Tamar did kill Roland Brant, was it because . . . because *he* was the one who raped her? My God, could that be true? Of Roland Brant?" Neva seemed stunned beyond words. Glynis didn't reply, and after a minute Neva went on, "But if that's the case, you must know that I couldn't possibly condemn her. You do know that, don't you?"

"Neva, you should not say that the girl was raped by Roland Brant, and neither should I! Her being raped will not save Tamar from hanging for his murder. I hope you understand that."

Neva brought her open palm down on the table with a resounding slap. "It's outrageous! It is just outrageous that a man can violate—"

"Yes," Glynis interrupted, "but that is the way it is. And has been so for centuries. Neva, do you believe for one minute that a jury of men would set that girl free because she claimed Roland Brant had raped her? Of course not! If nothing else, they would choose to believe it wasn't true—that she was lying to save herself."

"I can testify to her condition!" Neva snapped.

"But you cannot state absolutely that she was raped," Glynis argued, concern bringing her to her feet. "And certainly not that she was raped by Roland Brant, who in death seems to be taking on all the trappings of sainthood. No; all you could do would be to say that there is some evidence that she *might* have been raped. By someone. And how do you think a prosecutor would approach that? By saying she was unchaste, that's how. Just a wanton, little baggage who seduced leading citizen Roland Brant—enticed him so as to win her release from servitude or for myriad other reasons. The girl has no protection and no standing, Neva—even Clements, another *servant,* described Tamar to me as 'only a kitchen maid.' "

Neva had slumped into a chair, and was staring at her with an expression of incredulity. "You, Glynis, I regret to say, are beginning to sound exactly like Jeremiah Merrycoyf. That is not, by the way, meant as a compliment. I have never seen you so . . . so antagonistic. And to me, your supposed friend!"

"You are my friend, Neva. But I am afraid for that girl. If you so much as imply to anyone that she should plead rape as justification for killing Roland Brant, a prosecutor will snatch it up and run like the wind with it. And Tamar will be lost."

Neva shoved her chair away from the table and stood up, her voice clipped when she demanded, "So what, Madam Prosecutor, is your solution? Since the girl has confessed to murdering Brant."

"That wasn't quite what I heard yesterday from Cullen," Glynis answered with caution, "and he ordinarily is very accurate. So what Tamar said must have been distorted by the time it reached the newspaper. And I have to assume it reached there by way of someone in the search party."

"So what *did* she say?"

"She talked—undoubtedly in shock when she did—about a knife. Her knife, she said, killed him."

Neva groaned. But then, her forehead creased in thought, she said, "It may be splitting hairs, but that's not precisely the same as saying *she* killed him."

"No, it's not," Glynis agreed. "But it evidently sounded like a confession to the men who heard it."

"Speaking of your friend the constable," Neva said brusquely, "I saw him on my way here. He said to tell you that Elise Jager has filed a petition with the court clerk in Waterloo. For custody of her daughter."

Glynis drew in her breath. "Did he say when it would be heard?"

"Heard?"

"The application. Heard by the court."

"As I said, you sound far too much like Merrycoyf. But to answer your question, Judge Endicott is back from circuit court, so Cullen said he would probably get to Elise Jager's petition this afternoon. He, Cullen, wants to know if you plan to attend."

"Yes, I think I should."

"Fine," Neva said, turning to leave the kitchen. "Now if you'll excuse me, I need to get to work."

"Neva, I apologize if I said something offensive. Or something that hurt you."

"That's quite all right," Neva said over her shoulder.

But Glynis knew by the stiff set of the shoulder that it was not all right.

Several hours later, a light breeze sent the smell of honeysuckle and freshly tilled earth through the open windows of the Seneca County Court House. Glynis sat waiting in the second-floor courtroom, as did everyone else there, for the appearance of Judge Tobias Endicott. Just a handful of people were present, and Glynis, the better to observe them, was content to sit alone at the end of a row halfway down the center aisle, grateful that she would not be testifying this day. She'd been required to do so on previous occasions, but could still at times be gripped by her lifelong fear of speaking in public.

With Cullen and Neva and Jeremiah Merrycoyf, she had traveled in a four-passenger phaeton the six miles west to the town of Waterloo. During the ride, there had been little conversation. That was not unusual for Merrycoyf. Glynis knew from past experience that he rarely talked before a court appearance. The lawyer, a stout St. Nicholas figure, had sat beside her on the rear carriage seat, the only indication that he was not asleep being an occasional nudge of the spectacles which had a tendency to slide down his small, round nose.

Neva's silence, however, had been unusual. The only breaks in it had come when she replied in perfunctory fashion to Cullen's infrequent comments. After he had directed the carriage around the heavily treed square in front of the courthouse, and had reined in the horses under a rustling canopy of tall elms, they climbed from the phaeton, and Neva took Glynis aside to briefly apologize. But the doctor's rage at what had happened to Tamar did not seem to have abated; nor, Glynis thought, had her own rage. She and Neva simply had different ways of seeking resolution. And Glynis did not view all men as the enemy.

Realistically, it was time, not rage—no matter how justified—that would free the girl from a murder charge. Time to find the real murderer, because Glynis was nearly, if not completely, convinced that Tamar was not Brant's killer. In addition, the girl's highly publicized confession was now seen by Glynis as quite possibly useful. It might give the killer a sense of security, perhaps just enough to be caught off guard and to make a careless mistake.

Of one thing Glynis was absolutely convinced: that for months Tamar Jager had lived with terror and shame; preyed upon by the town's leading citizen and philanthropist Roland Brant. But if it were to be told, few would believe it. Since his death there had even been talk of naming a grammar school for him. And Glynis had to admit that she wouldn't have believed it either, had she not known the history behind Gerard Gagnon's fury, had she not caught the cook Addie's cryptic remark, had she not heard a stableboy's hesitant whisper. There must have been other instances of Roland Brant's casual violence, his exploitation of power, but they had perhaps been better-hidden ones.

The incident of Brant shooting a sound horse nagged at Glynis; it surely had been meant to serve as a graphic warning to Tamar—to what would happen to her if she "talked." But why had a warning so explicit been necessary? Had she already told someone? Or had Roland Brant believed that someone had guessed and might question the girl? Whichever, the warning clearly had worked.

The most confounding puzzle, though, was that Tamar,

despite her confession, did not know whether it was she who had killed Roland Brant.

The night before, after she'd blurted "I killed him," Glynis had persuaded her to tell what she knew about Brant's death. The persuasion had not been effortless. Even now, seated here in the courtroom, Glynis was ashamed that she had implied to Tamar that Gerard Gagnon could be charged with complicity—as Cullen had suggested—unless the true killer was found. A harsh strategy. But as Neva herself had said earlier that night, was it worse than allowing the girl to die? For a crime she had not committed?

And the threat to Gerard had proven to be the key.

Glynis had begun by asking Tamar: *Why had she spoken of a knife, her knife?* Several days before Roland Brant's death, Tamar had answered, she had taken a knife from the kitchen, then hidden it under the mattress in her room.

Why had she taken it? She had vowed to kill Roland Brant, or to kill herself the next night he came to her room. But on that last night, he had been interrupted.

How? Someone had called him. He had gone upstairs, and after what sounded like an argument, he must have fallen into bed, because she'd heard a thump and the bedsprings had squealed, or maybe it had been someone crying. She'd thought he was hurting someone.

No, she didn't know what time it had been. Only that a humpback moon had been climbing into the sky.

What had she done after that? She thought she might have slept, because there came what seemed to be a dream where she was standing over Roland Brant, plunging a knife again and again into his heart. Blood was spurting everywhere and she didn't know how to stop it. Or what to do with the knife. She tried to run, but she could only take a few steps and then, when she looked behind her, she could see a trail of bloody footprints. It had seemed so real. She didn't remember waking. And she had thought: What if it hadn't been a dream?

She was so terrified by what she might have done that she'd left the house by way of the kitchen door—no, she didn't know what time it had been, but the sky had barely begun to pale. And there was mist rising from the grass. She had started to run toward the stable for a horse, when she saw from the corner of her eye that the door of Roland Brant's library stood open. It had frightened her, because the door was always kept bolted.

What did she think had happened? She'd feared that Brant might have gone from the library to the stable him-self—he sometimes took an early ride—so she'd crept along the house toward the library to see if he was inside.

That was the last thing she could remember clearly.

But where had she been all that day—Monday? She might have run to the stable. But if the stableboy and groom had been there, she would have hidden in the loft. She'd done that before sometimes, hidden there, and later she had found pieces of straw clinging to her wool cloak.

Then it had been late afternoon when she'd taken the horse? She didn't know. She had a faint memory of a horse rearing, and of waking up in the swamp. And then, in the swamp, she'd had a picture in her mind of seeing herself above Roland Brant's body. Her knife, the knife with the bone handle, had been in his chest. So what she had thought was a dream must have been real.

And then Gerard and the dog had found her.

"But you said Gerard is all right?" Tamar had again tear-fully asked Glynis, while the shepherd lying beside her bed stirred slightly in his sleep.

"Gerard is fine. And I will do my best to find the answer to this terrible thing," Glynis had promised her. She'd not had the heart to press the girl for more, but simply sat with her until she had slept.

This morning, directly after the scene with Neva in the

refuge kitchen, she had gone straight to Merrycoyf's law of-fice. The newspaper had been lying open on his desk. And despite his protestations, Glynis had recounted to him all that Tamar had said. Only that, however. Not her own uncer-tain speculations.

"Jeremiah, is it possible for you to believe Roland Brant capable of such evil?"

"My dear Miss Tryon, almost anything is possible to be-lieve when it comes to human depravity. I seem to recall that we have discussed this topic before."

"You must represent the girl."

"As it happens, Adam has already informed me of the un-fortunate Tamar Jager. And I told him, unequivocally, that I could not represent her. I am retired."

"You are here in your office, Jeremiah!"

"To finish some small items of business."

"I will never be able to forgive you."

He had peered at her over his wire-rimmed spectacles. "Are you quite serious, Glynis?"

"Quite serious." She had almost stammered, so startled was she to hear him use her given name.

"I am too old, my dear, to be dashing to the defense of maidens in distress."

"If you don't, this maiden may die. And you are in the pink of health."

"I am tired, which is why I have *re*tired."

"I will not permit you to set foot in my library again." A hollow threat, she realized, since he was on the library's board of directors. "I meant what I said, Jeremiah—I will never forgive you!"

Thus here they were, shortly past midday on a warm spring afternoon, seated in the Seneca County Court House. The courthouse had stood in Waterloo for more than half a cen-tury, and the generous amount of polished wood trim in the small courtroom where Glynis waited, uneasy and impatient, smelled of linseed oil and age.

At last, in the front of the courtroom, a narrow door to the side of a raised platform swept open to admit the judge.

"All rise!" called the bailiff. "The Honorable Tobias Endicott presiding."

22

---※---

*And king Solomon said, Bring me a sword. And
they brought a sword before the king. And the king
said, Divide the living child in two, and give half
to the one and half to the other.*

—First Book of Kings

*J*udge Tobias Endicott, a thickset man with broad forehead
and reputation for suffering little foolishness in his courtroom, strode to the bench with his black judicial robe swinging about the ankles of his boots. He had more than once
visited Glynis's library, and she liked this intelligent man,
not in spite of but possibly because of the fact that he was
known for an occasional eccentricity. He was also known
for his common sense.

After he put on his spectacles, took them off and examined them closely, then put them on again, he nodded to the
court clerk. While the clerk came forward to read the hearing calendar, Judge Endicott briefly scanned the room, and
when his eyes came to rest on Jeremiah Merrycoyf, Glynis
caught his suppressed smile.

"The first item, Your Honor," said the clerk, "is a request
by the deputy coroner of the Village of Seneca Falls, Dr.
Neva Cardoza-Levy, on behalf of the People of New York,
for permission to conduct an autopsy on the deceased
Roland Brant. In opposition to the request for autopsy is the
deceased's son Erich Brant."

"Are both parties here?" asked Judge Endicott.

"Here, Your Honor."

"Come forward."

Neva rose and started down the short center aisle. Erich Brant also got to his feet and followed her through a waist-high, swinging gate; the gate connected two sections of elaborately carved wood railing, and brought Neva and Erich to stand before the triple-tiered enclosed bench on the raised front dais. Both managed to behave as if the other was not there.

"I have read your petition, Dr. Cardoza-Levy, and your response, Mr. Brant," said Judge Endicott. "Do you have anything to add, Mr. Brant, to your stated opposition in this matter?"

"Yes, sir, I do."

"Proceed."

"In the past twenty-four hours, there has been a confession made by my father's murderer. Which makes the purpose of an autopsy completely immaterial."

"Now, Mr. Brant," the judge cautioned, "I am the one to decide what is material or immaterial here. You have argued in your response that an autopsy is unnecessary because the cause of your father's death by stabbing is obvious. And that you object to the desecration of his remains. Do I understand that your opposition is now based on the recent confession of . . . whom did you say?"

It must be, Glynis thought, that His Honor did not read the Seneca Falls newspaper. A commendable practice.

"I didn't say, Your Honor, but she is an indentured servant girl."

"This servant girl presumably has a name?"

"Jager. Tamar Jager. She has confessed, sir, to stabbing my father. It was in this morning's newspaper," he added.

"Are you relying for information on some *newspaper?*" Judge Endicott scowled, removing his spectacles to dangle them from his hand.

Erich recovered rapidly. "No, sir. Her confession was heard by Constable Stuart, as well as by two deputies of the Seneca County Sheriff's Office, and members of a search party. She was captured, Your Honor, while trying to escape."

Glynis heard from behind her a soft intake of breath, and turned to see an elegantly gowned Elise Jager just entering the courtroom. She appeared to be alone, and she seated herself across the aisle, several rows behind Glynis. A man then also entered, but Glynis, afraid of missing something, turned back to face the bench before taking the stranger's measure.

"Dr. Cardoza-Levy," the judge inquired while replacing his spectacles, "in view of this recent development, are you prepared to withdraw your request?"

"No, I am not."

Neva looked too small, Glynis thought as she often did, to be possessed of such a robust voice. Her words carried as clearly as the peal of a cast bronze bell.

Judge Endicott looked down at her over his spectacles, and then shuffled quickly through a sheaf of papers. After a minute or two, he said, "I must tell you, Doctor, that if a confession of stabbing has been made—and you have stated here in your petition that there was a knife in the body of the deceased—I can hardly see good reason for an autopsy."

"Your Honor, first I wish to address the confession of Tamar Jager."

Glynis moved uneasily in her chair. She was still worried, considering this morning's argument, that Neva would try to claim that Brant's murder might have been justified by reason of rape.

"Very well, Doctor, address the confession," allowed Judge Endicott.

"The girl was in shock when she was brought to my dispensary, Your Honor. I don't know when the so-called confession was made, but in my opinion, my patient at the time may well have been delirious. Few people would be capable of rational thought immediately following that kind of injury."

"What kind of injury?"

"She was shot, Your Honor."

"That doesn't mean," Erich Brant protested, "that she didn't know what—"

"Mr. Brant," interrupted Judge Endicott. "When I want your opinion I will so inform you."

Erich's rigid posture indicated his displeasure, but he gave the judge a brief nod.

Judge Endicott, now frowning, asked, "Who brought the Jager girl to your dispensary, Doctor?"

"Constable Cullen Stuart and his deputy."

"Constable Stuart, please come forward," directed the judge.

When Cullen stood before him, Judge Endicott said, "Please enlighten me, Constable. What is the background of this situation?"

Glynis listened as Cullen related the search for Tamar Jager; it coincided with what Zeph had told her.

"And, as I described, she was wounded by the bounty hunter, Your Honor," Cullen concluded.

Judge Endicott's frown had deepened, and he asked, "Would you be able to state, Constable, as Dr. Cardoza-Levy has claimed, that the suspect was in shock when you first saw her?"

"I think she probably was, yes."

"And when she made the confession?"

"I wouldn't call it a clear-cut confession, Your Honor."

"What would you call it?"

"Some phrases spoken by a very sick girl."

Bless Cullen, Glynis thought, with a glance at Erich Brant, who looked angry. But then he always did.

Judge Endicott sighed deeply, removed the spectacles again, and rubbed the bridge of his prominent nose. "Very well, Constable, that will be all for now."

As Cullen went back to his seat, the judge said, "Now, Dr. Cardoza-Levy, your petition stated that you observed two different wounds on the body of the deceased Roland Brant. Explain the particulars of that observation."

"There was a knife protruding from the deceased's chest in the area of the heart. There was also a bruise on the left temple made, I believe, with a small blunt object—which has not to my knowledge been identified."

Both Neva and Judge Endicott looked at Cullen.

"It hasn't been clearly identified," Cullen agreed.

"Either of those injuries," Neva continued, "could conceivably have caused Roland Brant's death. An autopsy might show which indeed *did* cause death, and which blow was struck first. That might also answer the question as to who would have been able to inflict such injury on a strong, and to all appearances healthy, man. Also, since the deceased's body was not discovered for some time—or so we have been led to believe," she added, provoking a scowl from Erich, "an autopsy would allow the time of death to be, if not fixed absolutely, at least narrowed down. As of now, we are simply speculating about an unknown period."

Judge Endicott had replaced his spectacles and when he now looked down at Neva, he was again frowning. "Are you saying, Doctor, that there are viable suspects in this murder other than the servant girl?"

Glynis waited, increasingly alarmed at a possible revisitation of Neva's rape defense. She thus heard with relief a simple, "I believe so, yes, Your Honor."

A few rows ahead of Glynis, a stout figure heaved himself out of his chair. "Your Honor," said Merrycoyf, "may I have permission to approach the bench?"

"Yes, indeed, Mr. Merrycoyf," said the judge.

As the lawyer lumbered forward, Judge Endicott commented, "When I saw you earlier, Mr. Merrycoyf, I thought perhaps you were here for sentimental reasons. But it would seem that rumors of your retirement have been premature."

"No, Your Honor," Merrycoyf replied as he went through the gate, "they were not rumors, nor were they premature. But I have this morning been beseeched, not to say besieged, by my dear friend Miss Glynis Tryon to emerge temporarily from retirement."

Glynis felt all eyes turn to her, and she very much wanted to sink beneath the floor; Merrycoyf, who knew her all too well, was exacting his small measure of recompense. She tried to hide her embarrassment by meeting Judge Endicott's bemused gaze with a bemused one of her own.

"I must offer my apologies to the court for a lack of preparedness," Merrycoyf explained. "I was retained by Miss Tryon to represent the aforementioned Tamar Jager shortly before departing Seneca Falls, thus I have not met my client, nor have I talked with my client. But I have been well informed of her need for counsel by Miss Tryon."

Glynis could only believe that her face by now must be a livid pink. And she could see Cullen making little attempt to conceal a smile.

"Well, my congratulations on your return, Mr. Merrycoyf," said Judge Endicott. "May I assume you wish to speak to this autopsy request?"

"Yes, Your Honor," Merrycoyf answered. "Now that I have some better understanding of these lamentable circumstances, I believe an autopsy to be absolutely essential. My client's feverish ramblings dealt with a knife, I am informed, not a head injury caused, in the learned doctor's words, by a blunt object. My client, Your Honor, must be protected by a fair determination of the cause of death."

"I tend to agree," Judge Endicott said, "that too much doubt has been cast to avoid an autopsy. Request granted. Will the clerk call the next item on the calendar?"

Glynis wondered if anyone else in the courtroom had caught the subtle but powerful shift that had occurred when Tamar Jager was no longer referred to as merely the Brants' "indentured servant girl," but, instead, became the eminent attorney Jeremiah Merrycoyf's "my client."

Erich Brant, to his credit, did not take vocal exception to the judge's ruling; not that it would have done him any good if he had. But when he came down the aisle past Glynis, she received not even an angry glance, so disturbed did he seem. When she heard the door behind her open, then close with a sharp report, she wondered if Erich's objection to an autopsy was truly based on a belief that his father's body should not, in his term, be desecrated. Or could he be more concerned about what an autopsy might reveal?

In the meantime, Merrycoyf had gone lumbering back to his seat. And Neva, before she sat down, sent Glynis what appeared to be a conciliatory nod; as if to say, *You could have been right.* Glynis breathed easier.

The clerk called the next item on the calendar. "Petition for sole custody of Tamar Jager, filed by her mother, Mrs. Elise Jager. In opposition to the petition is the father, Mr. Derek Jager."

"May I assume," asked a surprised-looking Judge Endicott, "that this is the same Tamar Jager about whom I've just heard? Mr. Merrycoyf?"

Again Merrycoyf rose to his feet to answer, "Yes, Your Honor, I believe it is."

"Very well. Are both parties here?"

Glynis had sat forward with a start, looking around the courtroom for Derek Jager, whom she hadn't seen enter. As Elise Jager passed her on the aisle, Glynis was troubled to note that the Waterloo attorney Orrin Makepeace Polk was also going forward, Polk's resemblance to a ferret more pronounced every time she had the misfortune to see him. How could he be involved in this?

"Your Honor," said Polk in his shrill voice, "I am here representing Mr. Derek Jager, sir."

"And where is your client?"

"Mr. Jager received the show cause order late yesterday,

Your Honor, only an hour or two before he was scheduled to leave Seneca County. On important business," Polk added. "At that time he retained my services."

"Are you ready to proceed on such short notice, Mr. Polk?"

"Oh, yes, indeed, Your Honor! Absolutely ready, and eager to proceed."

Judge Endicott's thick brows raised only slightly before he turned to address Elise Jager. "You are the petitioner, Mrs. Jager?"

"Yes, I am, sir."

"According to the calendar, you are appearing, madam, on your own behalf?"

"Please, Your Honor," came the voice of a rather young, nice-looking man who was hurrying up the aisle, and whom Glynis recognized as M. B. Blaustein of the Waterloo law firm of Blauvelt & Blaustein. "Your Honor," said Blaustein somewhat breathlessly, "I hope you will accept an apology for my tardiness. I have just this morning been retained as counsel for Mrs. Jager, sir."

"I am very glad to hear it," Judge Endicott responded, removing his spectacles. "I've had only one prior case involving the recent statute allowing mothers to request custody, and the new law has raised some profound issues. And, given what has already come to pass here this afternoon, I would imagine there will be some complications. Are you ready to proceed, Mr. Blaustein?"

"No, sir, I am not ready. My client and I came today solely to answer the calendar. I need more time to prepare, as there are contentious matters in this case, Your Honor. I need to investigate all the factors involved, and would like to have this hearing scheduled for next week."

Judge Endicott had begun to nod, when Orrin Polk stepped forward.

"Your Honor," protested Polk, "I have a subpoenaed witness here and, frankly, sir, I don't want to take the risk of him leaving the court's jurisdiction. I therefore earnestly request that this witness be heard today."

Whom could Polk be talking about? Glynis wondered uneasily. The witness must be a hostile one, else Polk would not be so worried about a possible disappearance. She turned to look over the courtroom and then saw the man several rows back who had come in just after Elise Jager; in his early fifties, Glynis guessed, the man had a short-bearded jaw thrust forward in a combative manner. His brows were the same light brown color as his hair, and his blue eyes were deepset and sharp. Glynis felt certain that she hadn't seen this man before today.

Judge Endicott, his frown and spectacles back in place, asked Polk, "Just who is this witness—and is his testimony critical to this case?"

"Extremely critical, Your Honor! His name, sir, is John Humphrey Noyes, and he is the leader of the infamous Oneida Community just east of Syracuse."

Oh, dear Lord! Glynis thought, gripping the seat of her chair. She recognized the man's name immediately, having seen it often enough in newspapers, usually being denounced by members of the western New York clergy in connection with his "free love" commune at Oneida. Judge Endicott's expression didn't change, though, so perhaps it was not only the Seneca Falls newspaper that he avoided.

In contrast, Elise Jager's response to Polk's request was unmistakably distressed. And now Glynis remembered Liam Cleary's stammered report about the man in Mrs. Jager's hotel room. Might that man possibly have been, by some long stretch of the imagination, the controversial John Humphrey Noyes? If so, heaven help her.

Attorney M. B. Blaustein had in the meantime sent Elise Jager a baffled look. And she, hiding her words behind her hand, was now telling him something that made him suddenly swivel toward the judge.

"Your Honor," said the attorney, in a voice less confident

than that of his previous statements, "we filed as petitioners, sir, and we have the right to be heard first. Therefore I urgently request, again, that this hearing be scheduled on the court's calendar no sooner than next week."

"Mr. Polk," said Judge Endicott, "is it my understanding that you wish to call this witness now?"

"If you please, Your Honor," Polk responded in an excessively deferential manner that Glynis found grating. "There is considerable legal precedent, sir, for allowing a witness to be called out of turn."

"I am aware of the legal precedent, counselor," retorted the judge. Therein followed a long silence while Judge Endicott again removed his spectacles, this time examining them minutely as if for flaws. He finally replaced them, saying, "Under the circumstances, Mr. Polk, and since your witness is not a resident of this county, it makes sense to allow him to testify today—out of turn."

"Thank you, Your Honor!"

"But sir," Blaustein argued, "I've had no time to prepare for—"

"You'll have opportunity next week, Mr. Blaustein," came the short reply from the judge. "I hereby schedule the testimony of the witness Mr. Noyes, in this custody proceeding, for three o'clock this afternoon. Mr. Clerk, continue the calendar call."

The clerk, however, handed the calendar up to him.

Judge Endicott frowned, and said to no one in particular, "It seems we have yet another item today which concerns Tamar Jager, one just added to the calendar. You might want to stay for this with your client, Mr. Blaustein. You, too, Mr. Polk."

The judge nodded to the clerk, and sat back in his chair, reaching under his robe to withdraw a white handkerchief. Glynis had no doubt as to what purpose it would be put.

The clerk read, "Petition for protective custody of Tamar

Jager, submitted by the constable of Seneca Falls, Cullen Stuart."

"All right, Constable Stuart," said Judge Endicott, employing the handkerchief with vigor to his spectacles. "What is *this* about?"

Cullen, who had already walked to the bench, answered, "Your Honor, I am requesting protective custody for the girl, pending her recovery from shotgun wounds. Since she has made a confession—whether under extenuating circumstances or not—she should, theoretically, be locked up. But Dr. Cardoza-Levy has said the girl isn't well enough to be removed from medical care at this time."

"Is that true, Doctor?" asked Judge Endicott.

"Yes, Your Honor. She remains absolutely in need of medical care."

"I can anticipate," said the judge, replacing his handkerchief and his spectacles, "that we have the potential for a murder trial here. For how long will this medical need exist?"

"I can't say exactly, sir. The girl is extremely malnourished"—Neva shot a glowering look at Orrin Polk— "and that will certainly retard the healing process."

Judge Endicott turned to Cullen. "What is your suggestion, Constable?"

"That Dr. Cardoza-Levy be granted protective custody at this time," Cullen answered.

"Mr. Merrycoyf," the judge said, "do you have any objection?"

Merrycoyf again hoisted himself to his feet. "None whatsoever, Your Honor. It is, I believe, a most satisfactory solution." That said, he sat down rather heavily.

"Excuse me, sir," M. B. Blaustein interjected as he came forward again, "but I understood that custody of Tamar Jager was to be decided upon the petition of my client. Since her daughter has confessed to murder, Your Honor, Mrs.

Jager wants to be sure she will take part in selecting the best legal defense available."

She *has* the best, Glynis thought with some irritation.

And indeed, to her satisfaction, Judge Endicott gave Elise Jager a wry smile, and said, "You needn't worry about that, madam."

Orrin Polk's long neck snaked forward as he immediately objected, "Your Honor, with all due respect to my colleague, Mr. Merrycoyf, my client will most certainly want an attorney of his own choosing. For *his* daughter, sir."

Off came the spectacles. After which Judge Endicott appeared to be staring into space. What he saw there remained a mystery until, the spectacles again in place, he asked, "Does anyone here know the story of the judicious biblical king Solomon?"

Glynis, despite her anxiety, had to smile at the singular aptness of the question. The judge evidently saw the smile, as he nodded to her, saying, "Yes, I expect a librarian would know."

He leaned over the bench toward the clerk and said, "Until I've ruled on the petition of Mrs. Elise Jager, I direct that protective custody of Tamar Jager be granted to Dr. Cardoza-Levy. And we will now adjourn until the proceeding scheduled for three o'clock."

23

When the will of God is done on earth as it is in heaven, there will be no marriage. . . . In a holy community, there is no more reason why sexual intercourse should be restricted by law, than why eating and drinking should.

—John Humphrey Noyes, 1837

A short time later, Glynis again entered the courtroom. Merrycoyf, however, together with Neva and Cullen, had pleaded the necessity of returning to Seneca Falls. Opportunely, M. B. Blaustein had requested and received from Merrycoyf permission to speak with Tamar Jager, and the lawyer offered Glynis transport if she wished to stay in Waterloo for the afternoon hearing. Since she thought there was something to be learned here, she accepted his offer.

After taking the seat she had earlier occupied, only a minute or two passed before Elise Jager, looking strained, and M. B. Blaustein, looking preoccupied, filed back into the room. They were followed by the tall, seemingly unconcerned John Humphrey Noyes. Orrin Makepeace Polk entered alone. Deservedly so, Glynis thought.

She was scolding herself for this meanness when the Waterloo bailiff appeared, shouting "Oyez! Oyez! Let all who have business before the court come forward and you shall be heard. All rise."

When Judge Endicott had settled himself on the bench,

the small group reseated themselves. Apparently satisfied that his spectacles were securely placed, at least for the time being, the judge straightened. At which point Orrin Polk sprang to his feet to say, "Your Honor, may I approach the bench?"

"We haven't begun yet," said Judge Endicott, a frown already restored.

"No, sir, but I have a matter that I would like Your Honor to address before we do," stated Polk.

"Very well, come forward."

If Polk had expected a private conference, Glynis guessed he must have been disappointed when Judge Endicott motioned for M. B. Blaustein to join them. There followed several minutes of hushed but apparently lively conversation, which Glynis strained unsuccessfully to overhear.

Judge Endicott then addressed the courtroom, which consisted of the bailiff, the clerk, the two lawyers, Elise Jager, John Humphrey Noyes, and Glynis. Not exactly a standing-room-only crowd, she thought, her curiosity aroused.

"It has been brought to my attention," Judge Endicott announced, and Glynis found to her surprise that he was looking straight at her, "that portions of today's testimony may prove inappropriate for the tender sensibilities of a lady. Since one of the only two ladies present is directly involved in this hearing, the caveat would seem to be directed solely at yourself, Miss Tryon."

Glynis was so dumbfounded that she couldn't respond. She just sat there, thinking that she must look like a simpleton, and also thinking that now wild horses couldn't drag her from this room. However, she could *not* think how to phrase this in unmistakable but, of course, lady-like fashion.

"Would it be safe to assume, Miss Tryon," asked Judge Endicott, and she saw a twitch at the corners of his mouth, "that as a librarian you may occasionally have contact with material that would not be, shall we say, seemly for those with delicate constitutions?"

"Yes, that would be safe to assume, Your Honor," Glynis managed to reply.

"Then you are capable of exercising your own judgment in this matter. Needless to say, if you are at any time offended, you should leave."

Glynis nodded, murmuring "Thank you, sir," but decided that this was a damned-if-she-did, damned-if-she-didn't proposition: if she left she would miss the promising testimony; if she didn't, she would be branded less than a lady. But probably only by the ignominious Polk, who had brought up the subject, she'd wager anything, to embarrass her—and, by association, Polk's nemesis Merrycoyf.

"Therefore," Judge Endicott was now saying, "since everyone has been well and truly cautioned, I would like to think we can at last move forward. Mr. Blaustein, do you have something to say regarding your client's custody petition before Mr. Polk's witness is called?"

"Yes, Your Honor."

"Proceed."

M. B. Blaustein rose and went forward to stand before the bench. "I would like to again state for the record, Your Honor, that I need opportunity to investigate this situation with thoroughness. Petitioner's daughter was sold into servitude by her husband, the girl's father, Derek Jager. Against the express wishes of my client."

"Objection!" declared Polk. "Your Honor, that is completely irrelevant."

"It is not irrelevant, Mr. Polk," responded the judge. "This application is governed by Section 9 of Chapter 90, adopted by the New York state legislature." He removed his spectacles and for several minutes shuffled, scowling, through a stack of papers, until he raised his head to ask, "Mr. Blaustein, do you by chance have at hand that section of Chapter 90?"

"I do, Your Honor." Blaustein quickly went to his table to the right of the bench and, almost immediately, extracted from a folder several sheets of paper.

"Please read the pertinent section into the record, Mr. Blaustein," directed the judge, donning his spectacles.

M. B. Blaustein began, "Chapter 90 is entitled 'An Act Concerning the Rights and Liabilities of Husband and Wife.' And Section 9 states: 'Every married woman is hereby constituted and declared to be the joint guardian of her children, with her husband, with equal powers, rights, and duties in regard to them, with the husband.' "

"Your Honor," protested Polk, "that piece of legislation will unquestionably be ruled unconstitutional, and hence overturned. Women are not by nature suited for the responsibility which that law entails. It passed only because of the disruptive public pressure brought to bear by subversive females who are unworthy of motherhood to begin with."

"That will be enough, Mr. Polk," remarked Judge Endicott, although Glynis wished he did not look quite so amused. "Let us have no more lobbying."

Polk sat down abruptly, but looked not in the least chastened.

"Proceed, Mr. Blaustein."

M. B. Blaustein, not visibly intimidated but clearly irritated by this exchange, continued, "Your Honor, in the course of the girl Tamar's servitude, the girl became mute. The reasons for this phenomenon are at present unknown, but the matter deserves thorough investigation. And, in addition, there is a further complication in that the girl's father, Derek Jager, was a business associate of the recently deceased Roland Brant."

Judge Endicott whipped off his spectacles and stared at Blaustein for a moment before turning his stare on Polk, and asking, "Is this true, counselor?"

"Yes, sir. But the only relevance it has here is that the death of Roland Brant has precipitated Mr. Jager's natural concern for his daughter's future welfare."

Glynis couldn't be sure whether the muffled groan she heard came from herself or not, but she was the recipient of raised brows from Judge Endicott. Nonetheless, Polk's statement raised in her mind the stark question of why Derek Jager was contesting this custody request by the girl's mother. Retribution against his wife? Pride? Or so that he could sell Tamar to someone else?

"As you see, Your Honor," Blaustein concluded, "it is imperative that these important issues be scrupulously examined before custody can be awarded. I thank you, sir."

Polk was on his feet even before Blaustein sat down. Judge Endicott made a few notes, then said, "Very well, Mr. Polk, proceed. No, on second thought, I would like to know why your client indentured his daughter."

"The long and the short of it, sir, was that my client took this action to protect the girl—and so indentured her to one of the leading families in this county, Your Honor—because his wife was then, and remains now, an unfit mother."

Glynis risked a glance at Elise Jager, who, although pale, sat in rigid silence.

And when Blaustein rose to object, Judge Endicott waved him back into his chair. "May I assume that we will have substantive evidence of that serious charge, Mr. Polk?"

"Yes, Your Honor, and to that purpose I would like Mr. John Humphrey Noyes called to the stand."

Judge Endicott peered over his spectacles and said, "Mr. Noyes, please come forward."

After Noyes was sworn in, he settled himself into the witness chair with aplomb. At the same time, he radiated an almost palpable energy, as if at any moment he might spring from the chair like a jack-in-the-box. The pugnacious thrust of his chin, which Glynis had noted earlier, did not appear to have receded.

Mr. Polk began, "What is your name and place of residence, sir?"

"John Humphrey Noyes, and I reside in Oneida, New York."

The man's manner was affable and his voice pleasant; both held warmth and a controlled intensity.

"Did you receive a subpoena requiring you to appear today, Mr. Noyes?"

"You should know, Mr. Polk, since you ordered it," the man answered, smiling.

Polk said to the judge, "May I instruct the witness to answer yes or no, Your Honor?"

Judge Endicott, even now beginning to show signs of strain, answered, "I think I can gather that this is a hostile witness, if that's what you're after, Mr. Polk. Now please get on with it."

"Mr. Noyes," continued Polk, "are you a friend of the petitioner, Elise Jager? Answer yes or no."

"Yes and no, Mr. Polk."

"Your Honor—"

"Yes, yes, Mr. Polk," sighed the judge. "Mr. Noyes, please answer the question."

"I am Elise Jager's spiritual advisor, Your Honor," replied Noyes.

Polk started to protest, but a look from Judge Endicott cut him short. "Very well, Mr. Noyes," Polk snapped, "you are Elise Jager's spiritual advisor."

"That is what I said."

"And was it in the capacity of spiritual advisor that you spent last evening in Seneca Falls in the company of Mrs. Jager? *In her hotel room?*"

"Yes," said Noyes blandly.

There was no doubt that Polk now had Judge Endicott's complete attention.

"Isn't it a fact, Mr. Noyes," Polk went on after a melodramatic pause, "that you have known Elise Jager for many years?"

"Yes, for some years."

"Did you know her when she was performing as an *actress* in New York City, Mr. Noyes?" Polk asked with a curl of his lip.

Ah, thought Glynis, that answered some of her questions,

and she glanced at Elise Jager, who sat ramrod straight with her eyes trained on Polk as if waiting for an entrance cue. While actresses were seldom viewed with favor, Glynis doubted that this in itself would sway Judge Endicott. Although a man who clearly eschewed newspapers, she knew his reading taste to be cosmopolitan.

John Humphrey Noyes had answered, "Yes."

Polk, with a quick look at his notes, then asked, "Isn't it a fact, Mr. Noyes, that Elise Jager followed you to the Oneida Community?"

"Elise Jager follows God, Mr. Polk, which is why she came to us at Oneida," Noyes answered with amiable calm.

"God. Oh, yes, God," Polk intoned, gazing upward. "And is it true, Mr. Noyes, that you claim to have direct communication with God?"

"I wait and watch for indications of God's will."

"So your answer is yes?"

"I am the spiritual father and liberating authority of the family at Oneida, just as God is the—"

"Thank you," interrupted Polk, "for that succinct description of your position in the Oneida commune. And as father of the family, and one called upon to relay God's intentions, did you draw up something for your children called 'Rules for Sexual Intercourse?'"

Judge Endicott, who had begun to reshuffle his papers, stopped with brows lifted.

"I did, yes," answered Noyes.

"And isn't it true that members of your family indulge in unrestrained sexual activity?"

"On the contrary, restraint is what my rules address. I alone have the spiritual authority to ensure that godliness prevails in sexual relations."

While Polk looked gleeful, Glynis observed, Judge Endicott seemed to look . . . wary.

"Mr. Noyes, isn't it a fact that you do not permit marriage in your community of followers?"

"Not marriage in the conventional sense, that is true, because it encourages selfish love. We follow the doctrine of what we term *complex marriage.*"

"Yes, it certainly must be complex," agreed Polk, "what with women and men indulging themselves in sexual intercourse whenever the spirit moves them. And isn't it a fact, Mr. Noyes, that they are urged by you to do so?"

"It is a natural function—"

"Ah, yes," said Polk, "natural. I believe you have stated that carnal activity should be approached in the same manner as eating and drinking, correct?"

"Not quite, Mr. Polk, but it is simply another expression of God's love for us."

"For *us,*" Polk repeated. "But isn't it true, Mr. Noyes, that at Oneida young girls at puberty are introduced to sexual practices by you personally? Isn't that contrary to your protestations of unselfishness?"

M. B. Blaustein rose to say, "Your Honor, I object. Surely this salacious line of questioning is totally irrelevant."

"I will sustain that objection," Judge Endicott ruled. "Mr. Polk, do you suppose that at some point you might share with the court what exactly this has to do with the subject of today's hearing? Which was not scheduled, to my knowledge, to offer a discourse on sexual codes, however interesting they may be."

"Your Honor, there is relevance here, and I am getting to that."

"Please get to it soon, Mr. Polk."

"Yes, Your Honor. Mr. Noyes, let us return to the subject of family. Do the children who live at Oneida have parents? Fathers and mothers?"

"Not in the usual sense, no—"

"Don't you mean," Polk interrupted, "not usual in the biblical sense? The legal sense? The decent and moral sense?"

"All members of the community act as parents, in order

to obliterate the sin of possessiveness," Noyes explained patiently.

"Mr. Polk," the judge reminded, "*soon!*"

"Yes, sir. Now, Mr. Noyes, is Mrs. Derek Jager—oh, excuse me, that would be too conventional a title—is Elise Jager a member of the Oneida family?"

Noyes's smile indicated that he took no umbrage at Polk's gibe, and answered, "Elise Jager lives at Oneida, yes."

Polk very nearly levitated. "And *this,* Your Honor," he addressed the judge, "*this* is the depravity to which the poor, young girl Tamar Jager would be subjected if custody is given to the woman who claims she is a *mother!*"

"It does bear serious consideration, Mr. Polk," acknowledged Judge Endicott. "Now, if you have completed your questioning, and I sincerely hope that you have . . . ?"

Polk, with great indignation, declared, "Your Honor, there are other illegal, sacrilegious, and immoral practices that take place at the Oneida den of iniquity, but I will rest if you so direct."

"I so direct, Mr. Polk."

"Your Honor," said M. B. Blaustein, now on his feet but looking a trifle pallid, "before I cross-examine this witness, may I have a few moments to confer with my client?" When the judge frowned, Blaustein reminded him, "I've had no chance to prepare for this, Your Honor." He shot a look of contempt at Polk, who was smiling with self-satisfaction.

"Very well, I will recess for fifteen minutes," said Judge Endicott.

Glynis had been waiting at M. B. Blaustein's table, and when he returned, she handed him a note she had written during the recess. It contained a question that she requested he put to John Humphrey Noyes. Blaustein scanned the note, and although he looked mystified by it, he nodded.

"Proceed, Mr. Blaustein," said Judge Endicott, once again settled, his spectacles again in place.

"Mr. Noyes," began M. B. Blaustein, "at your Oneida Community, isn't it true that no one is forced to participate in your complex marriage . . . activities?"

"Yes, that is true, though all are urged to do so. But no one is compelled to do other than the routine chores of the community, which are divided equally—equally between men and women."

"Would you give the court an example of that?"

"The cooking and the laundry. Those duties are assigned on a revolving basis, so that no one is unnecessarily burdened for any great length of time with tasks he or she might find distasteful."

"Is there leisure time available?" asked Blaustein.

"Oh, yes, there is sufficient time for recreation."

As Polk snickered, Judge Endicott sent him a flinty look over the unusually motionless spectacles.

"What kind of recreation, Mr. Noyes?"

"We hold Sunday afternoon picnics for our neighbors, and frequently conduct musicales. And theater as well."

"And does Elise Jager participate in those theater events?"

"Indeed, yes. She often directs as well as performs in many of the productions. Elise is a splendid actress, which is why I encouraged her to come to Oneida. Her husband, I understand, forced her to abandon the theater after their marriage."

Standing at his table, Blaustein picked up Glynis's note, scanned it again, and asked, "Mr. Noyes, did you ever have occasion to meet Roland Brant at the Oneida Community?"

"Objection," Polk barked, jumping to his feet. "Irrelevant and immaterial."

"Objection overruled," declared Judge Endicott. "Mr. Polk, I gave you leave to pursue a prurient line of questioning in an attempt to reach the truth in this custody matter. Tamar Jager has been at the heart of all that has gone before me today, and if attorney Blaustein's question assists in any way to determine this girl's future, I will allow it."

Bravo, Judge Endicott, Glynis silently applauded. And

she suddenly saw that he had shown her another vantage point from which to view Roland Brant's murder. She also saw that for the first time John Humphrey Noyes was looking somewhat less than supremely self-confident.

"Mr. Noyes, shall I repeat the question?" asked Blaustein.

"No, no," he quickly replied. "I believe that, yes, I may have met Roland Brant on the perhaps one or two occasions that he came to purchase some of Oneida's fine cutlery," answered Noyes. He turned to Judge Endicott, saying, "You may have heard of our steel traps, the knives made in our own forge, and our invention of a revolving oven to temper steel."

Judge Endicott's expression indicated mild interest, but Blaustein looked unimpressed as, glancing again at Glynis's note, he asked, "Did you also have occasion to meet Tamar Jager's father, Derek Jager?"

Orrin Polk started to object, but apparently thought better of it after seeing Judge Endicott glower.

"I believe that's possible," Noyes nodded. "He was, as I recall, a business associate of Roland Brant's."

Blaustein swung around to look at Glynis, and she gave him a brief nod. He then turned back to the witness.

"Thank you, Mr. Noyes. I have no further questions of this witness, Your Honor."

At this point Noyes looked exceedingly cheerful, Glynis thought, for a man who had heard his life's work described as iniquitous. In fact, he sat in the witness chair, a slight smile on his face, and stared toward the window, perhaps listening for God's intent. Or Noyes might be thinking that, as Harriet Peartree would put it, Orrin Polk was small potatoes and few in the hill compared to God. And, needless to say, to himself.

Judge Endicott unexpectedly asked, "I am rather curious about something, Mr. Noyes. With all the activity that Mr. Polk has described as taking place at Oneida, how do you people manage to find time to feed and clothe and house yourselves?"

"Those are pleasurable religious obligations, Your

Honor," Noyes answered with a beneficent smile. "It is our duty to God to take joy in all that we do in His kingdom, and you have perhaps heard of our magnificent horticulture. You should visit our landscaped gardens, sir, and observe for yourself our guiding principle: that beauty is inseparable from utility."

Glynis covered a smile with her hand at Judge Endicott's obvious curiosity. If she'd had the opportunity, she undoubtedly would have asked Noyes the same question.

None, so far as she knew, were held captive at Oneida; they could leave anytime they chose. Moreover, the commune, when subjected to a particularly vicious attack from local clergy, had received the almost unqualified support of their neighbors, the largely Protestant farming community that surrounded Oneida.

Which, she supposed, was one thing for the adults that chose to live there—but what about the youngsters? Much as she disliked Orrin Polk, she thought his point well taken; as benign as Noyes appeared to be, she couldn't help but compare his use of power over young females to that of Roland Brant. A power that was centuries old and unchanging.

Judge Endicott, suddenly looking judiciously grim, said to the two lawyers, "I must tell you both that, given what I have heard here so far, I'm inclined to rule that Tamar Jager, at seventeen, has as much right to determine her own future as anyone in this room. And I will hear testimony from the girl herself before deciding this matter. Court adjourned."

Glynis was impressed, and wished she could say so. As she rose from the chair, she began to realize that Noyes's testimony today had cast light on some treacherous possibilities. She wondered if the man was aware of them. Or was he simply an unwitting accomplice?

24

I am more and more convinced that man is a dangerous creature; and that power, whether vested in many or a few, is ever grasping, and like the grave, cries "Give, give!"

—Abigail Adams, 1775

On the carriage ride back to Seneca Falls, Glynis listened with half an ear to M. B. Blaustein's measured and mournful analysis of the afternoon's proceeding. She tried but couldn't manage to keep up with his comments, and thus simply nodded periodically.

Over the past days she'd accumulated so many odd scraps of information—which she thought were somehow related if only she could bring them together—that her mind was behaving like a sieve. It wouldn't hold onto a single idea long enough to consider it before it drained away and another one came pouring in to take its place. Followed by another and another. She wondered how much this had to do with her feelings in relation to Roland Brant.

At first she had not believed him capable of such evil; and surely merciless assaults on a defenseless young girl could only be named evil. Then, when belief became unavoidable—listening to Tamar the night before—she had experienced a ferocious anger. But now the anger seemed to be joined with a grievous melancholy. She had tried to balance what she had recently learned of Brant with his many acts of charity, his contributions to numerous Seneca Falls organizations, even the bestowing of a new set of bells in his church. Had all that beneficence been simply to make the town beholden to him? To increase his influence?

And what had Shakespeare, the voice for all seasons, said? *The evil that men do lives after them; the good is oft interred with their bones.* It was probably true. No matter how hard Glynis tried, she could not see past the worst of Roland Brant to remember the best.

And the most frightening part of it was that the worst had been so nearly invisible.

In Waterloo she had learned some significant things. While she had believed that Roland Brant's family and staff members were those most suspect in his murder, she now included Derek Jager, whom Roland Brant might have admitted through that library door. She recalled Jager's angry words when he had been with Erich in the library; Roland Brant might have double-crossed his own business associate.

Would Brant have admitted to his library Gerard Gagnon? Glynis couldn't discount it. And since she'd learned long ago not to trust alleged arrivals by train, or stagecoach, or canal boat, she supposed Elise Jager might have secretly arrived Sunday night, rather than Monday afternoon. Glynis hadn't, after all, actually seen the woman leave the train. And if the girl's mother had suddenly discovered what Roland Brant had done to her daughter . . .

"Miss Tryon, I'm in Seneca Falls," M. B. Blaustein's voice cut into her thoughts. "But are *you* here?" he asked, smiling.

"Barely," she admitted with embarrassment, looking around to discover they had arrived at the livery on Fall Street. She shaded her eyes with a hand, as the sun had begun its descent and light shimmered off the surface of the canal with the blinding glare of a sunlit mirror. *A mirror,* she suddenly thought.

She thanked Blaustein, wished him well in the custody

proceeding, then walked briskly in the direction of the lockup. If she was correct, however, Judge Endicott might not have to make a custody decision.

She found only one deputy in Cullen's office.

"You don't have to worry about Sledge," Zeph told her when he opened the door to the lockup's holding cells. "He's gone. Long gone if he knows what's good for him."

"Cullen released him?" Glynis asked in surprise as they walked down the hallway.

"Nothing to hold him on. I didn't see him fire that shotgun, and Sledge swore it was his pal doing all the shooting."

"But Sledge would swear to that, wouldn't he?"

Zeph shrugged. "There was a wanted notice out for the girl, you know, so he didn't do anything illegal—least not that we can prove. Anyway, Constable made him sign a sworn statement that Gagnon had killed that runty guy in self-defense. Then he told Sledge to get out of his town and not come back."

"So for company, he's keeping *me* here!" came Gerard Gagnon's voice as he moved to the bars at the front of the holding cell.

The man sounded as angry as Glynis had expected.

"Zeph, I don't have to stand out here in the hall to talk to Mr. Gagnon, do I?" she asked.

"Since the constable's not around . . . what did he tell you?"

"Earlier today he said I could visit Mr. Gagnon. He didn't say I had to do it through the bars of a cell."

"Ah, but I'm a dangerous character, Miss Tryon," Gerard told her. "Certainly more dangerous than a half-wit bounty hunter armed with a shotgun!"

"Gagnon, why are you making this so hard on yourself?" Zeph asked as if he didn't expect an answer.

"Zeph, he's not a convicted criminal. So why don't you unlock this cell door," Glynis suggested, "and then leave that door into the office open. That way," she added, "you'll hear me if I cry out." She hoped this would be heard by Zeph as a poor attempt at gallows humor.

He stood looking at her, then gave Gagnon a longer look. "If anything happens, Constable will string me up," he said finally, reaching forward to unlock the cell door. "You give me your word, Gagnon, you won't try anything stupid?"

Gerard looked as if he were ready to deliver a less than cooperative reply, but after seeing Glynis's warning glance, apparently reconsidered. "My word, Deputy," he finally said.

When Zeph had gone back into the office, Glynis swung open the cell door and stepped inside. Gerard Gagnon's dark hair was shaggy, his face too lean, his frame too gaunt, but he had a quality that reminded Glynis a little of Jacques Sundown; she hoped, however, that he was more approachable than Jacques had once been. She didn't have years to wait while this man learned to trust her.

Gerard gestured for her to sit on the only thing available, a rumpled cot. "My home is your home, Miss Tryon," he said with a sardonic smile, and quickly lowered himself to the floor to sit with his back against the cell wall. "How is the girl?" he asked, the concern in his voice disputing his offhand manner.

"She was much improved this morning," Glynis answered. "One of the reasons I came was to tell you that. I hope that you'll be released soon and can see her yourself."

"You're not alone in hoping that. And thank you. But you said that was one reason?"

"Yes. I wonder if I might ask you several things that I'm curious about?"

"Depends," he said warily. "Would you mind telling me if you think I killed Roland Brant?"

"I think you might have. But you're not the most obvious suspect, at least not at the moment."

"Who is? Not Tamar!"

Glynis shook her head. "Not Tamar. But you're not really in a position to ask about anyone else, Mr. Gagnon. It would be more to your advantage, and to Tamar's, to help in finding the real killer."

He nodded. "Ask away. But since you've been fairly straightforward with me, I'll tell you that for months I had every intention of killing Roland Brant."

"Why didn't you?"

Gerard looked surprised. "You're not shocked by that?"

"Not particularly. Not after what I've learned about the man."

"What have you learned? Was it from Tamar?" he asked, the distress in his voice clearly genuine.

"Tell me why you didn't kill Brant."

He seemed to think about it before answering, "I couldn't. I just couldn't bring myself to do it. Call it lack of nerve—or maybe I just didn't want to dirty my hands on him."

Glynis was aware that she wanted to believe Gerard, and so she couldn't trust herself to remove him yet from suspicion. "Tamar told me that you found her in the swamp." When he nodded, she went on, "Did she speak to you then?"

"No. And she didn't say anything that made sense until that bounty hunter shot Keeper. My dog," he added.

"Yes, I know Keeper. Were you told that he's with Tamar at the refuge dispensary?"

"The deputy said he was."

"Dr. Cardoza-Levy removed the pellets from Keeper's shoulder. Did you meet her?"

"Yes, when we left Tamar there," answered Gerard. "Before we came here and the constable decided I was a menace to society."

"Constable Stuart is afraid you'll leave town. Leave quickly and lose yourself in the swamp, and possibly take Tamar with you."

"He could be right," Gerard said. "And I'd take her— if she wanted to go. You just asked if Tamar spoke when I found her. She didn't, not to me, but she said a few things in her sleep."

"What things?"

"The first night she cried, and while most of what she said made no sense, she kept repeating 'The blood, the blood.' As if she were Lady Macbeth."

Immediately Glynis made the biased decision that a man who knew Shakespeare could not be all bad. "Can you guess what that might have meant?" she asked him.

"I think so. I told her the next day that she'd had a few splotches of blood on her hands when I found her, but that they were probably from an open cut on her own arm. She seemed relieved."

As was Glynis. It had been the last obstacle to believing Tamar innocent.

"But I couldn't help with her other nightmare," Gerard went on. "She kept saying over and over 'Don't hurt me.' "

His tone suggested a growing anger that he didn't bother to restrain when he said, "At first, she was terrified of me, backing away and cringing every time I came anywhere near her. I guessed right away that someone had hurt her badly, Miss Tryon. I assume you know what I mean by that?"

Glynis wondered how much of his conjecture to confirm; the man was intelligent, and he had already recognized the substance of it. Her hesitation was for Tamar's sake, but she decided that she couldn't know what was best for the girl. And that the truth was not negotiable. "Yes, I know what you mean, and I'm afraid you're right," she said at last. "Tamar told me some of it."

"That filthy swine Brant did it! Didn't he?" Gerard demanded, leaping to his feet. "I should have damn well killed him months ago!"

The rage in his voice brought Zeph racing down the hall, revolver drawn.

"There's no danger, Zeph," Glynis insisted as the deputy

stood there with his gun trained on Gerard. "And he has every reason to be angry."

"Not with you, he doesn't."

"It has nothing to do with me," she assured him, thankful that Gerard was now silent. Not that he had to say anything; his eyes were fierce, his fury all too evident.

"You finished, Miss Tryon?" Zeph asked, his eyes still fixed on Gerard.

"No, I'm not. Would you please go back to the office?"

"Nope, sorry."

Glynis had supposed as much, and turned to Gerard. "Mr. Gagnon, he's dead. What he did is past and done and it can't be changed. But if you care for Tamar, you have to try to look, both of you, beyond that past. He's *dead!*"

She could see Zeph's confusion, but this was not the time for explanation. "I have one more question, Mr. Gagnon."

He had been standing with his back to her, and when he turned, the rage was still there, but she could see that he was controlling it. "All right, yes, what is it?" he said distractedly.

Zeph had stepped back into the hall, but he stood there with his revolver, watching Gerard's every move.

"It's about your father's factory," Glynis said, aware that by asking she risked another outburst, but she needed to know. "When Roland Brant foreclosed, did he give any indication what the building would be used for?"

"Not to me," Gerard answered, his voice tight but steadier than Glynis had expected. "Why are you asking?"

Ignoring his question, she said, "When did Roland Brant actually take possession of it?"

"Four months ago."

"So . . . early February of this year?"

"Yes! Why, what does it matter?"

"Because it's located across the canal from my library, and it occurred to me earlier today that I've never seen much activity over there."

"Could be it's standing empty," Gerard said bitterly.

"Maybe Roland Brant just took pleasure in grinding people under his heel."

Standing with Zeph outside Cullen's office, Glynis looked across the canal at the stone warehouse.

"Zeph, do you think Gerard Gagnon is a killer?"

"If he's not, he does a pretty good imitation of one!"

"Perhaps. But rage doesn't necessarily lead to violent action. I suppose you have to tell Cullen about that incident back there?"

"Yes."

"Of course," Glynis sighed. "Well, for what it's worth, it was my fault. I brought up something almost certain to make Gerard, or anyone, enraged. And he didn't try to attack me—or you, Zeph."

"I had a gun."

"So did that bounty hunter."

Zeph scuffed at some loose dirt with the toe of his boot, and then responded, "Yeah, but Gagnon knew my gun was already loaded."

Glynis, shaking her head, sighed again. And thought that before too much more time passed, someone should take a look at that warehouse.

FRIDAY
May 31, 1861

25

—〰—

*Over 3,000 men from Seneca County took part in
the [Civil] War and many branches of the services
were represented. Companies A, C, and K of the
New York 33rd were comprised of men from
Seneca County, most of them from Seneca Falls
and Waterloo.*

—From *Seneca County History,*
edited by Betty Auten, historian

Glynis finished dressing in a green muslin gown, then went
to open her bedroom curtains. White clouds like mounds of
popped corn moved across a bright morning sky on what
was surely the last day Emma could make a decision about
whether the wedding would take place. And, in fact, it was
already too late to reach those out of town; Emma's father
and brothers must have long since caught the train from
Springfield, Illinois. At least, Glynis thought, she'd been too
tired to lie awake all night worrying. She had, though, fret-
ted for some time about maidens Emma and Bronwen and
Tamar, while staring at the moon-streaked ceiling of her
bedroom, but when sleep had finally come it had been
sound.

She left her room and on the way to the stairs heard ham-
mering, as well as several male voices coming from the direction of the Usher house next door. Glynis stepped to the
hall window and looked out. By this time the Usher grounds

had taken on the aspect of a fairyland. The flowering trees, standing like mannequins dressed in voluminous pink-and-white ruffled petticoats, encircled an open area of blue-green grass sprinkled with white violets. In the center of the grassed circle, what looked to be a latticed arch some eight or nine feet high was being constructed with supple poplar slats. Vanessa, resplendent in rich crimson, stood directing the production. The pastel shades of the trees, shrubs, and flower beds were as lovely as the misty landscapes of Oneida County artist Charlotte Coman, but it was the color of Vanessa's gown that drew Glynis's eyes like moths to a flame.

A half-formed image rose in her mind, but before it could take shape, she was distracted by movement below. Only then did she see the two figures who stood close together among the pines growing between the Usher and Peartree properties. While the couple might have taken pains to remove themselves from Vanessa's view, they must have forgotten the Peartree window. Or perhaps, Glynis thought while smiling, they were too involved to think of anything other than each other. When the two merged in an embrace, she backed away from the window and took her time descending the stairs.

After she'd walked out the front door and around the house, she signaled her approach with an overly hearty "Good morning!"

Emma gave a start, but Adam, as if she might slip away from him like Cinderella at midnight, kept one arm locked around her waist. And if Glynis had any doubt remaining, her niece's radiant face told her there would indeed be a wedding on the morrow.

"Good morning, Aunt Glynis." Emma greeted her in joyous voice. "Just see what Adam has brought me."

Adam stood grinning at Glynis as Emma handed her a maroon leather-bound sheaf of gilt-edged paper, the cover announcing in gold embossed letters that here was a copy—

albeit a very expensive one—of New York State's Chapter 90 law. Glynis experienced an odd prickle of *déjà vu*, but did not let on that she had recently become closely acquainted with at least some of this document.

"A unique and stylish wedding present, Adam, I must say," Glynis commented with a smile.

"I thought you'd approve, Aunt Glynis," answered Adam, and Emma gave a delighted laugh.

"She *is* your Aunt Glynis now, isn't she," Emma said to him, "or almost." She moved to stand beside Glynis, lifted the title page and pointed to Section 1. "Look, Aunt Glyn, there it is!"

Glynis read the entire section, a lengthy one, which began by stating, in effect, that any property of a woman, no matter how she came by it, *shall, notwithstanding her marriage, be and remain her sole and separate property and may be used, collected and invested by her in her own name; and shall not be subject to the interference or control of her husband.*

"It's all there in black and white—and gold," Emma sighed. "I am just so happy!" She gave Adam a smile laced with love. "And just look at what Miss Usher has done," she said to Glynis, turning toward fairyland. "Have you ever, *ever,* seen anything like it?"

Glynis could truthfully say that she had not. "When are your father and brothers arriving?" she asked.

"Papa's telegram said four this afternoon, so Adam and I will meet the train. They'll be staying at Carr's Hotel, and so will . . . everybody!" Emma exclaimed with a breathless, child-like excitement, as if she were just now beginning to enjoy the prospect of her wedding. "And Cousin Kathryn sent a wire from New York City saying that her train arrives at five. This will be fun!"

Glynis smiled at Emma's infectious joy, and hoped against hope that she wouldn't inquire after her cousin Bronwen. Perhaps a change of subject? "Adam, do you expect to see Gerard Gagnon today?" Glynis asked.

"I talked to Cullen first thing this morning," he answered. "Told him I didn't want to spend the day before my wedding preparing a writ of habeas corpus, but that I would if necessary. Cullen said I needn't bother. He'll not press the other charges. He does, though, have cause to hold Gagnon a while longer on suspicion of Roland Brant's murder. And I can't do anything about that."

Emma seemed not to notice these asides, perhaps because she was watching, obviously entranced, the huge sprays of fragrant orange blossoms being carried across the Usher yard. They would probably be used to decorate the nearly completed arch.

She turned to Glynis, who was beginning to back away toward the Peartree kitchen and the smell of coffee—but not fast enough. "Aunt Glyn, where's Cousin Bronwen?" she asked. "I didn't see her at all yesterday."

Glynis supposed she could tell Emma that her cousin had gone off ballooning for the United States Treasury Department, but it would sound too bizarre to be believable.

"I would guess," she answered, "that Bronwen is busily flying around to complete some unfinished tasks. I expect she'll appear any time now."

At least Glynis hoped that she would!

After she stopped at the library to reassure Jonathan that she would sometime actually return to work there, Glynis went to the lockup, where she again found only Zeph in Cullen's office.

"Dr. Cardoza-Levy" he said, accurately guessing what Glynis would ask, "is doing the Brant autopsy now."

"Where is Constable Stuart?"

"He's gone out to Tyre. Couple of men got knifed there last night in a tavern brawl."

"And Liam?"

"Up the river a ways. Some canaler reported a stolen mule."

"So you're the only one here."

"I'm it. Why?" Zeph asked, giving her a searching look; searching until it turned dubious. "You planning to do something?" He now regarded her with an expression that verged on one of alarm.

"Nothing that need concern you," Glynis said firmly.

It was essential that she go to the Brant house, and what with her family arriving later in the day, she needed to do it now. With a carriage, she could go there and be back before anyone even missed her.

A short time later, the buggy she had rented from Boone's Livery was bouncing up the Brants' gravel drive. She slowed the small gray mare, however, when ahead of her she heard voices, pounding noises, and the clatter of a wagon. Surely, she prayed, the wagon could not be coming toward her down the narrow drive. She listened for a minute and concluded that it sounded too far away. But what was going on at the house? she wondered, as she urged the mare forward.

Cullen would not approve her doing this alone, but since there was no one available to go with her, she felt she had little choice. Not if she were to find what she needed before it was found by someone else. If that hadn't already been done. She relied on her belief, though, that no one but she— she and Tamar—would know of it.

When the buggy rounded the last curve of the drive and Glynis looked ahead at the Italianate house, it became clear that she could not have picked a worse time.

A two-horse dray wagon, on the side of which had been painted PROPERTY OF SENECA COUNTY, stood in front of the porch steps. Four or five men were stringing a thick rope between wooden stakes that other men were pounding into the ground, apparently intending that a barrier would surround the house.

Glynis, puzzled and apprehensive, pulled the mare to a

stop. It was crucial that she gain access to the house, but how could she with a mob of men between her and it? Before she could devise a course of action, she recognized the burly frame and iron-gray hair of the Seneca County sheriff, Matt Fowler, who stood on the porch, leaning against a pillar. His presence complicated things further, as she recalled that he had the eyesight of an eagle.

She sat revising her original plan until her curiosity became too forceful to contain a second longer. After climbing from the buggy, she lifted out of it a large, empty wicker basket, then tethered the mare to a fence post and walked to the house, carrying the basket by its curved handle.

"Morning, Miss Tryon."

"Good morning, Sheriff Fowler," she answered, looking up at him from the foot of the porch steps. "I fear I've arrived at an inconvenient time."

"Depends what you've come for," said Fowler, chewing on a long stalk of grass.

"May I ask what's happened?"

"Well, you come on up here, Miss Tryon, and I'll show you."

She climbed the steps with misgiving, expecting at the very least that Erich, or even Konrad, would come hurtling through the doorway, demanding that she leave the property. She had anticipated that, however, and had an excuse ready. What she'd not anticipated was the sign at which Sheriff Fowler was pointing. It had been nailed to the front door and read: "NOTICE OF LEVY AND ATTACHMENT. BY ORDER OF THE SENECA COUNTY SHERIFF." Beneath this, Matt Fowler's signature was scrawled.

"I'm afraid I don't understand, Sheriff Fowler," she said, thoroughly bewildered because she knew the general meaning of the notice.

"I'm impounding Roland Brant's property. Seizing it at the direction of a creditor."

Glynis couldn't believe what she'd heard. But she knew Fowler too well to think he would be joking.

"You look surprised," he said, "but not any more than I'll bet I did. It's a shock, right?"

"Yes! Yes, it certainly is, Sheriff. A creditor, you said. Someone to whom Roland Brant owed money?"

Fowler took her arm and marched her back down the steps and a short distance from the house, before he said quietly, "It seems Mr. Roland Brant left quite a few people unpaid. Substantially unpaid. You might give your friend Constable Stuart that piece of news"—his voice dropped even lower—"since I know he's got a murder investigation on his hands. But you've earned some reputation yourself in that department."

His smile didn't seem to be a mocking one, and he would probably answer more questions, but Glynis was so stunned by this turn of events that she had to think hard before she could find one to ask.

"Sheriff, does the levy include all the property of Roland Brant?"

"All of it. I have a levy against his personal property and his interests in any realty."

"But that wouldn't include Mrs. Brant's . . . Mrs. *Helga* Brant's dower interest, would it?"

"No, you're right, Miss Tryon, it wouldn't. Can't include that."

Glynis nodded, attempting to see how this latest irregular piece might fit into the puzzle of Brant's death.

"Heard there was a confession to Brant's murder," commented Fowler. "That true?"

"It was a tainted confession, Sheriff, and it's extremely unlikely that it will hold up."

"That so. Hadn't heard that. So why are you here today?" He eyed the basket. "A social call?"

"Ah, yes, more or less. The family members are all home, aren't they?"

"No, not all of them, but—"

"Sheriff Fowler?" The call came from one of his men. "Sheriff, can you come over here?"

"Excuse me, Miss Tryon," he said and walked toward the newly strung barrier, where men were fastening to the rope a number of flags which bore the same message as the notice on the door. The sheriff clearly meant business.

While Glynis couldn't begin to guess what the overall implications of this seizure might be, she decided that nothing had altered the purpose of her coming here. She began strolling toward the porch, but went on past the steps and around a corner of the house. Once she knew that she was beyond sight of Sheriff Fowler, she moved more deliberately, while hoping that one of the family inside was not looking out a window. She was taking a chance by trespassing, but she needed to confirm Tamar's story before she related it to Cullen. And she assumed attention would be focused on the sheriff's activities.

She slowed when she saw the small square of glass that was the window of Tamar's room. Just beyond it was the glass-paned door of Roland Brant's library.

Glynis went along the house wall and edged up beside the door. Humidity had caused condensation to form on the glass, and since the sun hadn't reached it yet, the moisture made it difficult to see into the room from where she now stood. If she moved any closer, she would be visible if anyone were inside there, but the risk must be taken. Quickly, she stepped forward and put her face to the glass with her hands cupped around her eyes like blinders.

There stood the desk, and from this close vantage point Tamar would have been able to see Roland Brant's body. A casual passerby would not. Which lent some credence to the family and staff's assertion that Brant's body hadn't been discovered until hours after his death. And Tamar had said that in her fright she might have pushed the door closed.

Glynis took a step back, and saw her face mirrored as if

through wavering water, an illusion created by streaks of condensation on the glass. Since there had been not only mist but fog last Monday morning, the reflection effect would have been even greater. And a deluded, panic-stricken girl might well have later imagined that she'd seen herself standing over the corpse of her tormentor.

Glynis turned and went back around the house, intending to enter it by way of the kitchen door, though by this time she had not much hope of doing it unnoticed. Where were all the Brants?

To her relief, she reached the door unchallenged. It was not latched, and when Glynis stepped into the kitchen, the first thing she noticed was the smell of pot roast. Addie sat at the table shelling peas, and glanced up at Glynis with no more reaction than if she'd been fully expecting her to appear.

"You're back," Addie stated, cracking open a pod and expertly running her thumb down the length of it, letting the peas drop like bright green beads into a wooden bowl.

"Yes, as you see." Glynis, holding up the wicker basket, explained, "I've come to collect Tamar Jager's things."

"Guess she won't be coming back here," Addie said, her square, brown face without expression.

"I think that's a safe guess."

"You hear the news?" Addie asked.

Glynis naturally assumed she meant the property seizure and replied, "I just saw the sheriff."

"Sheriff?" Addie echoed with a small frown. "What's the sheriff got to do with it?"

Confused, Glynis said, "Got to do with . . . with *what?*"

Addie reached for more pea pods. "With Mr. Konrad's going," she answered.

"Mr. Konrad's going *where?*"

"Gone to war, that's where."

Glynis felt her knees weaken, and she lowered herself

into a chair opposite Addie. "Konrad Brant has left town? When?"

"Went to the train station more'n an hour back. Gone to catch up with his company. He said the other men already done left here a few days ago."

"Konrad belongs to a militia company?" Glynis said, her memory belatedly bringing back the bright metal flag on his lapel, his elaborate toast to the Union.

Addie nodded matter-of-factly. "Joined up some weeks back."

"But . . . but why . . . why would he leave now?" Glynis stammered. "His father hasn't even been buried yet."

"All I know is that Mr. Konrad, he said word come that in the next couple days his company will be heading down to Washington. To protect the President, he said."

"Didn't his mother or brother try to keep him here at least until the funeral?" asked Glynis, although perfectly aware that patriotism had become an overriding passion in the minds of many young men.

Addie shrugged. "S'none of my business. But Mr. Erich took him to the station." Addie turned to glance out the window, saying, "He's not come back with the carriage yet, though."

Glynis followed Addie's gaze, suddenly remembering that the stable and carriage house were in full view from this kitchen window. "Addie, do you remember if, on the day after Mr. Brant was killed—"

"How you know when he was killed?" Addie broke in.

"I don't know for certain. You didn't see him Monday morning, though, did you?"

"I already told the constable ten times over I didn't!"

"But did you see the girl, Tamar Jager? Did you see her from this window anytime that day?"

Addie did not meet her eyes, but continued to strip peas from their pods.

"Please tell me if you saw the girl," Glynis pleaded. "It's important, Addie."

"Whose side you on now?" came the response, accompanied by a long look.

Glynis stared back at the woman. "I'm trying to keep Tamar from being charged with Roland Brant's murder."

"Well, why didn't you say so?"

Glynis held her tongue and leaned forward to cross her arms on the table. And she waited.

Addie stood up with the bowl of peas and started for the stove. As she passed Glynis, she said in a voice that was just above a whisper, "I seen her leave on a horse."

"When?"

" 'Long 'bout late afternoon. Figured she was running away."

"Running away? But Mr. Brant's body hadn't been discovered yet, had it?"

"Nope. Anyhow, that's not why I thought she was running."

Glynis looked straight at the woman and said, "You knew what was being done to that girl, didn't you? You knew!"

"I figured."

"And you never said anything about it? Not to anyone? You just let that poor, young— "

"I told you, I need this job!" Addie snapped. "And it weren't no worse'n what happens to slave women down South."

Glynis let out her breath in a long sigh and put her head down on her arms. *Power. Centuries old and unchanging.* The room was silent but for the ticking pendulum of a clock.

Not knowing if her legs would hold her, she rose from the chair. "I need to get into Tamar's room," she said to Addie. "Do you know if Mrs. Brant—that is, if both the Mrs. Brants are downstairs? In the parlor, perhaps?"

"Don't think so. First there was the uproar when Mr. Konrad left. Didn't tell nobody ahead of time, he didn't, so there was the devil to pay. Then that sheriff arrived. Think those two women went upstairs and took to their beds. But they're probably arguing like they always do. Don't even know if they're going to eat dinner," Addie groused, pointing at the iron kettle that obviously held the fragrant pot roast. "Nobody tells me nothing."

"Had Erich left with Konrad before the sheriff arrived?" Glynis asked.

"Yep."

So Erich Brant might not yet know of the sheriff's levy, although surely he must be aware of his father's debts. Which meant, Glynis suddenly thought, that the estate Erich would expect to inherit had no worth. But had he known that last Sunday? Perhaps not. Perhaps not until Derek Jager had come. She took a quick glance out the window, and then, not seeing anyone on the drive, she picked up the basket and walked to the doorway. After looking out into the hall to see if the way was clear, she hurried across into Tamar's room, closing the door quietly behind her.

She went immediately to the mattress and got down on her knees beside it. While she ran her hand between it and the floor, she kept an ear cocked for the sound of approaching footsteps, and inched her way around the mattress. And found nothing. She went back around the opposite way. Nothing. Straightening up on her knees, she glanced around the room. But Tamar had said she kept it hidden under the mattress. Had someone else already looked there and found it? The one thing that could all but clear Tamar completely? Glynis was about to stand when, in a last desperate attempt, she thrust her hand behind the mattress where it met the wall. And her fingers touched something cold.

She carefully withdrew the knife. Holding it by its bone handle, she looked closely at the long shining blade. Clean as a cat's whiskers. It could not be Tamar's knife in Roland Brant's body. Not unless three kitchen knives were missing.

Glynis let out the breath she'd been holding and quickly

got to her feet. Placing the knife in the bottom of the basket, she rapidly collected Tamar's few items of clothing and piled them over the knife. The hairbrush and book of poetry went in last, along with the Bible. Glynis cast a final glance around and started for the door, before she realized that something was missing. She searched the sparse room once again, and at last went back into the kitchen.

"Where are the knives kept, Addie?"

The woman gave her a startled look, but walked to a cupboard and opened the door, then pulled out a deep drawer. Glynis went to stand beside her and peered into it. Resting in slots were four bone-handled knives. There were six slots.

"Where are the knives that belong in those?" Glynis said, testing Addie by pointing to the two empty slots.

"Well," Addie said, her face again without expression, "I s'pect one of them is in Mr. Brant. And since you just come out of that room, you probably know better'n me where the other one is."

Satisfied, Glynis asked, "So you don't think Tamar killed Roland Brant?"

"Nope, never did. But before you ask another of your everlasting questions, I don't know who *did* kill him!"

Glynis believed this was probably true. She pointed again to the drawer. "Is that the only place where knives are kept?"

"Nope, there's smaller paring knives, but I thought those'd be the ones you'd want to know about."

Glynis nodded and pulled one of the knives from its slot. She looked at the sharp blade, as she had the one in Tamar's room, and again found the mark of its maker. The same mark that had been on the knives given to Emma by Helga Brant as a wedding present.

"These knives look fairly new," Glynis said to Addie. "Do you happen to know where they came from?"

"From Mr. Brant himself—"

"*Roland* Brant?" Glynis broke in.

Addie nodded. "Brought them back from a business trip, he said."

"A trip to the Syracuse area?"

Addie looked at Glynis as if she'd just pulled a rabbit from a hat. "That's so," she answered slowly, continuing to eye Glynis with suspicion. "He said those knives were made by—can't bring it to mind now, but the name sounded like one of them Indian tribes."

"Yes," Glynis said, "the Oneidas."

"Those're the ones."

Glynis stood there, thinking, and then realized that Addie was still staring at her. "Where are Clements and Phoebe?" she asked.

"It's Clements's day off, so I s'pect he's gone to town."

"Did he go before or after the sheriff arrived?"

"Before."

So there was another member of the Brant household who did not yet know of the disastrous turn of events. "And where's Phoebe?"

Addie frowned as she said, "That one! Touched in the head. She's supposed to be in the dining room cleaning the silver."

The silver that was about to be seized for Roland Brant's debts, Glynis brooded, her thoughts now scurrying down previously dim or unseen paths.

"Thank you, Addie," she said, as she left the kitchen. The woman did not reply.

Glynis went up the hallway toward the front of the house and looked into the dining room. Once she'd confirmed that Phoebe was indeed there—although the silver lay unpolished while she likely daydreamed of warlocks—Glynis went across the hall and was about to step into the parlor when her name was called from the top of the stairs. She looked up to see Tirzah Brant on the landing. The light coming from the stained glass window behind her made it difficult to see her expression, but Glynis guessed that it wasn't a pleasant one.

"So, Miss Tryon, come to witness the end of an era?"

When Glynis said nothing, Tirzah gestured to her. "Come up here, Miss Tryon, if you would."

Glynis, still gripping the handle of the basket, wondered how unstable Tirzah was at this moment—her hopes surely dashed by the property seizure—and she regretted not having told Zeph where she would be. But Tirzah clearly wanted something, and Glynis couldn't gamble on it being a mere whim. She climbed the stairs with caution.

"I've been expecting the constable," Tirzah said, and Glynis saw the puffy, red-rimmed eyes which had once beguiled, and the nervous twitch of hands which had played the harpsichord with such precision.

"Why did you expect Constable Stuart?" Glynis asked her, moving well away from the top step of the staircase.

"I thought he might at least have the courtesy to tell us the kitchen maid had confessed to murdering my husband's father."

"But apparently you already know that," Glynis said, stating the obvious. "As it is, I don't believe that confession, and I doubt that you do, either."

"Why shouldn't I believe it?" Tirzah demanded, then turned from Glynis and for a brief time stood staring up at the stained glass window. The pearl-white lilies had acquired, to Glynis's mind, a funereal cast she'd not seen there previously.

"I think my mother-in-law would like to see you, Miss Tryon." Tirzah's voice now held a commanding edge.

Glynis glanced toward the closed door of Helga Brant's room, and saw a tray of uneaten food on a table next to the dumbwaiter. "I can't imagine she'd want to see anyone now," she protested. "I think another time would be more appropriate."

"Let's find out." And before Glynis could object, Tirzah

had rapped sharply on the bedroom door and, without waiting for a response, pushed it open.

Helga Brant stood at the window. The room's flower motif resembled that of the parlor, with blossoms on every conceivable surface. Its occupant began to turn slowly toward the door.

"Tirzah, I refuse to discuss this further," Helga Brant began, "and . . . Miss Tryon? I fear I'm not in the mood for visitors today. You will excuse me. Tirzah, close the door as you leave."

Helga Brant turned again to the window. Tirzah didn't move, however, but stood with her eyes scanning the room.

"Close the door, Tirzah," repeated Helga Brant.

Her daughter-in-law began to slowly pull the door closed, but not before Glynis had caught a bright flash of red on the surface of a small writing desk.

She gave Tirzah a brief nod, and quickly went down the stairs. As she stepped out the front door, she was grateful for the clean, fresh air that met her.

An hour later Neva greeted her at the refuge door with, "I assumed you'd be along soon. Tamar is greatly improved, by the way—now if she'd just stop worrying about that Gagnon man!"

While they walked together across the yard and into the shade of a spreading beech, Neva said, "Honestly, after what that girl has been through, it's a marvel that she trusts anyone, let alone a man."

"I think she's learned that not all men are dangerous," Glynis answered with some confidence in what she was saying.

"And just where would she have learned that?" Saving Glynis a response, Neva went on, "Isn't your family about to arrive? We do have a wedding on the docket for tomorrow, don't we?"

"Indeed we do. And yes, I need to start behaving like a

maiden aunt—however that might be. But you know why I'm here, Neva."

"I'm afraid I don't have much to tell you. Cullen left here just a few minutes before you came, and I said the same thing to him."

"You did perform the autopsy?" Glynis asked anxiously.

"Yes, but again, there isn't much to tell. I can't say with any degree of certainty which blow killed Brant."

"You can't?"

"Glynis, either of those injuries could have caused death. He'd hemorrhaged from the blow to the temple, and the knife had been thrust directly into the heart. Directly. Since it's unlikely the blows were delivered simultaneously, about all I can say is that one must have followed soon after the other. I can *guess* that the blow to the head occurred first, because of the hemorrhaging, but guessing is all I can do."

"What time do you think it—they—happened?"

"There I'm on a little firmer ground. His stomach was almost empty, so we can assume that he hadn't eaten for some hours."

"*Almost* empty?"

"There was a fair amount of alcohol present. Now, everyone at the Brant house says he ate supper on Sunday night. No one saw him eat breakfast, although that supposedly wasn't unusual for him, but I don't believe he was killed during the day on Monday."

"Why not?" Glynis asked,

"Because of the rigor. Commonly, rigor mortis sets in around four to six hours after death. It lasts about twenty-four hours, and Brant was already stiff when we got there Monday night. I went to the icehouse to check it Tuesday morning around seven A.M., and he was moderately stiff, but the rigor was leaving. I went back at ten o'clock and at that time, even given the effect of the ice, there was no rigor remaining. Are you with me?"

"Yes," Glynis said. "So he couldn't have been killed later than—"

"Later than Monday morning, and *before* he ate breakfast or lunch. But remember, there's a considerable amount of leeway in the rigor time."

"Let's imagine, for the sake of trying this out," Glynis proposed, "that Brant was killed, one way or another, somewhere around three A.M. Monday morning. Rigor mortis would have set in about seven to nine A.M.?"

Neva nodded.

"So," Glynis went on, "if we add twenty-four hours to *that* we can say that the rigor should have worn off—"

"All things being equal, which they never are," Neva cautioned, "but yes, ordinarily the rigor would have been gone by nine A.M. Tuesday."

"And it *was* gone, when you checked at ten. Although you say there's leeway, is it unreasonable to assume that he was killed a few hours after midnight Sunday, or even at midnight—but probably not before, since he'd eaten supper, and you found no food in his stomach?"

"No, it's not an unreasonable assumption, but can't you imagine a lawyer like Merrycoyf tearing that apart? Look, Glynis, I'm just trying to help you narrow down this time period. I doubt it would stand up in a court of law," Neva emphasized.

"Maybe it won't have to stand up there," Glynis said quietly. "I think it's time to set a few things in motion."

26

—∿∿—

I do not pretend that I have brought aerial naviga-
tion to perfection. . . . I have no doubt, but cherish
a fervent hope, that the time is not far distant
when we can travel in air without the aid of bal-
loons for buoyant force.

—letter from Thaddeus Sobieski Constantine Lowe, 1859

*T*he strangest thing about sitting for hours in the dusky
sky, Bronwen decided, was the silence. Once she heard a
hawk's high-pitched scream, and occasionally an upward
tug made the manila mooring ropes of the balloon groan, or
the willow rattan basket would creak some, but otherwise
the quiet was absolute. There was not much to make noise
one thousand feet above the ground.

The stately, fifty-foot-high *Enterprise,* a huge, silk, gas-
filled envelope varnished with rice starch, towered above
the waist-high basket in which she and Professor Lowe were
riding. Bronwen was perched on a narrow bench that ran
around the basket's interior, scanning with field glasses a
five-mile stretch of the Oswego River. Lowe insisted that
she should be able to see the smoke of a campfire twenty-
five miles away. About this, she had her doubts. Campfires
at the end of May were scarce.

The balloon was anchored five miles west of the Oswego
River, and ten miles downstream from the Lake Ontario port
city named for the river. From where Bronwen sat, she could

see twenty miles of that river: north to the city and south to where the Oswego and the Oneida Rivers met. The river traffic at this time of year was scant because farmers had not yet begun shipping crops, so the few canal and river boats she observed rode fairly high in the water. These she ignored.

An hour before, however, scanning some distance to the south, she had spotted three boats, all of which were riding low, indicating heavy freight.

"Professor Lowe, I think I've got something," she had said, pointing to the southeast.

Lowe had picked up his own glasses, followed her finger, and after a minute or two he nodded. "Could be. Could very well be," he'd agreed. No silk top hat or Prince Albert coat on this trek; just a long smock-like coat, high cavalry boots, and a sleek cap of black hair.

They had both swung their glasses to the north to survey the riverbanks. "I haven't found anything peculiar along there," Bronwen had told him. "The farms all look pretty average and the few wharves are empty."

"We didn't think there would be any activity until dusk," Lowe had reminded her, putting down his glasses and taking a swallow of water from their canteen. "But things should liven up soon, I expect. Carry on," he'd said, smiling.

Lowe was, without doubt, Bronwen thought, one of the most even-tempered men she had ever met. Nothing much seemed to faze him, yet nothing much happened that he didn't observe with keen curiosity. He also assumed that if anything went wrong, he could fix it. If he ever worried, Bronwen had yet to see it; even during the perilous descent into Seneca Falls he had remained the soul of equanimity.

After the ascent of several hours ago, Lowe had checked the mooring ropes and then spent most of his time making copious notes in his logbook, recording barometric readings, latitude and longitude, and altitude as indicated by the altimeter he had developed. Since the balloon was anchored, Bronwen decided that he must be building a case for the re-

connaissance flights he was trying to convince the War Department to approve. When she and Treasury chief detective
Rhys Bevan had been in Cincinnati, Major General McClellan had enthusiastically backed the idea of a Balloon Corps
to assess Confederate troop positions, so this present assignment was more or less a practice run.

"See anything yet?" Lowe now asked her, then hoisted his
own field glasses.

"Nothing but those three suspicious northbound boats,"
Bronwen replied.

She still worried that the balloon would be observed, but as
the sun behind them grew to a great bronze ball and began to
roll below the horizon, she became more confident. She had
seen the *Enterprise* aloft at dusk, and she knew that from a
distance it resembled nothing more than a pale, thin cloud.
Trees would of course make it difficult for men on the ground
to see very far. Unfortunately, most of this area was farmland.

But once the balloon was freed from its mooring and
moving east toward the river, it would become a much more
visible target.

They knew from a Treasury agent stationed in Oswego—
the same one who'd been tracking the activities of British
espionage agent Colonel Dorian de Warde—that the Enfield
rifles had been unloaded from a Canadian ship late the previous night. There was nothing illegal in that. From the Lake
Ontario wharf, said the agent, the guns had been put on wagons; again nothing illegal. Some hours later the guns were
loaded from the wagons onto canalboats, which then headed
south on the Oswego River. The agent followed on horseback, hidden by trees growing along the bank, but after five
miles he'd finally been spotted. Before the men on the boats
had fired at him, he'd done the prudent thing and taken himself out of range. The boats had continued on.

This agent's report had considerably narrowed the zone of
their present search.

Circuitously evading Lincoln's blockade of Southern seaports, British Enfields not only had been secretly transported through western New York and Pennsylvania twice before, but had, in the process, been equipped with sword bayonets. All of which *was* illegal. Was, in fact, high treason.

Treasury calculated that the guns and bayonets, to travel undetected to the South, needed to be disguised, thus they were probably being repackaged and falsely labeled. This operation would require a quiet, isolated place, and since Treasury knew the guns were disappearing somewhere along the Oswego River, they guessed that a farm, a barn, and a good size wharf would be necessary. And these must be, from what the agent had reported, at a location at least those five miles south of the Ontario port city, but north of where the Oswego River joined the Erie Canal system. They also figured that the location, remote enough to avoid observation, would likely be north of the hamlet of Fulton. Thus reducing the area under surveillance to a five-mile stretch of river.

So they figured.

As Rhys Bevan had said, the men who loaded and unloaded the guns were small fish. They might not even know where the cargo was ultimately headed, and if picked up, their arrest would only serve to warn those who masterminded the operation. The job now was to catch the big fish.

Bronwen swung the glasses east to scan the ground. On horseback, somewhere down there, Jacques Sundown and Rhys Bevan and a band of Treasury agents were waiting. There would be only a small opening of time in which to identify and seize the contraband; Bevan's greatest worry was that a premature ground attack might give the ones in charge an opportunity to escape.

Slowly, slowly, Bronwen moved the field glasses to sight along the river. Then she stopped, moved the glasses back a fraction, and held. "Professor, I've got something on the river! Almost due east!"

"Please give me a point of reference."

She squinted, running through the calculations he had

taught her to determine distance. "Maybe a mile or so above Fulton on the west bank. I just saw wagons come out from behind some trees. There's a big clump of willows hanging into the water and beside it I can see the end of a wharf— must be a big one the way it's jutting out into the river."

She concentrated as she moved the glasses to the south. "I really think this is it!" she said a minute later. "Those three boats that've been coming north—they're past Fulton now. It looks like they could be heading for that wharf! And all of a sudden there's a lot of activity that wasn't there the last time I looked."

Lowe's glasses were now moving beside hers.

"Yes, I see them!" he exclaimed. "Boats heading north with heavy cargo, probably the bayonets, while the ones with the rifles head south from Oswego—and they rendezvous at a location mid-river. Very clever."

He watched for another minute, then he lowered his glasses. "Time to get under way!" he said. "Keep watch while I contact the ground crew."

He reached beneath the bench where his equipment was stored. Bronwen had heard in his voice an excitement that echoed her own, but she knew without looking that his movements would be steady and methodical.

She felt the basket tilt slightly as he leaned over the side, and then "Loose ropes! Loose ropes *now!*" came booming from his megaphone. The basket listed again, as Lowe leaned farther over the side to watch those below who were releasing the mooring ropes from their anchors.

And now would come the part she dreaded. The worst thing about ballooning, hands down, was the stench of the coal gas; the closest Bronwen could come to describing it would be to say that it smelled like an open sewer filled with rotten eggs. While it didn't seem to bother Lowe much, whenever Bronwen saw him reach for the gas valve, she held her breath.

The air seemed still and Bronwen, with her eyes glued to

the river activity, couldn't tell if the mooring ropes had been loosed, but she risked a sideways glance at Lowe, who was throwing out several sandbags of ballast. Then—she sucked in her breath—he turned the valve at the base of the silk envelope to let a small amount of the gas "blow off." The *Enterprise,* with a diameter of forty-two feet, could hold over thirty thousand cubic feet of gas. If released all at once, Bronwen imagined, the stench would topple a herd of elephants.

While her glasses were trained on the wagons, three more canalboats, which must have been concealed by the willows, suddenly appeared. "Professor," she insisted urgently, "I truly think we need to get moving. Right now!"

She heard a soft chuckle behind her, and looked down to see the mooring site on the farmland below receding. It astonished her, as it had the first time she'd been aloft, that there was no sense of motion. And yet they must be floating somewhat faster than usual on a whisper of breeze from the west.

"You'll be on your own for a minute or two, Miss Llyr," Lowe said, ever courteous. "Please keep them in your sight and report, because I'll be busy."

He climbed up into the hoop, a ring between the basket and the balloon envelope on which the guide ropes were fastened, to check the lines. Bronwen now scrutinized the ground to find Jacques and the Treasury men, who were divided into two groups: one to the north of the *Enterprise,* the other to the south.

Yes, she had them! A number of horses and riders were standing some distance ahead on a grassy hillock—she guessed it was a hillock because she had no sense of depth perception from the air—the men waving white flags to signal they saw the balloon.

"Professor, I've got Treasury men in sight." She could hear her voice beginning to tighten. "How far are we from the mark, do you think?"

Jacques and Rhys would have field glasses, and she was

supposed to signal them when the *Enterprise* was a mile and a half from the target.

Lowe climbed down beside her and raised his glasses. And put them down almost immediately.

"Get ready to signal!" he said, and she reached for a portion of the flexible, telescoped wand that he was elongating. On the end of it was hanging a large banner of bleached canvas.

He and Bronwen leaned over the edge of the basket, both gripping the now fifteen feet of wand and extending it as far as they could to point to the target. Bronwen could see that one of the horses below was already galloping hard toward the river. While Lowe collapsed the wand, she hoisted her glasses, and grinned. That first horse, furlongs ahead of the others, was of course Jacques Sundown's black-and-white paint.

A minute or two later the *Enterprise* passed directly over him. He never even glanced up.

As the balloon approached the river, a barn appeared set back a ways from the water; in front of it stood several flatbed wagons loaded with crates. Another wagon stood at the wharf, and men were hauling more crates to it from the barge-like canalboats. But what interested Bronwen most were the tall wooden kegs standing near the end of the wharf. They might well hold black gunpowder.

She felt a jolt of tension as she again smelled the gas, which meant they were about to descend. This did not seem too smart. It wasn't as if the men on the ground had to look very far for weapons.

She heard faint shouting, and saw in her glasses the men on the riverbank making startled jerks as they looked up and found the *Enterprise*. Which, it seemed, was now barely moving. Below, the activity had slowed, and then, for a long moment, everything stopped completely. The scene ahead resembled a carving in ice, frozen in place, and nothing in it stirred.

It came suddenly alive with a storm of activity, as if a

giant had stepped on an anthill. And Bronwen again smelled gas. They were descending still farther!

She put down the glasses and whirled to shout at Lowe, "We're supposed to keep them distracted, not serve as their bull's-eye!"

She was still more dismayed to see Lowe smiling as he heaved a sandbag over the side, and they lifted: he was *enjoying* this. Then, with a twist of the valve, down they went again.

She heard the muffled report of a rifle, then another and another, and frantically told herself that the basket and balloon must be too distant to hit. And the men were shooting upward at a moving target—how accurate could they be? The professor, however, was again reaching for the gas valve. Was he crazy? They hadn't discussed this part of the assignment, and she felt a flare of temper at her own neglect. It hadn't crossed her mind that Lowe might be suicidal.

Even without the glasses Bronwen could now see that what had looked like a sagging picket fence was actually a ragged line of guns pointing upward. And every second the *Enterprise* was getting closer to them. She heard a volley of gunfire, and decided she wasn't ready to die.

She reached under the bench and grabbed her weapon. Snatching it from its nest and holding it up, she yelled, "O.K., I'm doing this, Professor!"

"No, wait!" he shouted at her, and the stench of gas nearly knocked her off her feet. She grabbed the side of the basket, regaining her balance just as she heard more rifle blasts. They sounded way too close. The balloon was descending over the roof of the barn and in less than a minute would be over the wharf and the dark river.

Bronwen steadied herself against the bench, while eyeing the powder kegs at the end of the wharf; she waited, waited, waited. Then hurled the grenade.

Nothing happened. There were at least a dozen rifles trained on the basket, firing at it, and nothing happened. The damn grenade was a dud! Or had she forgotten to insert the plunger?

BANG-BAMMM! The explosions came as the basket lurched downward. Water sprayed beneath her, tossing up pieces of wood and metal; she couldn't see much else because the *Enterprise* was now over the river, descending fast to the farmland beyond. But on the riverbank behind her, a score of horses were thundering into the smoking, roiling, mass of confusion.

"They're here, Professor! Bevan and his men!" she shouted at him, pointing at the agents. He was manipulating the ropes and just nodded, smiling broadly.

She braced herself for the coming jolts.

They made a rocky landing in a field of scrub, and when Bronwen crawled out of the basket, she staggered when she first tried to walk. It felt as if every inch of uncovered skin was scratched. Professor Lowe was now concerned only with securing his balloon, and seemed to ignore with the clamor coming from the riverbank.

Bronwen ran in the direction of the noise and the smell of gunpowder, her hair whipping around her face, although it had not so much as ruffled during the flight. She tripped over the cuffed legs of her too-large, men's trousers, and had to stop and haul them up, pulling the drawstring at the waist so tight she could hardly breathe. Then she drew her Treasury-issued pocket revolver and dashed forward.

She was stopped short by the river; it was not wide, but it was wet. Rhys Bevan, not more than thirty yards away on the opposite bank, stood with his revolver trained on several scruffy-looking men.

Bronwen shouted, "Everything O.K.? *Sir!*"

"Top-notch!" he answered, and jerked his free thumb over his shoulder. He was smiling, but it was probably because for once she'd remembered to respect his rank.

It looked less chaotic here than from the air; Bronwen saw half a dozen men herded together and wound tightly with rope like an upright bundle of logs. Other men with crowbars—a few of whom she recognized as fellow Treasury agents—were prying open crates and hauling out Enfield rifles. And sword bayonets.

She was missing everything. Casting a quick look around her, she spied several small rowboats beached along the riverbank. With some effort, she shoved the first one into the water and scrambled into it.

Shortly, she was standing beside Rhys Bevan, looking down at numerous crates on which had been stenciled bold black letters: PICKAXES. SHOVELS. RAKES. Some crates were empty, some were still full of weapons.

"A shrewd operation," Rhys commented in his pleasant Celtic lilt, and his eyes glinted like pieces of clear blue glass. "Well planned. Not particularly well executed, but almost good enough."

"Where's Jacques Sundown?" Bronwen asked.

"In the barn, I believe. It's a shame about him," he added.

"Why?"

"I've never seen a man act faster—never a moment of hesitation, never a wasted motion, never a false move. I'd give a great deal to have him in the detective unit."

"You know he won't join."

"Yes, and even if he would, McClellan's the one who could claim him first. He wasn't pleased about Sundown leaving Cincinnati right now, not with Confederates in western Virginia threatening the railroads."

Bronwen grinned. "Jacques would never pass up an excuse to come back here."

"And we both know why, don't we," Rhys commented, watching Jacques stride toward them. Behind him, lanterns were being lit, their glow keeping at bay the gathering dark.

"Everything wrapped up?" Rhys asked.

"It's done." Jacques gave Bronwen a short nod.

"Did you get everybody?" she asked.

"All but one."

"De Warde?"

"No," answered Rhys, "I doubt very much we'll be able to hang this on Colonel de Warde. He's too cunning. Most of the men know only their immediate contacts, which was a smart move by the one who masterminded it, because that way nobody knows too much. There's nothing to trace back to the man at the top. It won't be de Warde, though—I'll wager he saw an opportunity, collected his money, and kept his coattails clean. But we did have some very fine luck. Winged a canary who wants to sing. You guessed a few days ago who he might be, Agent Llyr, and I think we'll know soon enough who's behind *him*. What we don't know, though, is where the bayonets came from."

"I think I do," offered Bronwen.

Both Rhys and Jacques stared at her. "Well?" demanded Rhys.

"Have you ever heard," Bronwen asked, turning to Jacques, "of the Oneida Community?"

Jacques's flat expression almost changed; which, if it had, Bronwen would have seen as a near-supernatural phenomenon. "They make steel knives," he said.

"What are you two talking about?" Rhys asked with impatience.

"I think three of those boats"—Bronwen gestured in the direction of the demolished wharf—"came into this river from the Oneida River. And they made it into *that* river by way of Oneida Lake. The Oneida Community, as Jacques said, is noted for its steel cutlery—among other things. It has a forge, and its own foundry. But while the people there are a little . . . strange, they might not have known where their swords were going."

"Good work, Agent Llyr!" Rhys said to her. "Oneida makes the swords that someone orders, then someone else entirely puts the weapons on boats and brings them to this spot. Here they're fitted to the Enfields come down from Canada to Oswego, and crated as farm tools. Then they're stored until they can be delivered to the South. Think I'll pay a call on this Oneida Community."

Bronwen looked toward the moon just rising over farmland to the east. "Chief, could I borrow a horse—please, sir?" she asked. "I need to get to a train station, because by morning I *have* to be in Seneca Falls. My cousin's being married there tomorrow . . . maybe." She looked down at her scratched arms, imagining Emma's reaction.

Rhys nodded to her. "What about you, Sundown?"

"Heading back to Ohio."

Rhys smiled. "But I distinctly heard you tell McClellan—when he was ordering you to stay in Cincinnati—that you are not a Union soldier."

"I'm not. Going back because I want to. There's a difference."

"I really have to leave, now!" Bronwen stated. "But I don't want to abandon Professor Lowe. Chief, can some of the men put the balloon on a wagon, and take it to the rail station?"

Rhys nodded again, and Bronwen started for the tethered horses, then stopped as two men approached, one of them an agent, the other a man whose hands were bound and whose face was rigid with fury.

"And here we have our treasonous canary," Rhys said, gesturing toward the captured man. "I believe you guessed the name of this angry gentleman, Agent Llyr."

Bronwen looked at the man. "Yes, he lives east of Syracuse—which is where the Oneida Community happens to be located," she answered. "His name, I think, is Derek Jager."

SATURDAY
June 1, 1861

27

—⟁—

*Men are April when they woo, December when
they wed. Maids are May when they are maids, but
the sky changes when they are wives.*

—Shakespeare

$\mathcal{G}$lynis stood with her brother Robin under the branch of a cherry tree in full bloom, while every now and then a pink petal floated down into her crystal punch glass. Vanessa Usher must have made prodigious offerings to those spirits who command the weather, as the morning had dawned just as she'd promised Emma: fair and warm, a flawless June day.

The fragrance of mock orange blossoms and opening roses drifted over a magical scene of women in hoop-skirted, pastel gowns and men in courtly morning coats, while servants continued to bring forth enough elegantly prepared food to feed half the Union army. The virginal, white wedding cake stood nearly two feet high. Violins, harp, and harpsichord sent music rippling from under the flowered arch where Emma and Adam had just been wed. Adam still looked somewhat dazed. Grooms usually did, Glynis had noticed.

Besides which, Adam had earlier managed to work himself into a frenzy, because by eleven o'clock Bronwen had not yet arrived.

"Marriages must, by law, take place before noon!" he'd

announced in agitated voice so many times that the entire wedding party had threatened to toss him into the canal. Even the ordinarily unflappable Reverend Mr. Eames had shown a brief spurt of annoyance, before he then joined Adam in worrying.

Emma, however, had stood firm. "She'll be here," she'd kept saying with an unexpected faith in her cousin that Glynis for once feared might be misguided.

All the while, Adam had paced back and forth across the Usher grounds and, when not intoning the legal statute of doom, muttered under his breath as to what bodily harmful, and illegal, things he planned to do to Bronwen if she failed to show up. Glynis thought his plans displayed an imaginative streak she hadn't previously seen in him. Vanessa began to complain about her grass wearing thin.

But at last Bronwen, racing a buggy at breakneck speed up Cayuga Street, had arrived from the railroad station, her hair wildly tangled, her neck and arms covered with scratches. The hair, however, had quickly been tamed with brushes and combs and flowered wreath, the scratches mostly concealed with powder.

The wedding ceremony had begun at a quarter to twelve, only fifteen minutes late.

After the ceremony, Bronwen had told Glynis the story, at least those parts of it, her aunt realized, that Agent Llyr was at liberty to tell. Glynis had not mentioned what she'd deduced about the mastermind behind the contraband. She thought she knew, even if Treasury didn't.

Her brother now asked her, "Can I get you more punch, Glyn?"

"Please, yes." As Robin went off toward the punch bowls, she glanced around, deciding that men never looked more handsome than when, complaining every minute, they were forced into formal dress. Today they were decked out in colors of fawn and dove gray, and the portly Merrycoyf, Adam's best man, looked as if he had stepped directly from the pages of *Harper's,* or a sketch of Dickens's more well-to-do characters. Adam himself wore a velvet coat the color of claret wine. Which had undoubtedly been Emma's choice.

At the moment, her three nieces were seated under a white dogwood, undergoing a photographer's endurance test, which made them pose in the same steadfast position for what seemed hours at a time. It was no wonder that even Emma had lost her smile. How different they were from one another, Glynis thought, as she had thought many times before. Any similarity was to be found only in their size, which was almost the same, with Bronwen perhaps a shade taller than her sister and cousin. Emma, her dark hair partly concealed by veiling, her gray eyes glistening like stones under sunlit water, radiated the glow which a wedding was commonly thought to bestow upon a young woman. And if this was too rosy a picture of some brides, today it appeared to portray Emma perfectly.

The lovely Kathryn, she of honeyed hair and midnight blue eyes, had arrived late the previous afternoon, having just completed a nurses' training period in New York. Last evening, it had been Kathryn who, alone of the family, had tried to deflect the anger directed at her younger sister's conspicuous absence. Glynis, chafing under sworn secrecy, had been grateful when Kathryn had said in her gentle voice, "I think Bronwen must be involved in something for the Treasury. She would never deliberately slight us—it's not in her nature."

Coming from someone else, this might have sounded persuasive, but everyone there knew that Kathryn would try to find, if at all possible, a reason to excuse Caligula. It was her nature.

"Aunt Glyn!" Bronwen's voice now called. "Aunt Glyn, would you come over here, please?"

Bronwen, having escaped the photographer, was standing at the edge of the Usher grounds' bordering pine trees. Glynis went toward her, threading through groups of family and friends, wondering with some unease what intrigue Bronwen might be hatching now, because her voice had held an unmistakable note of urgency.

"What is it?" Glynis asked when she reached her niece.

Bronwen took her arm and all but dragged her in among the pine trees. "Sundown's here! You know he won't come over where the crowd is. See you later," she said over her shoulder with, Glynis thought, remarkable tact.

She walked through the remaining trees to Harriet's back yard, where the black-and-white paint stood patiently, its rider astride.

"Wanted to see you before I left," he said.

"Are you going to Ohio?"

"For a while. Gave McClellan my word I'd be back."

And that would be enough, Glynis thought, if McClellan knew this man at all. He seldom gave his word. When he did, it was uncompromising.

He reached into a pocket of his buckskin jacket and withdrew a small wooden box on which had been carved dogwood blossoms in an intricate design. "To keep you out of trouble. When I can't be here," he said, handing the box down to her. "Don't open it now."

Glynis brushed at her eyes with her gloved hand.

"Got to go," he said. His warmed gold eyes looked down at her for a long moment, then he wheeled the paint around.

"Please take care, Jacques," Glynis said. "Let me know where you are, how you are."

"You know I will."

When he rode off, Glynis stood there until he was out of sight. She took the lid off the box—the carving must have taken him days—and withdrew a sterling silver link chain from which hung the silver figure of a running wolf.

She put it around her neck, slipping it under the bodice of her gown, then tried to compose herself enough to return to the wedding party. It took some time.

As she went back through the pine trees and stepped onto the grass beside a flower bed, she felt something snag her satin sleeve. She looked down to see a rose bush, some of its full, scarlet buds beginning to open; her sleeve had been snared by one of its thorny stems. As she carefully unhooked herself, something skimmed across her mind. She frowned, trying to recover it, but she was halfway across the grass before she turned around to stare back at the bush.

Even at the far edge of the grounds, and even dwarfed by the pink and white trees and shrubs, the red blooms drew the eye like a magnet. And Glynis realized she had very nearly made a serious mistake.

She believed that she knew who had murdered Roland Brant. Since there seemed little in the way of proof, she hadn't as yet spoken to Cullen. She had also waited to speak in deference to those who were not guilty, as Brant had been buried at dusk the previous evening. But earlier this morning she had given Liam a letter to take to the Brant house.

"Don't wait for a reply," she'd told him. "I doubt there will be one."

She now saw that she had been misled, deliberately misled, by the ancient trick of dragging a red herring across a trail to cover a scent and thus divert the hunter. The red herring here had taken the form of a rose.

Somewhat later, after Emma and Adam had left for their wedding trip, the Usher grounds remained crowded, as if all were reluctant to leave this ephemeral Garden of Eden to rejoin the real world. Glynis, walking back from the road where the couple's carriage had just rumbled off, looked over the beautiful grounds and all at once experienced a profound sadness. Some of those here today, she thought, may never be here again.

The war could claim them. Her nephews, the brothers of Bronwen and Kathryn and Emma, and Bronwen's rugged young Marsh, who had come this morning from a small

Pennsylvania town named Gettysburg. Jonathan Quant, Liam Cleary, Danny Ross, and even Adam. And if Negroes were allowed to fight to free their brothers, she knew Isaiah Smith and Zeph would go.

It was said by many that the conflict could not last long. That the South would soon drop to its knees. But what if it did not? And if the younger men were not enough to feed the war, would the call come for older men? Her brother Robin. Brother-in-law Owen Llyr. Abraham Levy. Cullen and Jacques . . .

How many of them would not come back? How many women, both North and South, would be left impoverished, widowed, unable to fend for themselves and their children? How many would need to care for men so badly wounded they had little life remaining?

Glynis shook her head. This was not the time to think of the uncertain future. *Carpe diem.* Seize the day, this warm, loving day, and face tomorrow only when it came.

She gathered up the skirt of her gown, and went across the grass.

SUNDAY
June 2, 1861

28

—∞—

*While the nation's life hung in the balance, and
the dread artillery of war drowned alike the voices
of commerce, politics, religion and reform, all
hearts were filled with anxious forebodings, all
hands were busy in solemn preparations for the
awful tragedies to come.*

—Elizabeth Cady Stanton,
History of Woman Suffrage

*C*hurch bells were tolling to gather the faithful, and Glynis
flinched as she recalled the frowns relaying her family's dis-
approval when it became apparent that neither she nor Bronwen would be joining them. They had left the breakfast table
in the Carr's Hotel dining room, ostensibly to powder their
noses; the euphemism employed even though everyone
knew it meant use of the water closet. The original plan
called for them to maneuver with some degree of finesse,
but alas, at the hotel door they'd been caught, and it had become all too transparent that they were not sneaking out to
attend church. Fortunately no one had seemed to notice the
ungainly bulge in Glynis's large book bag: the shortened
crowbar ordinarily put to use opening crates of library
books.

"We are in utter disgrace," she said to Bronwen now, as
they hurried across the Seneca River bridge.

"When you've been in disgrace as often as I've been,"

Bronwen replied, "you get used to it. You even begin to expect it. Besides, by now everybody's in church—supposedly learning forgiveness!"

"I fear that your mother is right—I'm a bad influence, Bronwen. And if I weren't so worried that the evidence might be moved, I would have waited to do this until after you'd all left town. As I had planned to do. But that was before your account of the Oswego River raid. Now I'm worried that it might be too late. You, though, should have stayed there with the others."

"Do you think I'd miss *this?* Don't look so upset, Aunt Glyn. If you're right, Rhys Bevan might raise my salary. And we'll be heroes."

"People are seldom considered heroes by their own families. Having usually, in the process of becoming heroic, offended almost everyone. And I may not even be right about this."

"Even if you're not, it's better than sitting through church. Reverend Eames is fine, but we heard him say it all yesterday. I thought that wedding ceremony would never end."

"Now there is a real hero," Glynis said. "Do you know how much Reverend Eames has risked, working with the Underground Railroad? People like Eames can go to jail for a long time, Bronwen, when they help escaped slaves."

"I know," Bronwen said, "and a lot more people are going to die in this war over slavery. What we're doing right now could mean a few less will die, so I honestly don't think Reverend Eames would object."

Glynis had stopped midway across the bridge to look at her niece. "I didn't know you had any feelings at all about slavery."

"I didn't used to," Bronwen agreed. "Seeing it firsthand, I've learned to hate it. And I've heard all the rubbish that people say—that this war is about everything *but* slavery. Who could believe that? If there were no slaves, there would be no war!"

It was somewhat refreshing, thought Glynis, that Bronwen had not lost her intolerance of ambiguity.

They reached the south side of the bridge and turned to walk down the towpath along the water, then passed under the wooden sign for Serenity's Tavern; it swung from a shiny black beam that jutted out over the path and creaked softly in the warm morning breeze. Ahead of the tavern stood a gray stone warehouse.

"I wonder," Glynis said, "if anyone in the tavern has ever noticed activity at that warehouse?"

"Do you want to stop in and ask?"

"Certainly not." Glynis saw Bronwen's sideways glance and the grin, but continued, "On a Sunday morning, that would really raise some dust. Or on any other morning for that matter."

"Cullen would do it."

"We are not Cullen. We are to all appearances respectable women. Women who want to appear respectable do not go into taverns. One has to draw the line on public conduct somewhere, Bronwen, and that would be well over mine."

She knew her niece was regarding her with amused skepticism, but chose to ignore it.

As they approached the warehouse, they could see the door fronting the canal, and nailed to it the sheriff's notice of attachment.

Bronwen went forward to try the door handle. "It's locked, which is no surprise. But if there's no one around to—"

"No! We are not breaking in."

"How else do you propose to get inside?"

Glynis sighed. "I expected a guard to be here."

"On Sunday morning?"

"Why not? I rather doubt that thieves take Sunday off to attend church," Glynis answered. "It never occurred to me that the sheriff wouldn't have someone posted here. Now I really am concerned."

"I'll take a trip around it, see if there are any broken windows."

Glynis started to protest, but then decided that this would not necessarily be an unconscionable way to enter. Broken windows should be repaired, after all, lest they tempt those without scruples. Such as her and her niece.

This sophistry aside, Glynis needed to know, and quickly, if her speculation had been correct. She had worried all day yesterday, but could hardly leave her niece's wedding party to traipse down here; there'd been difficulty enough this morning. And now, while Bronwen was exploring ways to break the law, she supposed that she should gaze earnestly at the trees along the canal and hope that, in the event anyone was watching, she would be taken for a Thoreau enthusiast.

"Well, well!" came a throaty voice from the direction of Serenity's Tavern.

Glynis whirled round to see the tavern's statuesque proprietor coming down the steps of her establishment, gowned in a thinly striped, rose-and-green taffeta that was unmistakably one of Emma's creations. Spills of frothy cream lace at neck, sleeves, and hem gave the wearer a virginal appearance. Knowing this woman, the irony could well be intentional.

"When I saw you pass my window, I couldn't believe my eyes," said Serenity Hathaway, her smile filled with mischief. "Out for an early morning stroll, Miss Glynis Tryon?"

"Would you believe me if I said yes, Miss Serenity Hathaway?"

"No." Serenity's smile broadened.

"I thought not. Although it isn't particularly early."

"It is for me!" Serenity grinned, and tossed her thick, coal-colored hair. "Now, we've known each other too long, darlin', to dance around a subject. I think you smell a rat. Question is, why are you sniffing around for it down here in my neck of the woods?"

Bronwen came around the building, saying, "No luck, Aunt Glyn, the windows are—"

"And who's this?" Serenity asked.

"My niece, Bronwen Llyr. Bronwen, this is Serenity Hathaway. She owns the tavern," Glynis added gratuitously.

"Your niece?" Serenity repeated the word, eyes flashing between Glynis and Bronwen in sharp-eyed appraisal as if looking for firm evidence of kinship. "Well," she finally conceded, "she does have red hair. Is it God-given or hennaed?" she asked Bronwen, who for once seemed to be struck dumb.

But nearly everyone was at their first glimpse of this woman. Whatever the expectations, Serenity didn't meet them. She just might be the most ravishingly beautiful woman ever viewed by human eyes, and that she was also the owner of a tavern-cum-brothel did nothing to diminish the impact.

Bronwen had recovered enough to say, "Yes, I'm her niece. Yes, it's God-given. Good morning, Miss Hathaway."

"Come to think of it, I've heard about you," Serenity said with a knowing smile. "You're Miss Emma's cousin, right? The one who's always raising hell. Detective for some outfit down in Washington. In town for the wedding."

Bronwen blinked, several times, before saying, "That about sums it up."

"Ah, Serenity," Glynis ventured, trying to keep the reason for being here central before they traveled too far afield, "since you asked, I need to know something about this warehouse."

"Why, what are you on to now?" Serenity asked, a small frown line appearing in the smooth ivory forehead. She looked at Bronwen again. "Detective, huh? The acorn doesn't fall far from the tree, right?" She jerked her thumb at Glynis.

Bronwen grinned. "Right. It's passed on along with red hair, but only to female acorns."

As Bronwen and Serenity chortled, Glynis felt a growing frustration. She had to get into that warehouse. She would have thought her niece wanted that also, but Bronwen was enjoying herself too much.

"Excuse me, Serenity," tried Glynis again, "about the building here? Do you ever see people going in and out of it?"

"Not often, as a matter of fact. Why?"

"Is it being used, do you know?"

Serenity studied Glynis, seemed to deliberate, then answered, "As I recall, the only activity I've seen there has been after dark. Kind of like my line of business," she said, smiling. "So what's your angle?"

"I'd like to get inside," Glynis said. "Until I do, there is no angle."

"You should have said so! If you don't mind a little dirt, I can get you in easy enough."

"You can?" said Bronwen, obviously surprised.

Glynis was not surprised, as over the course of the past few minutes, she'd remembered the tunnels that ran under the tavern like spokes from a wheel. They'd originally been used—and some still were—by those involved in the Underground Railroad, and some years ago, she'd been in one of the tunnels herself. From what Serenity had just said, the warehouse must be connected to the tavern by means of a subterranean passageway.

"How do we get in?" Bronwen asked Serenity, while Glynis debated whether to go through with this.

She supposed the prudent thing would be to fetch Cullen—if she could even locate him. But Bronwen was now walking off with Serenity, and Glynis very much doubted that her niece would wait, not with the opportunity that possibly lay ahead. And the warehouse must be searched by someone, because Gerard Gagnon remained in jail, and a shadow still hovered over Tamar; if what Glynis guessed was true, it might help to free them both. And expose a murderer.

After all she'd had to say about respectable women, however, she would now be forced to eat her words. She cast an extremely careful glance about before following the others, but she probably needn't worry about anyone seeing her. All respectable women were, or should be, in church.

The grimy windows gave them barely more light than the tunnel had, and Glynis held up Serenity's lantern as she and Bronwen stood, baffled, in the middle of the warehouse floor.

"I was so sure this must be the place," Glynis said, their lack of success gnawing at her. And there was the added worry of being caught at this, although she hoped Serenity would warn them if wagons appeared. She brushed cobwebs from her hair and skirt, while Bronwen again began using the crowbar to pry the lids from what were proving to be rows of empty crates.

But why would there be *empty* crates in a warehouse? It made no sense. Unless they were there on the open floor to thwart suspicion and conceal the real purpose of the building. Meaning there was something to hide. So where was it hidden? In another warehouse entirely? She'd quietly checked around some, and had even asked Sheriff Fowler, who should know, but no other building in Roland Brant's name that was big enough had been found. Though that did not mean there wasn't one.

"Aunt Glyn, we're not getting anywhere," Bronwen groaned, casting aside another lid from another empty crate.

"I know."

"If we're going to find something, we'd better do it fast. Before we get some so-called help. Because we didn't tell Serenity what we're after, she thinks there's something really valuable in here—which there might be, but it won't be the jewels or gold that she probably expects. And she said if we didn't reappear in half an hour, she was going to send over her . . . her . . . what is he?"

"Brendan O'Reilly? I'd rather not say what he is."

"Well, I don't want *him* to get credit for this!"

"Credit for what? We've been in here at least fifteen minutes and haven't seen anything that looks remotely like rifles or bayonets. I must have been wrong—"

Glynis broke off, because she suddenly noticed something odd. A pale sliver of light was coming from under the windowless, far wall. From *under* the wall? She walked toward it, and held the lantern close to the floor. When she straightened, still mystified, she tentatively reached out her hand, balled it into a fist, and rapped the wall. A hollow sound. It was wood! Painted gray, she now saw, to look from a distance like the other stone walls.

"Bronwen! Come here with the crowbar!"

In an instant, her niece was beside her. "Did you find something?"

Glynis nodded. "I think so. There must be some point of access—but we've already checked the four corners of this place," she said, pointing to the wall. "Wait! I remember something the Underground Railroad uses. A wide slat of wood that blends with a wall, but can be lifted out to conceal runaways."

They inched away from each other, holding up the two lanterns as they searched the wall, their hands sliding carefully over its surface.

"Here it is!" Bronwen said. She set down the lantern to insert the crowbar into what Glynis now saw was one of two long vertical cracks, some fifteen to twenty feet apart.

"Watch out!" yelped Bronwen, as the large section of false wall fell toward them.

It was thin wood, and they both jumped away in time, but it hit the floor with a tremendous clatter, raising a cloud of dirt. By the time Glynis had wiped her eyes enough to see,

Bronwen was already scrambling into the previously con-cealed space.

"These blasted skirts!" she complained, and then Glynis heard a loud thud and a metallic rattle as something struck the floor.

She took a step inside with the lantern, although there were now several windows exposed. It was a larger area than she'd expected, and Bronwen was on her knees franti-cally prying open a crate, one of many crates, which had been stacked one on top of another. There must be several hundred, Glynis thought, moving closer to read what was stenciled on the crates in large black letters. And her hopes plunged.

"Never mind, Bronwen, they're nothing but tools. Just shovels and pickaxes and—"

She was stopped by Bronwen's yell. Having pried off the top of the crate, she'd tossed it aside, and was now beaming down at its contents.

Try as she would, Glynis could not shake off the bereft feel-ing she'd had at the train station after watching her family ride off down the rails. She hated good-byes. And the bleak question continued to haunt her: would all of them ever be together again?

After Bronwen had wired Rhys Bevan, the guns and bay-onets had been loaded onto a special freight car. Then Cullen and Bronwen, along with Zeph and what appeared to be most of the men of the Seneca County Sheriff's Office, had boarded the eastbound train, which would take them to the state capital. Treasury agents would meet them there in Albany.

Cullen had been so involved with the contraband that Glynis had been unable to tell him of her conclusions. And now he might be gone for several days. In the meantime, Liam Cleary was holding down the fort, with the newly hired Danny Ross backing him up. But neither of those youngsters were equipped to deal with the Brant household, and Glynis at this point regretted having sent yesterday's letter. She had thought Cullen would be there to deal with the consequences.

It was now late afternoon, and, without thinking, she found herself walking from the station toward Neva's refuge. Neva had told her yesterday that Tamar's physical wounds were healing rapidly, but that she seemed despondent. All things considered, this hardly seemed surprising, given what she had endured. And with the only person in whom she had some trust confined to a jail cell. Glynis felt a spurt of anger toward Cullen and his stubborn nature. He still thought Gerard might have killed Brant. Which to Glynis seemed preposterous, although she was disgusted with herself for having lacked the wherewithal to drag him away from those rifles. Roland Brant's rifles. It seemed there was no end to the man's treachery.

She abruptly turned, thinking she had heard someone call. And, in fact, Danny Ross was running down the middle of the road toward her.

"Miss Tryon," he panted, cheeks like fat, fall apples, "this just came for you." He held out to her a cream-colored envelope, her name written across it.

"This was sent to the constable's office?" Glynis asked him.

Danny shook his head. "No, it was delivered to your boardinghouse, but Mrs. Peartree just now brought it to the office, thinking that maybe the constable could find you, because—" he stopped for breath "—because she, Mrs. Peartree, told Liam and me that the servant, the servant person who brought the letter, said it was urgent that you get it right away." Another deep breath.

Yes, Glynis thought after she had sorted out this barrage of information, Harriet probably wouldn't yet know of the warehouse affair.

"Thank you, Danny, I appreciate your finding me." She

badly wanted to see what the envelope contained, but the boy deserved a minute. "I've heard about your new job," she said to him, "and Constable Stuart says you are a good scout. Obviously, I agree. Perhaps now Zeph can leave his bloodhounds at home."

He grinned at her. " 'Fraid not, cause he gave 'em to me to take care of while he's gone to Albany, and I hope he gets back quick 'cause they eat an awful lot."

Glynis smiled as Danny turned and went running back toward Fall Street. She walked to stand under an elm and leaned against its trunk while she tore open the envelope and read the short note. Then read it again.

She tucked it into her book bag, lighter now that the library's crowbar had been commandeered by Cullen, and considered whether she should reply to this note. She thought for a moment or two, then walked quickly toward Boone's Livery. There was such a thing as striking while the iron was hot. If she waited longer, she could lose her nerve, and there might never be an end to what Roland Brant's murder, like a pebble tossed into a quiet pond, had set in motion.

29

—∞—

*To men, glory, honor, praise, and power, if they
are patriots. To women, daughters of Eve, punishment still comes in some shape, do what they will.*

—Mary Boykin Chesnut, 1861 entry from
A Diary from Dixie

$\mathcal{T}$he Brant house appeared to Glynis no more friendly than usual this early evening. The sun was still high, however, the summer solstice nearing, and she would be gone from this place long before dark. Still, she had to admit to herself, much as she disliked to, that it might not have been quite as wise an idea to come here as she had originally thought.

After tethering the gray mare to the hitching post, she had reached the foot of the porch steps when Erich Brant came through the front doorway. He didn't look well—he looked pale and anxious—and before directing his eyes toward her, he glanced at the door holding the sheriff's notice.

"You're not welcome here," he informed her curtly, as if she couldn't possibly have known that. "There's no reason to bother us again," he went on, although she couldn't imagine that he would think she was dropping by on a whim.

She remained silent, mostly to see what more Erich might offer, since it didn't appear that he knew about the letter. About either letter. And she didn't think he could have heard yet what the warehouse had yielded.

He just stood there, looking at her with what she began to

sense was nervousness. Finally, he said, "Just what is it you want?"

"I was asked to come," she answered, withdrawing the envelope from her book bag, wishing now that she had not relinquished the crowbar. She held up the envelope, saying, "I'm certain you recognize the handwriting."

"She can't be disturbed," Erich said immediately.

"That's not what she indicated in this note. She said that she wanted to see me, and as soon as was convenient. Since it's convenient now, perhaps you might tell her that I'm here."

Having said this, Glynis briefly wondered where she had acquired such bravado, and decided it must be Bronwen's questionable influence. In any event, Erich did not seem impressed. He continued to stand in the doorway like a sphinx, during which time Glynis searched her mind for whatever elusive words she might say to be allowed entrance. Then she heard above her a window being raised and looked up at it to see Helga Brant standing there, as still as an image in a daguerreotype.

"Please come in, Miss Tryon," she directed in a clear, commanding voice.

Glynis saw Erich's chagrin as he moved back into the entryway. As he'd left the door ajar, she waited a short time, then went up the porch stairs and stepped inside. And found herself alone in the foyer. Erich must have gone upstairs to confer with his mother. But where was Clements? And Phoebe? Was Addie, at least, in the kitchen? Glynis suddenly had the disturbing thought that the servants might have been dismissed. It shouldn't have come as a surprise, given the notice of attachment and its every indication that the Brants' financial status had abruptly altered. It was something she should have thought of before now.

When she had first entered, she'd heard the notes of a harpsichord, presumably coming from the music room. The sound continued, and as she followed it through the parlor's flowers and greenery, she found she needed effort to push aside her uneasiness. Tirzah, after all, was someone she needed to see.

"Here again, Miss Tryon?" Tirzah struck a jarringly unpleasant chord. "Like a nosy neighbor, you just keep intruding where you're not welcome," she commented, shifting on the music bench to face Glynis.

"But surely you expected someone to come," said Glynis, "after taking such pains the other day to ensure it."

"What pains were those? I'm afraid I don't follow you."

"Oh, I think you do. You made absolutely certain that I was forced to look into your mother-in-law's bedroom. In fact, you insisted upon it. Trailing, as it were, a red herring across my path."

Glynis almost didn't catch the flicker in the dark eyes, but she'd been watching for it, for anything at all to confirm that she was right.

"I have no idea what you're talking about!" Tirzah insisted, her voice tense. "Are you quite well, Miss Tryon? Perhaps the strain of having a wild imagination has clouded your reason. Either that," she went on, her face now flushed, "or the labors of this morning's discov—"

She didn't stop soon enough. So she, and thus presumably Erich, *did* know that the rifles had been found.

"I have nothing more to say to you," Tirzah said, turning back to the keyboard.

"You've already said more than enough," Glynis responded, and was rewarded with a faint twitch of Tirzah's shoulders. "Whom did you think you were protecting with that diversionary tactic? Yourself? Your husband?"

Tirzah's fingers were poised above the keys, but they didn't resume play. Instead, Tirzah turned again to Glynis, and said, "Protecting from what?"

"From a charge of murder, as you well know."

"And just how was I doing this protecting?"

Glynis was aware that she'd rattled Tirzah, and debated

whether to just leave it at that for now. But the woman rose from the bench and stood with her hands on her hips, apparently thinking that an aggressive stance might work more successfully than a disdainful one.

"Just tell me what you think I've done," she demanded. "Do you believe, for instance, that *I* killed my father-in-law?"

"I've certainly considered it. But a better question might be, why do you think that your husband killed him?"

As Glynis had always supposed, highly emotional people who lacked self-discipline did not make good actors. Tirzah's face alone was proof of this. Her bluster dissolved, and she sank back onto the bench, her eyes wide with alarm. "Does . . . does Constable Stuart believe that Erich killed his father?"

"At the moment, the fact that you believe it is more important," Glynis said, listening carefully, as she had been, for the sound of footsteps in the parlor. "Isn't that why you moved the Millville Rose paperweight? Moved it from your mother-in-law's bedroom into the library to divert suspicion from your husband to her?"

"I was afraid," Tirzah said, tears now threatening, "that the paperweight might have been the murder weapon."

"An odd thing to fear," Glynis said, "considering there was a knife protruding from Roland Brant's chest. Unless you had heard a violent argument take place between Roland Brant and his son. And unless, when your father-in-law was found murdered in his library the following day, with a bruise on his head, you assumed that your husband had first struck him with the paperweight. The Baccarat crystal paperweight. But since it had disappeared by the time the body was discovered, I imagine you thought Erich had permanently disposed of it. But the knife . . . did you think Erich had stabbed his father while he was unconscious from the blow to his head?"

"I don't know. I don't know anything about the knife,"

Tirzah cried. The tears that now ran down her cheeks made untidy furrows in her face powder.

"It must have been a shock for you," Glynis went on, wishing that she didn't feel some sympathy for Tirzah, and praying that Erich wouldn't walk in, "when I appeared here with that crystal paperweight—it was you watching from an upstairs window that night, wasn't it? So while Konrad and his mother were in the parlor, and your husband was occupied on the porch with the constable and Dr. Cardoza-Levy, you took the Millville Rose from your mother-in-law's bedroom. Then you brought it down to the library and put it under the desk—where you knew it would eventually be found."

"No, I didn't!"

"I think you did. That night, when I first came into the foyer, I saw you, Tirzah, rushing down the hall away from Roland's library. You assumed the paperweight would be traced to your mother-in-law. And that would have been convenient, wouldn't it? She stands between you and the sale of this house—one-third of which, by her dower rights, belongs to her. So, when things didn't seem to be moving quickly enough, and your mother-in-law didn't appear to be a suspect, you helped them along the other day by calling me upstairs—"

"What the hell are you saying?" Although she'd been expecting it, the voice from the parlor made Glynis start. She hadn't heard footsteps, and she wondered how long Erich had been standing there.

"I asked a question, Miss Tryon," he said. "Are you accusing my wife of murder?"

Before she could answer, Helga Brant's voice came from the upstairs. Glynis started to walk through the parlor, but Erich blocked her path. "Are you saying that Tirzah killed my father?" he repeated angrily.

"No, I didn't say that," answered Glynis. And realized, when she saw a flash of relief cross his face, that he cared very much for this difficult woman. Complicating matters still further.

"If my mother didn't insist upon seeing you," Erich told her, "I would throw you out of this house!"

"Which reminds me," asked Glynis, trying to stave off her nervousness, "where is Clements?"

"That's none of your business."

Helga Brant's voice now came more clearly. She must be on the stairs, Glynis thought, and apparently Erich thought the same thing because he moved aside. When Glynis passed him she could feel his intense dislike. But she had started this and would now have to see it through.

Helga Brant was halfway down the steps, gripping the banister of the staircase, when Glynis emerged from the parlor.

"Will you come upstairs, Miss Tryon," said Mrs. Brant, the peremptory tone indicating that what she'd said was not a question.

Glynis nodded, and as she followed the woman, she couldn't help but note that Mrs. Brant was considerably steadier than she had previously appeared. Perhaps Neva's comment about the frailty of some wives was not merely speculation. When they reached the landing, Helga Brant turned and went straight to her bedroom, and once inside the room, closed the door behind Glynis.

"You may sit down," instructed Mrs. Brant, gesturing to a wing-back chair covered with flowered chintz.

Glynis tried not to glance around, as the cluttered, flowery furnishings made her even more uneasy; it was by no means a restful room, but looked rather as if the occupant had deliberately attempted to overwork the effect of a garden. It was even more evident here than in the parlor. Glynis recalled the woman's words: *My husband did not like flowers.* She also recalled the tightness of voice with which the words had been spoken.

Mrs. Brant went to stand at the window, her hands quiet at

her side, her profile serene. Thus Glynis was not prepared when the woman said, "I despised my husband." She turned to face Glynis. "Does that shock you, Miss Tryon?"

Glynis found herself groping for an answer. Helga Brant did not seem disposed to help her, but stood, waiting.

"I suppose," Glynis answered, "that it *should* shock me. But in the past days I have learned things about your husband that . . . Well, I doubt that I would be shocked by anything you might say. Assuming, that is, that you knew these same things."

"Oh, I knew. I knew within days of our marriage. He immediately started using my dowry money. Then he began dunning my father for more. It was that money, Miss Tryon, that and my inheritance, which paid for everything you see here. Paid for everything that Roland owned. Even his many financial ventures returned little of it."

"Were you aware of the nature of his investments?" Glynis asked.

Helga Brant looked at her with what might have been amusement. "If by that you mean," she said, "was I aware of his latest scheme of gunrunning to the South, yes. But I only discovered it a week ago. Last Sunday, that creature Jager came here, demanding his share of the payment, or so he said. He must have discovered that the well had run dry. The argument that resulted was rancorous and noisy enough for anyone to hear who cared to listen."

"That was in the afternoon?" Glynis asked.

"Yes. But the reason I requested that you come here, Miss Tryon, was in answer to your own letter, stating that you had certain questions to ask of me. You are an intelligent woman, who I believe has already come to some conclusions about my husband's death—servants do talk, as I know you've learned. I also believe you are a kind woman, and might understand better than Constable Stuart what I'm about to say. And to do."

Helga Brant walked with only the trace of a limp to her

writing desk. She carefully lifted the heavy glass dome of the Millville Rose, her hand dipping slightly with its weight, drawing from beneath it a piece of cream-colored vellum that Glynis assumed was a letter, and returned with it to stand by the window. A faint tremor in the blue-veined hands made the sheet of vellum quiver.

"I suppose," she began, "that there is no agreeable way to phrase this. Perhaps it is best if I simply tell you, Miss Tryon, that this"—she glanced at the paper—"is a written confession. I am the one who killed Roland."

Whatever Glynis had been expecting, it was not that, and she gripped the arms of the chair in astonishment. She had known there was no positive proof. That almost everything would have to turn on circumstantial evidence, but she'd never considered that Helga Brant would confess to murder. As she tried to recover from the jolt, she began to wonder at the woman's purpose.

"You look surprised, Miss Tryon."

"Well, yes, I am. And I really don't know what to say. Forgive me, but would you mind if I asked a few questions?"

"Not at all. Please do, in fact, as I know Constable Stuart has left town, and that was a deciding factor."

"A deciding factor?" Glynis repeated.

"I hoped I might prevail upon you to permit me some small amount of time before you notify him. I have several things to which I must attend."

"I doubt if I can do that, Mrs. Brant. What kind of time would you need?"

"Until tomorrow morning should be sufficient. I will not leave this house, and on that I give you my word of honor, Miss Tryon—if you believe that murderers can have honor. I believe that I do, and I am hardly a danger to anyone."

"Perhaps, Mrs. Brant, if you would answer a question or two?" Glynis said again.

"Yes, certainly."

"Well, for one thing, I don't believe your husband was . . . that is, I *didn't* believe he died in his library."

Glynis had thought, ever since she'd heard Tamar's account, that Roland Brant had been killed upstairs. Here in this bedroom directly over Tamar's room. But since she couldn't imagine Helga Brant moving his body to the downstairs library, she'd excluded the woman from suspicion. Obviously, she'd been wrong; Brant *must* have died in his library.

She became aware that Helga Brant was watching her, again with a faintly amused look. The woman now moved from the window to seat herself in another wing chair, saying, "But you were correct, Miss Tryon. He died in this room. His bedroom adjoins this one—through that door over there—as I'm sure you have learned."

Glynis stared at the woman. "Was . . . was he stabbed here?"

"Yes."

Glynis looked down at the vivid, floral-patterned Brussels carpet under her feet. In places, it was a trifle worn, as she had noticed when Tirzah had encouraged her to look; there were no spots that looked as if the carpet had been recently cleaned.

"I'm afraid I don't understand then," she said. "For one thing, there must have been blood. Unless he was already dead when you . . . when he was stabbed. Which I came to believe was actually the case."

Mrs. Brant frowned slightly, but added nothing.

"Was the Millville Rose paperweight the real weapon then?" Glynis asked, trying unsuccessfully to avoid looking at it. "The paperweight that Tirzah correctly identified, but identified in the wrong hands?"

"Yes, it was. I struck him in the head with it, and he fell. Rather heavily. You look somewhat doubtful, Miss Tryon. I am much stronger than I appear, I can assure you."

That would have been the noise that Tamar had described. The thump she had heard.

"But why?" Glynis asked. "I understand that there was an argument, but still—"

"Oh, yes, there was an argument," Mrs. Brant interrupted. "I had learned, as I told you, that Roland had added to his other perfidies by smuggling arms to the South; that his guns might actually kill young men fighting for the Union cause, in which I believe. I have known my own particular variety of slavery, you see, and I am sympathetic to the arguments of the abolitionists. Konrad is now on his way to the South, Miss Tryon, as he had intended before Roland's death, and there was the possibility that one of those smuggled guns might be used against my own son. It was, simply, intolerable!"

Glynis nodded. She could understand the rage that the gunrunning would occasion. And she could accept it as a motive to spark murder, fueled by years of betrayals and ill treatment. But there were other things that she had more difficulty understanding.

"Mrs. Brant, I am sorry to ask this, but I must. Did you know what . . . what happened to Tamar Jager?"

For the first time, the other woman displayed emotion, and it was unmistakably that of shame. Her eyes, which had been trained levelly on Glynis, dropped, and then her gaze went to the window.

"Yes," she answered in a voice no more than a whisper, "yes, I knew. And I did nothing. Tamar Jager wasn't the first, or the only young girl. However, the first one I managed to free. I sent that girl away. When Roland discovered what I had done, though . . . well, I would rather not go into the consequences that I suffered. And so I was afraid to do it again, with Tamar. It was cowardly of me, reprehensible, and I am greatly ashamed."

Glynis sighed, as the staggering ugliness of Roland

Brant's evil continued to grow. But there were still other questions.

"Mrs. Brant, if I might go back to the night of Mr. Brant's death. Why did you stab him with that knife? If he was already dead?"

"I wasn't convinced that he *was* dead. I wanted to be absolutely certain. I had planned to kill him for some time, Miss Tryon. I was simply waiting. Waiting for my anger to give me courage. I imagine a prosecutor will call it premeditated murder, and indeed, I admit that it was."

Glynis straightened in the chair and drew a breath. "Mrs. Brant, again forgive me, but I am finding this difficult to accept. Your husband's body was found in his *library*. And while I may appreciate that rage can generate unusual strength, I simply cannot see how you managed to move your husband's body down those stairs. Steep stairs. And I must admit, but for that fact, I would have considered you the most likely person to have been your husband's . . ." She stopped, searched, then said, "His executioner."

"As I told you, I am stronger than I appear. No, don't shake your head, Miss Tryon, it is true. It is also true that I had some assistance."

"Assistance?"

"You are an observant woman," said Helga Brant, "so it surely has not escaped your notice that there is a door just outside this bedroom. And another door directly below it. Next to Roland's library."

Glynis slumped back into the chair, stunned beyond words. Of course she had seen the doors. But she had not made the connection.

It was probably her expression that nearly brought a smile from Helga Brant, since she was not the type of murderer who would enjoy the cleverness of the crime.

Glynis finally found her tongue. "The dumbwaiter."

Helga Brant nodded. "I dragged Roland's body to the dumbwaiter—he was rather a short man, if you recall—and quite easily lowered it to the first floor. Then I simply dragged it into the library."

"What time was that?"

"I believe it was an hour or two after midnight. Roland had been drinking heavily that evening, more so than usual after Derek Jager had left—and I knew what the drinking might mean. When I heard the door to the library open, and then heard nothing more, I feared he had gone to the girl. That was when I made the decision to act. And I called him."

"Was no one else in the house awakened?"

"It is a large house, and the other bedrooms on this floor are at the far end of the corridor. A great many things that have happened in this room have gone unheard."

"And you created the disarray in the library? And removed the Baccarat crystal paperweight I found on the drive?"

"Yes, I took the crystal outside. Riffled and also removed several documents from the safe. And opened the library's glass door. They were simply melodramatic and, again, cowardly ways to attempt to shift the blame to an outsider. I almost thought I could get away with it, Miss Tryon."

"But you almost did. And, frankly, it puzzles me that you are now confessing. Why are you?"

Helga Brant sat forward in the chair. "Because I am not the monster that my husband was. I cannot allow that girl, or Gerard Gagnon, to take the blame for something that I have done. I've already harmed Tamar enough, and I agree with young Gagnon that Roland all but killed his father."

There followed a silence that Glynis did not feel strong enough to breach. Finally, she asked, "Did you know that your daughter-in-law attempted to point the finger of blame at you?"

"By taking the rose paperweight to the library?" Mrs. Brant said. "Oh, naturally, I knew. Tirzah is unhappy, and unstable, and she didn't know then of Roland's looming financial problems. I'm aware that she wants to leave this house, and this town, and that if I were to stand firm and refuse to waive my portion of the dower rights, the house could not be sold. And Erich would probably insist upon staying here."

Glynis nodded, then asked, "How much did Erich know about his father's financial difficulties?"

"Very little, I imagine. Roland never gave either of his sons much credit for shrewdness, or venality, and thus would not involve them in his business schemes. I also believe that neither Erich nor Konrad realized the extent to which Roland was prepared to injure not only his family but his country."

Glynis sat trying to absorb all of this, and yet much of it she had suspected for several days. "I have one or two last questions," she said. "How much, in regard to his father's death, did Erich suspect?"

Helga Brant shifted in the chair, as if uneasy. "I don't really know," she answered. "Since I have confessed to the slaying, I would assume that he cannot be charged with anything, if that is what you are asking."

But Glynis thought that Erich *had* suspected his mother, or very possibly his wife, and so had tried to block the autopsy, because he'd feared what it might reveal. What, in fact, it *had* revealed.

"Mrs. Brant, why have you told me all of this? Why not just send your confession to Constable Stuart?"

"Two reasons. I knew there would be more questions than I could anticipate and answer in writing—and you, Miss Tryon, have certainly more than proven me correct! But I was also afraid that something—or someone—might prevent a written confession from reaching the constable. Do either of those explanations sound irrational? Well, perhaps they are, and I admit I have not been myself recently. Guilt does exact a toll."

Glynis shook her head. "I don't think they, or you, sound irrational, no."

"Then, if you have finished your questions," Helga Brant said, "may I again ask the favor? That you not contact the authorities until the morning?"

"You are placing me in a difficult position, Mrs. Brant. While I might sympathize with the motives for killing your husband—and I believe that I do sympathize—I can't knowingly ignore the law. I grant you that our law can be absolutely wrongheaded—the issues of slavery, of suffrage, are the most obvious examples—but women especially need the law. Otherwise, we'll be faced, as we have been for centuries, with the principle of 'might makes right.' Men are larger, stronger, more powerful, and, I assume, always will be. It's only the law that can balance the scales."

"The law did not protect me, or the girl, Miss Tryon."

"No," Glynis sighed. "No, and I look to the day when it will. However, Mrs. Brant, I can say this. I honestly do not know where Constable Stuart is at this hour. By the time I get back into town, and by the time I send a wire to Albany, there will be no trains running west. Not until the morning."

MONDAY
June 3, 1861

30

Everything comes to light ... sooner or later.
When God Almighty wills it, our secrets are found
out.

—George Eliot, *Silas Marner,* 1861

*M*orning had been too late.

Glynis, with a deep sadness settling over her, put down the newspaper to gaze out the window of her library office at a sky absent of clouds; there was only a stark, cold, uninterrupted arch of blue. No, the first morning train had not come soon enough. By the time Cullen had received her wire and arrived by rail in Seneca Falls, Helga Brant was dead.

The murderer of Roland Brant was also dead.

Glynis started at the knock on the office door. She rose and opened it to Cullen.

"Neva will do an autopsy," he told her, "but it seems straightforward enough—everything points to a massive overdose of laudanum. And we found the empty bottle on her night table. Glynis, did you have any idea that Helga Brant would commit suicide?"

"I may have guessed that she might."

"What? You knew—"

"No," she broke in, "I didn't say I knew. I said I guessed she might. And what would you have had me do about it? Post Liam Cleary and Danny Ross inside her bedroom? To prevent her from doing what she apparently was bound and determined to do? I very much doubt those lads could have stopped her. She was a remarkably strong-minded woman."

"But what about her son and daughter-in-law?"

"She would have found a way around them. Everyone in the household deferred to her, Cullen, even her sons."

Cullen nodded. "I noticed that more than once. It probably answers the question I've had since the beginning—did that entire household know of Brant's death for hours before I was notified?"

"I think they did—at least the family members must have. But everyone waited until Helga decided the time was right to make the murder public; the more hours that passed, the less likely the murderer was to be implicated. And Helga Brant was very persuasive. She almost persuaded me that *she* had killed her husband. Almost."

Cullen stood there, staring at her, obviously searching her face for meaning when he said, "Would you repeat that? Since I have her signed confession."

"You haven't read this morning's paper, have you?"

"I just glanced at the headlines—it's all I've had time to do. Glynis, tell me what you're talking about."

"Take a look, then, at that item across the bottom of the front page."

Cullen snatched the paper from her desk, and quickly scanned it. Glynis watched his eyes stop, move back, and read once more. When he lowered the paper and looked at her again, she could see from his expression that the truth was still elusive.

"All right," he said. "Sort this out for me."

"Everything that Helga Brant told me about the murder of her husband was true—the motives behind it and the means of executing it—except for one thing. She was not the one who killed Roland Brant."

"Did you know that?" Cullen asked. "While she was telling you, did you know she was lying?"

"That's hard to answer," she said, moving to the window

to look out. The canal was busy with boats passing through the locks, their towlines harnessed to teams of surefooted mules plodding ahead on the gravel path. At the crest of the opposite slope, barely visible from where she stood, the old village cemetery lay serene and still, waiting.

Had she known without a doubt?

Glynis turned back to him. "I couldn't be absolutely certain, Cullen. There were two things which at the time made me believe that my original conclusion was correct. But they could never have been used to convict the killer. At least I didn't think so. I still don't. I intended to tell you this yesterday morning, after Bronwen and I found the rifles. By then I was fairly sure I knew *who* killed Brant because I knew *why* he was killed. But you were involved in transporting the contraband, and I thought one or two days more wouldn't matter. Perhaps, I was wrong—" she gestured at the paper "—but I don't believe so. It would probably have ended pretty much the same way."

"Two more men are dead," Cullen said. "No, make that three."

"How many young soldiers might have died from the Enfield rifles that those two gunrunners in the South were receiving?"

He shook his head. "O.K., why didn't you believe Mrs. Brant?"

"For several reasons. First, the bruise on Roland Brant's temple was on the left side of his head. Cullen, I'm right-handed; so if I, facing you in fury, were to strike you with a heavy object—intending to kill you with *one* blow—which side of your head would take that blow?"

Cullen paused before saying, "The left side. So? Helga Brant was right-handed, wasn't she?"

"I observed her enough to think she was, yes. Most people are. Significantly, though," she added, "Erich Brant is not. Which helped to eliminate him from suspicion, because I thought the killer was most likely right-handed."

"But Glynis, Helga Brant might not have been facing her husband."

"True enough. But the smooth glass dome of that rose paperweight is slippery and unwieldy. I know because I picked it up myself and nearly dropped it. Helga Brant's hands were palsied—you must have seen the tremors. I just couldn't believe her capable of the necessary strength, or, more important, the needed dexterity. But the real key, the thing that most convinced me, was that I didn't believe Helga Brant capable of such astonishing accuracy. That was the telling flaw in her story. Accuracy was also the reason, especially after I heard Neva's account of the autopsy, why I suspected whom I did."

"You've lost me," Cullen said. "*Accuracy* told you who killed Brant?"

"Cullen, that single blow to Brant's temple was done by someone who knew precisely, *precisely,* where to strike. To make a single, small bruise that would hardly be noticed—or could be explained away as something that happened in a struggle—particularly since he was found with a knife in his chest. But the knife didn't kill him. Remember the biblical David and Goliath? The giant warrior felled by a small pebble from a boy's slingshot? A far-fetched tale, even for a parable, unless you believe that David and his pebble were guided by the Lord. And perhaps this killer was guided, too, for all we know. But the deadly accuracy of that one blow to Roland Brant's head offered another explanation."

Cullen, now obviously following her, nodded. "And when I think about it, so did the knife in Brant's heart."

"Exactly. I don't think many people could make a single, clean thrust guaranteed to go, as Neva said, *directly* into the heart. But there is one kind of person who could do it. Someone who had studied anatomy. Who had attended medical school."

"Someone," Cullen said, "like Konrad Brant."

Glynis nodded. Cullen sank into the chair in front of the window, while she seated herself behind her desk.

"So Helga Brant confessed to protect her son," Cullen murmured. "Not an unheard-of reason."

"No, but I believe, as she stated, that she also wanted to free Tamar and Gerard Gagnon from blame."

"But, Glynis, how did she know it was Konrad?"

"Oh, she knew because she was there. For most of it, anyway. I think that when Roland Brant went upstairs after she'd called to him, it was with the intention of . . . of doing what he had intended to do to Tamar. As he had likely done often enough in the past. But this time there was a difference. Konrad was either in his mother's bedroom, or he overheard his parents' loud voices—which was the way Tamar described them. Remember, too, that he would have just heard, on Sunday afternoon, what Helga Brant characterized as a 'rancorous and noisy argument' between Roland Brant and Derek Jager."

"And Konrad," Cullen said, "learned then that his father was the mastermind behind smuggling arms to the South."

"And we know," Glynis added, "that Konrad was a patriot, dedicated to the Union, and a member of the Seneca Falls militia. In other words, he could well imagine those guns being used against his own company—his own friends and neighbors."

Cullen drew a breath, and exhaled sharply. "I hadn't thought of it that way."

"I imagine, though, there was another element in Konrad's hatred of his father. I would be willing to wager that when the authorities locate his belongings, they'll find among his things a carved wooden moth. I think that Konrad cared for Tamar. Just a few weeks before Roland's death, she told me, Konrad had given her a book of poetry with two telling lines that he'd marked: 'Maidens like moths, are ever caught by glare. / And Mammon wins his way where Seraphs might despair.' Mammon means riches or wealth, and specifically the wealth that creates evil. Roland Brant."

"And the girl was the caught—trapped—moth," Cullen added. "Trust a librarian to make that connection," he said, giving her a dry smile.

"Not that it was what Byron had in mind when he wrote those lines, but it was what Konrad read into them. So not long ago," Glynis went on, "he must have discovered what his father was doing to Tamar. But it was likely the gunrunning that pushed him over the edge."

"But why stab Brant, if he was already dead from the blow to the temple?"

"Perhaps, as Helga Brant said, it was to make sure he *was* dead. But that was another reason I didn't believe her story—why would she have a kitchen carving knife in her bedroom? A knife that was part of a set, and certain to be missed? I think it's just as likely that Konrad did it after he used the dumbwaiter to take his father's body downstairs to the library—and when he found those names that Derek Jager wanted. Names of the two men in the South who were receiving the rifles. The kitchen was close by, and that knife to the heart could have been an act of pure rage."

"And then Konrad went after those men."

"They're both dead, according to the newspaper."

"But not before Konrad was fatally wounded himself."

"Another victim of war, to my mind," Glynis replied. "On a field of battle Konrad would have been considered a hero. And, in that sense, he was."

She sighed heavily, then rose and went back to the window, saying, "Those of us here in the North who believe we'll remain untouched by this war had best take another look."

But they had already been touched, she thought, glancing back at the newspaper that, in an item on an inside page, told of a cannon which had exploded just outside Washington, killing three Union soldiers. One of them was the young man with whom, only a week before, Faith Alden had been standing at the rail station.

Cullen's expression was thoughtful as he got to his feet. "It's a war, Glynis, that has to be fought."

"I wonder. Does any war *have* to be fought?" she questioned while she walked with him to the door.

They went through the library proper, and stepped outside into a brilliant, sun-warmed day.

In the side yard of the refuge, the girl sat on a bench in the sunlight, the shepherd dog Keeper lying beside her. She looked down at the bandages wrapped around her arm and thought it was strange that her heart was hurting more than her arm.

Early this morning a large man with spectacles had come to see her. He told her that he was a judge. He had come, he said, to talk about something that was very important.

"Miss Jager," he had said, which startled her because no one had ever called her that. "Miss Jager, I have just spoken with your friend, Miss Glynis Tryon. She has told me some things about you. Things I was very sorry to hear. I need to know if you wish to be with your mother. To live in the place where she lives. It's not a place I would want to go, or one where I would insist you go, but I believe that *you* should make the decision about that."

She had told the judge she did not want to go with her mother. That she wanted to see the man Gerard. But the constable had put Gerard in jail. Gerard was not a killer, but the constable thought he might be.

The judge had told her that he would look into it.

It didn't matter what the judge did, though. Even if Gerard got out of jail, he wouldn't want to see her. She was the reason he went to jail to begin with.

She would never see Gerard again.

The tears, always there, started down her face, and to stop them she pushed the heels of her hands against her eyes. So she didn't see the dog leave her. But she heard him barking. Barking and barking, and running around in circles. She wiped her eyes and looked up.

Gerard was coming across the grass. And he was smiling.

"Incidently," Glynis said to Cullen as they stood in front of the library, "did Rhys Bevan discover if the members of the Oneida Community knew where their steel swords were going?"

"All he said was that John Humphrey Noyes absolutely denied it," Cullen answered. "Hell, naturally he did. Noyes is a profligate scoundrel. Bevan told him that Treasury would be watching him. I don't know about Bevan, but I sure won't be on that watch!"

As they walked up the steps to Fall Street, the scent of village roses reached them, and now silken clouds began to float before the sun like white balloons. Empty hay wagons rumbled past, but they would soon be weighted down with the harvest of winter wheat. A glorious summer was promised, and the great storm gathering in the South still seemed distant from Seneca Falls. But what would the morrow bring? A morrow, Glynis feared, that would fast be upon them.

Cullen took her arm. "Miss Tryon," he said, "may I have the pleasure of your company at lunch?"

"Yes, you may indeed, Mr. Stuart."

Seize the day, thought Glynis. This day.

Afterword

—∿—

But to you, women, American women, a few words may not be addressed in vain. One here and there may listen.

—Margaret Fuller, 1844

The fears of Emma proved to be entirely too valid, and the predictions of Orrin Makepeace Polk entirely too accurate, when, in a chilling lesson for women of all times, the New York state legislature, in April of 1862, adopted "Chapter 172: *To Amend the Act Entitled 'An Act Concerning the Rights and Liabilities of Husband and Wife.'*"

With this amendment, the Eighty-fifth Session of the male legislature effectively nullified Chapter 90.

HISTORICAL NOTES

—⚓—

Ballooning Western New York State has had a long tradition of ballooning and for 125 years has been a hot spot for the sport. Its tradition began with the Civil War when Ira Allen of Dansville met Thaddeus Lowe (see *Lowe*) and assisted in Lowe's reconnaissance balloon flights for the Union. After the war Allen went home to Dansville and developed, among other things, the smoke balloon. The Allen name is still one of the best known in the history of ballooning. It was my great pleasure this past summer (1998) to meet Florence Allen Wood, of the renowned "Flying Allens," who, many years ago, began her ballooning career when in her early teens. This intrepid lady related a number of her flights, and also told of being shot out of a cannon as part of the Allen repertoire.

Carr's Hotel This tavern and inn, originally called the Clinton House, was built in Seneca Falls around 1850. Thomas Carr, an Englishman, purchased the property in 1856 primarily to serve travelers on the stagecoach, railroad, and canal. After changing hands again in 1866, the hotel burned in the "Great Fire" of 1890. It was rebuilt by Norman Gould of Gould Pumps, and, as the Hotel Gould, subsequently changed hands a number of times. Although the building still stands on a corner of Fall Street, its future as of this writing remains sadly uncertain.

Coman, Charlotte Buell (1833–1942) Born in Waterville, Oneida County, New York, Coman studied in Paris and is often cited as being one of the artists responsible for bringing the Barbizon landscape tradition from France to the United States. She created misty landscapes, usually done in greens or blues, influenced by the tonalist movement. By the time of her death, she was considered to be the dean of American women landscape painters.

Enterprise Yes, indeed, fans of *Star Trek,* one of Lowe's favorite silk balloons was the first spaceship using this name to explore the heavens. And it is said that there is nothing new beneath the sun.

Fuller, Margaret (1810–1850) Feminist author and essayist who, with Ralph Waldo Emerson, edited the *Dial,* a Transcendentalist journal that was considered to be a criterion by which to judge early nineteenth-century American literature. She later became the political and literary editor of Horace Greeley's *New York Daily Tribune.* Susan B. Anthony considered Fuller to be the earliest and most influential author in the embryonic women's movement.

Lowe, Thaddeus Sobieski Constantine (1832–1913) Lowe's research flights with the aeronautical balloon made him a forerunner of modern aviation; during the Civil War he also pioneered the use of the balloon for espionage reconnaissance and aerial photography. The Lowe Observatory in California is named for him. For some reason, this man has remained mostly unknown, and yet he is clearly one of American history's more interesting characters. My research suggests to me that Jules Verne very likely created Phileas Fogg, the main character of *Around The World In Eighty Days* (1873), with Thaddeus Lowe in mind. Eyewitness accounts describe the brilliant, eccentric Lowe as stepping from his various balloon flights dressed in an elegant Prince Albert coat and tall silk hat.

Millville Rose In the mid–nineteenth century, glass paperweights became extremely popular. Miniature fruits, reptiles, birds, commemorative portraits, and flowers were encased in heavy domes of clear glass that served to magnify the objects. The Millville Rose eventually became perhaps the best-known American-made paperweight.

Montezuma Marsh (and Black Brook) Until some seventy-five years ago, Black Brook was a flowing body of water of substantial size. Although sections of it today can still be traveled by canoe, it has been 90 percent channelized for irrigation, so its flow is greatly diminished, except in the spring. The brook flows north from Seneca Falls into what is called today the Montezuma National Wildlife Refuge. Prior to the turn of the twentieth century, the Montezuma Marsh extended twelve miles north from Cayuga Lake and was, in some places, eight miles wide. During construction of the New York State Barge Canal, which included a dam at the outlet of Cayuga Lake, and subsequent alterations of nearby existing rivers, most of the swamp was drained. In 1937 the U.S. Fish and Wildlife Service purchased 6,432 acres of the former marsh. Since Montezuma lies in the middle of one of the most active flight lanes in the Atlantic Flyway, it is today an important refuge and feeding ground for migratory birds.

New York Infirmary for Women and Children The infirmary was founded on New York City's Bleecker Street, in 1857, by Drs. Elizabeth and Emily Blackwell and Marie Zakrzewska. It was the first infirmary to be run entirely by women, and its practice consisted of both medical and surgical services. Despite criticism from the male medical community, threatening mobs, and financial uncertainty, the infirmary quickly outgrew its original facilities, and in 1859 moved to a new location on Second Avenue, with a dispensary as well as space for several female medical students.

Noyes, John Humphrey (1812–1886) The charismatic leader of the Oneida Community (see **Oneida Community**). He also authored the weighty tome *History of American Socialisms,* published in 1870, which studies the nineteenth-century socialist community movement, also referred to as "Utopian Socialism."

Oneida Community This was but one of many religious groups that experimented with utopian communities during the early to mid-nineteenth century. The western section of New York State is often called by historians "The Burned-Over District," referring to the flames of religious revivals, fanned by the period of the "Great Awakening," which swept the area beginning around 1825. Oneida and John Humphrey Noyes rose out of that fervor. Oneida was unquestionably one of the, if not the, most successful of these communes, as it lasted for more than a generation while others disbanded. This success was due in great part to the leadership of Noyes. And it left its mark, as Oneida Ltd. became one of the world's largest manufacturers of stainless steel knives, forks, and spoons. The community prospered financially during the Civil War, and while questions were raised as to where its money originated, no charges of treason were ever substantiated.

Scientific American Founded in 1845 by Alfred Beach, *Scientific American* is one of the oldest of American periodicals still being published.

Wollstonecraft, Mary (1759–1797) English feminist Mary Wollstonecraft is considered by most to be the first major essayist on women's rights. Her most accomplished work is *A*

Vindication of the Rights of Woman. Wollstonecraft died with the birth of her daughter, Mary, who, after marriage to the poet Percy Bysshe Shelley, became best-known as the author of *Frankenstein.*